MW00467369

The End of the Dating Moratorium

Stephanie Celeste Perkins

The End of the Dating Moratorium
Copyright © 2012 by Stephanie Celeste Perkins
All Rights Reserved
ISBN 13: 978-0615649764
ISBN 10: 0615649769

This is a work of fiction. Names, characters, places, and incidents are either the product of the author's imagination or are used fictitiously, and any resemblance to actual persons, living or dead, business establishments, events, or locales is entirely coincidental.

To my parents, with all my love

Acknowledgements

First and foremost, I'd like to thank my wonderful parents for their undying love and support. I could never write better fictional parents than the ones I already have in real life. And the same definitely goes for my brother Keith.

I'd also like to thank all my friends and family for their constant encouragement and excitement for me over the years. If this book makes you laugh even a little, I will feel as if I've done right by all of you.

Thank you as well to my friend, Ann A. Massey, for allowing me to interview you about your "former life" in the wedding industry. Your stories over the years helped to inspire Shelby's career.

And a big thanks to both my reader and friend, Melanie J. Brenneman, for taking time to give my book one last go-over, and to my editor, Erin Brown of ErinEdits.com, for loving my manuscript and helping me to make it that much better.

p.s. Dad: Mom and I both know you will always sneak one—or three—homemade chocolate-chip cookies from the batch, even when you claim you won't.

And Mom: Every "Hot damn!" is just for you.

One

"You know when you have one of those sneezes that you think is going to be all nice and clean and it turns out you just spray snot all over yourself?"

Oh, good grief.

I could barely watch as my blind date for the evening used his starched dinner napkin to loudly blow his nose, after which he balled it up and then began wiping off the sleeve of his suit jacket. He snorted and sniffed with gusto as he worked.

Out of the corner of my eye, I saw the well-dressed couple at the next table looking distastefully our way. I, too, had a hard time hiding my revulsion. And I was going to kill my cousin Jake for setting me up with this guy who—besides feeling the need to discuss the less-appetizing facets of sneezing—talked with his mouth full, held his fork in a death clench like a two year old, and called Cesare, our very proper, tuxedo-wearing waiter, "dude."

Speaking of…

"Yo, dude," he said, stretching his left arm out to stop Cesare, who was trying to breeze by with two desserts called *La torretta di cioccolato,* or the tower of chocolate. The tiered layers of ganache-covered chocolate cake jiggled as Cesare abruptly halted just centimeters before hitting my date's arm.

"Do me a favor and bring me a fresh napkin, okay?" my date said, leaning over and stuffing his snot-laced one directly into Cesare's pocket. "Thanks, man," he said, adding a thumbs-up.

Turning toward me with a big, unconcerned grin, my date didn't even notice the thoroughly disgusted sneer Cesare gave him for a full two seconds before our waiter pushed his considerable nose in the air and marched on with a dignified expression to his previous destination, the chocolate tiers of the desserts wobbling dangerously with each irritated step as the ends of the white napkin bounced merrily from his jacket pocket.

Next time I get an offer to be set up, I thought to myself as I picked up my glass of wine and took a healthy slug in lieu of meeting my date in the eye, I'm damn well going to say no.

Not only no, but Hell No.

Through my continuing dark thoughts of how I'd just about had enough for this particular evening, a deep rumbling sound reached my ears. Wine glass still in hand, my jaw nearly dropped when I realized that the sound, a belch which had reached a level comparable to that of a bellowing bull elephant, was coming directly from my date.

"Okay, then!" I sang out with false enthusiasm as I shot out of my chair. "I think it's time to go. Shall we?" I folded my napkin hastily and placed it on the table with one hand and grabbed my black Kate Spade clutch with the other.

"What?" he said, apparently truly bewildered. "We haven't even had dessert! I wanted one of those chocolate thingys our waiter was carrying. And we haven't paid our bill."

Trying to ignore the disapproving looks of the other patrons, I leaned toward my date and gave a cheery smile. "You know what, Kevin? You are in luck tonight because *I've* decided to treat *you* to dinner. No, I won't hear anything of it," I continued with a serene shake of my head as he tried to protest. "It would be my honor. But we're going to pay at the hostess stand, okay?" With my smile still plastered into place, I turned and briskly walked off before he could say anything else.

And on my way to the relative safety of the front door, I grabbed out my iPhone, surreptitiously tapped in a short text message, and prayed for it to be seen immediately.

Finally out in the parking lot and the fresh air, I walked as slowly as possible next to my sulky date who, despite not having two brain cells to rub together, had figured out that I was not happy with him. His childish pouting only irritated me further, though, and in the ensuing silence I found myself completely unbelieving that this guy had made it to thirty-two years old without being shown at least once how to properly behave in a nice restaurant. Or seemingly any restaurant, for that matter.

And Kevin's a pretty cute guy, too, on the outside, at least. How was it that no former girlfriend ever gave him a talking to, even if his mother never did?

But his mother wasn't there and I had no desire to give Kevin the Caveman a belated lesson on etiquette in her stead. In fact, I never really wanted to go on this blind date to begin with and now I just wanted to get the hell out of Dodge.

Just as I was going over my options for getting out of this evening should my text message not be received, my brooding date decided that it was time to put his petulant attitude into words.

"Are you mad at me, Shelby?"

Oh, for Pete's sake! What are we, in the third grade?

Glancing at him and finding his hands in his pockets and his shoulders hunched, I didn't feel the least bit of pity for his sorry, ill-mannered ass. He had brought it on himself. Still, I just clenched my cell phone tighter in my left hand, willing it even more fiercely to ring, and stupidly went against my honest nature in favor of a lie.

"No, Kevin, I'm not angry with you. I'm just a little tired. And I've got a big day tomorrow with several appointments and that contractor I told you about who's coming to start on the office renovations, so I need to get a good night's rest."

"Are you sure?" he said, turning his chiseled face and Caribbean-blue eyes directly on me. A lock of his dark, wavy hair fell perfectly into place onto his forehead and with the light of the street lamp shining directly down over him and creating a halo effect, he looked like some well-built, broad-shouldered cherub. All he needed now was some wings and a harp...

"Shelby? Are you sure you're not mad at me? I mean, I thought we were having a good time back there. You do still want to go see a movie, right?"

My irritation getting the best of me, I opened my mouth to tell him just how much I had *not* been having a good time at dinner, how slovenly his manners were, and how much I did *not* want to be in his presence for even a nanosecond longer.

Saved by the bell. Or, rather, by the quietly vibrating cell phone in my hand.

Closing my mouth abruptly, I looked down at the screen and read *Hilary*. I inwardly cheered even as I put on a face of surprised curiosity.

"This is my best friend calling," I said with a straight face to my date, whose own face was losing its puppy-dog look and becoming harder with frustration. "She knows I'm on a date and wouldn't have called unless it was important. So just excuse me for a sec, okay?"

Not waiting for his answer, I turned around and walked off a step or two. "Hello?" I added the appropriate amount of concern in my voice to make it authentic.

"I called, as requested," Hilary's voice replied. "So, start your spiel."

"Get outta town. Really?" I fairly squealed.

There was a small silence where I could hear the rustling of paper. Hilary, a middle-school history teacher, was undoubtedly trying to grade papers. "Um, yeah, really," she finally replied in a nearly inaudible way that said that her red pen was clenched between her teeth.

Okay, the ball is obviously back in my court.

"I knew Marianne was about to pop," I said with even more conjured excitement, "but I didn't think she'd have the baby tonight!" I turned and looked at my date with what I hoped were sparkling eyes. Kevin just stared broodingly back at me. He obviously didn't like our conversation being interrupted.

"Oh, that's where you were going with this," Hilary replied with a laugh. "Even though we both know my sister had her baby two weeks ago. Well, if you're going to do it, you gotta really sell it. Bring it home, baby."

"Yes, of course! I'd love to go up to the hospital with you to see her new little boy. Oh, I bet he's *gorgeous*!"

"Emmy-worthy, but not Oscars. C'mon, Shelb. Work it some more."

I was going to throttle Hilary when I saw her next. My best friend was loving it just a little too much that I had to invent an excuse to get out of my bad date.

A frown creased my forehead. "You mean you want to go right now? But Hil, I'm on a date." I let the exasperation tinge my voice.

"That's what I'm talking about. Now give him that fake concerned look of yours and let's wrap this thing up. I've got twenty more essays to grade before I go to bed."

"Oh, okay, *fine*," I said with an irritated cock of my hip. I then turned back to give Kevin my best I'm-so-sorry-about-this look. "Yes, yes, I'll just wait here at Bernatello's for you so that you don't have to 'backtrack'." I did air quotes and rolled my eyes dramatically.

Kevin did not look impressed. Damn, but onward ho!

"Okay, yes, fine. I'll be here waiting for you and I'll just let Kevin go on home. Okay, bye, Hil." I ended the call with an amused shake of my head. "That girl is like a dog with a bone. She's been looking so forward to being an aunt that she can't stand even waiting until the morning to go see her new nephew. And obviously she wants me to go with her."

Kevin was silent for a moment and just stared at me.

"You know, I'm not as much as a dumb-ass as you think, Shelby. I know you faked that call. You don't want to continue our date, do you?"

Even as much as my stomach dropped from being found out, my twelve years as a wedding planner had taught me how to remain calm and cool in the face of adversity. So, instead of blustering, I went right for a stone-cold reply.

"Kevin, if I didn't want to be here with you, I would just say so. My friend Hilary really did call and her sister really did just have a baby."

Two weeks ago was still worthy of being called "just," wasn't it?

"Yeah, right," Kevin said scathingly with a look on his face that made him go from cherubic to downright ugly. "You're a real bitch, Shelby."

Shocked, my mouth could only gape even as another male voice from the direction of the restaurant interrupted our conversation (if you could call it that).

"Excuse me, is everything okay here?"

Kevin turned toward the guy, blocking my view. "Dude. Butt out. This woman is my date and I'm dealing with her."

Boy, did my hackles rise up on that one. But I was beaten to the punch by my unseen Lochinvar.

The voice of the other man became very cold, but stayed relaxed. "Look, I don't know what's going on between the two of you, but I don't think you should be talking to her like that. It's disrespectful."

"It's okay," I said, moving forward and thinking that, although I was smart enough to be grateful that someone else had shown up since Kevin's demeanor had changed so abruptly and negatively, I didn't want anyone fighting my battles for me. "I'm handling this just fine."

When I finally got a look at my accidental knight-in-shining-armor, I saw that he was tall and lanky, with brown hair that curled at the edges. A beautiful brunette with the long, gracefully toned legs that my five-two self had always wished for stood on his right, looking concerned, but not saying anything.

"Are you sure?" he asked me.

"Dude!" Kevin said loudly. "She said she was fine!"

That was it. I decided to end it right there. Sucking up my humility and aiming where I should have gone in the first place, I took a deep breath and turned with a stony look toward my date who obviously had the temper straight from hell.

"Kevin," I said icily, "you were right—about one thing. I did fake that call. I couldn't stand to be around you or your appalling Neanderthal manners for even one more minute and so I sent my best friend a text asking her to call me."

Kevin looked momentarily shocked and then his lips curled into an acidic smirk. "I was right. You *are* a bitch."

The lanky guy took an angry step forward that Kevin didn't notice. My warning glance toward the brunette told her to get a hold of her date and she responded immediately by grabbing his arm. I heard her whisper, "Don't."

Squaring my shoulders, I continued with a poison-laced voice of my own. "You know, Kevin, I wouldn't have had to call my friend had you exhibited even one shred of gentlemanly behavior throughout this whole night." I put my index finger out onto my palm in a counting fashion.

"First of all, when you came to pick me up, you were twenty minutes late and honked your horn instead of coming and ringing my doorbell as is simply polite. Then, when I got in your car—and you didn't even try to open the car door for me or apologize for being late, mind you—you were playing your music so loud that I had to ask you to turn it down so that I could hear what the hell you were saying."

I felt heartened when I heard the merest of chuckles from the brunette. "Then," I said, adding another finger onto my palm to indicate a third wrongdoing, "you kept answering calls on your cell phone during dinner, which you never bothered to set to vibrate, of course." A fourth finger went onto my palm, "And every chance you got, you maneuvered the conversation back to yourself, how *awesome* your so-called sports supplements business is, and how much richer you've become than any of your buddies!" My voice had gotten louder and it only became stronger when I saw the surprise on Kevin's face. Apparently no woman had ever spoken to him that way.

And ye shall know the truth, and the truth shall make you free, right?

"And *then*," I said, swinging my arm out in an emphatic gesture, "you acted like Fred Flintstone's less-socialized cousin in one of the nicest restaurants in town! Not to mention one I regularly do catering business with! I couldn't believe that burp you let rip! And stuffing your snot-filled napkin in our waiter's pocket? How un-*believably* uncouth!"

"Yeah?" Kevin said, finally regaining his bulldog-like stance and cutting into my diatribe as he jerked his thumb at his chest. "Well, at least *I* didn't lie."

And he turned and stalked off, leaving me stunned, out of words (which can be hard), and with megawatt blush creeping up my face that would easily be visible to the people who had come to help me.

And ye shall know the truth, and the truth shall come back and bite you in the ass.

Damn it. I hate it when that happens.

Two

I heard the taxi cab drive off as I shut my front door and breathed out a sigh of relief, grateful that the night was finally over and I didn't have to be kissed goodnight by a creepy frog named Kevin who would never turn out to be my prince.

Not that I really need a man to be my prince, you know. In the last two years of my life, I have been quite happy—dare I say even happier—being single than being in a relationship.

I'll admit that it wasn't always that way. Throughout the bulk of my twenties, I absolutely loathed being single each time I found myself that way. And since I tended to go many moons between relationships, I found out just how much I could pity myself, doubt my looks and my abilities, and whine like a baby to my very married best friend, who really is the poster child of patience, thank goodness.

Then, in my twenty-ninth year, with the big 3-0 looming over me like a billboard screaming out *THIRTY YEARS OLD AND STILL NOT MARRIED*, I had a bout of Temporary Singleton Insanity and went on a rampage of short-term boyfriends. I guess subconsciously I had this wild hope that if I went through more of them at a faster pace, I would find myself that Right One who I had been looking for all my life and who my mother has been praying I would meet since the day I graduated from college. My mother, in fact, has been regularly lighting candles at St. Matthew's Catholic Church in hopes of this event. She's known as a regular now and gets a five-cent discount from the usual thirty-five cents it costs to purchase a candle from the nuns. She buys them in bulk.

Anyway, I went out with five guys during this year of my life who Hilary collectively referred to as The Morons and I simply classified as disappointing.

The first guy had a thing for telling dirty jokes—loudly, in public, and often with descriptive hand gestures. The second was a litigation lawyer who was always trying to pick fights with me just because he thought I was cute when I got mad. The third constantly touched himself (yes, down there). And the fourth one was five years younger than I and kept introducing me as his sugar mama.

But the last one was the kicker. Why? Because he consistently referred to himself in the third person. Not just by his name, which was David, but by his own personal, self-given nickname of "Davey." (I asked. His entire family always called him David.) In my defense, we dated for two whole weeks before I ever heard mention of Davey and, at first, I thought he was talking about someone else entirely.

We were sitting out on the porch of my 1930s one-bedroom bungalow in Houston's historic Heights district, sipping iced tea and enjoying the warm, humid afternoon (or I should come clean and say we were gulping our teas post sex-on-the-sofa) when David turned to me and said, "Davey is hungry. Davey would like a hamburger."

And no, I'm not yanking your chain here.

Well, because David had seemed fairly normal up to that point and was the last person I expected to refer to himself in the third person, I chose to give him the benefit of the doubt and said, "Who's Davey? One of your friends?"

Okay, so the hope that springs eternal obviously didn't flow down my street because the relationship was over two weeks after that. Now, I'm a firm believer in giving people second chances and I applied that rule firmly to David because I had liked him very much at the start, but the more Davey came to call, the less I wanted to be anywhere near the actual David.

And it wasn't long after I broke up with him that I pretty much woke up and realized I was tired of the whole thing. I was tired of dating, tired of the game, the active hunt for a husband—or even a normal boyfriend—and, mostly, the sheer fact that I felt as if I had to have a man in my life.

So I declared a dating moratorium. I liked the sound of that better than just "taking a break." It sounded more official in capacity.

I decided in said moratorium that I would spend exactly six months just not worrying whatsoever about men, dating, or the fact that I was about to turn thirty and was nowhere near to getting married and having babies (which is another thing I've always wanted and the absence of which in recent years has caused the nuns at St. Matthew's to double up on their candle orders in the name of Frances Waterlane).

So, that's exactly what I did. I stopped worrying, I stopped thinking about where my next date would come from, and most of all, I stopped putting pressure on myself.

And you know what? It was freakin' wonderful. And it ended up lasting two years instead of six months.

Believe it or not, I got to where I actually looked forward to either going out to a fun dinner with just my girlfriends or just coming home to a quiet house after work where I fixed dinner for myself and watched whatever I wanted to on television. I also got to where I could go into any store or restaurant in town and not immediately scan the entire place for cute guys who didn't have something shiny on their third finger, left hand.

It really was blissful, let me tell you. I'm not going to sit here and tell you that not having sex for the past two years has been a bed of roses, but I've survived without the world imploding on me or anything. And there are other things one can do when needed, if you get my drift…

Anyway, I digress. The best part of it all turned out to be that I learned to truly like myself. I don't know how it happened because it came on so slowly, but I just found myself being more accepting of who Shelby Amelia Waterlane was innately and also the adult person I had become, faults (and there are tons of 'em, let me tell you), cellulite, crows' feet (and there are a good bit of both of those, too), and all.

And lastly, I found that, although I still *wanted* a man in my life, I no longer felt that I *needed* a man in my life. And there's a big difference, you know.

Hallelujah! Miracles do happen! Even to single women!

On the topic of my career, during my moratorium I also moved from doing event planning and catering at the Chatsworth Hotel, one of Houston's largest and fancy-schmanciest hotels, to having my own event-planning business, with weddings being my specialty. I called my company Waterlane Events Inc.

Long story short, the first year of my self-imposed moratorium was also my first year of being my own boss and getting my company up and running. And when you're that busy, time flies even more swiftly. However, just when Waterlane Events Inc. had celebrated its second year as an established force in the event-planning industry and my moratorium was running on cruise control, the Hounds of Hell came calling.

Or, rather, Frances Waterlane and her sister and near-constant companion, Priscilla O'Keefe, decided that they'd had enough of my so-called moratorium—Mom would say it with a wrinkled nose, as if it were something unseemly—and declared it open season on setting me up with any man they could find. And this included using coercion on Pricilla's son Jake, who is the owner of a fitness gym near uptown Houston and "must know tons of single men," as my mother and Aunt Priscilla apparently put it to him when they hijacked him, took him to lunch, and insisted that he set me up.

Too bad for me that Jake, a consummate romantic at heart, was only too willing. Having just gotten married himself to a cute little redhead named Livvie—I did their destination wedding at the Lady Bird Johnson Wildflower Center in Austin; it was absolutely gorgeous—he and Livvie were all in the mode of wanting the whole world to be happy and in love right along with them.

I love them and all, but, seriously? Gag me.

Only my younger brother Colin seemed to be able to dodge the clutches of the evil Franzilla, as Hilary and I had dubbed the monster that my mother and aunt had become, and that was only because Colin was completing his last year of his medical residency and my wonderful and usually laid-back father Robert had threatened Mom with the deepest cut of taking her American Express Platinum card away if she bothered Colin when he needed to concentrate on his burgeoning medical career.

Mom is so desperate for me to be married that she almost—*almost*—chose to voluntarily hand over her Platinum card to my father. Visions of me marrying a doctor were obviously dancing around in her head and it was only my father's quick-thinking move of casually mentioning how worn out some of Mom's legions of shoes were looking that made the visions in her head go away in favor of the ability to purchase some of the latest expensive footwear fashions.

Thank God my mother is a shoe whore, no?

But before I knew it or could activate my deflector shield, I was fielding a call from Jake who had this "great guy" named Kevin to set me up with, and would I be available on Thursday night?

That's what they all say, I had thought. But after hearing Jake's description of the guy—and Livvie's voice in the background yelling, "He's a total hottie, Shelby!"—I had to admit that my interest was definitely piqued.

If I had to reintroduce myself back into dating society, who better to do it with than a total hottie, right?

Well, now we know *that* thought was a dumb one.

"It doesn't matter anymore," I murmured to myself as I finally drifted off to sleep, the tension in my muscles loosened by a combination of a hot bath, a double dose of lavender bath salts, two chapters of my latest mystery novel, and the satisfying knowledge that there were no more blind dates on my horizon. I could once again concentrate on my clients and, at least for the next four months, on the renovations to the Waterlane Events offices.

Maybe after that I would consider going on another blind date. But until then? Not only no, but Hell No.

Three

The next day after Caveman Kev and I came to our mud-slinging understanding, I went into work feeling a lot more chipper than I thought I would.

I think it was because I honestly didn't realize that I, in fact, had been trapped back in the dating world and I would need the Jaws of Life to cut me loose again.

Regardless, everything on this Friday morning started out just fine. I left my little bungalow and drove all of five minutes through the Houston Heights subdivision to the 1920s two-bedroom house that served as the offices for Waterlane Events Inc.

On a tree-lined street with several others that had been converted into businesses, the twelve-hundred-square-foot house was painted a cheery buttercup yellow with white trim and black shutters. A brick walkway in a herringbone pattern led to the porch, which had a white railing and was just big enough to hold a swing. In the front yard, an artfully notched wooden sign announcing Waterlane Events and the phone number hung from a scrolled iron hanger.

I never ceased to feel a surge of pride when I drew up. I had worked hard over the past twelve years at becoming a respected event planner in Houston and had meticulously saved every extra penny I could just so that I could have my business in just such a prime location. Then I had saved some more to afford the renovations that were about to begin, which would convert the living room and the adjacent dining room into three offices for my employees. The pride I felt gave way to excitement as I trotted up the porch steps and opened the glass-paned front door.

It was going to be a good day, I could feel it.

My head held high and a smile on my face, I breezed into the office sporting my favorite ice-blue sleeveless dress and nude patent-leather four-inch Jimmy Choo heels. There is something about this ensemble that makes me feel very chic, very trim, and very powerful. I sometimes feel my three employees sit up a little straighter when I walk in wearing this outfit.

My assistant Bryan certainly does. Those gay guys understand about women and their power outfits sometimes even better than other women do. And I love 'em for it. Seeing me, Bryan's face immediately split into a wide, cheeky grin as he made his way from the former master bedroom (and now my office, naturally) to the former living and dining rooms, temporarily partitioned to make three offices, to put copies of the coming week's schedule on the desks of my two other full-time event coordinators, Lauren Avaldi and Emily Lynford.

"Well, well, well, aren't we looking all gorgeous this morning in our power outfit and everything," he said approvingly, with a quick once-over as he breezed by.

See what I mean? They just get it.

"I take it the date went well last night, hmm?"

From the kitchen located in the back of the house, I heard the clickety scurrying of two women in heels who'd heard my arrival. I caught a glimpse of Lauren's and Emily's excited faces as I made the right turn into my office, with it walls the color of toasted almonds, white built-in shelving, and a sofa and two chairs in blue toile that were situated by the picture windows that looked out over the front lawn.

"You gotta tell us, Shelby! We want to know everything!" Emily called out as both girls' strides lengthened and the sound of their heels became more like beats from a snare drum.

If I had been a little more paranoid about being dragged back into the dating scene at that moment, it would have sounded to me like a fashionable Revolutionary War brigade was after me, counting cadence with their kitten heels so as to march me into the battle of Will He Call Me or Won't He Hill.

Instead, I was oblivious to more thoughts of dating and, after putting my King Ranch laptop bag and purse down on top of my desk, I turned to face my three expectant-looking employees with a placid smile.

"Actually, no, the date didn't go well at all."

Lauren, who was tall and lean, with wavy dark brown hair and eyes that were the exact color of my secretly hidden bottle of Wild Turkey, looked crestfallen for me like the sweet-natured, very forgiving person she is.

Okay, okay, I'll explain about the booze. It's really very simple. I bought my big, ornately carved oak desk at an estate sale when I first opened my company and one day found that it had a hidden niche underneath that was just the perfect size for a bottle of liquor and a couple of stacked rocks glasses. But don't worry, I'm not a lush. I keep the Turkey strictly for Son-of-a-Bitch Days. One large finger of the hard stuff and, as I choke and gag while my throat feels like it's being sliced up, I'm instantly reminded of my blessings.

Emily, on the other hand, put her hand on her *zaftig* hip and ruefully shook her highly styled mane of Scandinavian Blonde No. 5 hair. And yes, I'm saying she has Texas Big Hair. But it's the classy kind or I wouldn't have hired her. Emily is what my grandfather would call a pistol. She speaks her mind and isn't afraid of anything. She's also a hell of a good wedding planner and I fear for the day that she leaves me to start her own company.

And lastly there was Bryan. His grin fell like the soufflé I tried to make at home the other night and I could see through his tailored gray suit coat that his very correct posture sagged a bit.

"What?" he said, obviously expecting some other answer than the one I gave him. "But you've got your ice-blue dress and Jimmy Choos on...and you look so refreshed...I thought surely...." His voice trailed off and the papers he still held in his hand seemed to just wilt with disappointment, making Emily take her hand off her hip to put it around Bryan's shoulders for a sympathetic squeeze.

I suppose I should explain further about Bryan before I give the impression that he bursts into dramatic, high-pitched wailing at any given moment. Bryan is the most laid-back, relaxed, and non-dramatic gay man I've ever met in my life— and believe you me, honey, I've met a ton of 'em. Except when it comes to yours truly.

At risk of sounding like I'm in need of some humble pie, I basically discovered Bryan Monahan five years ago when he was working as the reception clerk in some dump of a motel outside of Beaumont, Texas. I was on my way to Beaumont as it was where one of my first freelance gigs as a wedding coordinator would be taking place, on the QT from my general manager at the aforementioned fancy-schmancy hotel where I worked as the catering manager, of course.

This job was a last-minute, day-of gig where the bride, a sorority sister of mine named Mitzi Lambert, decided one week out that she suddenly couldn't handle everything on her big day and somehow remembered hearing that I'd been working at a hotel doing weddings. The *Reader's Digest* version is that she hunted me down and hired me at an ungodly amount of money to come in for the day of the wedding and just be there to handle everything that she needed.

How could I say no?

So there I was, driving my leased white Audi like the proverbial bat out of hell toward Beaumont at seven o'clock in the morning because I'd just gotten an utterly hysterical call from the bride where, between gasping sobs and the occasional Harpy-esque scream at her mother, had found out that all the boutonnieres for the ten groomsmen, eight ushers, and her father and three brothers had all been unceremoniously put down the garbage disposal by her three-year-old cousin and ring bearer.

And to someone who isn't getting married, that sounds like a ridiculous amount of drama for a few rosebuds, right? But to a bride? Well, a bride is a beast unto herself and is more easily set off than a heroin addict who's trying to quit the smack cold turkey. They're scary and there's not much you can do with them but relinquish your own petty dramas and do whatever the hell the bride wants.

If you don't want your throat metaphorically torn out by the lovely bride's bare hands, that is.

Anyway, my first job as a freelance wedding planner was officially on before I'd even had my morning cup of coffee and, wouldn't you know it, I heard a muffled *pow*! as I was cruising at top speed on I-10 toward the city whose former ban of dancing and rock music was the inspiration for the classic Kevin Bacon grain-mill dancing, establishment-bunking movie *Footloose*.

Moments later I was pulling off the highway, my right back tire deflating rapidly with each revolution, and I just barely made it into the parking lot of Moe's I-10 Motel.

I was so frantic at that time, not because of my flattened tire from what turned out to be the longest nail I'd ever seen in my life, but because time was a-wasting and I was no closer to finding a reputable florist who would make twenty-two boutonnieres at the last minute that I wouldn't have cared if the motel had been called Larry, Moe, and Curley's I-10 Motel. I was going in and I was going to show my boobs if I had to in order to get someone to drive me to the nearest rental car place.

Hey, give me a break, I figured you just never knew.

It turns out my peek-a-boob would not have done me any good even if I had tried, though. Because what I got was Bryan. And by the way he was sucking his cheeks in as he primped himself in a small mirror, I knew him instantly as one of My Friends.

See, yours truly and the gay boys get along like peanut butter and jelly. I love 'em and they love me and it's been that way since my freshman year in high school, when my friend Josh confessed to me that he had a crush on our star quarterback and I didn't laugh. The bond was created at that point and the gay boys just seem to sense it like Coco Chanel could sense the next fashion trends.

And Bryan was no exception. He had looked up from his primping to find an utterly freaked out (and moonlighting) catering manager, and when I whimpered the words "Help me," he locked his moss-green eyes onto my baby blues, sensed my gay-boy mojo, and literally jumped into action.

And within the next hour I knew I just had to hire this twenty-four-year-old guy whose stepfather had kicked him out of the house a year earlier when he—Bryan, that is—had come out of the closet. Not because I pitied Bryan, no siree. He wouldn't have liked that. I wanted to hire him because he had the resourcefulness of McGuyver with the panache of St. Laurent. And he was smart, well-spoken, and had impeccable manners to boot.

Within minutes of hearing my plight, Bryan had turned on the No Vacancy sign at Moe's, locked up, and had led me out to his old yet still snazzy red convertible, where we hopped in and tore up the highway to a local florist known for opening early.

And before I knew it, we were back at Moe's and Bryan himself had made me all twenty-two boutonnieres at no charge. They were absolutely gorgeous, too, and he'd found just the right shade of hot pink that Mitzi favored over any other color.

It seemed that in his spare time, and because he was so insanely bored working at Moe's with nothing to do but wait for the next businessman to bring in his hooker for the hour, he would fiddle with the small batch of flowers that the owner always kept on the tiny reception desk and knew how to wrap the stem of a rose with florist tape so beautifully that it made me want to cry with happiness.

But when I took one good look around the conditions in which Bryan made his daily life, it was clear that he deserved a shot at something better. He was living at the motel as he had nowhere else to go and was too proud to live with any of his relatives or friends. He wanted to make it on his own, he told me, and not rely on others. And so as he wrapped the stem of the last boutonniere, I asked him if he had a decent suit.

"Of course, darlin'," he had said, not taking his eyes off his work. "I wouldn't dare leave my mama's house, forcibly or not, without my good suit."

"And could you leave here and help me at the wedding when you're done being Super Florist?" I had asked.

Bryan had looked up, his fabulously long, dark lashes making his suddenly hopeful eyes look even bigger than they already were and also, heartbreakingly, incredibly vulnerable.

"Do you mean it?" he had whispered.

"Bryan," I'd said, "You've obviously got more talent than you've displayed here for my pathetic, unprepared ass today. I'm going to take you along for the wedding as my assistant and, so long as you don't try too hard to impress me—and I'm saying that you need to be yourself and not fake what you think an assistant should be—and if I think you're right for the job, I have a catering-assistant position currently open at my hotel in Houston. I've been given sole discretion as to who to hire as well."

As Bryan's stunned face continued, I had said, "You've impressed me already more than you realize. If you show me that you've got what it takes, then I can guarantee you a job at my hotel. And I have a small apartment at my place where you can hang your hat until you find an apartment of your own."

I had just bought my little bungalow and there was a tiny apartment above the detached garage that was clean, even if it was about as big as a thumbtack. I had a feeling Bryan would think it heaven after his life at Moe's.

"Sweet Jesus. Are you serious?" Bryan's face had lit up, second by second, with guarded excitement.

I'd nodded, and my instincts were telling me I wasn't going to be sorry. "There will be some rules, of course, like no parties while you're staying at my apartment, you have to clean up after yourself, and you have to find your own place within six months. And if I find out you do drugs or go overboard with the booze, you're evicted immediately."

"I don't. Do drugs or get drunk, that is." Bryan had replied. "My dad died of alcoholism and I refuse to go there. And I won't even date a guy who I suspect of being a druggie. I promise, Shelby, I won't let you down."

And he didn't. Bryan outshined every assistant I've ever had in my ten years as someone who was actually high up enough to have one. I took him to the wedding with me and he touched up the bridesmaids' makeup, shined the father-of-the-bride's shoes to a high gloss, spruced up some sagging flower arrangements, gave Mitzi a Perrier when she got nervous to make her burp and get the excess air out of her stomach, distributed last-minute necessities such as aspirin, hairspray, bobby pins, an extra bow tie, and some breath mints to members of the wedding party from my big Samsonite full of emergency extras he came to call the Suitcase o' Tricks, and did a million other errands for me without questions, without drama, and without attempting to take the limelight away from me.

Not that I didn't try to give him some of my limelight, he just wouldn't take it. He told me later, when we were sharing a bottle of champagne after the reception, that he actually liked being a behind-the-scenes kind of person and would never want to be thoroughly in charge, as I prefer to be.

See what I'm talking about? Peanut butter and jelly, baby.

And good as my word, I got Bryan a job at my hotel and he became my Guy Friday from the moment he hit the lobby's highly polished marble floors running. His confidence and abilities grew exponentially, too, and was in line for promotion after promotion within his first year. Bryan, however, chose to remain my assistant. I made sure he got pay raises and the title Executive Assistant to the Director of Catering (as I had become), but otherwise he was very comfortable to be looking after me and doing all the little things I needed to get done to make an event top notch.

So you can probably guess that I made damn sure he was coming with me to my new company when I left the hotel to make it on my own. I would have done and will do just about anything not to lose Bryan. And he still feels the same way about me; hence, the incredibly emotional attachment he has to my personal happiness. And he also wants to be Uncle Bryan about as badly as my mother wants to be MeeMaw, and so this first foray I had back into the world of dating and (possibly) mating was as much of a big deal to Bryan as it was to Frances "MeeMaw Hopeful" Waterlane.

Anyhow, as my three co-workers stared at me with disbelief on the bright morning after my fiasco with Kevin, it was Emily who put it all into perspective. "So the beautiful, healthful, and satisfied look you're sporting today is the result of, what, a big plate of linguine with clam sauce?"

I gave her a haughty look and told the truth, as is my predilection, despite what I tried to pull with good ol' Kev. "No, it just so happens to be a combination of linguine with clam sauce, some really nice wine…" I saw their faces start to become slightly hopeful again. Time to lower the boom. "And a long, hot bath by myself with my newest mystery novel."

I'd never seen three more disgusted looks in my life.

"You're kidding me, right?" Emily said.

"No, I'm not," I returned as I made my way around my desk to my chair. "It's a very good novel and I thoroughly enjoyed myself. And that, in addition to a good night's sleep, is why I look so refreshed."

Stares, from all of them.

"And I happen to think I always look beautiful, thank you."

No response. There was no pity happening from the Dating Brigade. Instead I think they were about to lower their bayonets and charge.

Bryan, however, recovered some of his aplomb and leaned one arm on my desk. "Okay, honey? Are you seriously going to tell me that the gorgeous sexed-up essence you're currently radiating is from *a bath and a book?*"

Ever seen someone who had just taken a bite of a rotten banana? Yeah, his look was something like that. Luckily, sweet Lauren came to my rescue.

"Well I happen to like a hot bath and a good read myself," she said. I smiled warmly in return until she said, "Only, my hot baths are with my boyfriend Chris and some wine and the only reading I do is to make sure I'm pointing the faucet lever at hot instead of cold."

Okay, strike that. Evil Lauren is now her name.

"All right, fine," I said. "And do any of you horrible people happen to care as to *why* my date was so bad that I resorted to a bath and a mystery novel to make me happy?"

Emily, ever the one with the mouth on her, examined her nails in a bored fashion and said, "Why? So you can tell us that he had one eyebrow higher than the other or that he missed a spot when shaving and then we'll be okay with you slinking back to your self-imposed existence as the Future Crazy Cat Lady of the Heights?"

"Is that any way to speak to your boss?" I asked archly.

Obviously not archly enough. Either that or I am such the not-scary boss.

"Yes," Emily said without batting an eyelash, and Bryan, my assistant extraordinaire who always had my back, had the absolute gall to second her.

And Evil Lauren earned the title Very Evil Lauren by saying, "It's about time someone laid it out on the table for you, Shelby. You're walking far too placidly into old maid-dom. You need to realize that no guy is perfect—"

"Hear, hear," drawled Bryan, making Emily grin wickedly.

"—and you need to start accepting some faults or you'll never have one single good date again!"

Apparently I was mistaken. Her name is Very Evil and Bossy Lauren.

Anyone else besides me think it might be time to whip out my trusty Wild Turkey? I do, that's for sure.

But even though the pointy toe of my Jimmy Choo began to lovingly caress the small hidden niche underneath my desk, I decided to attempt one more time to explain myself.

"Are you three going to listen to my story or are you just going to judge me before you know the truth?"

Yeah, that tactic didn't work, either. Emily just quipped, "Oh, I think judging you is good."

And Bryan, acting as if he were admiring a perfect blue sky: "Hmmm, yes. It's a beautiful day for judging."

And Very Evil and Bossy Lauren: "No, y'all, she's right. We should at least listen to what she has to say about her date. Go on, Shelby."

Ahh, there's my Sweet Lauren again. I knew she was around somewhere. I looked at her gratefully. And launched into my story of Kevin of the Prehistoric.

"Good God, Shelby," exclaimed a now-reformed Emily once I was done. "How did you not clock that guy when he called you a bitch?"

"If I would have been there, I would have clawed his eyes out for you, sugar," snarled Bryan, his eyes positively glowering with fury.

"Oh, Shelby! You were so right to leave. What a jerk!" gasped Lauren.

Oh, to be back from Coventry! I was now basking in the collective on-my-behalf indignation of my employees.

Sort of.

"Well, at least we found out quickly that he was an ass," said Emily with a keen glare in her eyes. "But we're not going to let that stop you from getting out there again. Shelby Waterlane is officially dating again!"

Wait a minute. What's this "we" business?

That's when I realized that they were all in cahoots. With Franzilla. The scary ideologies that my mother and Aunt Priscilla have been spewing forth had settled on the heads of my trusted employees and permeated their brains. They were no more the level-headed, even if romantic, people I had hired and had come to think of as some of my best friends. They were converted. They had been swayed.

They had gone to the Dark Side.

I was about to put my head in my hands and start whimpering (or screaming out "Sanctuary!") when Lauren happened to look at her watch. "Oh my God! I'm supposed to be downtown setting up for the Houston Women in Sports event in ten minutes!"

And the office leapt into action. Bryan turned and yelled, "Go, go! I'll finish them and bring them to you at lunch!" to Lauren as she sprinted out while squealing frantically that she didn't have the contracts ready for her off-site afternoon appointment.

Emily had turned and was rushing out as well. "Gotta run, too, guys. I'm due to meet a prospective bride and her mother at the Galleria in less than an hour. We'll talk more later, Shelby!"

Fantastic. Just what I needed to cap the day off. More harassment. I looked up and saw Bryan standing over me with a kind smile. He stretched out his hands and I gratefully took them. He pulled me up and into a big hug, knowing that it was just what I needed after being picked on.

"I know I was mean to you, sweetness," he said, putting his chin on top of my head as I breathed in the scent of his cologne. "But I want what's best for you and I just don't think that you really want to not have someone in your life anymore. So that's why I push you and let the other girls do it, too."

"I know," I replied, reluctantly pulling away. "It's just hard to get ganged-up on sometimes. But I'm okay."

Bryan stooped his six-foot frame to look into my eyes head-on. "So will you try again sometime soon?"

I pushed one side of my chin-length blonde bob behind my ear as I digested what he just said. It sounded suspicious. Like I was being set up for a fall.

"Um, yeah. Sure. You know I want to get married someday, so of course I'm going to go on other dates."

"Possibly one this Saturday night?"

I wondered if the police would find solid evidence of Bryan's fingerprints on my power outfit when they recovered my body from the cliff off of which he'd just pushed me.

"Bryan, no."

"Shelby, I promise you that you will like this guy. He is totally your type." Bryan's words were rushed and, to my ears, rehearsed as well.

Madame Bryanna hath foretold my resistance (probably by looking deeply into his crystal Tiffany paperweight).

My hands went to my hip and my indignant, pissy side came out. "And what, pray tell, is my 'type'?"

"Tall, smart, funny, laid-back…"

"Okay, fine, so you know my so-called type," I growled, cutting him off and hating it that he knew me so well.

"And you have a bizarre thing for guys with bird legs that I so cannot understand," Bryan said with his eyes looking heavenward in disappointment and his hands up in a get-that-shit-away-from-me style.

I glared at him. "So I happen to like guys who have skinny legs. Is there anything wrong with that? Huh?"

Emily stuck her blonde head back into my doorway. "You do have a thing for guys with bird legs, my friend. It's positively odd."

As she sashayed out, I yelled, "It doesn't mean they're not still muscular legs, you know!"

I turned back to find tears of laughter in the vulnerable-no-more eyes of my dear, faithful assistant.

Four

Later that morning, I looked with satisfaction over the plans for the office renovations even as I hugged my office phone between my shoulder and ear and listened to Dierdre Zuckerman, one of my June brides, vent about how her mother was insisting that she dance the *horah* at her reception when she flatly did not want to.

"It's so cheesy, Shelby," she whined, sounding much more immature than her twenty-four years. "I don't want to dance around like some ridiculous peasant and have a bunch of guys lift me up in a chair. Please help me convince my mother that it's an outdated tradition and that I'll be, like, *so* embarrassed if she makes Hunter and me do the *horah*."

"Listen, sweetie," I said, "You are my client and I am here for you in whatever you need. And I will be happy to have a talk with your mom if that's what you really want—"

"Oh, I do, Shelby," she gushed. "I want, like, a modern wedding, not one full of stupid, old-fashioned traditions just because Mom says I should."

"And I understand that," I replied soothingly, "but what you need to remember is that dancing the *horah* is not exactly the equivalent of doing the Chicken Dance or watching your great aunt Harriett shake her booty in a conga line. As you know, the *horah* has great cultural and religious significance in a Jewish wedding that I think you'll come to respect as you get older."

"Yeah, I know," Dierdre said. "That's what Mom and both my grandmothers keep saying, too. I'm really sorry, Shelby, but I am so sick of hearing it!"

"I know you are, honey. But what you also need to remember is that I can't give your wedding back to you ten years from now."

"Ten years from now?" she repeated. "What are you talking about?"

"I'm talking about that moment when you wake up and realize that you regret not incorporating more Jewish traditions into your wedding. That moment that you wish you had done things a little bit more like your mother and your grandmother had done at their weddings—those moments that you've heard so much about that still bring smiles to their faces. And as cheesy as you think doing the *horah* is now, Dee, I guarantee you that you won't see it that way the older you get, especially when you have children of your own and start explaining to them the beautiful and age-old facets of your religion. It's a special moment in time that connects you to all your ancestors, and it's something that I can't give back to you once your wedding is over."

I paused and waited. Sure enough, moments later I heard an audible sniffle on the other end of the line. I smiled into the phone and said, "Okay, sweetie, you just take some more time to think about it and let me know. If you decide a few days from now that you still don't want to dance the *horah*, then I promise you that I'll help you talk to your mom."

Dierdre thanked me in a choked-up voice and said she'd see me next Tuesday, when I was to meet her with her fiancé to go over the wedding program I had mocked up. As I hung up the phone, I smiled. If I read my bride-vibes correctly, Dierdre and Hunter would be dancing the *horah* at their wedding and be feeling grateful the next day, and in the years to come, that they did so.

It didn't take long for me to sag in my power outfit once more, though.

"Sweetness," Bryan said as he strolled into my office a few minutes later. "Bad news. I just got a call from KT Construction. Bob Kappler broke his leg while playing in a charity golf tournament this morning and won't be able to start the renovations today."

Although I felt genuinely shocked that something bad happened to such a nice man, I instead asked the most pertinent question: "How in God's name does someone break his leg playing golf?"

Bryan shrugged his shoulders. "Apparently it involved a sand trap, that's all I know. The main thing you need to know is that his nephew is going to be taking over the project."

While still feeling bad for Bob's run-in with a wayward sand trap, I nevertheless felt a shade irritated. Bob Kappler, now in his late sixties, had been a major force in the small-scale home renovation business for over forty years and his work was both thoughtfully executed and expertly completed. He employed only top-notch workers and oversaw each and every single day's work personally. He'd renovated my parents' house, Hilary's parents' house, and many other houses belonging ~to~ people I knew. I simply didn't want to use anybody else. I had saved up to get the best and it was the best who I wanted.

Steadfast pickiness is still a virtue, right?

"Do you know who this nephew character is? Does he have any experience at all?" I asked Bryan, who had sat down in the leather barrel chair across from my desk and crossed his legs elegantly.

"He's apparently the 'T' in KT Construction, so I'm guessing that unless extreme nepotism is to blame, he might be qualified for the job. And his first name is Luke. All I can tell you beyond that is that I hope he's easier on the eyes than your friend Bob. The man's a dear, but his super-sized beer belly and obsession with pearl-snap shirts gives me the shivers." He added a tiny shiver for effect.

"And that's all we know of this guy?" I asked.

"The only other thing I know is that he will be here at two-thirty this afternoon to meet you and then, barring any problems, the demolition of the wall separating the dining and living rooms will go ahead as scheduled on Saturday morning."

"Fabulous." I grumbled, knowing there wasn't much I could do about it but feeling the urge to brood anyway.

Bryan, after years of knowing me as intimately as any gay man could know a straight chick, knew I needed some time alone to regain my humor. As he got up from his chair, he asked, "Flowers to Bob, then?"

"Definitely. And send along a six-pack of Shiner Bock beer while you're at it. No, make that a case. It's his favorite and the poor guy obviously deserves it."

"Gotcha."

"You're the best, Bryan," I replied.

"Don't I know it." He sent me a wink and walked out. He'd only gotten two steps out my office door before he called back, "Heads up, sugar. We have a walk-in and her mother coming up the lane. Square those shoulders and apply some gloss—she's got that look." A pause, and then a delicious note came into his voice. "And better yet, so does mummy."

I didn't need to be told twice. Whipping open my desk drawer, I pulled out my emergency mirror, compact, and gloss and primped at high speed. *That look*, as Bryan had called it, was code for someone who looked like she was well bred and knew it. And if she was a walk-in, then that meant she was most likely a little desperate, too, meaning that either she'd left her wedding preparations until the last minute or possibly that her wedding would come just weeks before the stork did. (It does happen, you know.) Regardless, a walk-in was very often a sure thing. Especially if she had good hair and an engagement ring that you could see clearly from across the room.

I was looking every inch the professional event planner by signing off on some contracts when Bryan, chatting charismatically, ushered in a well-dressed woman and her daughter.

On the mother: Black linen cropped pants, pressed and well fitting (check); white three-quarter sleeve button-down graced with appropriately large turquoise necklace and earrings (check); a looseness at the neck that belied her sixties, but with a well-preserved look and expertly colored short hairdo that decreased her overall age by ten years (check); two diamond eternity bands on her left hand that guarded her diamond ring and a tote-bag–sized Gucci handbag (double check).

On the daughter: Sassy halter-neck sundress in a chocolate brown with small Tiffany-blue polka dots (check); stylish wedge sandals on her pedicured feet (check); glossy, long medium-brown hair freshly highlighted and fashionably cut (check); beautiful, pimple-free skin and minimalist makeup (check); and one hell of a big rock on her left hand that could have guided ships in from sea (Bingo!).

And even better, both ladies were all smiles and had open, honest expressions. Bryan had been working his magic as well, charming them right out of their skin as they walked up to my desk. I stood up with a smile and felt the need for a shot of my Wild Turkey fading very fast.

"Shelby," Bryan said to me with his eyes twinkling, "This beautiful bride-to-be is Maggie Treadwell. And she obviously gets her looks straight from her mother, Virginia. Ladies, this is my boss and the owner of Waterlane Events, Shelby Waterlane."

I grinned, said my how-do-you-dos, and warmly shook hands with both ladies even as Maggie's mother twittered like a turquoise-laden songbird. Bryan, proving his weight in gold once more, gently steered Maggie and Virginia to the blue toile couch by the windows told them that he would be right back with some mint iced tea and homemade chocolate chip cookies.

Have I mentioned yet that Bryan bakes the most fabulous cookies? His secret is a teaspoon of cinnamon in the flour before it gets mixed with the rest of the dough ingredients. I'm not ashamed to admit that Bryan's cookies have been my substitute for sex these past two years.

Okay, maybe I'm a little ashamed to admit it, but they're still to die for.

"We're so happy you had the time to see us on such short notice," Virginia began as I settled myself in the adjoining chair.

"Yes," agreed Maggie, her huge hazel eyes wide with earnest. "We were expecting to be turned away because we didn't have an appointment, but we couldn't keep ourselves from seeing if you had some time. So, thank you so much for being willing to meet with us, Ms. Waterlane."

Ahh, some respect from someone today. Feels nice after being summarily thrown to the wolves of romance by my co-workers.

"Please, call me Shelby." I said, smiling at both ladies. "And we always welcome walk-ins when we can accommodate them. I'd love to know how you happened to hear about Waterlane Events, though."

Maggie giggled. "Well, you did the wedding of one of my friends from college, Monica Beresford..."

"Oh, absolutely," I said, nodding. "Such a cute girl. Lovely parents. Her wedding was one of the most fun and beautiful events that we did last year."

"It's what I'd like to model my own wedding after," Maggie continued, a blush of absolute happiness lighting up her pretty face.

It was that kind of look, the one of pure love and the most genuinely heartfelt hopes for the future of two people who had found each other and didn't want to let go, that made me truly love my chosen career. I never got tired of it. And seeing this look was what kept me willing to look for that right guy, too.

When I'm damn well good and ready to give up my moratorium, that is.

"And tell her the other thing," Virginia said with a grin that made her daughter start giggling again.

"The other place I heard about you is from my uncle and my brother, Bob Kappler and Luke Treadwell."

Well, now, my brain wasn't working properly at that point (probably still reeling from the lashing it received from my three employees) and so I didn't get the implications of what I'd just been told. Instead, the rest of the conversation with Maggie and Virginia went like this:

"Bob!" I said with a big grin of recognition as I sat up straighter in my chair and began to babble like most of us do when we realize we have somebody in common. "Oh, how funny that he's your uncle! He's an absolute doll. But I was horrified to hear about his accident! I just asked Bryan to send him a case of Shiner Bock and some flowers from all of us at the office, in fact. Is he feeling okay? I'm so disappointed that I won't get to work with him on the remodeling project. We had a great rapport and that's so hard to come by between a contractor and client."

Virginia laughed and made a humorously exasperated motion with her hands, "He'll be just fine, the big lug. His wife Nell just called from the hospital. His leg is thankfully just fractured and the doctor said it should heal easily. But you are so sweet for asking after him and sending him a get-well basket. He'll definitely appreciate the beer."

"I'm so glad he'll be okay," I replied.

"We were relieved as well," she smiled. "But I have to tell you that although my brother is a talented contractor to be sure, he is also one of the biggest klutzes ever to be seen on a golf course. This is his third time hurting himself playing golf. The third time! You'd think the man would learn by now. Nell is threatening to ban him from the links for good and I wouldn't blame her if she did."

We all laughed at that one and, things being as they were that day, I still hadn't totally clued in to all of what Maggie had said. Until…

"But now you'll be working with *my* brother Luke!" she exclaimed. "He's really talented as well. And he told me that I would like you and he was right." She was absolutely beaming, and so was her mother.

34

Luckily, my brain was starting to function again and I could feel my face finally showing the proper expression: confusion. "Well, I was told I'd be working with him since Bob is out of commission, but I don't think I've ever met your brother."

"Yes, you did," Maggie said. "You met him last night. At Bernatello's. He told us all about it."

I must stop here and plead with you to believe me that I really am a smart person. But at that moment the only person who came to mind from the night before was Caveman Kev. And even as I inwardly shuddered at the thought of him, Kevin's last name wasn't Treadwell, so I knew that I was still missing something from the conversation. Maggie delivered me the final key, however.

"He was there with Claudia. They met you in the parking lot."

And the hand of awareness slapped me square across the face.

Oh, God. Maggie's brother—Virginia's son—was my Lochinvar from last night! The guy with the leggy brunette (obviously named Claudia)! And Maggie and Virginia apparently knew the whole sordid story!

How. Incredibly. Embarrassing!

I struggled to keep from sliding under the coffee table in my power outfit in total mortification. I could feel my face burning, just as it did with Luke and Claudia when Kevin called me a bitch and a liar. (How quaint that the entire Treadwell family could now bear witness to this event.) I was only saved by Bryan's breezing in with a silver tray laden with iced teas and chocolate chip cookies.

"Here we are, the perfect mid-morning snack, in my opinion, cookies and iced tea," Bryan said in his most chipper voice. Since he usually stayed as quiet as possible when I was talking to clients, I could tell that he'd either heard what Maggie had said or he'd seen me turn my ninth shade of red and knew I needed a moment to compose myself. He took two of our Waterlane Events Inc.-monogrammed cocktail napkins and used them to pick up a cookie each for Maggie and her mother.

"Now ladies, if you don't mind me tooting my own horn for a moment, I won a blue ribbon at a bake-off with these just six weeks ago and so I'm proud to be able to tell you that what you're about to eat is a truly award-winning chocolate chip cookie." When both ladies made more excited twittering noises and took their cookies with eager fingers, Bryan merely smiled proudly and said, "The iced tea is freshly made as well. Please, enjoy, and I'll let you two get back to talking about your wedding with Shelby." He stole a surreptitious glance at me to find me smiling once more before excusing himself politely.

I could just kiss that boy! Praise be the day that I found him in that seedy motel!

With Maggie and Virginia munching delightedly on their cookies, I reached out to take one myself and brought the subject back up of Maggie's brother, who I had decided in the time it took my blush to fade was a mean-spirited toad who reveled in other people's embarrassing moments. But I did so now on my terms.

"You know, it's truly amazing how small the world is sometimes," I began with a tinkling laugh in my voice that I didn't really feel. "I had no idea that the guy who was so kind to help me out last night was your brother, Maggie. You see, after my date and I decided we'd had enough of each other, I caught a cab and left Bernatello's so fast that Luke, Claudia, and I never properly introduced ourselves. Or, I should say that my manners went out the window along with my evening because I failed to introduce myself properly to them. It's amazing what one bad blind date will do to your social graces, you know? But I will be sure to thank him again when he comes this afternoon to go over the plans again with me."

More likely, I was going to be sure to rake his skinny ass across hot coals for airing my dirty laundry to his sister and mother for his own amusement.

I saw that both ladies were wanting to reply but their manners prevented them from doing so as they had mouths full of Bryan's blue-ribbon cookies. So, with relish, I changed the subject.

"Now, Maggie, I'd *love* to hear more about what you want for your wedding," I said, leaning forward as if nothing could have excited me more.

And, just like magic, I was off the hook for any more embarrassing repartee about my evening with Caveman Kev. (And may it stay in the past.) Maggie needed no further encouragement to launch into all the details she wanted for her wedding, from the nearly five-hundred-person guest list, to her penchant for ball-gown style wedding dresses, to her desire to have huge arrangements of vibrant flowers filling both the church and the reception hall, to the look she wanted for her seven bridesmaids, how she wanted one of those fun photo booths at her reception for the guests to have an instant take-home memento, and much, much more.

It came out as well that the reason for their walk-in status was not because of procrastination or the impending stork. It was because Maggie's fiancé Barton had just found out that his company was transferring him to London on the first of October—exactly five months and thirteen days from the current date on the calendar. So, they had to move faster than initially expected. And when Bob had heard that I was one of the coordinators on their list to interview, he had apparently had given me a glowing reference and said they should try me first. And they had.

So, God bless Bob and his healing leg, he was now my hero. And with each enthusiastic nod of my head and suggestions here and there, I felt myself getting more and more excited about planning Maggie's wedding. Beyond being smart and having a good sense of humor, she had great ideas, knew her budget, had brought along pictures of the type of bouquet and flower arrangements she wanted, already knew she wanted her colors to be raspberry, peach, and apple green, and was clear that she wanted a Great Britain theme to honor her fiancé's Scottish heritage, her own mostly English heritage, and their impending move to England's capital. She also had already put a deposit down for St. Anthony's Episcopal Church for three separate dates in September in hopes that she would be able to find a reception venue to match, though she was nevertheless aware that she would have to be flexible. She knew what she absolutely had to have to be happy with her wedding day and knew what she could live without. She was obviously a dream client.

I gotta say, the embarrassment I had felt upon finding out that my newest potential clients had found out how horribly I'd handled my blind date with Kevin was fading quickly with each time Maggie's and my thoughts seemed to mesh—which more often than not foretold a good working relationship—and each upscale amenity that Maggie mentioned and Virginia seconded, making it very clear that she and her husband wanted the very best for their only daughter's wedding. Regardless, I still intended to make it clear to Luke that I didn't approve of him giving out the details. It's important to lay the ground rules out first thing, no?

Still, I found myself genuinely enjoying both Maggie and Virginia's company, and so I knew that my association with them was going to be pleasurable as well as profitable. It only takes a newbie event planner a couple of clients to figure out that some weddings are going to be easy and some just plain aren't. And those that aren't, even if the bride-to-be is a nice person in and of herself, are the equivalent of a never-ending root canal. When situations like that happen, every minute spent preparing for the bride's big day seems to be a chore and, for me, it takes everything I've got to keep my good humor intact and not feel like I want to bitch slap the bride into oblivion. But thus far in my career I've been able to hand out measured doses of honesty when needed and otherwise keep my smile and my humor intact. It was one of the core reasons for my success.

Now if I could just do the same thing with Luke "Sings Like a Canary" Treadwell...

I was still planning to find a way to put the fear of God into the man about disclosing any more details of my evening with

Kevin, until the rug that was Maggie's sure-to-be-fabulous wedding was gently tugged out from under me.

When our meeting finally came to an end, I had written everything down, we had discussed the event coordinators' holy trinity of rates, dates, and space—with rates actually being discussed last, as every good coordinator knows—and Maggie and Virginia had many times had included me in their future plans. ("You'll come with Mom and me to help me choose a gown and a reception hall, right, Shelby?") But at the very last minute, when I began talking contracts, the person I had already begun to think of as my client began to shift uncomfortably like there was something she hadn't told me.

Now, here is another secret to my success: I start the aforementioned measured doses of honesty out first thing when I meet a new client. I don't pussyfoot around and make them think I'm going to be sweet and easygoing and then bring the hammer down upon their heads when they start becoming the bride from hell. Instead, I start off immediately by steering them down the straight-and-narrow path to the altar so that we all have a good, open relationship and the wedding preparations get done with as little drama and mishap as possible.

Because, I don't know if you know this, but the bride and her mother both go from being two nice and intelligent people with whom someone can easily hold a conversation to being two frazzled, even if still well-dressed, spokespeople for stress-management classes by a month or so before the wedding. They truly go off to La-La Land because they're so overwhelmed and it's hard to get any decisions made after that point. By that time, the only sane person you can deal with will be the bride's father and he is so ready to get the thing over with that he'll usually just wave his hand out in front of him to stop you from saying things like "nosegay," "tulle," and "crinoline," then he'll whimper, "Whatever you need, really," and hand you the first credit card his trembling fingers can reach.

So, when I saw my first red flag go up in the form of Maggie looking a tad on the shifty side at the mention of a contract with Waterlane Events, I pushed her unceremoniously right into the honesty waters by saying with, "Okay, sweetie, I see you looking like you'd prefer to fade into the wallpaper right now. So, 'fess up. Is there something you need to tell me?"

Maggie blushed and, with a glance at her mother for courage, said, "Well, I'm embarrassed to have to admit this, but I did sort of promise another wedding coordinator that I would come interview with her before I settled on one person or another." And then she cried out, "I'm so sorry, Shelby! I should have told you before!"

Well, it was a tiny blow to my thinking this would be an open-and-shut walk-in coup, but it was all part of the business. Actually, I would have thought her a bit of a fool if she didn't shop around a little bit. Finding the right wedding coordinator is like finding the right guy: Pick the wrong one because you've chosen too fast and more than likely you'll be in for a world of misery.

Maybe I should remind Franzilla and my three wonderful employees about that fact…

Anyway, I calmed Maggie's nerves by telling her that, by all means, she should shop around and to just let me know soon because of our short, five-month deadline that was already looming. We all got up and shook hands warmly and I wasn't the least bit worried. But then my rug got a slightly rougher tug.

"Well, then," Virginia said to her daughter as she pulled her sunglasses out of her handbag and put them on top of her head. "Do you have the directions to the other wedding planner's office? What was her name again?"

I was smiling and putting the cap back on my pen when I heard Maggie mumble, "Kendra Everitt." And then she said in slight exasperation: "And for the tenth time, Mom, yes, I have the directions."

Virginia turned to me and I had the presence of mind to hold my pleasant expression in place even though I really wanted to start gagging at the mention of my toughest competitor's name. "Shelby, do you know Kendra Everitt? Is she any good at planning weddings?"

"Mom!" Maggie said with a horrified look. "We can't ask one wedding planner about another!"

"And why not?" Virginia asked and looked at me pointedly.

Virginia Treadwell was tougher than she looked. She was putting me on the spot to check to see if I would deliberately bad-mouth Kendra just to score Maggie's wedding. And good for her. I don't like wimps. And I don't like to bad-mouth the opposition to clients, either, thank goodness.

Even though Kendra Everitt is a platinum-haired, back-stabbing, rate-gouging, lying anorexic bitch from hell who wouldn't have anything nice to say about me even if someone pulled out her titty-dancer–length nails out one by one with excruciating slowness. It was just my own dumb luck that she is also admittedly an excellent wedding coordinator when she wanted to be. The only one who could really hold a candle to me in this city when it came to organizing upscale nuptials, if I may pull a Bryan and toot my own horn. I know this because it was I who hired her and trained her seven years ago. And then it was I who fired her two years later after finding out that she had mounted a smear campaign against me out of nothing but jealousy to some of my most trusted vendors. Luckily, one of the vendors had enough doubts to approach me and the whole mess was eventually cleared up, much to Kendra's intense frustration, and at the expense of her job.

Nevertheless…

"Kendra does beautiful weddings," I replied truthfully. "She's got an eye for detail and is very good at what she does."

"Really?" Maggie said, clearly astounded that I would say something like that about the competition.

I nodded. "Really. And if you like Kendra, then you need to sign with her. It's important that you feel comfortable with whomever you choose to handle your wedding, Maggie, and I mean that more than you know. You'll be spending so much time with your coordinator that she will get to be like a family member after a while, so it's imperative that you choose someone who you can respect and share all your wants and needs with, without hesitation. *You're* the one who needs to be happy, Maggie, and so make your decision on what you want, not what anybody else wants, okay?"

Maggie nodded, looking like she might be following in Dierdre's footsteps and developing a little emotional-bride lump in her throat. And so to save her saying anything she shouldn't, even something potentially good for me like, "I'm signing with you right now, Shelby!" before she had explored all her options, I began walking both ladies out of my office while asking Maggie about her dress and complimenting Virginia's turquoise baubles. We spent another few minutes discussing accessories before they left, happy, relaxed, and promising to contact me by Monday morning with their decision.

But although I felt at peace with myself that I had done the right thing with Maggie Treadwell (as I always do, because I realized early on that honest business practices will get you further in the end), I was also keenly aware that I no longer had the edge when it came to dealing with her big-mouthed older brother, who was due to show up on my doorstep in a little over three hours. I realized the moment I had heard Kendra's name coming out of Maggie's mouth that I was going to have to be nice to the jerk if I wanted to still have some pull in possibly getting his sister's business.

Damn! And I wanted to read him the riot act, too.

This day just wasn't going to give in without a fight, was it?

Five

Once Maggie and Virginia left, I did my usual post-first-meeting routine of typing up every thought, observation, and detail from my conversation with the bride-to-be. Not only did this help me to get a fully formed picture in my mind of what the bride wanted her wedding to be like, but it usually gave me a lot of great ideas, too.

And, in this instance, another thing it did was keep me from brooding over my impending meeting with Loose Lips Treadwell.

Not that there was much time to brood in the first place. At eleven-thirty Emily and I went to a luncheon for small-business professionals at the gorgeous Junior League of Houston building where we each nabbed a potential client with our charm and good looks. (I'm still in tooting-my-own-horn mode, apparently.) Then later I accompanied Lauren and Bryan to the office supply store to stock up on necessities like sticky notes, printer paper, and pens. There my two employees kept my mind occupied with their playful fighting on which of the two of them was going to have to work in the kitchen during the renovations.

With Emily claiming the file room, which was the former second bedroom, as her domain upon my first utterance of the word "renovations," it had come down to a tongue-in-cheek battle to the death between Lauren and Bryan as to who would get to share my office with me and who would be setting up shop in the kitchen, where, of course, tempting snacks were always kept on hand for clients.

In the end, though, Lauren knew that she would lose out. Since Waterlane Events' inception, Bryan had been both the office manager and our one-person welcoming committee who ushered in the new clients to their respective coordinator's domain. He would need to be where he had street-facing windows so that he could witness the arrival of any client and then perform the duties he had expertly honed over the last five years.

And after his stellar save of my embarrassed ass this morning with Maggie, I would have gladly rigged a coin toss in his favor had it come down to it. Thank goodness for one easy thing today, right?

I should have known not to count my chickens before they hatched, though.

When Bryan, Lauren, and I walked into the office using the back door by the kitchen, we trooped noisily into the file room with our wares and found that Emily had already moved the bulk of her things to the room while waiting for our return. Her desk had been moved as well and was positioned in the center of the room, which had honey-colored walls, one large window, one small closet that served to house all our office supplies, and several sets of light-brown metal file cabinets around the perimeter. I immediately thought the presence of her desk was odd because of the fact that it could not possibly have been moved by one person, but I didn't have to wait long to get my answer as to how Emily had performed this feat.

"Hello, ladies," she said with a wide grin to the three of us as she walked into her new pseudo-office carrying her framed black-and-white poster-sized picture of two golfers watching a third finish a beautiful swing at foggy St. Andrews in Scotland. Emily is a golf freak, has been since she was five. She plays better than most men, even though you'd never know it by looking at her voluptuous curves and ability for always being the best-dressed and accessorized person in the room.

Bryan, who was turned around and lowering a heavy box of printer paper into the nearby supply closet, wiggled his butt at her and I replied, "Hello, dahling. Anything exciting to report in the last hour?"

"Oh, not much," she said.

"Good," I returned, handing two cellophane-wrapped packs of sticky notes into Bryan's outstretched hands. I gestured toward her desk with my head, "So how'd you get your desk in here all by yourself?"

"I told you, Shelby," Bryan said. "She practices witchcraft when we're not here. She probably levitated it in here while we were gone using a wand she hides in that antique putter." His eyes went dramatically to the artfully mounted putter that was also atop the filing cabinets and then ducked when Emily launched a needlepoint pillow that said *The Princess Is in Residence* at his head.

"I had some help, actually," Emily said casually. Too casually, I might add.

"Who?" Lauren asked for me. "Did Percy come over?" Percy was Emily's boyfriend of three years and his huge six-foot-five, could-have-been-a-football-player frame made up for his kind of wussy-sounding name.

"Nope," Emily replied, cocking one eyebrow evilly. "It's our stand-in contractor, come a little early. And I gotta tell you, not only is he a looker, but he's also got one nice set of bird legs on him."

Then she had the audacity to look pointedly at me.

As I froze on the spot, it took about a half second for the room to fill with the excited high-pitched whispering that generally befits a group of teenaged girls when a group of cute boys are standing within earshot. And it all came from the mouths of my thirty-year-old co-workers.

"Shelby's Superman from last night?" Bryan asked, all agog.

"Hey!" I protested. Loose Lips was definitely not my Superman anymore. Nor my Clark Kent, for that matter. Clark knew how to protect his sources.

Bryan grabbed Emily's hand in excitement. "And he's hot?"

Emily nodded in a way that could only be termed salacious. Hearing the drumbeats of the Dating Brigade starting up again, I tried not to listen, but their voices kept shoving their way into my ear canals in a full-on charge.

"And is he wearing a ring?"

"Nope," my sassy and meddling blonde employee confirmed.

"Oh my God!" squeal-whispered Lauren, looking at me with lit-up eyes. "Shelby! He sounds perfect for you! And he's going to be working right here, every day, for the next four months at least! We're going to have to get you two together somehow."

Okay! This was going too far. I was feeling too many metaphorical hands on my back pushing me toward a man I could not have. And did not want, for that matter! And it was pissing me off royally. So, I went for the jugular.

"I doubt very much that Claudia would like that."

The coldness of my voice seemed to do the trick as much as what I had said. I rarely took that tone with anyone I loved, but when I did, they snapped to attention immediately.

With wide eyes, Lauren squeaked out, "Who's Claudia?"

I snatched up my purse from the top of Emily's desk and said, "She's his girlfriend. The beautiful, leggy brunette I told you about. And all three of you know I will not have anything to do with guys who are married or in a relationship, so we're ending this conversation now. I don't want Luke messed with when he's here to work, not to mention that he's getting paid and paid well to work, for Christ's sake. Are we clear on this point?"

Emily looked slightly miffed (like I said, she's not afraid of anything). Bryan and Lauren looked like they should, though. Like they knew they had stepped one foot over the line. I heard them say, "Sure, Shelby," and then Emily finished with, "He's in your office as we speak, going over the plans. And he's very nice, too, Shelby, so please don't skewer him for something we've done wrong, okay?"

I was going to stalk out and skewer the guy anyway. I *so* wanted to, it would have been so much fun. But instead I took a deep breath and sighed loudly, letting the anger flow out of me. I then grabbed Emily, Bryan, and Lauren into three quick hugs, saying, "I'm sorry. It's been a long day."

They each hugged me back fiercely and smiled at me as I walked out the door to meet Loose Lips (Okay, fine! I mean Luke) Treadwell properly for the first time.

Now I should explain something about me before we go any further. When I know that a guy I'm meeting with is either married or dating someone, I have a little thing that I do naturally and without really thinking that I find to be a godsend. I call it my Inner Wall.

What happens in simple terms is that I more or less shut down any part of me that might find said new guy attractive, no matter how attractive he, in fact, may be. A wall comes up, so to speak, between me and whatever part of the brain or heart that would allow me to be physically attracted to a guy who is not free to return those feelings. I have become so adept at signaling this wall to come up over the years of being both single and meeting men who aren't single, and being in the wedding business and working with men who are engaged, that I can almost *feel* an actual wall rise up within me that allows me to be charming, friendly, and helpful, but still arms me against doing anything stupid, such as giving off signals to any man when I shouldn't.

But far from depressing me, I find my Inner Wall comforting. It keeps me professional and able to do business with quick-on-the-jealousy-uptake brides and their fiancés who, often because of the fear of the "'til death" aspect of "do us part," often fool themselves into thinking that the grass may be greener on the other side of the fiancé fence (at least temporarily). I'd known more than one young naïve young wedding planner who had fallen for a man who was about to get married, his fear of marriage serving to make the aforementioned wedding planner seem more attractive than she actually was. It all blew up in the end, of course, and all of the naïve young wedding planners I knew had made some lifelong enemies and are now practicing other careers.

I, on the other hand, had watched and learned. And it has served me well. I would not be so uppity as to deny that I once had minor romantic feelings for a prospective groom in my own very early days of doing weddings. In all, I had been just lucky enough to find the willpower to tell him I was ending things well before anything irreparable happened (anything more than a few days' worth of flirting, to be exact). It's possible that my willpower was bolstered since I'd once been cheated on once myself and I never wanted another girl to feel what I had felt after finding out that the boyfriend I had trusted had betrayed me. Who knows? The point is that my Inner Wall was in its early stages back then but is now a steel-reinforced bad-ass that comes up and protects my sensibilities, my friendships, my clients, and my business faster than any guy can flash me a knees-melting smile.

So, when I came within two steps of turning left into my office, I stopped, took a calming breath, and felt a blessed calm come over me when I felt my Inner Wall rising solidly into place. Luke Treadwell and his Emily-certified hotness would have no effect on Shelby Waterlane. No siree. Even if I already had to admit to myself that, from what I had seen of him in the dark last night, he was of the general type of guy my eyes found pleasing.

And it would take me only a split second to see that in the daylight he was even better.

I walked into my office with my best professional smile in place and immediately saw what Emily was referring to when she'd said he had a nice set of bird legs on him. His back was to me as he was examining the plans for the office renovations that he had spread across one end of my desk. He was wearing a blue long-sleeved oxford, untucked with the cuffs rolled up to his elbows, running shoes, and khaki cargo—oh my God—

shorts. Shorts that easily displayed a long length of tanned and toned skinny-ass legs to absolute perfection.

Hey, it's my own brand of perfection we're talking about here. Work with me.

I fear I may have made a slight choking noise at the sight of his sexy gams because Luke Treadwell looked over his shoulder and right into my eyes.

"Shelby, hi." Crinkling eyes, which turned out to be a nice shade of blue when not hidden by lamplight glare. Same slightly wavy brown hair as before. He still had all of it, too. Wide smile with a dimple in the right cheek. Deep, relaxed, utterly sexy voice—the works.

Damn it. Inner Wall, send for reinforcements! Stat!

He turned around fully and covered the distance between us, holding his hand out to shake. I, Shelby of the Malfunctioning Inner Wall, was having a hard time keeping my eyes from his cute legs, though. And I hated my employees for pointing this fact out to me beforehand. I probably wouldn't have noticed them half as much had Emily not made a fuss over them. And I say that because not only would my Inner Wall have been firmly in place, but my lesser-used You Have Been Contracted Out to Do a Job and No More Wall would have been solidly up as well. Instead, it seemed that all my normally helpful walls were on the fritz because my employees had harassed me into taking my mind off the original end game: That I was a professional woman who had no current interest in dating and only wanted my office renovated.

And with that slightly miffed thought, my Inner Wall seemed to strengthen once more and I felt my usual calm and professional power come back to me. I snapped my eyes upward to their rightful destination (his face, of course), smiled one to match his, and held out my hand, which thankfully hadn't yet found the time to go all sweaty and clammy in the face of the type of guy who normally made my heart flutter.

"Luke. It's a pleasure to meet you properly." I ignored it when his hand engulfed mine in a good way. "Thank you so much for coming today to go over the plans with me since Bob is so unfortunately out of commission."

"I'm glad I finally get to meet you again, too," he said. His grin was one that said he had intimate knowledge of what I looked like when I had my foot firmly transferred to my mouth, and I didn't like it one little bit. He continued, oblivious to my growing irritation: "Though it didn't come from the greatest situation, I'm happy to be here to take over for my uncle, who, I've been instructed to say immediately, sends his regards and profuse apologies." Releasing my hand, he pulled at his oxford and said with a wry look, "I need to apologize myself, though, for being so informally attired. It seems that in a fight between my khakis and an open bottle of Dr. Pepper being carried by a plumber at high speed around a corner, the Dr. Pepper will win. These shorts and running shoes were all I had with me."

My co-workers' voices popped into my head at that point and dared me to get a good look at his long legs again. "You know you want to," came from the little voice that sounded suspiciously like Emily. I mentally doused all of them with ice water and held my gaze on Luke's face. "Absolutely no problem," I said. "Would you like something to drink before we get started?"

"Emily already gave me a bottle of water, so I'm good, thanks." Then amusement lit up his face as we moved to my desk, "And she obviously thought my impromptu work clothes highly entertaining—" He apparently didn't notice the compulsive jerk in my step at that comment. "Is she always that much of a…"

"Smart-ass?" I finished for him. "Yes, so prepare yourself. Bob learned quickly that if you can fire it right back at her then she'll respect the hell out of you. If you show fear, though, watch out. Emily's humor has fangs and she eats wusses for breakfast."

Luke Treadwell laughed deeply and loudly, two things I also have to admit I like in a man, dang it. "I'll remember that," he said.

Speaking of things he should remember, I felt it was time to gently remind him that, when it came to my own private and embarrassing moments, *en una boca cerrada, no entran moscas.*

Which is Spanish for silence is golden. Okay, it really means something like, "Flies don't enter a closed mouth," but that's just a little too unappetizing, so I went with the prettier paraphrasing first.

Anyway, I must confess that I never really stopped having an internal war between sucking up my pride and being nice to Luke in order to not hurt my chances with snagging his sister's wedding and going through with my original idea of having his head on a silver platter for blabbing the details of my parking-lot slam-fest with Kevin. In the end, I decided to pull a Johnny Cash and walk the line between the two extremes: Tell him how I felt, but do it nicely.

Fingers crossed, right?

When Luke began rolling up the plans so that we could take them with us while we walked through the parts of the house to be renovated, I laughed oh-so casually and said, "I wanted to thank you and Claudia again—now that I know both your names, of course—for coming up and trying to help me out with my date last night." I glanced up at him to see that he was grinning with knowledge again and I felt another stab of irritation. "It had just turned into one huge mess of a blind date, but I'll admit that it was ninety percent my fault by that time we got out into the parking for simply not being honest with him in the first place."

"It's never your fault when someone else's temper gets that out of control, Shelby," he returned. Like a big brother talking down to his completely off-the-turnip-truck little sister, I might add. I had to mentally yell "Down, girl!" to my own rising temper.

"I realize that," I said, forcing my voice to remain sweet. "And believe me, I don't take responsibility for his lack of control. But I am big enough to accept my own responsibility in what went wrong. Nobody likes being lied to, not even bull-headed cavemen."

As he was now finished with rolling the plans, he turned around and leaned up against my desk, looking at me thoughtfully. Respectfully, even. Then he laughed. "Okay, you're right. I can accept that. And for Claudia and myself, you're very welcome. After seeing what a jackass the guy became, we were just glad we were there, even though—" he grinned widely, "you looked mad enough to take him out by yourself."

He pushed his long, rangy self (Down, girl!) off the desk, obviously thinking that was the end of the conversation. Even though I was slightly mollified by his assessment of my abilities, the fiendish part of me continued to relish surprising him.

"Yeah, I probably would have tried to take him out if he had pointed his finger at me for even one more second," I laughed, doing a slow-motion right hook in the air for effect. "But how wild is it that, after what amounts to a chance meeting in the parking lot, you turned out to be my contractor's nephew? I mean, what an incredibly small world. Not to mention a totally embarrassing one when your sister and mom turn up the next day not only to interview me, but also fully aware of how foolishly I had acted last night. I was floored, let me tell you. Completely and totally floored."

I expected—I guess I wanted—him to defend himself and fight me on it. With all the crap I'd taken in the last twenty-four hours, I was itching to scrap and take out my frustrations on somebody who I thought deserved my wrath.

Instead, he just looked confused. And then his features smoothed into understanding.

Gotcha, you long, lanky, good-looking, loose-lipped ape! C'mon! Gimme your best shot! I practically heard the theme from *Rocky* in my head as I mentally danced in place and prepared to spar.

However, the look of understanding did not come with a side of hot temper. Instead, it came with the equivalent of liver and onions: a cool-headed explanation.

"Well, if what you mean by 'fully aware' is that I told them how you found yourself being verbally abused by your jerk of a date and then Claudia and I witnessed you cutting him down to size without any help from us, then, yes, they were fully aware of what happened." And he said it all with a calm, easygoing smile that bore me no resentment.

Okay, rational people officially suck.

"That's all?" I heard myself say. I wondered if my jaw looked as slack as it felt.

"Promise," he said.

Once again, I found myself utterly mortified in the presence of Luke Treadwell (thankfully without his arm candy as a secondary witness, though). He had obviously read me like a petite, blonde, power-outfit–wearing book and figured out exactly what I was so pissy about and took no time in correcting it. Not to mention the fact that he had deliberately made me look like a much better person than I was to his sister and mother.

If I slunk out of the room and never looked Luke in the eye again, do you think his sister would still hire me as her wedding coordinator? No? Damn.

Taking a deep breath, I linked my fingers together in front of me and called upon the shreds of my good manners to stand up and be counted. "Well, this makes twice that you've seen the absolute worst in me, Luke, and I must apologize." I had to tilt my head back to do so, but I looked him straight in the eye and felt stronger. "No, I should say I'm sorry. You don't know this about me, but I never say the words 'I'm sorry' unless I truly mean them—and I do mean them because I've treated you unfairly." I gave a self-deprecating chuckle. "I just hope you believe me that I can actually be a normal, level-headed person who doesn't make a habit of jumping down guy's throats at the least little thing because I want us to have a good working relationship with no hard feelings."

He grinned infuriatingly again and looked at me sideways. "You've been mad at me all day, ever since Maggie and Mom came to see you, haven't you?"

Here's another news flash: People who can read my mind suck, too.

I thought about it for a second. "If I admit it and say yes, can we shake hands, call it a truce, and get back to what you're here for in the first place?" I nodded at the plans he held in his right hand, and cocked an eyebrow, feeling more lighthearted even though he had called me out...again.

"Absolutely," he said genially, switching the plans to his left hand and holding out his right.

But I discovered with a shock that my own hands were no longer shake-worthy.

"Dang it," I said, finally busting out laughing despite myself as I vigorously rubbed my sweaty right palm on my leg. "You've embarrassed the hell out of me and made me all nervous. I hope you're happy." I held out my hand, grinning at both my own foolishness and sudden ridiculous clamminess of my palms. I figured that, since nothing else had worked, it was time to throw every ounce of pride out the window and see if that made for a friendship with my new contractor and erstwhile Lochinvar.

It worked. Luke's baritone laugh came out again and he grasped my hand and gave it a good shake before releasing it with a big smile. Then he gestured with a swish of the rolled-up renovation plans for me to be the first to walk out the door.

Okay, and I gotta say thank God that worked out. Otherwise I was going to have to make a swan dive for my desk and throw back a Big Gulp-sized finger of my secretly hidden Wild Turkey.

Six

Shockingly, the rest of the day went fairly smoothly. In the quiet of the afternoon, I returned messages, did my week-out confirmation calls to all the vendors for my client Janelle Rutherford's wedding next weekend, helped Bryan move his desk into my office, and then made arrangements to pick up two extra cases of wine for a huge bash Emily and I had co-planned this evening for a local city councilman's re-election celebration-slash-sixtieth birthday party.

But at four-fifteen came the call that made the whole day, crappy parts and all, worth it.

"Shelb," Bryan's voice came through my phone's intercom system, "line one is for you. It's Maggie Treadwell and she sounds fit to jump out of her skin with excitement. It's a good sign, sugar, I'm sure of it."

"Here's to hoping," I replied. "Put her through and thanks."

A moment later, Maggie's voice was coming through the line and aimed straight for the point.

"Shelby," she said. "I just couldn't wait any longer to call you and say I want to hire you to do my wedding."

"Oh, that's wonderful!" I exclaimed. "I'm thrilled—and I accept."

And although I didn't ask why she chose me (I never do, it would be tacky), she went ahead and told me anyway.

"Well, Mom and I met with Kendra Everitt and she obviously very knowledgeable about the wedding business like you said, but I got the feeling that she would try and steer me in the direction that *she* wanted to go, instead of helping me to truly fulfill all the dreams I've had for my wedding since I was a little girl. I just got the opposite feeling from you, you know? In fact, I felt like you and I clicked immediately and I liked your honesty."

"I'm flattered," I said. "Thank you."

"Well, there was just no contest," she returned. "But, Shelby," she then continued, suddenly talking to me as if she were one of my best friends. "Why didn't you just tell me that it was you who trained Kendra and that's how you knew she was so good at planning weddings?"

I laughed and replied, "I learned a long time ago that it does me no good to be that kind of person. Either you and I would click, like you said, or we wouldn't and no amount of bragging about whatever I've done in the past will make you and I work well as bride and planner if our personalities aren't suited to begin with."

"Well, then Luke was right again."

"Right…?" I repeated.

"I told him about how you encouraged me to check out all my options and how you said that Kendra knew what she was doing. I also told him how Kendra reacted when Mom mentioned that we'd seen you first—"

"You don't have to tell me what happened," I interjected.

Maggie ignored me and said, shock in her voice. "She *sneered*, Shelby. The woman actually sneered when I told her about how we'd just walked in to your office without an appointment and how you were so nice and wanted what was best for me instead of best for your business. I mean, let's face it, I'm planning a really big wedding and I'd be a fool to think that that kind of business wouldn't be good for any coordinator, but I just didn't get the vibe that the price tag on my wedding was the thing you cared about most, as I did with Kendra."

Now I was blushing again, but this time it was actually a good thing.

"And then she just sounded hateful when she warned me that what you said was all for show and that you really didn't mean it. But then I talked to Luke and he said that he's had two experiences with you now and that you don't know how to lie."

"Um, Maggie, I wouldn't go that far." As nice as it was to hear, I didn't want anyone making me out to be an angel when I knew that, although I tried to be one, my halo definitely fell by the wayside at times. (Okay, a lot.) Anyway, I'd rather people saw me as I really am—a nice, hardworking person who strove for honesty, but still made mistakes as much as anybody else. Being put up on a pedestal only meant one thing: a hard, rough fall with disappointment all around when you finally fell off.

"I know," she replied. "Luke explained it better. Something about how the honest side of you always came out in the end. And I like that. So deal with it, Shelby. You're hired."

Did I say this day had been a crappy one? Well, I officially retract that statement. It hadn't been so bad after all. I got up and practically danced my way back to the kitchen to tell my co-workers the news.

And, to make the suddenly nice afternoon even better, Bryan kept his yap mercifully shut about the guy he'd mentioned setting me up with earlier.

Yay! I had slain the dragon. I was free from another blind date!

Yeah, not so much.

Exactly seven minutes before Emily and I were to leave for the city councilman's party, Bryan walked innocently into my office with a couple of folders and a sticky note. I was typing up Maggie's contract and, being the trusting person I normally am, I didn't even look when he put the folders down on my desk, stuck the note on top of the folders, bent down to give my cheek a quick kiss, and said "Happy Friday, sugar. Have a *wonderful* weekend."

"You too," I said without looking away from the computer screen. "And give Gabriel a hug for me," I finished, referring to his sexy French boyfriend who worked as a translator and had just come home from a month-long work stint in his native country.

"Will do!" was Bryan's enthusiastic reply. I heard the front door close just as I saved my file. I moved my cursor up, clicked File, then Print, and then I turned my head and saw the hot-pink sticky note on top of the folders.

And felt my heart clutch in fear.

Okay, that's a little dramatic, but you know what I mean.

The note said:

Sweetie:
You have a date tomorrow night! I know you're thrilled. You can thank me later.

His name is Lars Michalski (Good Polish name—and you know what they say about those Polish boys, don't you?)

He is expecting you Saturday at Bistro Poitiers (I chose your fave French restaurant just for you!)

Time: 7:30 p.m. He'll be waiting for you outside the front door.

I met him at the airport while picking up Gabriel and have no way of getting in touch with him. So you <u>must</u> show up.

Have FUN! Love you most!
—B

Love? Love?! Yeah, I was not feeling love for Bryan at that moment. He had ambushed me! And that fairy bastard knew my sense of right and wrong would not let me stand this guy up at the restaurant, so I was stuck! I didn't even get to say Hell No to the idea of another blind date. That was just so wrong. Damn him and his sneaky ways!

And if you're wondering about the crack about the Polish boys, it comes from a joke about a woman who meets a guy on the airplane and tells him she studies ethnicities in relation to penis size. She goes on to say that the American Indians have the longest length while the Polish have the widest girth. Then the guy turns to her, holds out his hand, and says, "Pleased to meet you, I'm Tonto Kowalski."

Ha, ha. Yeah, if only.

That's it. I was going to tie Bryan to my couch, force him to watch monster truck rallies on TV, and make him drink Lone Star beer out of a can. That's right, regular, high-calorie beer. Cheap beer at that. Sneaky gay bastards don't get their prissy-ass wine. It will just about kill him.

Emily breezed in just as I was relishing the thought of how much Bryan would suffer under my torture regime. Walking up to my desk, she read Bryan's note (I have nosy people working for me, don't I?), smirked in a self-satisfied way (cahoots, they're all in cahoots), and told me to get my rump in gear because we had to be at the Dickinson's house for the birthday soiree in less than half an hour to make sure that everything was up to snuff.

Sometimes I wonder who runs the show at this place.

Anyway, I gave her my best snappy salute, which she cheekily accepted with a regal nod, and, after leaving Lauren to lock up, we were on our way.

And, like scores of Southern women before me, I invoked the mantra of our most sacred patroness, Scarlett O'Hara, in that I chose to push aside any thoughts of my impending blind date and think about it tomorrow.

Seven

Saturday morning I woke up early, stretching languorously and feeling good with the thought of landing Maggie Treadwell's wedding. But then my mind remembered Bryan's late-afternoon ambush on my moratorium and my stomach instantly turned with a feeling of dread at the idea of going on another date when I really didn't want to.

And, though I tried, I could not reach Bryan to bitch him out about it. The boy had done the unthinkable and let my call go to voicemail. And the message I left, which I intended to be scathing and fear-inducing, turned out to be more of a completely un-scary stuttering dispersed with phrases such as "you big, mean bastard," "such a traitor," and "really big, mean, horrible bastard." Try as I did to believe he would be affected by it, even as I hung up, I had visions of Bryan doing nothing more than snickering evilly as he listened to my attempt at being tough.

Nevertheless, like the big girl that I am, I shook off the feeling of Blind Date Dread with a two-mile jog through the tree-lined neighborhood followed by a good, hot, soaking shower. Throwing on some jeans and a watermelon-pink V-neck tee, I left just enough time to go by Shipley's Donuts to get coffee and a dozen glazed for Luke's four-person demolition team before hightailing it to the office to open up.

Once the workers had begun knocking down the non-load–bearing wall that separated the living and dining rooms, I made sure my Inner Wall was firmly in place before I quietly took Luke aside to thank him for what he had said to his sister on my behalf that made her want to hire me.

"First of all, she had it in her mind to hire you even before I said that," he said, but with a charming smile that indicated he was altogether very pleased that the whole thing had worked out, "and changing Mag's mind is about as hard as I figure it would be to change yours." I gave him a look of shock at that dead-on assessment, which made him laugh. "And secondly, I wouldn't have said that to her if I didn't think you were the right person to work with her, but you're welcome anyway."

I was very glad that I could escape to my office to do some paperwork after that because, although his cute legs were now hidden under faded jeans and beat-up work boots, he was sporting another thing I found ridiculously sexy and therefore felt immense relief that I even had an Inner Wall at all: Saturday Morning Scruff. And he wore it well, too—he had neither too much nor too little, and didn't apologize for not shaving. He was comfortable in his manhood and there is little (besides the bird legs, of course) that is more sexy to me than that.

But, alas, he was taken by the beautiful Claudia and I had such immense respect for people who enter into relationships that I would never be privy to doing anyone's relationship any harm. Therefore, I turned my energies and attentions elsewhere for the rest of the morning, catching up on paperwork and sending off a multitude of e-mails, all while listening to the semi-melodic sounds of accordion-driven Tejano music and the banging and scraping noises of wall, shelving, and baseboard removal. And through every bit of it, I couldn't tell you how blissful it was to have a morning free from people harassing me about my love life.

That was, until Hilary showed up.

Being as it my best friend lived down the street from one of Houston's best Mexican taquerias, I had arranged for her to pick up the order of twenty tacos *al carbón* with sides of beans, rice, cheese, sour cream, and pico de gallo for the workers, Luke, and ourselves and bring it to the office for lunch. When she walked into the house, which was beginning to quiet down since all the really hard demolition was now done, I watched from my office in amusement as my best friend poked her riotously curly strawberry-blonde head into the war zone across the hallway, raised her eyebrows, and said a silent, "Wow," before coming into my office.

"They've done a lot of work in a short period of time," she said, after placing the bags in the barrel chairs and giving me a quick hug.

"Well, there wasn't a whole lot for them to demolish besides the one wall and all that hideous shelving that the previous owners had installed sometime in the seventies." I said as I handed her the money for the food.

"True," Hilary conceded with a grin. Then, motioning with her head of curls back across the hallway, she said, "So, who's the skinny, six-two *gringo* amongst all our friends from across the border in there?"

I heard the note in her voice that said she'd noticed he was about our age and probably had seen his lack of a wedding band as he helped to sweep up the debris that was collecting on the drop cloth-covered hardwood floors. That's my Hilary to a hilt. I've been calling her Eagle-Eyes MacIntosh since I met her in the sixth grade. Only now she's Eagle-Eyes Petrakis after marrying Dimitri, a fourth-generation restaurateur, almost seven years ago.

I played it cool and pretended to look in the bags of tacos to make sure everything I'd ordered was there. "He's our contractor," I said.

"Really?" Hilary replied with a calculating glint in her clear green eyes. "I thought Bob Kappler was your contractor. And unless I'm mistaken and a whole lot dieting and plastic surgery has occurred, not to mention the discovery of the Fountain of

Youth, that boy in there with the long legs and Saturday Morning Scruff is *not* Bob Kappler."

Okie dokie. It was obviously high time I learned to keep my blabbering mouth shut around ol' Eagle Eyes MacIntosh-Petrakis. She not only saw too much, but she also remembered too much as well.

As I turned around, I heard the Tejano music shut off, signaling that somebody knew it was lunch time. Hurriedly, I leaned in toward my friend's beautifully freckled face and said in an undertone, "Hil, knock it off. The boy with the scruff is completely taken. And he really is our contractor. Bob broke his leg and Luke is both Bob's nephew and his partner in the company. He's the 'T' in KT Construction. Our relationship is very strictly professional."

Hilary, who was smart enough to know better than to push something with me when pushing wasn't an option, immediately dropped the cute-boy-for-Shelby-at-fifty-paces tone in her voice and nodded her head. "Gotcha. Backing off the subject." Then, turning around to see five hungry men pretending that they weren't looking to pounce on our bags of tacos, she said, "Let's feed these poor guys, shall we?"

"Good idea."

When all the tacos and their corresponding condiments had been doled out and the workers had all filed outside to the front porch to eat, Luke—who had brought up the rear of the taco line like a good boss—got to talking with Hilary and me and we invited him to stay in the office with us for lunch.

And within minutes, while we feasted on the deliciously seasoned and grilled strips of tender beef cradled in warm, freshly made flour tortillas, it was as if Luke had been our friend since way back. Using my desk as a table since the couch and chairs were temporarily occupied by some of Bryan's many stacks of files, the three of us ate and talked about food, movies, and the undeniable fact that baseball games were boring as hell to watch on television yet somehow really fun to watch in person. And then later, during one of Hilary's hilarious stories of her first few dates with Dimitri that involved a Houston Astros baseball game, lots of beer, a big, ridiculous fight about the origins of ketchup, and Hil's teary call to yours truly, an innocent and totally offhand comment was made by my best friend that changed the course of events to come:

"And that's my one story that even comes close to matching Shelby's repertoire of lousy dating experiences."

Luke glanced across my desk at me. "So what I witnessed the other night was about par for the course with you?" His eyes twinkled with friendly humor as he took a huge bite of his second taco.

"Pretty much," I replied and then, seeing Hilary's confused face, I explained, "Luke and his girlfriend Claudia were the nice couple I told you about who came up and tried to help me when that guy Kevin became such an ass."

Out of the corner of my eye, I saw Luke stop in mid-chew and stare at me even as Hilary squealed in delight as she pointed at him, "Oh my God! You mean *he's* your Loch—" hearing her own error, she stopped herself mid-sentence and tried to correct it, "I mean, this is Luke?"

After apparently struggling to swallow as fast as he could so that he could say something, Luke seemed to change his mind when he heard Hilary's flub and said, "What do you mean, 'your Lock…'? Lock, what?"

Hilary's red-faced, sheepish look sufficed for a non-verbal apology after I momentarily flashed her the evil eye. Then, all at once, I figured, what the hell, why not just tell him? He's going to hear similar things from my employees when he works here, so he'd better know how it all works. It's not as if it would make a difference anyway since he's got a girlfriend and everything, right?

So, I let the cat out of the bag.

"What Hilary almost told you is that you have been referred to as 'my Lochinvar' for attempting to help me out the other night."

Luke, who had been casually bringing his bottle of Coke to his lips, froze and his blue eyes widened slightly as they looked into mine. I couldn't really read his expression, but knowing that to a guy with a girlfriend, referring to him as your knight-in-shining-armor verged on unwanted flirtation, I rushed make myself clear.

"Okay, you need to relax here and let me explain. There's something you should know if you're going to be working in close quarters with my employees and me," I said, wiping my hands on my napkin and wadding up the aluminum foil of my first taco. Luke continued looking apprehensive, which somehow made the whole thing ridiculously funny to me and I couldn't stop my wicked grin.

"Starting five years ago when I first hired Bryan and he heard about my uncanny knack for bringing out odd traits in my dates and boyfriends far sooner then they would normally have shown these traits to a date or girlfriend, he began a tradition that survives to this day. Every time I have a bad date, the guy in question ended up earning himself a rather unflattering nickname based on whatever goofy or strange personality trait he exhibited most."

"But...," Luke began, his expression veering toward bewildered.

I smiled kindly. "Bear with me, I'm trying to explain and still keep a shred of your respect for my intelligence." He visibly relaxed and so I soldiered on. "So, for instance, my date from the other night was Kevin. And as he had the manners of a Neanderthal, he was duly christened Caveman Kev."

I instantly saw the humor light up in his eyes again and his mouth quirk upward. Points for the former Loose Lips—a nickname I would *not* be revealing to him, thank you very much—for being a good sport. "Anyway, the nickname thing is a tradition that has sort of gotten out of control over the years. So much so that I tend to give most guys, regardless of whether or not they're normal or loony tunes, a nickname in my head that usually comes out in some way, shape, or form when I'm relating the story of my date to Bryan, Lauren, and Emily."

"And don't forget me. You do it all the time with me," Hilary piped up, not wanting to be left out.

"And Hilary, of course." I grinned. "And if no name occurs to me, then rest assured that one of my *treasured friends*," I batted my eyes at Hilary, "will come up with one for me."

"And...so...um...Lochinvar...?" Luke inquired, looking distinctly uncomfortable at having to say the word.

I sheepishly pushed my hair behind my ears. "Well, the name Lochinvar just came out because of how you gallantly tried to step in with Kevin and everything and was not meant, I assure you, to be anything but harmlessly amusing."

"You mean how I tried to step in with Caveman Kev, right?" he said, smile telling me that he'd finally decided that the whole thing was as funny as I'd hoped.

I clapped my hands together in glee. "By George, I think he's got it! Oh, my employees will be so proud!"

Laughing, Luke aimed his half-eaten taco back toward his mouth and asked, "So what are some of the other names you've saddled your wayward dates with?"

"Oh, God, where to start?" I said, turning to look at Hilary.

"Well, you gotta go with the classic one first." she said.

"Ahh, yes. That would be The Jimmy. Whose real name was, in fact, David."

Hilary turned to Luke. "Are you a *Seinfeld* fan by any chance?"

Mouth full, he nodded his head in a heck, yeah, kind of way.

"So you remember the episode with the guy who referred to himself in the third person?" she continued, cocking an eyebrow to see how quick on the draw he was.

Luke stopped chewing again, looked incredulously at Hilary and then even more incredulously at me. He knew instantly that the totally obnoxious *Seinfeld* character in question had been called The Jimmy. And it very clearly registered with him, too, that I had actually been dumb (or desperate) enough to date a guy who referred to himself in the third person.

"You're kidding me." he said, nearly choking as he tried to swallow and laugh at the same time. I nodded, saying, "But he didn't just refer to himself as David, he went one worse and called himself Davey."

"I repeat, you're kidding me," Luke laughed.

"With my dignity voluntarily in such shreds, how could you think I would be making this up?" I replied, hand to my heart, faking an insulted look.

"And how long did this relationship last, might I ask?"

"A little over a month. But Davey didn't show himself until the last couple of weeks, so I don't feel like a *total* ass."

"Just somewhat of an ass," my best friend said, nodding sagely as she added more cheese to her second taco.

"Thanks a lot, Hil." I returned dryly. "Way to be on my side."

"Anytime, my friend."

Looking like he couldn't be enjoying a conversation more, Luke asked, "Any other particularly choice names or dating escapades you want to offer up? Just so, you know, that I have the same amount of embarrassing inside information on you that Hilary here and your co-workers do."

Ladies and gentlemen, I think I have created a monster.

"Oh, no," I replied, trying hard to look appalled. "We couldn't have that, now could we?"

"Well, I wouldn't want to be working on half a tank of information here or anything. It's unfair." He leaned back in his chair and, just before popping the last bite of taco in his mouth, the scoundrel grin came out again in full force.

I leaned over my desk and wiggled my fingers in a confused kind of gesture, "Did I say we called you Lochinvar? Actually, what I really meant to say is that we call you Pain in the Ass Treadwell."

"I've been called worse," he responded, adding an infuriatingly cute wink that Hilary completely missed since her napkin had dropped to the ground and she had reached down to pick it up.

Inner Wall, stand strong!

Hilary, placing her napkin back in her lap, suddenly popped her eyes wide and said, "Wait a minute. I've got another one. Who was the guy who kept touching himself in public? The one with all the cats. He was a really spiffing one."

Luke blinked. "The guy played with himself in front of you? And owned cats? Where did you find this winner?"

Trying to keep a straight face and losing, I said, "I met him at an SPCA fundraiser that I organized. At first I thought he was just, you know, adjusting a little too often, but after two dates I found out that he couldn't stop."

Hilary drawled, "And it got worse when he thought he was going to get naked, too."

"Hey," I said. "I broke up with him before we got naked, thank you."

"Well, before *you* got naked," Hilary returned. "He was all too willing to strip down and be friendly with himself right smack dab in front of you after one good kiss."

Luke rushed his hands through his hair and then covered his eyes in a combination of laughter and disgust for a member of his own sex. "What did you call this guy?" he finally asked.

I grinned. "Well, in honor of his love of cats, we went with Rum Tum Tugger."

It took Hilary slapping Luke on the back a few times to get him to stop coughing.

And then my best friend, being the teacher that she was and thusly feeling the need to explain and inform no matter what the subject, gave Luke yet another interesting little tidbit of insight into my life: "You know, it was due to guys like the Jimmy, Tug, and a couple of others that Shelby decided to go on her dating moratorium."

Luke went to grab a third taco from where they sat in the middle of my desk and his smile, predictably, changed to a look of confusion.

"Okay," he said, opening up the foil to his taco and looking thoughtful, "now, I know what a moratorium is, but I've never heard of it in relation to dating." He angled his head and gave me his sideways I'm-trying-to-figure-you-out look that I was quickly learning was a common Luke Treadwell expression.

And of course, I found it shamefully cute. In fact, I was starting to wonder if my own moratorium wasn't trying to taunt me by sending me a cute, but utterly taken, guy who I could have really liked otherwise just to blow a big ol' feel-the-emanating-spittle raspberry right in my face. It would have been about on par with everything else, wouldn't it?

Anyway, Luke said, "So, do you want to explain this to me?"

Lest I be thought of as even weirder than before with the disclosure of some of the oddballs I'd allowed myself to go out with? Oh, sure, what the hell.

I shrugged and said, "It's very simple. I got tired of always meeting and dating the wrong guys, so I decided to take some time off from dating."

"A dating moratorium…," Luke stated, narrowing his eyes and sounding like a scientist trying to analyze a freaky, two-headed byproduct of a lab experiment gone wrong.

"Precisely," I returned, squaring my shoulders. "I just decided to take myself out of the game for a while."

"And when did this start?"

I wondered when he was going to start prodding me with some sort of pointy tool to see if my other head would start moving.

"Um—"

I hesitated just a fraction of a second too long.

"Two years ago," Hilary supplied for me. "In fact, it's now *over* two years since Shelby has been on any dates at all." She looked at me kind of sadly.

Awww, now the two-headed lab experiment is being pitied. How nice for me.

Dr. Treadwell decided to throw me a bone, though. "Except for Caveman Kev, you mean."

Both my heads grimaced at him and he asked, "So you haven't been dating…at all…in the past two years? Voluntarily?"

"Voluntarily," I confirmed. "And I know it sounds strange to you people, but I've actually enjoyed the time off from the dating scene. It's been, I don't know, refreshing."

"And are you still on your moratorium?" Luke asked, his face inscrutable again.

I answered quickly: "As far as I'm concerned, yes. For right now, I happen to like being single and I just don't know that I'm ready to start dating again yet." Then, I nodded toward Hilary and said, "But as far as my so-called best friend here, my employees, and Franzilla are concerned, I'm up for grabs to the highest bidder."

"Um, *Franzilla?*" Luke queried.

"Oh, right," I laughed. "Franzilla is what we jokingly named the combination of my mother, Frances, and her sister, my Aunt Priscilla."

(Speaking of freaky, two-headed...)

"Seriously?" he asked me, the blue eyes lighting up again, making me decide their color was definitely of the Wedgwood variety.

"Yes, very seriously. I love my mom and Aunt Prilly with all my heart, but they never accepted my moratorium and have been harassing me from minute one to get back in the game. They backed off for a while when I opened up Waterlane Events," I said, gesturing with my hand to indicate the offices, "but now they're back at it and at full force. Franzilla, in fact, is the responsible party behind my cousin Jake—who is Priscilla's son—setting me up with Caveman Kev. Jake got ambushed and then coerced. He said it wasn't pretty."

Luke gave a commiserate laugh and replied, "Been there— at least sort of."

"How do you mean?" I asked.

Without looking up from doctoring his taco with pico de gallo, he said, "Oh, my best friend is always jumping on me to set her unmarried girlfriends up with my other friends. I try to resist every time—basically because it has never, ever worked out—but then she uses that feminine knack for inducing guilt that all you chicks possess in droves and I end up giving in. It always turns out horribly, but within a few months she's at it again."

"Brazen hussy," I joked.

Hilary, being a married woman, picked up on the point that interested her the most, though. "Your best friend is a woman?"

When Luke looked back up, I read in his face that he'd heard that particular challenging tone before that had shown up in Hil's voice. Nevertheless, his reply was easygoing. "Sure. She's a great girl. We've been friends since our first week of college."

"And Claudia doesn't mind?"

Luke's responding smile said that something in his own mind was suddenly funny. "Nope. In fact, it suits her quite well."

At Hilary's look of disbelief, he added, "It just so happens that *her* best friend is a guy, so we understand each other and it's not a big deal at all."

"Oh," was all my pal could say in return since her argument had been so quickly deflated. Being a wise person, Luke then took the opportunity to smoothly change the subject back to something he found much more entertaining: my dating moratorium.

"So, since you consider your moratorium to still be in effect," he said, "does that mean you're not going on any more setups?"

"I wish," I said, making a face at the thought of more bad dates.

He seemed to be surveying me even as Hilary the Informer put in her two cents again. "She's already got another blind date tonight. Bryan set her up."

Now it was Luke's turn: "Oh?"

I would have liked to say I heard disappointment in his voice, but I figured what I heard was probably closer to morbid curiosity than anything.

"Yeah," I said grouchily. "Bryan met some guy while waiting to pick up his boyfriend at the airport and apparently they got to *chatting*." I said it like Bryan talking to some other person was positively indecent. "Then, wouldn't you know, he goes and pimps me out for this Saturday evening—without even asking me first!" I looked at both my lunch partners with incredulity and hoped to receive some back in return at what Bryan had done to me.

I should have known that Lady Luck would thumb her nose at me as she flew by to help someone else out.

Luke, his lips twitching in the face of my despair, said, "That's a dirty shame, Shelby. Just...terrible."

It seemed I had another smart-ass friend on my hands, no?

"Thanks a million. I'm glad you find this all so funny."

Hilary, who had been quietly holding back her snickering, let out a loud snort of laughter, causing Luke to lose it as well.

"Both of you are mean, horrible people," I grumbled, sending what I hoped were glaring looks their way. Neither seemed fazed.

Apparently, I had little or no ability to intimidate any of my friends. This was so not good.

Eight

As the afternoon began to gallop at top speed toward the evening, I became more and more grumpy at the idea of having to meet another blind date for dinner. Hilary, being the optimistic type, tried to make me see the bright side of things as we sat out in the April warmth on the porch swing while Luke and his demolition crew finished up their work inside the house.

"After all, it's just one dinner," she said as I stared out at pink climbing roses that were beginning to unfurl on the porch railing. "And you really do need to start getting out there again."

I didn't snap at her and say that it wasn't her decision to make since Hilary had been one of the few people in my life who had actually supported me when I had decided to begin my moratorium. Mother, bless her and her dying-to-be-a-grandma heart, had been so disappointed in me that she didn't talk to me for a week, which is a record for both of us. Nevertheless, I still could not bring myself to agree with my friend, even when she made a good point.

"Since you are in a business where you never meet single men—and the only ones you've ever worked with have been gay—you will never have a chance to meet anyone unless you start allowing people to set you up more often or unless you start going out more and meeting people at parties and such, like you used to."

"I'm just not ready yet, Hil," I said.

She put her arm around me and said, "Shelby, you've gotten so set in your ways because of your moratorium, will you ever really be ready?"

I gave a frustrated sigh as my answer. But we both knew that she was right. I had already been a fairly independent and picky person even before my moratorium, and after two years of being single and loving it, I was even more so.

I guess the idea that one day the right person would wander into my life and make me *want* to give up my dating moratorium was just pathetic wishful thinking, huh?

Yeah, well, bite me.

"You're right, Hil, you really are," I told her as I used my toes on the wood plank floor to give the swing a small push, "but I'm not going to suddenly fall in love just because you and everybody else want me to. It will have to happen naturally or it just can't happen at all."

Hilary was ready for me, it seemed. "Yes, but sometimes 'naturally' needs a little bit of a helping hand."

"I don't deny that..." I stopped when I noticed the front door had opened. The Tejano music had shut off for the final time that day; the demolition crew was finished. Luke stepped out onto the porch, followed by his men, each carrying tools or a bag of trash out to Luke's dark blue Chevy crew-cab pickup truck. White lettering on the front door panels gave out KT Construction's phone, website, and the motto *Small jobs are our biggest business!*

"Well, we're done for today," he said, stuffing his hands in his jean pockets.

"Oh, great!" I said, feeling extra relief at having a reason to talk about something else than my impending date. When the porch swing swung forward again, I hopped up and walked two steps forward toward Luke, intending to offer my hand for him to shake as I thanked him and his crew for his work. I didn't get the chance, though, because one of the workers who was coming out of the front door lugging a huge industrial vacuum tripped over the threshold and rammed right into Luke, who stumbled forward, hands still in pockets, and right into me.

Or, specifically, my nose got unceremoniously planted directly into Luke's sternum.

Before I ricocheted backward, however, his hands shot up out of his pockets, caught me, and held me to him for the briefest of seconds (pretty much as I let out a totally unprofessional-sounding *oof* noise).

"Jesus, Shelby, are you okay?" I heard him ask when my next sound was, "Okay, ow." The poor worker behind him was apologizing in both Spanish and English and it was his concerned dark eyes that I first saw as I slowly stepped back from Luke's really good-smelling chest, which, without any active thinking to speak of, reminded me of a mixture of soap, fresh wood shavings, and leather.

I smiled at the worker and assured him in decent Spanish that I was just fine.

Hilary, who was not as concerned for my welfare, moved to Luke's side and said, "Way to go, graceful."

"Glad I could amuse you—yet again," I replied, now holding the back of my hand to my nose as it had opted to start running. A white handkerchief appeared before my eyes and I took it from Luke's hand.

"You really okay?" he asked me. When I glanced up, however, he looked like he really wanted to laugh at me. Wryly, I made a hand motion that encouraged him to let loose and the dimpled grin showed itself. Then he reached out with his index finger and lightly patted the tip of my nose. "Glad to know that thing is tougher than it looks, Waterlane."

"Yeah, yeah," I said, using the handkerchief on my nose again. "Does this count as a good enough reason to not show up at dinner tonight?" I gave a hopeful, pity-me look in the direction of my best friend.

"No," she said.

"Damn."

"It was a good try anyway," Luke chuckled. "Well, I'd better be going to get all the trash to the dump so my workers can go home. We'll be here bright and early on Monday, though."

"Sounds good. Tell Claudia hello for me," I said as he turned to walk down the steps.

He paused, his hands going back into his pockets. He didn't look at me. Instead, his gaze rested on the now-empty porch swing. "I'll certainly do that. See you on Monday, Shelby." With that, he bounded down the steps and his long legs quickly covered the short space of brick walkway to his truck.

The next moment I heard Hilary's chipper voice in my ear. "So, what are you going to wear on your hot date tonight?"

If my best friend isn't the four-star general and leader of the Dating Brigade, I don't know who is. The girl doesn't let up for a moment, does she? I figured it was time to put up a show of strength on the rebel side...

"Hilary, sweetie, I'm going to send you home now," I said. "I've got to formulate a plan for all the places Maggie and I are going to go to on Monday and I don't want to think any more about tonight until I absolutely have to."

"All right, all right," she said, holding her hand up in surrender, "I give. I'll leave you be. But I want a full report tomorrow morning, okay?"

I replied wearily, "I always do," and reached out to give her a hug.

And when everything was finally quiet, excluding my sniffing as my nose continued to run for another twenty minutes, I breathed a huge sigh of relief.

Still, it was a while before I stopped smelling Luke's scent every time I breathed in.

About a half hour before I was to leave for my date, I grudgingly got up off my comfy chenille sofa where I had been watching television and trudged slowly through my little bungalow, moaning dramatically the entire way. At a little under nine hundred square feet, I only got three or four good moans in. Still, my little one-bedroom, one-bath plus-a-study was pretty darn cozy and I loved it.

Smooth under my bare feet were the original wide-plank wood floors, darkened with age and good care to a lovely hazelnut brown. Windows in every room let in lots of natural light and shutters were at the ready for privacy. I didn't have a dining room to speak of, but the long, thin rustic wooden table in my little two-way galley kitchen did multi-duty as an island, chopping block, breakfast nook, wet bar, and occasional party-time buffet station.

At the back of the house was my bedroom, which stayed neat by virtue of the fact that all I did in there was sleep since it was only big enough to hold my queen-sized bed, one bedside table, and nothing else. And the closet? Yeah, it was so small it was downright laughable. Thus, I'd turned it into a linen closet and the study had become my eight-by-ten walk-in. Literally.

Freestanding modular wooden racks and drawers, stained mahogany, held my clothes and shoes while an antique tallboy housed all my jewelry. In the middle of the room was a leopard-print area rug, on top of which sat a chaise lounge upholstered in oxblood-red velveteen. Hilary or Bryan often reclined there, sipping a glass of wine and offering up their unfiltered opinions as I tried on outfits. At the far wall was a full-length, three-way mirror and in the corner was a bamboo tri-fold screen that hid my wicker laundry baskets. Colorful art-deco advertising prints decorated the walls and underneath each of the two windows were large Chinese blue-and-white urns holding delicately leafy ficus trees. Besides my kitchen, it was easily my favorite room in the house.

And hey, when it comes to closet space, a girl's gotta do what a girl's gotta do, right?

No sooner had I entered my bathroom, with its sage-green walls, white pedestal sink, tub-and-shower combo, and a slightly warped door that never closed properly, that I heard my home phone ring. Could it possibly be Bryan calling me to say he was just joking and I didn't have to meet some random guy at my favorite French eatery, perhaps? I trotted with a gust of hope into my bedroom.

No such luck. The Caller ID said it was the Fran in Franzilla.

Actually, it said "Waterlane, Robert," which really means, "Waterlane, Frances." My father, even though we were very close, was not one for calling me to chat. Or calling anybody to chat, for that matter. He viewed all telephone-like communication devices as a necessary evil that must be used on occasion, not the friendly lifeline that my mother viewed it as. Mother, in fact, liked her lifeline in the speakerphone variety, which drives most everybody crazy.

I picked up the cordless phone and said, "Hi, Mom. How's it going?"

"Shelby, don't you ever just say 'hello'?" another voice admonished.

Uh-oh. I was wrong. It was the full-on Franzilla! My Aunt Priscilla's voice had rung loud and clear into my ear, and more so due to the fact that she was one of those people who thought they had to talk twice as loud because of the speakerphone.

"No, she doesn't," my mother's voice said to her sister. "She almost never says hello since the invention of that person ID thing."

"It's 'Caller ID,'—and hi, Mom. Hi, Aunt Prilly."

"Hello, dear," they said simultaneously, their voices just a fraction different from one another in pitch, Mom's being the shade higher. There was also a hint of an echo when they spoke that had nothing to do with using the speakerphone.

"Y'all are holed up in the Death Star, I presume?" I said, as I tucked the phone into my shoulder and padded back into the bathroom to turn on my curling iron and begin my pre-date primping.

"Must you and your brother always call it that?" Mom returned exasperatedly.

"Dad calls it that, too," I reminded her as always.

The Death Star is what we call Mom's personal sanctum sanctorum. In normal terms, it's actually a library-slash-office, but since it happens to be mostly round in layout and is also Mom's personal space that she guards with a territorial attitude worthy of Darth Vader, my brother and I had christened it the Death Star beginning with its inception during our high-school days when my parents first remodeled the house (with a thirty-pounds lighter Bob Kappler at the construction helm). The name became even more fitting recently when Mom positioned her desk at the bay window that faced south—which, if you looked at the blueprints, made it kind of resemble the Death Star's crater-like laser station—and added two futuristic side-by-side flat-screen computer monitors on top so that she could have her e-mail up on one screen and then work on her volunteer group's newsletter on the other screen. When she sits at her desk typing furiously away, she looks like she's guiding a book-filled spaceship out into intergalactic war. And Colin, Dad, and I think it mighty funny.

I heard Mom say to her sister, "I have the most incorrigible family," and I laughed out loud when Aunt Prilly replied, "I know, honey."

I easily envisioned the two of them each sitting in one the office's comfy chintz chairs, designer-sandaled feet up on the available ottomans, with the phone on the little glass table between them. They would most likely both be wearing some sort of springy linen outfit—brighter shades for my honey-blonde and fair mother, and darker jewel tones and browns for my auburn-haired aunt—and their respective blue eyes would occasionally flick toward the muted television atop on of the library shelves that was undoubtedly tuned into the Food Network.

"But Shelby, dear," Mom continued. "We're calling because Jake told us that your date didn't go well last night."

"Uh-huh," I said as I freshened my mascara.

"Well, he didn't tell us any specifics or anything, but he did say that the two of you, shall we say, exchanged words and then the date ended early," Mom said primly, and with a certain dual-themed note in her voice that said that while she did not approve of my having a tiff with someone in public, she was still looking for more information that what she already had. I cast my eyes heavenward in exasperation and silently called Jake a knucklehead for not giving them enough information to realize that I'd done the right thing by sticking up for myself and giving this guy the boot.

"He seemed so nice from everything we heard about him before your date," my aunt said. "Jake pointed him out to us at the gym and said Kevin had started his own business from scratch two years ago. If that's true, he couldn't be that bad. Starting a business takes a certain strength of character that most people don't have—you yourself should understand. Are you sure you didn't just misjudge him?"

"That's right, sweetie. You must have just misinterpreted something he said." Mom chimed in.

Poor Aunt Prilly. Poor Mom. They were reaching in a big, bad way.

"I didn't misjudge him, believe me," I responded calmly as I picked up my eyeliner and leaned closer to the mirror. "And as for his business, did Jake tell you what kind of business he runs?"

Franzilla was momentarily (and uncharacteristically) silent. So I jumped in. "He sells so-called dietary vitamins and sports supplements over the internet. Teenagers and college kids are his biggest demographic."

More silence. But this time I knew it was because my beloved elders had no clue what I was talking about.

"These supplements are marketed toward kids as a way to help them build muscle and improve their athleticism, even though those claims are pretty much bogus. The supplements are legal to sell, but most sports organizations have banned their use. Colin told me that some of them even cause serious health problems."

"You can't be serious!" my mother exclaimed after a pause to digest what I had said.

"That nice-looking boy is selling drugs to children?" Aunt Prilly seconded my mother with a shocked gasp.

"More or less," I replied. And then I told them the abbreviated version of how and why the parking-lot fracas has ensued in the first place while I dusted my face with powder and combed my hair so that my tousled side part was once again straight and neat.

"Well!" Mom said when I was done, the anger at Kevin now clear in her voice.

"That awful boy!" Aunt Prilly huffed, making me feel altogether vindicated. But a heartbeat later my aunt's voice changed to one of interest. "Oh, look, Frannie, Ina's making her filet of beef bourguignon that I was telling you about. It's delicious."

"Mmmm, it certainly looks delicious," Mom agreed, her voice back to its normal happy timbre as well.

I shook my head in amused exasperation. Just like that, what I had gone through last night with Kevin had been reduced to something far less important than what the Barefoot Contessa was making for dinner.

"Um, Mom? Aunt Prilly? Did you two need anything else? I'm kind of getting ready to go out." I said this as I eyed my curling iron and wondered if I would burn myself if I tried to talk on the phone and curl my hair at the same time. I decided not to risk it and walked back into my closet to pick out a pair of earrings that would go with my new plum-colored boatneck cashmere tee, black Capri pants, and my black patent Kate Spade slides with a kitten heel.

I had no intention of trying too hard with my outfit. Mr. Michalski was not getting the ultra-spruced-up version of Shelby Waterlane until he proved himself worthy of the goddess-like vision I could become if I tried.

"Where are you going, dear?" Mom asked, the distraction in her voice telling me that she was concentrating more on reading the closed-captioning of whatever instructions Ina Garten was no doubt giving on how to perfectly braise the beef than on my plans for the evening. Or so I thought. Because just as I was going to give some vague answer about going to dinner, she said, "And who are you going with?"

For a split second, I considered fibbing about my plans to my mother and my aunt. But a flash in my mind of the scene that had occurred after I'd tried lying to Kevin made me instantly reconsider and go back to my truthful ways. Still, I hoped that if I slanted the whole thing properly by making it clear that I wasn't happy about being set up, then maybe my female family members would get the picture. Or, at least, not make too much of my impending date.

Silly, silly me.

"Well, it seems that you two have started some kind of rage with this whole set-up thing because Bryan met some guy while he was picking up his boyfriend at the airport and now I'm being forced to go on yet another blind date tonight." Just for clarity, I added, "And I'm not happy about it."

Nary a pause was heard before my mother cried out, "But that's wonderful!"

"Hot damn!" Aunt Priscilla seconded.

"No. Not 'hot damn'," I said. "This is not a fun thing for me like you two think." I then aimed to further lecture my relatives on the fact that setups rarely work out and that I didn't intend to be some guinea pig for my friends and family, but I didn't get the chance.

"Oh, Shelby," Mom said, "Don't be so dramatic. It's just a date and I'm sure you'll have a good time."

I gritted my teeth. First of all, I tried very hard *not* to be dramatic, thank you, and yet Mom had still decided I had been just so that she could say those irritating words. I absolutely hated that.

"Yes, Shelby," Aunt Prilly added. "I went on many blind dates before I met your Uncle Wes and I loved them. It was always so exciting to meet a new person and get to know them over a nice dinner. Even if it didn't work out, I felt I still had made a new friend."

"And don't forget that your father and I met on a blind date when we were in college," Mom said with a hint of smugness in her voice.

"Mom," I returned through my still-gritted teeth, "for the umpteenth time, it is not called a blind date when you forget to check your rearview mirror and you back over Dad and two of his geeky engineering buddies in your '57 Studebaker."

"It was a '58 Studebaker," my aunt corrected me, "and it wasn't hers, it was your granddad's. Your mother was just borrowing it for one of the skits we put on for the rushees at the Pi Phi house."

"Thank you, Prilly," I heard my mother reply in her fake hurt voice.

"You're welcome, dear."

Oh, for crying out loud! Which I then actually articulated: "Oh, for crying out loud, you two! This is ridiculous."

"We're not being ridiculous, Shelby," my mother answered, as if she had been biding her time for just such a perfect opening. "You are the one who is simply making too much of this. Your friends and family are just trying to be kind and set you up with men who they think you might like so that you can get some experience dating again. The very least you can do is to just thank them and then go and enjoy yourself while getting to know another human being. It's as simple as that. Please don't make it into a life-or-death situation, because it's not that big of a deal."

I took a deep breath and looked at my reflection in the mirror, only to see a flushed, rapidly angering Shelby staring back at me. So, instead of trying to defend myself and have a full-blown argument ensue, I did the only thing I could do to save me from saying things to my mother and aunt that I would really regret later. "Did either of you have another reason for calling me?" I asked, "Because otherwise I'm late for a real, true blind date." And, without giving them even a nanosecond to answer, I said, "No? Well, that's good. Because I've heard about enough from my so-called loving friends and family for one day. I'm going to try and calm down while I finish getting ready and then I'm leaving for the restaurant. Tell Dad hello for me and have a good night."

I heard a distinct, "So dramatic!" from the other end of the line just before I punched my phone's OFF button. In frustration, I hit the button much harder than I meant to, causing my finger to buckle, the phone to drop out of my hand onto my right big toe, and a long stream of blue words to come out of my mouth.

Hey, my motto is repression is bad for the soul. I never claimed to be Pollyanna, you know.

Nine

The clock on my dashboard said nine thirty-four when I hit a speed dial on my cell. He answered on the second ring.

"Hey."

"Hey yourself," I replied. "What are you doing?"

"Talking to you."

"Smart ass."

"You asked."

"I meant besides the obvious, Colin."

"Ohhh," my brother chuckled, apparently amusing himself with his own wittiness. "I'm watching television. Some show about Roman aqueducts on PBS. There's nothing else on."

"Hey, PBS is great television. Don't knock it."

"Spoken like the true geek you are, Shelb."

I gave an insulted snort, but my brother and I both knew, along with everyone else who knew and loved me, that I was a big ol' history-loving, museum-patronizing, biography-reading nerd and I wholeheartedly embraced it. Regardless, I shot back, "At least this geek had a date tonight while you, Dr. McWannabe Studmuffin, are home alone on a Saturday night—your only Saturday night off from the hospital in ages, I might add—watching public television instead of bedding that saucy new Latina nurse from pediatrics you told me about."

Colin groaned. "That was cold, Shelb. Ice-freaking-cold."

"So, she shot you down again, huh?"

"Don't remind me, please," he said.

"Okay, well, then since you're a big ol' loser tonight, how about meeting your big sister out for a drink at Lawson's?"

"Yeah? What's the occasion?"

"Oh, nothing really. Just had a not-so-great night and I'm not ready to go home." And before he could ask, I finished with, "And I'm not in the mood to answer to my personal gang of ruffians tonight, so I decided to call you instead."

Colin deftly ignored my backhanded compliment. "I take it the date you just referred to whilst slamming my own evening has something to do with this?"

"Yep, it does. But I'll only tell you about it over a couple of beers."

Proving himself a tried and true Waterlane, Colin sighed as if his life was over and then replied, "Fine. But I'm only doing it because I pity you and I want to make fun of your miserable love life."

"So that, what, yours seems fabulous by comparison?"

"Shut up," he laughed. "I'll see you there in twenty. And you're buying."

Lawson's Pub, founded in 1971, was situated on the corner of one main thoroughfare named Yale and a street called McKay Avenue that rarely saw much excitement due to the fact that it became completely residential just a few yards beyond the property boundaries of the pub. I live one street north of McKay and three houses down, making it very convenient for me to just park at my house and walk the short distance to the bar to meet my brother.

I found Colin standing at the polished dark-wood bar talking animatedly to one of the female bartenders. I could have predicted that he would be wearing jeans and a polo shirt that was some shade of blue (tonight it was sky blue). For all his attributes, Colin had missed out on the sharp-dresser gene and felt that jeans and polos were the height of fashion under most circumstances.

As I made my way through the crowd toward him, I wryly guessed that my call to ask him to meet me out had been a welcome one. Though it had barely been fifteen minutes since I'd talked to him, he'd obviously been at the pub long enough to order himself a glass of Guinness and make a dent in its contents; he must have bounced right up off his couch and hightailed it over to Lawson's as soon as he'd made his smart-mouthed comment about me buying the beer. The fact was, while Colin was nowhere near the needy type, he just wasn't as good as I was about being alone. But his love of being around people was a substantial portion of what made him a good doctor. Simply put, I was proud of Colin because he was a good man, with strong principles, a kind heart, and a generous nature.

And yet, he still managed to absolutely relish infuriating the living tar out of me. I guess some things never change, no?

"Hey, Shorty," he said as I squeezed in beside him at the crowded bar. He was only five ten, but he was one of those types who looked taller than he was, not to mention that he had almost a good eight inches on me to begin with. And he loved every centimeter of his height advantage, basically because he said he always felt like a giant around me. I stuck my tongue out at him in reply and Colin's arm immediately shot out, put me into a headlock, and gave me a quick noogie on the top of my pate even as I growled out a muffled protest.

Okay, so I probably egg on my little brother and that's why he loves driving me up the wall. It's an ingrained response; I can't help it.

Making grumbling noises about idiotic brothers as I smoothed my hair again, Colin cheerfully ordered me a pint of Harp and we moved out toward the belly of the pub, grabbing a four top that was conveniently close enough so that Colin could still eye the cute female bartender. Settling back in his chair, he said, "So what happened on your date tonight? Did the guy try to paw you or something?"

"He wanted to," I replied. "And if I had left the restaurant with him, he surely would have."

My brother's eyes narrowed for a second in a way that told me he was not liking hearing that his sister had been in a state of near-pawing without her consent. But then his look switched to puzzled. "You mean you didn't leave the restaurant together? What did you do, fake a trip to the bathroom and then walk out on him?"

I was shocked that he had unceremoniously foiled my story, but the way he said it, with all seriousness, suddenly amused me and I couldn't help but grin and ask, "Um, do we have any personal experiences with this so-called fake trip to the bathroom scenario, Colin?"

Colin gave me a ha-ha-you-are-just-*so*-funny look and replied. "No, I haven't. My dates can't get enough of me and I practically have to use a cattle prod on them to keep them out of my pants." And before my scoffing got too loud, he said, "I heard one of the nurses talking about doing that a couple of weeks ago. I couldn't believe that a date with some guy could really be that bad so as to actually make a girl pull a stunt like that just to get away from him."

Well, that sobered me up a tad. I took a drink of my beer and said, "You'd better believe it, honey. Because some dates *are* that bad. And yes, the fake trip to the bathroom was exactly what I did." After my date became thoroughly drunk and horny, which made him reveal his narcissistic, bigoted, and decidedly homophobic side, specifically.

Colin looked astounded and leaned forward so that his elbows were on the table. "You really walked off and left this guy sitting there waiting for you, Shelby? You stiffed him with the check and everything? Good God!"

Okay, maybe I should have called my girlfriends instead. So much for brotherly love and support.

"I did not 'stiff' him on the check," I returned, making a scornful face. "I had a waitress deliver money for my half of dinner. Including a generous tip!"

"Well, at least that's something," my brother replied, sitting back in his chair again and taking a swallow of his Guinness.

"Whose side are you on anyway?" I snapped back.

"Right now," he said, "I'm on the side of the guy who you publicly embarrassed at a restaurant simply because you decided that you no longer enjoyed his company. He may have acted like a jerk, but guys have it pretty tough with you women, you know. Especially on first dates." He sat up straighter and declared, gesturing toward me with his beer. "Especially on blind first dates! They're hell, Shelb. Even for the most confident of guys."

Damn it. My infuriating bigger-than-me little brother had a freaking point. Brothers who show some common sense when you don't want them to have now been added to my Things That Suck list.

"Do the details of the evening even matter to you or have you condemned me without so much as a trial?"

Colin's face lit up in a delighted grin. "I love it when you do Mom's wounded poor-little-ol'-me voice. It just makes my day."

Did I say that my brother had a big heart and a generous nature? Yes? Well, I take it back. Pardon me while I proceed to scratch my brother's eyes out...

"Hey," Colin said, his eyes flicking back toward the bar.

"What?" I snarled, pissed that I hadn't yet formulated my comeback to him telling me that I was doing the ungodly and emulating my mother.

"What does this guy who you had a date with look like?"

"Why?" I asked, still snappishly.

Colin's eyes flicked back to me, and then back up at the bar. His body language was tense. "Because there's a guy up there who's been staring at you for the past few minutes. He's been glaring at both of us, actually. And if this is the guy who upset you tonight, then I'm going to take out his spleen with my bare hands."

I felt a shade apprehensive as I turned around in my seat. I expected to see the long, tall, blond vision of Lars Michalski staring menacingly at me for walking out on him at Bistro Poitiers, only to find me casually having a drink at another establishment. What I saw when I zeroed in *was* a long, tall vision of a man. But it wasn't Lars.

It was Luke.

Ten

As I stared at Luke in surprise, he gave me a grim look and raised his beer glass at me a fraction by way of a greeting. He seemed as tense as Colin, but also like he was determined to be non-confrontational. It took me only a split second to realize that he'd seen me snapping at my brother and, knowing that I was to be out on a blind date tonight, he thought I was in trouble again and was surveying the scene and wondering how to act. Only this time my Lochinvar was being good and trying to let me fight my battles myself before charging in on his white horse. He had learned! God, that was cute. And before my Inner Wall shot it sturdy way up, I broke into my own delighted grin at the sight of him.

"Shelb?" my brother asked. "Do you know that guy?"

"Yes," I said as I saw Luke's face register confusion, then surprise at my smile, then something close to an embarrassed happiness. "And he's not the guy from tonight. That's Luke. My contractor for my office renovations." I beckoned enthusiastically at Luke to come over to us and turned back to my brother as Luke eased away from the bar and started our way. "And he's a very nice guy. I think he thought *you* were my date and that *you* were the one making me upset."

Colin feigned surprised. "Me? Making you upset? Never."

I laughed but then abruptly fixed my brother with a steely eye. "Now you mind your manners, Colin James Waterlane, or I'll have your head on a silver platter."

"And why should I mind my manners, hmmm?" Colin asked. "Does my big sister have a crush on her contractor perhaps?"

I glanced back to see that Luke was only three good steps away. Thank goodness it was loud as all get out in the pub so he didn't hear my reply as I whipped my head back around to attempt a mean glare at my brother. "No, you big brat, he's got a girlfriend. He's just a nice guy, nothing more." I shook an admonishing finger at him. "So you be good!"

Colin leaned back in his chair once more and batted his eyes at me like a prima donna just before looking beatifically up at Luke, who was suddenly standing slightly awkwardly at our table in his very Colin-esque attire of jeans and a navy-and-white striped polo.

"Shelby, hi."

"Luke! How are you?" I said with gusto as I stood up from my chair. Luke's smile widened in a way I really liked as he looked down at me. I was suddenly very aware of our closeness that was amplified by a very weird moment where I didn't know whether to shake Luke's hand or hug him like a friend or what. (My Inner Wall kept me from doing what I would have liked to do, but I'm going to be a good girl and not even go there.) Luke seemed to be letting me decide what to do and so I finally just kept my hands to myself, nervously gesturing to my brother, who was getting up from his chair like someone who actually knew his manners.

I introduced Luke to my brother and they clasped hands and said the obligatory "Hey, man, nice to meet you," specifically using the deeper octaves of their voices. I inwardly chuckled. Guys are so weird sometimes.

"Your brother, huh?" Luke smiled at me.

I nodded. "Yep. My one and only."

Luke looked at Colin and then back at me. "Now that I'm closer, I can definitely see the resemblance between you two."

Because we got this a lot, Colin and I both pointed at our eyes and said, "It's the eyes." We both had distinctive big, round, eyes set decently wide apart. But Colin got the thick lashes, dang it, as most guys unfairly do.

"You've got the same facial structure, too." Luke said. "Except for the noses." He looked at me but motioned with his head back toward Colin. "His isn't all pointy like yours is. How's it feeling by the way?"

My fingers went to my nose (which I inherited from my mother) even as I ignored my brother's inquisitive eyebrow. "Oh, it's fine now. No worries."

"Did you show off your clumsy side again, Shelb?" Colin of the Straight, Not Pointy, Nose asked.

"You hush," I replied, blushing and deliberately not mentioning that it was directly into Luke's broad chest—which smelled really good, if I can add that in again—that I had planted my nose. Luke and Colin looked all chummy and chuckled at my expense.

It had been less than a minute and already I could see that a contingency on the scale of Franzilla was developing between Luke and Colin. Just what I needed, right?

I threw up my hands to indicate that I was giving up and said to Luke, "Would you like to sit with us?"

Colin seconded the invitation and Luke accepted as we settled back in our chairs, with Luke sitting to my right.

Then it hit me that I didn't know if I had taken him away from anybody when I motioned him to come over, so I swiveled around and looked back at the bar in curiosity, "Who are you here with, by the way? Is Claudia with you?" I didn't see anybody who even gave us a second glance.

Luke cleared his throat. "No, Claude is out with her girlfriends tonight. I was here with some guys who occasionally do some work for Uncle Bob and me. We'd been here for a while and were about to leave when I, uh, saw you and your brother over here." He looked sheepishly at me and said, "I have to confess that I saw the two of you, ah, acting like you were having a heated discussion and I thought that maybe Colin here was that blind date that Bryan had set you up with. So, I left the guys to go back home to their wives and decided I would at least stay for a few more minutes to, you know, just to be sure." He grinned, shrugging his shoulders, and while I couldn't be sure because of the low lighting, I thought I saw him blushing. "I know I said I wouldn't do that again, but..." He looked at Colin as if for moral support. "I've got a sister, too, and a couple of good friends who are women and I guess it's just not in me to leave when I think that they might be in an..." His palm turned upward in a flustered manner.

"Uncomfortable situation?" I finished for him, not unkindly.

He looked at me like he was ready for whatever reprimand I could dish out. "Yes."

My brother piped up immediately before I could respond. "Well, as her brother, I'm glad to know that someone is watching out for my pipsqueak of a sister. She may act tough, but she's really easily squashable, like a little blonde bug." He then made a very bratty-younger-brother face at me.

Ahh, the eloquence of Dr. Colin J. Waterlane. It brings tears to your eyes, no?

"I am not *squashable*, thank you very much," I shot back.

Colin made a *pshaw* noise. "Wanna bet? I can take you with one hand tied behind my back. Remember last Thanksgiving?"

I put my hands on my hips. "Pushing me down on the couch when I was literally dizzy from one of the worst head colds I've ever had in my life and then sitting on me and threatening to fart on me so that you could keep me from getting the last slice of pecan pie does not make me squashable, Colin. Don't forget, I've kicked your ass once before and I can do it again."

Luke was laughing into his glass of beer and my brother said, "This 'ass kicking' to which my sister refers with such confidence, Luke, happened when she was thirteen and I was ten. I caught her reading her diary out loud and professing her love for a pudgy boy with huge Coke-bottle glasses poetically named Sheldon Fishburn. I laughed so hard I nearly pissed my pants and, when my eyes were closed at one point from hysterical laugher, Shelby here punched me in the stomach and I fell over. Two weeks later I got a big growth spurt and she's never dared to try to 'kick my ass' again since then because she knows I could take her *down*."

Try as I might to stay huffy, it was all over from there and I planted my elbows on the table and buried my face in my hands in (okay, I admit it, amused) mortification. Luke and Colin practically busted their guts and could barely get out a "yes, please" when the waitress came around and asked if they wanted a refill on their beers. It was all so charming and urbane. Like a roasting that had no ending.

I peeked one eye out from the shelter of my hands. "I guess after all you've heard from my friends and family, Luke, I have absolutely no chance of ever looking cool and sophisticated again in your eyes, huh?"

The huge grin—dimple and all—that I got in return was my answer, even as I said, "Don't answer that."

"Do you still keep a diary after the Sheldon Fishburn debacle?" Luke asked me.

"Hell, no," I said loudly, sending my brother and my contractor into fits of snickers again. I tried looking pissy and calling my little brother a couple of choice names, but it didn't get me very far, especially when I saw Colin reach into his back pocket and pull out his iPhone, which was lighting up with a vibrating call. Before he answered it, he leaned across the table, pinched my cheek like an Italian grandmother, and said in a pitying voice, "Awww, you're so cute when you try to be all tough and unsquashable, Shelb." Ignoring the withering look I gave him, he answered his cell phone with a professional-sounding "Dr. Waterlane speaking."

Luke gave me a questioning look and I nodded my head and gestured palm-up toward my brother across the table. "Yep. It's true. This man sitting here before you being absolutely horrid to his sister, who is the epitome of sweetness and light," I put my hand to my heart and looked heavenward for effect, "is, in actuality, a doctor. Currently a resident at St. Mark's Hospital who's set to specialize in internal medicine."

Luke nodded thoughtfully, his lips firmly pressed together in an attempt to keep a straight face. "The 'epitome of sweetness and light,' Shelby?"

"Damn. You're not buying it, huh?"

Luke smiled at me and leaned closer, making a little flutter happen in the pit of my stomach. (What gives? Does my Inner Wall need recharging or something?) "Nope, not for a second," he said. "I do think you're incredibly tough and virtually unsquashable, though."

I must admit that I turned beet red and gave him a big smile. You would think that it would have been more of a compliment to me to be called sweet, but instead the thing I cherished most about myself was my strength of mind, body, and character. All three working together had gotten me where I am today and so Luke Treadwell had just given me one of the best compliments of my life.

Thank goodness my brother interrupted because otherwise I might have sat there smiling at Luke for far too long than was acceptable for a single woman talking to a taken man.

Colin slid his chair back a few inches with a flourish and went to stand up. "Apologies, my fine companions, but I have to go."

"Emergency at your hospital?" Luke asked.

Colin affected a really good bad-boy grin. "Well, there is an emergency, but it's not at the hospital. It's the four-alarm fire known as Isabel Ramirez." He emphasized the name with a rolling-the-r's flourish the likes of which would have impressed Houston's entire Hispanic community.

"*Nurse* Ramirez?" I asked, astounded. "As in the wouldn't-touch-you-with-a-ten-foot-pole-and-willing-to-tell-you-so-in-front-of-the-entire-hospital Nurse Ramirez?"

"Shelby," my brother stated calmly, looking at me as if I were suddenly lacking my wits, "She was just taking her time coming around, that's all."

"Is that so?"

"You bet your clumsy little pointy nose, baby," Colin replied like the scoundrel he was as he dug out his wallet and extracted some bills to pay for his and Luke's pints, waving off Luke's attempt to help pay. "The fact is, she wants me. She has since the moment she walked her hot Colombian-born bod in the hospital doors and saw me."

"How romantic of you, Colin," I replied.

Luke, however, showed that he was still a red-blooded guy by saying, "Way to go, man. She sounds smokin'."

"Like you wouldn't believe!" was Colin's enthusiastic reply.

I tried my best to look shocked and reproving at Luke, who toothily grinned right back, but I was secretly a wee bit tickled. Sometimes, and especially when you know that they're just putting on airs—like I was positive Colin was, and I was pretty darn sure that Luke was—guys just being the sexed-up, permanently teenaged boys they were to their cores was kind of funny. Colin liked to harass me and play the playboy to the hilt, but in reality he treated women with respect and dignity. And I was guessing that Nurse Ramirez, who was the new girl at the hospital, had been finally set straight about Dr. Colin Waterlane by some of the other nurses and that is why she rang him up at ten-thirty on a Saturday night for what was probably a major booty call after a long shift at the hospital.

At least one of the Waterlane siblings would get laid tonight, right?

I leaned back in my seat as I prepared for my brother to hightail it at lightning speed out of Lawson's and into the waiting arms of his little Latin temptress, so I was surprised when he plopped back down in his seat and reached across the table to take my hand.

"Before I go, Shelb, are you okay? I mean, after your sucky date earlier?" He continued, his eyes searching my face, even as I felt Luke's gaze lock in on me, "We never really got to finish talking about it and…"

"No, no, sweetie," I said, shaking my head. "It wasn't a big deal. The guy was just a jerk and said some mean, homophobic things about Bryan. I was just going to vent about it some." I looked at Luke and then back at my brother, "But you two have done such a good job at entertaining me—or should I say humiliating and teasing the tar out of me—that I pretty much have already forgotten about the whole thing." I squeezed his hand and said, nodding my head in the direction of the pub's exit. "Really. Now you go and get yourself some of that hot tamale! Pronto!"

Colin looked at Luke. "And that is why I love my sister." He came around the table to hug me goodbye, but stopped before we could embrace. "Wait a minute, you probably walked over here from your house, didn't you?"

I rolled my eyes as I knew what was coming. Colin hated the fact that I would walk to Lawson's at night because of the dangers that could happen to anyone walking alone at night, even in a residential neighborhood. He'd seen too many things at the hospital and regularly scolded me on the subject. I knew the possible repercussions and respected them with my entire being, but I also knew almost all my neighbors on my street and I refused to live my life in fear when I lived on a quiet street in a safe neighborhood. Regardless, the truth came out of me as I grumbled, "Yes, Colin, I did."

Amazingly, I was spared the lecture this time, probably thanks to the saucy Nurse Ramirez and her waiting arms. Instead, he turned around to Luke and said, "Would you be willing to take my wayward sister home so that she's not being a dingy blonde and walking home late at night by herself?"

"Colin!" I said, outraged. I pointed forcefully in the direction of my house. "I live *right there*! Right there! And I've got my pepper spray!"

"Sure, no problem," interrupted Luke, addressing my brother and ignoring my protest. And when I gave Luke a blistering look that said I could handle myself in the two-minute walk to my house, he said with irritating calmness, "And I'm not going to take any of your lip, Shelby. I wouldn't allow Maggie to walk home by herself late at night no matter how safe her neighborhood was and no matter how close she lived. Pepper spray or not, it's not smart. So deal with it. I'm seeing you home safely and that's that."

My chin jutted and I fumed, but I said nothing. I knew he was right. My brother slung his arm around my shoulders and spoke to Luke with something close to awe in his voice. "Treadwell, you are the first guy I've ever known who's been able to shut my sister up. I'm impressed, man."

Luke shrugged nonchalantly. "I've got myself a sister who's as stubborn as a mule, too, so I know the ropes." And then he glared right back at me, his mouth quirking upward at one side, at my offended look and my insulted, "Hey!"

Colin pulled me close, laughing. In return, I shoved him away from me, growling, "Get your ass out of here before I string you up by your toenails."

My brother reached out and ruffled my hair and said, "You don't have to tell me twice, Shelb. Nurse Isabel *Caliente* Ramirez, here I come!" And he hoofed it out our sight by the time I flounced back down in my seat.

I looked at Luke. He looked at me. There was a moment of silence. "That was my brother in all his glory," I said.

"He's obviously a good guy. I liked him."

I snorted. Luke's blue eyes danced; he was loving this. And if I thought I had lost all shreds of my dignity after the Caveman Kev incident, and then the Trying-To-Pick-a-Fight incident, and then the Hilary the Bean Spiller incident, then I was sorely mistaken. The Colin and His Big Ol' Mouth incident had showed me that I still had some dignity to lose.

Now all I needed was to tangle with Franzilla in front of Luke. He'd never be able to look at me again without laughing, or without shaking his head in pity, possibly.

I fear I found myself staring out into the crowd in horror at the possibility of Franzilla meeting Luke when I heard him say, "So what happened with your date tonight? Did the guy turn out to be another Caveman Kev?"

I swiveled my eyes his way and he quickly said, "If you want to tell me, that is. I'll understand if you don't."

I shrugged, thinking about it, and said aloud, "I mean, why not, right? It's not as if you haven't heard every other sordid detail of my dating life, not to mention my embarrassing childhood moments."

"You have had some classic moments," he smiled.

"I prefer to think of them as unique."

"Definitely," he nodded, affecting seriousness. "Unique is a much better word."

"Bastard," I said without heat, and he laughed.

Then he leaned forward again, only inches from me and I could smell the soapy-woody scent of him. "But first things first. What I really want to know is whether or not this guy was bad enough to get a personalized Shelby Waterlane nickname." He gave me that sideways look of his, this time in a very cute jesting way, and I had to bitch slap my Inner Wall for a second to keep it in place.

"Um, yeah," I said, blushing just as much from how he'd just looked at me as the fact that he'd guessed I had already labeled my date for the worse.

"Well? Spill it, Waterlane."

I think you should hear the story behind it first, Treadwell," I chided.

Luke sat back in his chair, suppressing a dimple-inducing grin. "Okay, then, fair enough. Let's hear it." He made a c'mon gesture with his hand and hiked one of his—oh, good God, I'd almost forgotten about those gorgeous suckers—long legs up and rested his ankle over his knee.

I took a sip of my beer. "Okay, well, for starters, the guy's name was Lars Michalski, and he's a thirty-year-old financial adviser who told me that his life goal is to work as hard as he can and then retire early to wherever there's great skiing."

"I can't say it's a bad-sounding goal…," Luke said.

"Nope, it's not, but as soon as I heard him say that, I knew he wasn't interested in cultivating a relationship. But that didn't make me upset or anything. I mean, Lars was really good-looking, if you wanted to know—"

"Shelby, that's what guys always want to know. Really."

I giggled, "But I wasn't into him from the moment I met him. He was decently interesting to talk to, at least at the start, but I wasn't exactly expecting us to have a love that goes down in the history books or anything."

"So, no epic love story in your future with Lars the Polish guy, huh? No running across a field toward each other in slow motion, arms outstretched, with grand orchestral music building to a crescendo in the background until you fall into each others arms amongst the wildflowers?"

I clutched my hands to my chest and batted my eyes, "Actually, I was saving that for our second date."

Luke's eyes crinkled and he said, "So what ruined your potential for a Benny Hill moment?"

"Eh. Pretty much the fact that he managed to consume four glasses of wine by the time we'd finished our main courses and his drunken side also brought out his bigoted and homophobic side."

Losing all his joking around, Luke said, "You're not serious."

"Unfortunately, I am. Everything started off pretty well, I'll admit. Much better than with Caveman Kev, to be sure."

Luke's dimple flashed, so I kept talking to keep my mind on the right track. "We talked about movies, travel, college football, the basic stuff, all while he drank like a dehydrated camel and I drank like a normal person. I noticed after his second glass of wine that his opinions were becoming stronger and his voice was becoming louder, but I chalked it up to the fact that we were talking about the Olympics and I asked him if he had been smoking crack when he said how happy he was that golf would be coming back in 2016."

"Dare I ask why you believe golf is not Olympic-worthy?"

"Because golf is a game, not a sport."

He cocked an eyebrow. "But would you repeat those words in front of Emily?"

"Do I look like I want to be smacked upside the head with a nine iron by a woman wearing better accessories than I? Of course not. But it's the truth and I wasn't about to agree with Lars when he was clearly delusional about what makes a sport and what doesn't."

"Oh, *clearly*," Luke said.

I stared at him. "Treadwell. I can't believe you just mocked me. You're a mocker."

In response all I got was an evil laugh. And, of course, all it made me do was have to turn up my Inner Wall to eleven.

"Fine, mock if you will, but that's when Lars started his downhill slide. On his third glass of wine, he started getting pretty ballsy. He'd already complimented me a couple of times. He said he liked my shoes. Is that weird?"

"That's weird."

"I thought so too. But then he went and told me that he liked my lips and that he couldn't wait to kiss me later." I pretended not to notice when Luke's amused expression went to inscrutable. "Up until then, he'd been telling me the oh-so fascinating story of how he'd landed three Houston Rockets basketball players as his clients and so you can imagine how I nearly did a spit take when he abruptly switched from how he'd totally diversified their portfolios to informing me that we would soon be sucking face."

"It's a vivid image…"

"Then, not two minutes later, he called our waitress 'baby' and, as she walked away, asked me if I thought my ass was better than hers, because he said he knows women take notice of things like that and always compare ourselves to the other women in the room."

"And how did you respond to both, ah, invitations?"

"The first one I ignored. And I think my expression spoke for me, and may have also been the impetus for his personality's total descent into Loserville. As for the second, I turned around, got a good look at her ass, and told him I thought mine was better." I gave my own evil laugh and kept talking before Luke could comment.

"So I tried changing the subject to something I thought was neutral as he was pouring himself a fourth glass of wine, right? I asked him how exactly he and Bryan met at the airport…since, you know, that traitor who works with me deliberately didn't give me any information on the subject."

Luke's eyes just crinkled again as he took a languid pull on his beer.

I made a be-that-way face, then told him, "And this is where it went to hell in a handbag. He started by telling me—no, *laughingly* telling me—that he could tell Bryan was gay from a mile off because Bryan was wearing a tight black t-shirt with a red scarf around his neck. He said it was only a thing a queer would do. I kept my cool, you should know, and told him that Bryan wearing the scarf had significance for him and his boyfriend Gabriel. That the scarf was handmade and given to him by Gabriel's grandmother in a gesture to let Bryan know that she accepted Bryan and Gabriel as a couple. But that just made Lars start laughing even harder. He was so crass about it."

"What did you do?"

"Nothing at first. I was kind of stunned. He went on to tell me that normally he avoids gays at all costs because the queers swarm all over him like moths to the flame." Detestation thickened my voice, "But then he winked at me and said that he's recently learned that it pays to be nice to, and I quote, 'those sodomy-loving homos' because they fall all over themselves to set him up with one of their 'hot chick friends'."

Luke's eyes had darkened and a muscle flickered in his jaw. "I hope you told the jackass off. Worse than Caveman Kev. "

"Now I wish I had, but I didn't. I was seething, of course, but I had been pretending to listen politely once he started showing how small-minded he was because I wanted to be sure that I wasn't just misinterpreting what he was saying. I thought about laying into him once I was sure he was a total bigoted asshole, but I decided that causing a scene wasn't really what I wanted to do. I know that Bryan wouldn't have approved of my giving Lars' warped views any more credence, too, so I pretended that I needed to go powder my nose. But instead I gave money for my dinner, plus a tip, to our waitress and I left through the emergency exit."

"Seriously?" Luke said. His eyebrows had shot up sky high. "You walked out on him?"

I sighed with resignation and my crabby side came back out. "Yes, seriously. And Colin has already scalped me for doing so and told me how hard you guys have it on blind dates, blah, blah, blah, so you need not go there, if you don't mind."

Luke considered me for a long moment. "Jeez. Sometimes I could swear that you, Claudia, and Maggie were separated at birth."

"Meaning?" I said with an icy look.

A look that he was completely unfazed by, damn it.

"Meaning that you three are the most independent, funny, infuriating, intelligent, talented, and completely and utterly hardheaded women I have ever dealt with in my whole entire life. And if someone even remotely questions any of your decisions, your hackles come up faster than a cornered tiger and everybody around you better damn well watch out."

Was this a compliment or one hell of a slam? I couldn't tell.

"If you were so afraid of me criticizing you for walking out on the guy, then why did you tell me the story?"

Okay, fine. He had just made me realize that his opinion meant something to me and I've only known the guy for three days! What the devil was my problem?

"I don't know," I finally said, my stubborn voice fully intact. Oh, yes, we hackled-up tigresses do love our defense mechanisms…

He busted out laughing. At me, not with me. I glowered back in return.

"Have I already called you a bastard this evening?" I asked haughtily.

"Just once."

"Well, consider it said again." Though even as I said so, my cheeks were starting to hurt in my effort not to break down and smile again, and I was sure he could tell.

"So noted," he replied. We sat at our table in good humor, he looking out into the crowd at Lawson's and I finding myself staring at his profile, taking in a few human-making flaws and thinking that I liked him better for it.

"You ready to head home, then?"

"Huh?" I said, blinking at him. "Oh, yes, definitely." I fumbled to grab up my handbag, mentally yelling at myself for being caught staring at a guy who was in a relationship. What was I doing? Was I the biggest nitwit on the planet? God, Shelby, get a grip on yourself!

To show that I was ready to leap out of Luke's truck once it hit my driveway and barrel headlong into my house without skipping a beat, I pulled out my keys with a little jangling flourish and we walked out of the pub together to his truck.

Eleven

"Wow. You really do live close to Lawson's."

Being as there was little traffic, we'd pulled up to my house in under a minute. He put his truck in park and turned off the ignition. The combination of the porch lights on my little bungalow and the flood lights that lit up my one-car garage threw enough light into the cab that I could clearly see his face.

"See? I told you and my rat fink of a brother."

"Stubborn," he replied, shaking his head. "As a freaking mule."

"I take that as a compliment." Nodding my head toward the big plastic cup in one of his console's cup holders I'd noticed was filled with individually wrapped peppermints, I asked, "Like peppermints, do you?"

He grinned and grabbed out two, handing one to me and unwrapping the second for himself. "You've found me out already. It's my weird little quirk, picked up during my high-school days from working with Uncle Bob when he took to eating them after he stopped smoking. I can't go a day without one."

I unwrapped mine and popped it in my mouth. "Yeah? Well, this is a quirk I think I can actually handle. At least I know you'll never have halitosis around me, which is always a good thing."

He pretended to breathe on me, making me laugh. Then he relaxed into his seat.

"So, Maggie tells me that you are a high-end event coordinator—what exactly does that mean? And are people in your profession not just called wedding planners anymore?" He leaned away from me a little. "I'm not going to get hit for asking that, am I?"

Failing to convince him that the little bob-and-weave I did was the least bit frightening, I explained: "I'm one of the few who doesn't care what I'm called—wedding planner, wedding consultant, event coordinator, whatever. It's all the same to me and whichever term falls off my client's tongue is fine. I tend to switch out the terms myself, actually. Lauren is the only one of my staff who cares that she is called an event coordinator over any other title, but that's because she does a lot more true events than the rest of us do."

"And you prefer weddings, then?"

"I do, yes. Other events are fun, too, and I throw a couple in my schedule every so often because it gives me a break from hearing Pachelbel's 'Canon' every other weekend, but I like planning weddings over anything else."

"Why is that?"

I'd been asked that question a million times and, thankfully, the answer had never changed. "Because it's a big deal in two people's life. It's a life-affirming moment that's full of possibilities and a time when the love between two people and their wishes for a happy life together conquers everything else. I like being a part of that and I like helping someone to plan it the way they've envisioned it. Over the years I've realized that I sort of see myself as the bridge between a bride's dreams for her wedding and making it all happen, and I like that feeling. It's something that's very satisfying to me, even though it might not be all smooth sailing while it's happening."

The look on his face told me that he appreciated what I had to say. He probably saw his own job in similar terms, I realized. He was a contractor of new spaces, I of weddings—the two had many parallels.

"How did you get into planning weddings?" he asked.

I grinned. "It started as a part-time job answering phones for a wedding planner when I was a junior at SMU in Dallas. Well, my boss and I got along perfectly and, three months later, I was her second assistant. Six months after that I was her first assistant. Another six months later I was a junior wedding planner, and it just went from there. I found out very quickly that I was both good at the job and genuinely liked it, so the fit couldn't have been better for me. I stayed in Dallas for another year out of college before moving back to Houston and getting a job in the catering department at the Chatsworth Hotel when I was twenty-three. I saved my money while I moved up the ranks in my department, and, well, you know the rest from there."

He gave me his sideways look, as if he were arranging all the pieces of the puzzle that was Shelby Waterlane together in his head and he was missing a couple that completed the picture of me as a whole. "And so now you only do expensive weddings?"

I didn't take offense at his terminology. "I prefer to say that I handle weddings of a certain caliber. While more money gets you nicer services, it's not really the price that makes a classy wedding, it's the bride and groom and their choices. In fact, one of the nicest weddings I've ever handled cost only ten thousand dollars—but, of course, it was held in the bride's backyard, she wore her mother's wedding gown, and she only had thirty guests."

"I take it that ten grand is nothing when it comes to weddings, then?" Luke said, looking as if someone who paid that much to get hitched was off their rocker. He obviously had no idea how much his parents would be shelling out for his little sister's dream wedding…

"Let me put it this way," I said. "Depending on who you ask, the average wedding has between a hundred and fifty to two hundred guests. And you're lucky in any big city if you get to have a wedding reception for under a hundred dollars per guest. In New York, in fact, you're lucky if you get under two hundred per guest."

The math was easy for him. He gave me a sickened look and said, "Good God."

"And that doesn't count the gown, the flowers, the invitations, the wedding favors, the band, the limo, and a dozen other extra charges," I told him. "You should add at least another, oh, ten to thirty thousand to the number in your head—and that's just for what wedding planners would term a 'nice' wedding. While I'll still do smaller affairs a few times a year and quite a few of the so-termed nice ones, most of the weddings I do these days are about double that price, if not more."

He just stared at me, his mouth agape.

Thoroughly tickled by his reaction, I changed the subject, since talking about how much my clients paid for their nuptials was, in my opinion, a private matter and not information I cared to expound upon at length. "So, I've never seen you at Lawson's. Had you ever been there before tonight?"

"A few times," he replied. "I live across town in West University, but tonight I was there because the guys I used to work with live in this area. I wouldn't be surprised if I become more of a regular, though, because my brother John just bought a house a few blocks over in Woodland Heights. Claudia's in that area, too."

Ah, yes...Claudia. The mere mention of her name jolted my senses, easily revving my slacking Inner Wall back up to full speed. I'd only seen the brunette beauty once, but images of Claudia and Luke getting drunk at Lawson's and then going back to her place for lots of long-legged sex filled my brain and killed any warm, fuzzy feelings that had been brewing inside me.

"Speaking of Claudia," he said after pulling out a lit-up phone from his pocket.

"Um," I said, pointing for no reason toward my house with one hand and grabbing my purse with the other, "I'll go.

Thank—" I stopped when he made a motion with his hand that said *Don't worry about it; stay here* even as he answered his phone in a way that told me that he and Claudia's relationship was both tight and long.

In lieu of the standard greeting, he said, "Claude. Let me guess. Your car isn't starting again." And his eyes crinkled in amusement when Claudia replied in some way that obviously said he had pegged her.

"For the millionth time, why don't you trade that damn thing in on a new one so I don't have to come bail you out each and every time it acts up?"

She replied with something that made him do an exasperated roll of his eyes. "Where are you? And why didn't you ask one of your friends to stay with you to make sure your car started or not?"

I easily heard the squawking sound that said she was getting defensive, and I felt myself blush because it sounded as if Luke wasn't far off about the whole tigers-and-hackles thing when it came to the women with whom he regularly dealt.

Ah, well. Better to be a feisty tiger than a big ol' dull wallflower, no?

"Jeee-sus, Claudia." he laughed. "Yes, of course. You know I'll always come get you. No, it's no problem. I'm already out anyway. I'll be there in fifteen minutes."

Feeling that was my cue, I had my hand on the door handle by the time he hung up. "I hate to even ask," I said before he could speak, "But I would be very grateful if you would keep my confidence and not discuss the details of my date with anyone—even your girlfriend." I smiled. "I'm going to give Bryan the gist of the night, of course, but I think it would just be safer to forget the whole thing happened so that he never hears the worst parts of it." Feeling suddenly tired, I closed my eyes and rubbed them with my fingertips. It took me a moment to realize he hadn't replied, so I opened my eyes up again and looked at him. "Luke?"

He took a deep breath and then let it out sharply. He didn't look at me. "Yeah, sure, Shelby. Of course. I won't say a word."

He sounded frustrated, but I was too tired to question it at the moment. Besides, he smiled at me again and everything seemed okay once more.

"I'm glad we ran into each other tonight, Luke," I said. "Thanks for bringing me home, too. I appreciate it very much."

I went to get out of his truck, but Luke stopped me when he said, "Shelby, I wanted to make sure that you knew that you were very brave tonight."

My brows knitted. When was I brave?

"About walking out on your date." he explained.

I woke up a little bit. "You do?"

"Yes," he replied. "Don't get me wrong. No guy would want to have a woman walk out on him just because they weren't getting along on a first date—but this was different. This guy was very drunk and crossing more than one line."

And then he smiled sadly at me, "And this is where *I'm* going to ask *you* to keep a secret. A few years ago, long before she met Barton, Maggie went on a blind date with a guy who got plastered and thought that, since he bought her dinner or whatever, that she owed him something." I felt my blood chill and my eyes widen even as he said with quiet anger, "He tried to rape her in the car right in parking lot of her apartment complex after she told him that she would be going inside alone and that they wouldn't be seeing each other again. The only reason he didn't succeed is because, when she was struggling, she accidentally got a good swipe in at his face and broke his nose. She was roughed up pretty good, though, with several bruises on her arms, legs, and face, and she was scared to death to even talk to a guy she didn't know for a good six months."

"Oh...oh my God. That's horrible!" I was stunned. "I'm so sorry." I didn't know what else to say.

Disgust came heavily to his voice. "Yeah, well, John and I went to every emergency room in Houston looking for the bastard because we wanted to beat him to a bloody pulp, but we never found him. He actually lived in Austin and we're fairly certain he hightailed it out of the city as soon as he could stick some Kleenex up his nose. It's a good thing, too, because I'd still like to beat his brains out for what he did to my sister. He didn't succeed in raping her, but he did succeed in completely shattering her confidence for a long, long time."

I felt pressure behind my eyes and blinked to stave off tearing up in front of Luke. I now understood why he had even bothered to speak up when he heard Kevin speaking so rudely to me and why his posture had been so tense when he thought that Colin was Lars. He knew just how bad a situation could get. Wow.

"Anyway," he said in my astonished silence. "This Lars guy was obviously a drunken ass who had no respect for women. Or gays, apparently. It's highly possible that you could have finished the date and left without there being any problems, but I for one am glad you didn't take the chance. I'm glad you left, Shelby."

"Thanks," I said. "That means a lot to me."

There didn't seem to be anything more to say. He smiled at me, told me that he would see me first thing Monday morning with his crew, and his truck roared to life once more, filling my sleepy street with a deeply purring sound that only a big engine could make.

I was about to hop out of his truck when I remembered something.

"Lars the Loathsome," I blurted out. He looked hilariously perplexed and I said, "That's what I named him—Lars the Loathsome."

He grinned, "Not as snazzy as Caveman Kev, but still fitting."

"Hey, they can't always be classics," I replied. Getting out, I waved him goodbye and headed toward my porch steps with a light heart, noting with a pleasure I shouldn't have felt that he stayed in my driveway until I was safely inside my house.

Twelve

Two big hands cupped my face gently. "*Cherie*...I 'ave missed you."

"Oh, darlin', I've missed you, too," I said breathlessly and felt a little tingle on each of the spots where he kissed my cheeks. I looked up and was mesmerized by his soulful sloe-dark eyes.

"Good God, watching the two of you is like watching seriously bad porn," Bryan said loudly to my right as he walked up to us. He was holding a glass of iced tea in each hand and gestured with one of them in my direction. "And one of you has all the wrong parts."

I wrapped my arms around Gabriel's waist and he held me close in return. "Yeah, you just try to break us up," I returned with a devilishly wide grin and rested my head against his strong chest. The gorgeous Frenchman rubbed my back and rocked me gently from side to side.

I could have stayed that way for hours, believe me. Even if he's gay and wouldn't sleep with you if you paid him, being held by a man like that is one of God's greatest gifts to women. It's utterly delicious. But I eventually relinquished my hold on Bryan's boyfriend and transferred my arms to Bryan himself, just so that he never forgot that I loved him best.

"All right, enough with the love fest," came another voice. Hilary had walked up to the outdoor table we'd claimed for outside of a casual eatery in the Midtown section of Houston. Seeing Gabriel, though, she happily bounced into his arms for her own big hug and European-style kisses on the cheek. The man just had that effect on women. He was tall, built, snake-hipped, and pretty much the spitting image of Gregory Peck à la *Roman Holiday*. And of course that ridiculously sexy accent only bumped up his hotness factor by about ten notches. But if that weren't enough, Gabriel had a great sense of humor and was smart and kind, especially to Bryan. I had seen my friend through various relationships with other men who, because of their own issues, were either emotionally or verbally (and once, even physically) abusive and it had broken my heart every time. But then Bryan had met Gabriel and it was as if the two of them had found their other halves; they were two good people who were good together.

I just wish that some of that good-relationship mojo would rub off on me.

Once Hilary and I had gone into the self-serve restaurant to place our orders and get our drinks, we sat back down and Bryan got right to the point, looking me straight in the eyes from his seat across our round table.

"So, since Emily and Percy decided to go to Lake Conroe for the day and Lauren is having lunch with Chris and his family, we are all the audience you get. Now spill it, sugar. How was the date last night with the Polish hunk? I'm hoping your 'not so great' on the phone earlier was just to tease me and that you took him home and shagged him until his eyeballs rolled back into his head."

"Yeah," Hilary eloquently seconded before taking a sip of her Diet Coke.

I sighed. "I'm so sorry, Bry, but I wasn't teasing."

"Then how fast did you run this time?" he returned, looking perturbed.

Okay, it was true, but I was still stung. "Bryan!"

Hilary looked unmoved, but Gabriel gave Bryan an icy look on my behalf. Properly chastised, Bryan relented some. "I'm sorry, sugar, I really am. But what happened, then? Lars was so charming when I talked to him. He was everything you could have asked for—educated, funny," he leaned forward and added some umph to his voice, "incredibly gorgeous, lanky—"

"Homophobic," I interjected sadly.

Well, that stopped him in his tracks.

Byran said, "Excuse me?" while Gabriel, reverting to his native tongue, said, "*Pardón?*"

Even Hilary the Unmovable looked aghast. "Are you kidding us, Shelby?"

"No," I said. "I'm not. Bryan, he just pretended to be friendly with you because he knows that most gay guys have lots of women friends—or 'hot chick friends' as he so delightfully put it." The derision was evident as I proceeded to tell my three friends the gist of Lars' tacky commentary, leaving out the most derogatory remarks. I would rather have gone on a million more bad dates than hurt Bryan with the things Lars had said.

Though they picked apart every moment from the night before that I would relive for them, my three friends eventually agreed they were glad I didn't take the chance at having Lars become all octopus-handed (and possibly then some) with me when we left the restaurant. They did not, however, exonerate me from the possibility of any more future setups, so that sucked. But I decided to be content with my small victory and not push it.

Still, I did have to damp down their excitement when I casually told them about running into Luke at Lawson's Pub.

"Luke drove you home, did he?" Bryan said, arching one eyebrow and looking knowingly at Gabriel. "That's how you made your first move on me, remember? After Jud and Bob's party?" He turned to Hilary, since I already knew the story: "It was the sweetest thing. I had come to the party with some friends, but they left early, leaving me without a ride home." He gestured with his thumb back over his shoulder at a smiling

Gabriel, "But it turns out that this guy right here had told my friends that he was interested in me and that if they wanted to leave without me, he would like to offer me a ride home. So my friends hightailed it and I was left stranded until Gabriel, who I'd been eyeing all night, too, walked up. Can you believe that?" He then turned his twinkling eyes back to me, "And I'd bet you fifty bucks that Luke wasn't at all unhappy that Colin left so that he could drive you home, too."

Before Hilary or Gabriel could second his declaration, I interrupted, "People, relax. And please remind yourselves that the guy has a girlfriend. She even called. She'd been out with her friends and her car wouldn't start so he had to go give her a jump," I made a wry face, "probably both literally and figuratively. But regardless, all three of you know that I do not go after men who are in relationships. Period. No discussion." I turned my steely gaze onto my best friend.

"Hey, I didn't say a thing," she said, holding up her hands surrendering-style and shaking her strawberry-blonde curls.

"And you," I said, shaking a finger across the table at Bryan, "need to also remember that Luke is a hired contractor. It would be unprofessional for me to start something with him even if he were single, which he is most definitely not. So you need to behave, okay?"

Bryan sat back in his chair and didn't answer, but the mischievous look on his face had said that he would continue thinking exactly what he wanted about Luke and me no matter what I said.

Seriously, I was beginning to wonder if I've ever had any authority with this boy…

Monday came and I walked in dressed for reception-venue–choosing action in my black gabardine trousers, wine-colored short-sleeved silk top with ruffled trim, and black patent Ferragamo ballet flats. Gold hoops in my ears and a sparkly garnet cluster ring on my right hand, I felt stylishly comfortable for a long day ahead with Maggie and Virginia Treadwell.

Except first I had the dubious pleasure of getting a little kick in my gabardine trousers from Maggie's big brother.

I guess I expected that Luke would somehow be different with me because of the time we'd spent together at Lawson's Pub and the stories we'd shared later while in my driveway. I figured he'd be, I don't know, softer with me, maybe. Less likely to give me grief, if you will.

Oh, hell, that's bull. What I'm saying is that I expected him to be on *my* side from now on when it came to the Dating Brigade feeling the need for another skirmish with me.

Well, my bubble was unceremoniously popped on that one. Because my Lochinvar proved himself to be quite the long-legged turncoat.

It started almost the moment he and his crew walked in at their pre-established time of eight o'clock. After he supervised his men starting on the very first stages of true renovations to our former living and dining rooms, he sauntered into my office to find me cornered by the drill sergeants I used to call Lauren and Emily.

Let's just say that they didn't take the news of me walking out on Lars the Loathsome as well as Bryan, Gabriel, and Hilary had. They thought I had acted ridiculously, making it not Franzilla or Bryan who had given me grief for walking out on Lars, but Lauren and Emily instead.

My mother, and therefore by proxy Aunt Prilly, had actually been perfectly understanding as soon as I got into the part about Lars becoming inebriated. Neither of them wanted me to be with a man who became drunk and obnoxious, thank goodness. However, Mom did put the fear of God in me by ending our speakerphoned conversation with a cheery, "Well, we'll just have to find you someone who understands that he's much more of a man when he stays sober than when he gets drunk." And when I began to protest, Mom said an equally cheery, "Oh, that's my other line, dear! Must run. I'll call you for lunch this week, okay?" and clicked off before I could whimper out another, "Please don't!" I think she was inventing the call on the other line, too, which made me even more afraid that her tenacity about finding me a husband was increasing...

My two girlfriends-slash-employees? Nope, they didn't care all that much that Lars had become drunk at dinner. (Not that they didn't care for my safety, more that they just didn't see Lars' drinking as something that couldn't be curbed in the future.)

"Are you serious, Shelby? Did you really end *another* date early just because the guy had a few drinks and let you know he thought you were a beautiful woman?" Emily asked, looking at me as if I were the most cowardly person on Earth.

"It couldn't have been that bad," Lauren seconded, but with a more forgiving smile. "Maybe he got drunk because he was so nervous around you. I had a guy do that to me once, and when we kept going out, he finally started relaxing around me and he found that he didn't need to keep drinking so much just to give himself confidence. Some guys are just less sure of themselves than they seem and so they end up doing the wrong thing because they're nervous."

I was about to respond with some snappy comeback when Luke walked into the room, unaware of the conversation, and got immediately roped in.

"Isn't that right, Luke?" Lauren asked.

Luke, being wise, stopped in his khakis-and-oxford-wearing tracks about halfway between the door and my desk and his eyes did their Deer in the Headlights impression. "Um, is what right?"

"That guys can become nervous around women and do silly things like drink too much to boost their confidence," Lauren explained before I could scream out, "Run for your life, Luke! They've got you in their crosshairs!"

"Oh, good God," I said, dropping down into my office chair. "Guys," I said to my female employees, "Please don't mess with Luke. He's already been harassed enough before this job even started. And it's his first day of renovations..."

But this only stoked Emily's desire to put the screws to him. "No, I'd like to know the answer to that, too. It's been a long time since we've had a heterosexual man in here who can give us an actual, true-to-life male point of view."

"I heard that," Bryan said as he breezed in past Luke carrying a tray holding five cups of coffee. He offered one to Luke. "Would you like a cappuccino with your interrogation, sir?"

Luke chuckled (weakly, I thought) and thanked him as he took a coffee. I noticed that he still didn't move nor say anything when Bryan passed the coffees around to the rest of us, giving each of us a kiss on the cheek and a "Good morning, sugar," as he did.

Emily must have noticed that her powers of persuasion might be waning, so she picked right back up where she left off.

"So, what do you have to tell us, Mr. Treadwell?" she asked with lawyeresque formality. She began to walk around him, looking him up and down with a steely gaze, which made Lauren and me start giggling even though I tried not to. I had to admit that I just loved it when Emily became churlish around someone else. It was so refreshing to watch someone else sweat, let me tell you.

"Does she always do this?" Luke asked.

"Yes," Bryan said before taking a sip of his cappuccino. "It's kind of scary, huh?"

Luke's dimple came out as she circled around him slowly again, "Yeah, little bit."

"Then you might as well tell us what we want to know, because she won't let you go free until you do," Lauren teased.

Luke cleared his throat. "Well, yeah, I guess. Guys do get nervous on a first date and do stupid things. I've gotten too drunk on a first date or two myself."

"Really?" Lauren, Bryan, and I all said simultaneously, astounded.

Luke grinned at Emily and then the rest of us, "Well, I do have to admit that I was in college at the time."

"Oh," we all said disappointedly. Guys doing stupid things when they were still more or less kids was perfectly warranted, we all knew that.

Luke laughed at our reaction, "But the girls in question were so hot that I probably wouldn't have been able to make conversation with them at all if I hadn't had a beer or two first—or at least that was my line of thinking back then."

"But not now, right?" I said. "Not as a true adult who is over thirty years old and knows better, right?"

"No," he confirmed, regarding me with easiness. "Not now." But then he added, looking around at each of my employees rapt faces, "However, I can't say that I still don't do stupid things when I meet an incredible woman for the first time. And I would hope that I would be given a second chance if she thought me the biggest ass on the planet when we first met and not just kick me to the curb just because of, oh, say, some misunderstanding or something. I would hope that I would be given the chance to redeem myself."

Even as my jaw dropped to the ground, Emily turned around quick as a flash and pointed at me, "See! See, Shelby! You have *got* to stop making such snap judgments about these guys!"

Lauren agreed. "I think she's right, Shelby. Maybe if you went out with him again he would be better. He's probably very aware now of how drunk he got and feeling horrible about how strong he came on with you."

Bryan, reminding me suddenly that he was as determined as my mother to get me married off, raised his cappuccino to me in a sort of morbid toast and said, "I gotta say they're right, lovey. Lars was an ass for sure and I can't say that I'd want you to specifically go out with *him* again, but you're starting an ugly trend with this running-out-on-your-date thing that will only get worse until you realize that you've got to give these guys more of a fair shake than you are."

I looked through the throng of my employees—wherein Emily and Lauren were telling Bryan that I should call Lars for another date and Bryan was saying that, no, Lars wouldn't do because he was a homophobic putz but they'd just have to try again and find someone better for me—and eyed Luke, who still hadn't moved from where he'd frozen in the first place (and who was now sipping his cappuccino as if nothing significant had happened). "Thanks a lot," I said over my employees' voices to him. I gave him a sarcastic double thumbs-up for emphasis on how well he hadn't done for my team.

Luke winked at me and mouthed, "Anytime," before he turned to walk back out the office, a wide grin on his face.

"Benedict Arnold!" I yelled at his back as a last-ditch effort and, over Emily's and Lauren's voices (who were throwing around the word "spinster" a little too much for my liking), I heard his deep laugh echoing in the hallway.

Thirteen

Tuesday morning, with hammering and sawing noises in the background, I typed in notes from Monday's visits to six reception venues that fit Maggie's parameters and felt a dual rush of excitement and relief when I could erase the words *In Progress* in the database field titled Reception Venue and add in the words *Post Oak Country Club*. I could also firmly set the wedding date in her file for the second Saturday in September since the exclusive country club, which had just opened its doors to the weddings of non-members, had the date open that Maggie had wanted most. Maggie's fiancé Barton, who had been in meetings all day and could not join us, had given his approval to the club when she had described it to him over the phone in glowing terms. Everyone, including me, was thrilled.

"One reception venue down," I grinned as I saved the file and printed a copy to go in her paper file, "and one wedding dress to go."

Maggie and Virginia showed up at my office at ten o'clock, and I saw that Maggie had taken my suggestion and had worn an outfit that she could easily get on and off when going to the different bridal salons to try on dresses. She looked young and fresh in a kelly green strapless dress with a smocked upper bodice that relaxed into a knee-length skirt. She'd paired it with her grandmother's pearl earrings, necklace, and cuff bracelet that she wanted to wear on her wedding day plus a pair of nude heeled sandals the same height as those she would wear with her gown. I told her that it was imperative she do all of this so that she could get the best taste of what her entire wedding ensemble would look like when all was hemmed and altered. Virginia, who was in a very Franzilla-like linen capris-and-jacket outfit in a flattering lavender color with a crisp white collared shirt underneath and square-cut amethyst jewelry at her ears and throat, had agreed with me. And, thankfully, Maggie had listened to us both.

Remembering again the horrific story Luke had told me about Maggie's near-rape as I watched her hug her brother, I felt a little lump of gratefulness and emotion in my throat that the worst had not happened to her, and it also made me suddenly realize that I was already more invested in Maggie's happiness than I thought I was.

But just as quickly, I then I had to cover my mouth so as to not laugh out loud when Virginia fussed over her son, pushing the lock of wavy hair that had flopped down into his face away and telling him in the classic admonishing-mother manner that he needed a haircut. Luke winked at Maggie and, slinging his arm around his mother's shoulders, teased, "Sure, Mom, no problem. You like mohawks, right? I was thinking I'd try that style next."

It didn't escape my notice that Luke clearly loved his family—a trait that I found very sexy in a man—so, for the sake of my Inner Wall's strength, I separated my clients from my contractor and we were soon on our way to the first of four different salons.

Where, in short order, we were joined by an unexpected guest. Well, at least to me.

"Hi, Shelby!" a voice brightly said in my right ear while I checked my messages on my cell. I was standing next to one of the upscale salon's faceless, hairless, yet still somehow oddly chic-looking plastic mannequins that was decked out in the latest in mermaid-silhouette bridal gowns from designer

Monique Lhuillier. Hearing the voice, I looked up to see the beauty who had been on Luke's arm during the whole Caveman Kev incident.

"Claudia, hi!" I said, my voice unintentionally giving away the fact that I was surprised to see her. I felt my face begin to flush as well, which sucked rocks. Stupid Catholic guilt. Just a couple of minor naughty thoughts about Claudia's boyfriend and it showed all over my face like a huge billboard. I couldn't get away with anything, let me tell you. Nevertheless, the proper mannerly response kicked in and I held out my hand, taking envious notice as I did so of her even-toned skin and big, almond-shaped eyes. Her long brown hair was layered and fell sexily tousled around her face down to a couple of inches past her shoulders; her sleeveless crepe dress in a navy blue accentuated her svelte figure and model-like height. She was a stunner, for sure.

She shook my hand and her lips parted into a grin, showing uneven lower teeth that stupidly made me feel better. "I take it that Maggie forgot to tell you I was coming along for the gown tryouts. I hope that's okay."

"Oh, of course," I rushed out. "It's not a problem at all." I went to gesture across the salon to where Maggie and Virginia were standing. "Maggie's over..." Not seeing them, I stepped back and whirled around at the same time to look for them, my arm still stretched out...and I ended up with my hand planted firmly on the left boob of the chic, faceless mannequin.

Yes, obviously I was still not adept at keeping my embarrassing actions at a minimum around Luke and his girlfriend.

Still, after a nanosecond of a shocked face, I busted out laughing.

Claudia belly laughed right along with me and—earning her massive points in my book—reached out and squeezed the mannequin's other boob, saying, "Yep, these puppies are *definitely* fake, no doubt about it."

Our giggling didn't abate much, either, when a very disapproving salesperson came over to readjust the beautiful wedding gown that had now slipped down a few inches on the mannequin, threatening to expose both of her plastic breasts. Claudia and I scuttled away like naughty teenagers and went to rejoin Maggie and Virginia.

"Nice of you two to be feeling up other women when you're supposed to be oohing and aahing over me in my wedding dresses," Maggie teased us.

I looked at Claudia and jerked my thumb over my shoulder in the direction of the mannequin, "She was a bit of a tramp, wasn't she?"

"Oh, absolutely. We can do much better than her." Claudia returned.

"I am not hearing any of this," Virginia said primly, though her laughing eyes gave her away.

"I think we should definitely get on with the oohing and ahhing, then," I said. "Show us what you've picked out so far, Maggie."

Though I had warned Maggie to budget several days to find the gown that she liked the best, the right one ended up being at our last stop for the day, at a boutique called You Beautiful Bride. It was not the satin-with-beading Vera Wang ball-gown style that she had been envisioning all her life, but instead an organza sheath by a relatively unknown designer. Embroidered with a flower-vine motif that began as tight clusters around the sweetheart-shaped strapless bodice, the vines gradually decreased to where there only tendrils reached down to the floor-length hemline and onto the three-foot train. It set off Maggie's beautiful posture and toned arms and also served to make one long, gorgeous column of her slim figure.

In short, her dress did exactly what the perfect bridal gown should do: it took an already lovely woman and made her exquisite. So much so that seeing her come out of the dressing room absolutely stopped the conversation that Claudia, Virginia, and I were having dead in its tracks.

"Oh," I sighed as I saw her. "Oh, Maggie, it's heavenly. You're absolutely stunning."

Claudia put her fingers up to her mouth and her voice came out a little choked, "Oh, my God, Maggie. It's perfect."

Maggie gave a emotion-filled laugh and asked her mother, "Mom? What do you think?"

Virginia was so moved that she was at a loss for words and just hurried to hug her daughter, telling her over and over how beautiful she was.

With Maggie and Virginia off ordering the dress, Claudia plopped down next to me on the cream damask sofa we'd been occupying off and on for the last two hours. I was erasing files from my iPad, which had been playing a slideshow of Maggie in each of the dresses she had tried on, all from several different angles with as many different types of veils. I was not allowed to walk out of the bridal store with any pictures because of the high potential there was for a bride to simply take one of the pictures to a talented seamstress and say, "Here, copy this exactly," but I had a good relationship with most of the Houston bridal salons to the point that they allowed my little slideshow to happen so long as I erased the files while on premises.

"I didn't realize how exhausting all this would be," Claudia said, rubbing the back of her neck with her hand. "I mean, it's been such a blast, but it's still tiring."

"Did you not ever go gown shopping with one of your girlfriends?" I asked as I slipped my iPad back into its case.

"No, not really," Claudia replied. "The only time I've done anything close to this was for my sister, but she had already narrowed her dresses down to three styles and all I did was help her make the final decision." With a wry laugh at the fact that our watches now read eight forty-five at night, she said, "It took all of thirty minutes, not nine and a half hours."

Slipping my tablet into my roomy Coach satchel, I asked, "What about your best friend? Has she gotten married yet?"

An amused grin came across her pretty face as she replied, "Well, my best friend is Luke, and I don't think he would look very good in a wedding dress."

Well, crap. I had successfully avoided having any kind of conversation with Claudia about Luke for the last several hours and then like an idiot I went and skipped myself right into the lion's den.

Actually, it wasn't true that I'd been able to totally avoid the conversation of Luke and Claudia. There were several times where I had walked up to her, and then found some non-obvious way to sidle away, as she was talking to either Virginia or Maggie and saying things such as, "He came over this past Sunday and spent practically the whole afternoon waxing my car for me, Ginny. He even vacuumed it and put that shine stuff on the dashboard and everything—was that not the sweetest?" and, "Maggie, as much as I am totally and completely in love with your brother, he can drive me up the wall with some of his little quirks. The man can't stand rice. I mean, what is up with that? Who hates *rice*? It's the most ridiculous thing I've ever heard. Still, all he has to do is smile at me with that cute dimple of his and all and my knees still go weak."

Yeah, that last one, with her definitive declaration of love, shocked me. Especially when, right after saying that, she unraveled a peppermint and popped it in her mouth. To be honest, it made my heart sink, regardless of my Inner Wall's solid status.

Thus, when I was around Claudia, I found myself gently steering all conversations either toward Maggie and her dresses or anything that didn't have to do with any kind of romantic relationship between a man and a woman. It had worked very well for the most part and I had found myself liking Claudia Danneberg despite myself.

I found out she was an Amarillo native who now worked as an interior designer for one of the top firms in town. Her German and Cuban descent accounted largely for her height and exotic beauty and she loved to cook, her favorite things being anything fried because, as she told me, "I'm an etiquette nightmare—I love nothing more than eating with my fingers." And she also had a seriously bizarre allergy to gin whereby if she consumed even a shot-glass full, she would lose her normal sweetness and would literally turn mean and brusque, even to the point of becoming violent if someone pushed her too far. "It took ages for Luke and me to figure out what was happening to me," she'd said. "It wasn't until I got into an actual bar fight during our senior year at Vanderbilt with a girl three times my weight after drinking two gin martinis that we narrowed it down to the gin. Luke still calls me Bruiser because of it. I don't remember the fight at all, but apparently I left the other poor girl with a nasty black eye."

I had teased her by pretending to type into my phone, saying, "Note to self: Keep Bruiser—I mean Claudia—away from the Tanqueray..." I paused, grinning as I heard Claudia's fabulous laugh in my ears, and finished with, "...Unless extra bouncer is needed. Can easily take on those several times her size..."

So, throughout the most of the day, I had managed to keep from discussing anything that would force me to hear about how wonderful Luke and Claudia's relationship was and when Claudia herself might be needing the services of a wedding planner. But then I forgot everything I'd learned thus far and asked Claudia about her best friend. Who turned out, of course, to be Luke.

In effect, Luke had been teasing Hilary and me with a loophole during our lunch the previous Saturday—Claudia was both his girlfriend *and* his best friend.

Isn't that just sweet as pie?

Still, it wasn't anything to get all pissy about, so I grabbed my satchel as we got up from the sofa and replied, "You know, I'm not so sure. I'm thinking Luke might have looked quite fetching in that strapless, beaded A-line gown with the bow the size of Texas in the back that we saw that other girl trying on earlier. He certainly has the coloring to pull off the champagne-pink satin, that's for sure."

With a mulling look, Claudia said, "I don't know, Shelby...I'm thinking the mermaid gown with all the tulle ruffles at the neck and hem we saw at the last place would be more his style."

"What? You mean hideous and tacky is his style?"

Claudia said under her breath, "I'm telling you, if you would have seen the way Luke dressed before I got a hold of him in college, you wouldn't have been that far off. In fact, hideous and tacky would have been an upgrade." She looked at me and her brown eyes were sparkling, "He actually came over to my dorm room one day with his sweatpants tucked into his socks. I've never laughed so hard in my life!"

Yeah, well, at that point my prevalence for snorting when I laughed was exposed for all the bridal salon to see and my client, her mother, and the woman who would undoubtedly be an official member of their family before too long made sure to let me know they found it hilarious.

Chalk up another few people who would never again see me as calm, cool, and collected.

Oh well, as if it's a big surprise now.

Fourteen

"Close your eyes," I said, just loud enough to be heard over the soft, lighthearted jazz coming from the three-piece band. The nervous bride and her equally nervous father both did as I asked.

"Now take a deep breath…and hold it…one…two…and slowly release." As they exhaled, the tenseness in both their shoulders relaxed. They opened their eyes and grinned the same wide smile at one another, then back at me, as the music wound down.

"Ready?" I smiled.

They nodded and moved into position so that they were framed in the open double-doorway. I was a step behind the bride, carrying her train. When the trumpeter sounded a clear, regal beginning to what would be a jazz-infused version of the wedding march, we heard the sound, like a roll of thunder, of three hundred people rising to their feet and turning with expectant faces.

"Enjoy yourselves," I reminded them. "And walk in three…two…one."

I dropped down and let Janelle Rutherford's long ivory-lace train to the floor, fanning it out as she began to walk down the aisle on the arm of her father. When the last of her train went over the threshold and all eyes were riveted on her, I quietly closed the wooden doors so that I remained back in the vestibule. For the next thirty minutes, my client of the last eight months and her fiancé were in the capable, but often long-winded hands of Reverend Brickard. So until I was needed again, I busied myself gathering up the silk-covered guest book, its accompanying silver pen, and a handful of extra wedding programs announcing the wedding of LaShanda Janelle Rutherford to Dr. Omar Pierce Oyediran.

I was working alone on this Saturday night, two weeks into the office renovations. Bryan was down in Galveston helping Emily oversee an five-hundred-person wedding and Lauren was busy with the gala portion of a three-day charity event she'd designed for a Houston-based global marketing company. I'd barely seen any of them all week.

I had seen quite a bit of Maggie Treadwell, though. I'd spent every available moment that I wasn't working with one of my other brides helping her tick off items from her wedding to-do list.

I walked her through setting up a wedding webpage—maggieandbarton.com—and had researched hotel rates so that she could choose two options to give to her out-of-town guests; all of said information was included on the save-the-date cards she picked out that matched her overall invitation theme. Together we'd also perused magazines, online bridal sites, and my masses of photo albums for bridesmaids' dresses ideas. And on Wednesday, I'd spent my lunch hour at You Beautiful Bride with Maggie and three of her bridesmaids as they tried on different looks, wherein she eventually chose a strapless Lazaro satin dress in a deep raspberry with a pretty box pleat and a wide satin sash in a contrasting hue the color of creamed coffee. Two days later I had then taken her to three of my favorite florists, and was pleased when she chose to have Galliana at Bella Arrangements be the person to fulfill her floral dreams. Galliana's designs were always elegant, romantic, and full of joy, just like Maggie.

As for her fiancé Barton, he was content to let her make the bulk of the decisions. "Except for the things that directly concern me," he'd told me, traces of his Scottish accent lilting in my ears, at our first meeting at Post Oak Country Club for a scheduled tasting. "And by 'me,' I mean my stomach. So long as I get my say on the food and the cake, my Maggie here could have us get married in a pink room filled with bunnies and enormous hearts and I wouldn't care."

"Hot damn, Maggie," I'd said. "We've gotten the okay on the bunnies. That was quick, too. You didn't even have to beg." I'd whipped out my cell, ready to dial a number, "Was that a hundred and fifty you wanted, dyed purple? Or was it two hundred? The bunny wrangler will want a specific amount…"

Barton had threatened to force-feed us haggis if we did such a thing and, from that point on, he and I were big pals.

Though I blissfully had no need for my Inner Wall around Bart because he simply wasn't my type, I could still easily see how Maggie had fallen in love with him. I admit that I had it in my mind that Bart would be some big, rugged-looking, hot-tempered Scot. Instead, he was kind of your basic-looking guy, with medium brown hair receding at the temples, medium blue eyes, and a five-ten frame that walked the tightrope between in and out-of shape. The reserve he exuded at first, too, left one momentarily disbelieving that he could snag a girl as cute and outgoing as Maggie Treadwell. But Barton's charm proved to be the type that snuck up slowly, only to take hold and never let go. He kept Maggie and me in stitches with his dry-witted comments, but all the while I could tell that it was Maggie and her *joie de vivre* was what kept him constantly amused and besotted. They were the right kind of opposites, Maggie and Barton were. Each of their personalities—Maggie's more lively and often rose-colored-glasses in her optimism and Barton's more down to earth and even-tempered—served as a counterbalance to the other.

Yin and yang, baby. It was the kind of match I loved to see in my clients. It made the fact that I was planning their wedding more pleasurable because I knew within a short time of being around the two of them—watching the way they responded to one another, hearing the respect for one another in their voices, and witnessing all sorts of other little things that, to me, were telltale signs of a good relationship or not—that they were going to make it for the long haul. They were each other's Right One. They fit.

I'd also given Maggie and Barton a list of things to do for the wedding plus deadlines by which to have them completed, which included booking their honeymoon within the next two months, registering for gifts within the next month, getting their couple's portrait taken within three weeks so that they could submit their engagement announcements to both the *Houston Chronicle* and the newspaper in Barton's native Edinburgh, and, lastly, looking over a list of websites I'd e-mailed them of bands that played weddings. I insisted that they whittle the list down within the week to the two bands they liked best. I told her that she and Bart absolutely must see both of them in person and that they should stay for at least six songs at both places so that they could get a true feel of the band's range

"You're so bossy, Shelby," Maggie had teased as she sent Bart a text message to tell him that they were going out dancing on Saturday whether they liked it or not.

I'd planted my fists on my hips and squared my shoulders. "Damn straight. I am the lord of all things nuptial and you will obey me."

A voice from out in the hall had called out, "I'd listen to Wonder Woman here, Mags. She can kick your ass."

"Zip it, Treadwell, or I'll kick *your* ass," I'd tossed defiantly over my shoulder, holding my power pose. "And get back to work."

"Yes, ma'am, Mrs. Fishburn."

And when Maggie's giggles had turned into a bawdy laugh that said she knew all too well about Sheldon Fishburn and the diary of my youth, I'd declared that her loudmouth brother and mine were never again to be allowed within five hundred yards of each other.

Now, as I heard Reverend Brickard asking Janelle if she would take Omar for better or worse, richer or poorer, in sickness and in health, I didn't think it would hurt anything if I smiled when I thought of Luke and how much of a good rapport we had developed. I enjoyed being around him a little too much, I was aware of that, but I was keeping my Inner Wall running at full speed, so I felt I could give myself the tiniest of breaks.

All had been quiet on the fix-up front for the last couple of weeks, so I had relaxed some there, too. In fact, I had actually stopped being automatically suspicious that I was being targeted for another unwanted date whenever one of my employees showed more enthusiasm than normal around me.

Actually I had not realized that I had become tense at all until a few days earlier when Lauren had come dancing into my office with happiness at, unbeknownst at that point to me, landing a series of high-profile events for a big children's charity, and I had stood up from my chair, pointed at her, and shouted, "Absolutely not! No!" before she could even utter a word.

However, the unspoken peace treaty I had hoped I had negotiated with the Dating Brigade was not to last. In fact, it was the calm before the storm.

Naturally...

And in my defense, my Brutus Radar had been right on target that day when I had convicted Lauren without proof of trying to set me up, because it was she who betrayed my trust so willfully.

Okay, maybe that's me getting all dramatic again. Still, I had thought Lauren, with her sweetness of temper and usual lack of desire to piss me off—a trait Emily thoroughly lacked and Bryan only possessed when he felt like it—wouldn't even try to deliberately set me up. Oh, maybe she might help out one of the others in convincing me to go out on a date, but actually do the dirty deed? I didn't think there was a chance.

Obviously, I needed to revise my view of my so-called sweet Lauren, because I found out just how wily and coercive the girl could be.

Case in point was how she set me up...

It was the next Friday after Janelle's wedding and everyone at Waterlane Events had a rare free weekend to look forward to. The construction sounds from across the hallway had all but ceased, with sweeping noises and the sound of the front door repeatedly opening and closing taking over as Luke's men began hauling tools out to the truck and debris out to the truck's attached flatbed trailer. Otherwise, it was just Lauren and I left in the office as Bryan and Gabriel had flown out to Cabo San Lucas for the weekend and Emily and Percy were off to what Emily termed a "romantic golfing weekend." And so when Lauren had casually walked into the kitchen—otherwise known as her temporary office—where I was taking my turn at cleaning the day's coffee cups and other assorted utensils, I was, of course, totally unsuspecting.

"Hey, sweetie," she said as she straddled one of the barstools, punctuating her salutation with an it's-been-a-long-workday yawn.

"Hey, yourself," I replied, taking a dry dishtowel to the wet coffee pot. "I didn't get to see you after the Isgitt Corporation's annual charity auction this morning. How did it go?"

Lauren gave a dry laugh as she pulled her wavy chestnut hair back and secured it into a jaunty ponytail with a red hair elastic, instantly transforming her usual sultry Italian looks into something closer to cute cheerleader. "If you don't count a twenty-minute stretch just before the start of the auction when I couldn't find the celebrity emcee—the married celebrity emcee, that is—because he was swapping spit with one of the barely legal interns in the stairwell, it all went smooth as silk."

I grinned. "Niiice. Did anyone else besides you witness the emcee and the jail bait in action?"

"Nope," she said, shaking her head so that her ponytail swayed side to side. "But I did get bribed to keep quiet."

"Oh, really?" I laughed. "And what did he bribe you with? The offer of some sloppy seconds tonsil hockey of your own after the auction?"

"Ewww, Shelby, gross!" Lauren replied, pulling a face. "No, the guy had been given a hundred-and-fifty-dollar gift card to Leonora's Tex-Mex Cantina—you know, the place with the fabulous margaritas and the enchiladas that I've heard are absolutely to die for—and he gave me the gift card for my silence, with a wink and a, 'You're fabulous, babe,' if you can believe it."

"Well, notwithstanding the gag-worthy car-salesman charm he apparently displayed, that's not a bad bribe," I told her while wiping down the butcher-block kitchen island. "I've been there a couple of times with Hilary and the food is both amazing and not cheap."

"Well," Lauren said, concentrating on tracing an imperfection in the island with her finger (which should have been a clue, let me tell you), "Chris is actually out of town this weekend and so I was wondering if you might like to go with me to Leonora's tomorrow. I'd wait and everything, but I'm kind of craving chicken enchiladas, and I've heard theirs are some of the best. Besides, I wouldn't even have this gift card if it weren't for you because it was you who handed over the Isgitt Corporation account to me when you hired me."

"Ahh…," I said, looking wistfully up at the ceiling and clutching my pink-and-white striped dishtowel to my breast, "and just think that it could have been *me* who got bribed and winked at by a sleazy celebrity emcee instead of you…it fills my heart with sadness and joy at the same time." I finished with a loud sniff and dabbed my eyes with my dishtowel.

Lauren giggled. "So does this mean you want to go with me tomorrow night?"

"Sure," I replied. "I'd love to. You name the time, baby, and I'll be there with bells on."

"I'm counting on it," Lauren said, her happy smile suddenly bright enough to light up a black hole (which should have been another clue). "Meet me in the bar at seven, okay?"

"Done," I replied, and then within moments she had left me and headed home to start her weekend. I hummed to myself, like the village idiot I was, apparently, while I finished up in the kitchen, completely unaware that I had been thoroughly hoodwinked by the most honest and amiable employee I'd ever had. Because the girl turned out to be the Mata Hari of setups through and through.

Pulling open the heavy wooden door of Leonora's Tex-Mex Cantina, I was hit immediately by the semi-cacophonous sounds of way too many people talking over one another in way too small a place. Leonora's was, per usual, filled to bursting with people, and it seemed as many as half of them were standing in the bar area as sitting at tables. To make things even louder, the door to the large patio area in the back was being intermittently pushed open, which made the noises coming from outside (enhanced somewhat by the Mariachi band that was currently playing quite the peppy tune) ramp up the inside decibel level by another few notches with every tray laden with piping-hot Mexican food that was bustled in and out by the bolero-wearing waiters.

I'd come dressed for a casual night out in a pair of dark jeans, a cotton eyelet scoop-neck top in a tangerine color, and platform Tory Burch wedges. Not seeing Lauren as I looked around the room, I groped in my purse for my phone to give her a call and felt it already vibrating with a text message:

Running late. Drink a rita.

Unperturbed, I decided her suggestion wasn't half bad and went to the bar, where I got behind the shortest person I could find in the throng of patrons who were already standing at the bar. But naturally I was still height-challenged and had to stand on my tiptoes to try and get the bartender's attention. I was attempting to lean in between the two people in front of me when I heard a voice to my left say (or yell, rather, as it was so loud), "Are you Shelby, by any chance?"

I went back to an upright position and slowly turned, which put my eyes directly into the broad chest of a very big, very tall guy. Craning my neck upward to about six foot five, I saw a lopsided smile in a wide, square-jawed face, a nose that looked recently sunburned, a head full of dark, tightly formed curls that had been gelled so much that they looked like they might crack if they were touched, and two ice-blue eyes that, although much too small for his big frame and face, were crinkling in a lighthearted way.

Slowly but automatically holding out my hand to shake, I gave him a quizzical look and shouted back above the din, "Yes, I'm Shelby." His big paw clasped mine and I said, "Do I know you?"

"I'm Hale. Hale McCafferty. It's a pleasure to meet you, Shelby." He was still shaking my hand, and I was still looking at him like he was just a little bit nuts.

"Hi, Hale...," I replied. "Again—have we met before?"

"Lauren decided not to tell you, huh?"

Cue the shocked face. "Excuse me?"

Hale McCafferty dug into the front pocket of his faded jeans, and I noticed for the first time that his bulging thigh muscles were straining against the denim. A further glance down and I could just tell that the guy didn't exactly have my favorite cute bird legs, either. His were more of the tree-trunk variety, that was obvious. Looking up again when his hand came out of his pocket, I then saw something else that wasn't to my liking. He was holding up a cherry-red piece of plastic that in yellow, festive-looking script read out *Leonora's Tex-Mex Cantina, Where You'll Always Find an Authentic Taste of Mexico and a Lot of Texas Fun!* and then, in the corner, in white lettering: $150.

Mr. Big Thighs was holding Lauren's gift card.

And I obviously had myself another blind date.

"Hale, would you please excuse me for a moment?" I asked, smiling as sweetly as I could manage while some not-so-sweet language came into my mind in reference to Lauren setting me up (in every way the phrase could be used).

But Hale was apparently under orders from Ms. Mussolini. "No way," he said, shaking his massive head, which didn't make his frozen-in-time curls move even a millimeter. "Lauren warned me you would do this and she told me that I was in no way to let you go call her and yell at her for fixing you up with me."

Okay, shocked face, part deux...

He continued, "She told me that I was to tell you—" he leaned down a fraction and the lopsided grin was wide with how funny he found the situation, "—and I quote, 'Tell Shelby that she is to suck it up and enjoy herself.' And, although I'm not quite sure what to make of this, I'm also not supposed to let you leave until we both have finished our meals and I've gotten your phone number." Then he winked one of his tiny eyes at me and said, "Actually, I just made up the last part about your number, but I already know that I'd like to call you again, so I hope you'll let me have it."

Okay, here's the thing: While ninety-nine percent of me was in apoplectic mode (and, I'll admit it, wrathfully thinking, Oh, I'll let you have it, all right...), there was that little one percent of me that was giving Mussolini, I mean Lauren, some props for going to such lengths and pre-countering my every move. And that same little one percent of me found my blind date to be somewhat endearing. I couldn't exactly say that my romantic interest was piqued—and I tended to know for sure about that kind of chemistry right off the bat—but I couldn't say that I was repulsed by him, either. I mean, with the exception that I'd never find his legs to be as sexy as, say, Luke's, he wasn't all that bad in the looks department.

Well, the freeze-dried hairstyle needed to go, but I think any sane woman would have agreed with me.

Anyway, I decided to lean toward that one percent and give the evening a chance.

"Frozen sangria," I said, once more yelling over the crowd in Leonora's.

Hale looked momentarily perplexed. "I'm sorry?"

"That's what I'd like to drink, please. A frozen sangria."

And when he offered me a big grin, I tried out a smile in return and found it not all that hard.

Shocking, I know…

Fifteen

A little over two hours later, I was driving home again. Alone. Shaking my head in despair.

For it had happened again. Another guy had managed to throw my respect for him straight down the tubes within the course of one evening.

But this time, I could claim absolutely no part in the evening's demise. Not even a single shred. This time, it was all Hale McCafferty's doing.

And yes, I stayed for the entire dinner, thank you very much. All the way through a lingering dessert of thick, cinnamon-laced Mexican hot chocolate and several delicious deep-fried fingerlings of sweet batter rolled in cinnamon and sugar known as *churros*, to be exact.

And yes, I enjoyed myself, made conversation, laughed, and got to know Hale McCafferty fairly well.

Or so I thought.

Intending to go straight home, I changed my mind when I drove past Central Market, my favorite grocery store, and realized that it would be open for another two hours. I figured a little late-night shopping would be just the ticket to calm me down.

Like Leonora's, Central Market was still bustling with people even into the evening hours due to its popularity. I, however, didn't really take that much notice of all the other shoppers around me as I slowly pushed my grocery cart through the immense, winding produce aisle and browsed for the fruits and vegetables that suited my fancy while my mind raced through the evening's events and found them just as astounding as I had when they were happening right in front of my eyes.

When I'd watched my date get hit in the nuts with a set of brass knuckles, to be exact. By none other than his wife named Eden.

And, of course, it happened out in the parking lot. As if it wouldn't.

I took my time choosing a cantaloupe for breakfast in the morning and a couple of almost ripe avocados that would soon make perfect afternoon snacks with a drizzle of balsamic vinegar and a dash of kosher salt. I then moved on into the meat department, choosing some fresh chicken breasts to freeze and a small filet of wild salmon for my Sunday evening dinner that I would bake with teriyaki sauce and then place into sheets of nori with some sushi rice, wasabi mayonnaise, and thinly sliced cucumber to make myself some homemade hand rolls.

But as I was trying to navigate my shopping cart between two others whose temporary owners were busy inspecting the scallops and huge Gulf Coast shrimp, I heard a voice call my name over the display of Texas-brewed beers that served to separate the seafood side of the market from the meat side. I looked up over the rows of brown bottles and saw that it was my very first parking-lot pal.

"Well, well, well, if it isn't my Lochinvar," I said as I rested my forearm over a six pack of Shiner HefeWeizen and took in the sight of my friend and contractor as a bit of a sight for sore eyes (especially as the Saturday Morning Scruff was doing his face major justice). "Fancy meeting you here. What's new?"

Reminding me that Luke had uncanny powers of reading me and all my lovely moods, he rolled the peppermint that was in his mouth from one side to the other and said, "Uh-oh. What happened this time?"

"However do you mean?" I asked, fluttering my eyes as if he were saying something untoward.

Luke leaned over a couple of six packs of Saint Arnold Brown Ale and said, "I heard you had another date tonight and, if the very fact that you called me Lochinvar is any signpost, it didn't go very well. Am I right?"

"You suck," I replied in return, and didn't even bother to ask how he knew about the date because I was pretty sure that I had been, per usual, the last in the office to know in the first place.

"Ah-ha!" Luke said and, even with the scruff, his dimple came out to taunt me. "I'll give you five bucks if you make my evening and tell me all about it."

I studied him for a moment, feeling my spirits lift (and therefore calling upon my Inner Wall to wake its ass up and do its job). Then I held out my hand over the beer display, palm up, and looked at him expectantly.

"What? You want your five bucks now?"

"You betcha, my friend." I replied. "This chick no longer gives out embarrassing information for free. Cough it up."

Dutifully, Luke pulled out his wallet, extracted a fiver, and held it out to me in between his first two fingers. I used my own to grinningly snatch it out of his grasp.

"The Association for Women Who Can't Find a Decent Guy to Date thanks you for your kindness," I said, folding up the five dollars neatly and slipping it into my jeans' front pocket.

Rolling his eyes, Luke said, "Come on, Dame Shelby, let's get going."

When we met on the other side of the beer display, it turned out that Luke had only grabbed himself a small handheld shopping basket that contained nothing but a head of iceberg lettuce, a single huge russet potato, and a fresh thick-cut steak wrapped in white butcher paper. In his other hand he had one of the six packs of Shiner Bock.

"Let me guess—Sunday lunch?" I said.

"Yep," he said. "A few buddies of mine from college are coming over and we're grilling our first steaks of the summer. It's bring-your-own meat and potatoes. We do it a couple times a year."

"No girls allowed?"

Luke feigned manly derisiveness as he slid his basket and beer onto the rack under my cart and then came to stand next to me. "Absolutely. I'll even tack up my sign that says He-Man Woman-Haters' Club if I have to." He took hold of the cart handle with a grin. "Here, I'll drive and you talk. That way you can make all your normal gesticulations while you're telling me the tale of your evening."

I looked up at him like he was nuts, which was far easier than it had been with the way-too-tall-for-me Hale McCafferty. "What are you talking about? I don't make *gesticulations*."

"Sure you do. All the time. And especially when you're relating any kind of wild story." He made a couple of over-the-top dramatic gestures with his hand, nearly swiping another passing shopper with the second one. "In fact, if I couldn't tell that you do<u>n't</u> have a drop of Italian blood in you, I wouldn't have been surprised if you had told me your name was Shelby Soprano." And when I looked at him like I didn't know whether to laugh or be offended, he smiled at me, his eyes so blue, and said, "Don't worry, it's one of your most charming traits."

Oh, boy. Kick it into high gear, Inner Wall! Pronto!

I gave him a high-and-mighty look, "I happen to think *all* my traits are charming, thank you. And I do *not* make these so-called gesticulations."

Which I then completely negated when we came across a small display of wines from my favorite, but little-known California vineyard and I went a little bananas telling Luke about how fabulous they were and how you could literally taste the peaches in the chardonnay and what a surprise it was to find them being sold at Central Market because they were so hard to find. Finally witnessing my own multitude of dramatic gestures and Luke's I-told-you-so grin, I turned away from the display—with two bottles of chardonnay in hand, because I'm not stupid—and stalked off, saying, "Fine! So I make *some* gesticulations…"

Thereafter, with prodding from Luke to spill my guts or relinquish his five bucks, we slowly walked through the dry goods area and the bulk bins of nuts, milled flours, beans, and dried fruits, I told him of the first part of my evening with Hale McCafferty. And when he stopped me while I was perusing the wide selection of coffee beans and told me that the boring stuff I was telling him about how much fun I had been having getting to know "this six-five, former-football-player McCafferty guy" was totally not worth the shekels he'd shelled out, I then went into the good stuff.

I told him of how Hale and I had walked out, all smiles and easiness, into the quiet parking lot, and how I'd been thinking that I might have been willing to say yes if he had asked me out again.

"Then, as we got near his brand-new Range Rover, he saw something and shouted, 'I think someone's trying to break into my Rover!'"

Luke smiled. "I like how you deepened your voice there, Waterlane. Adds that little extra something to the story."

"You're interrupting my flow," I admonished before getting into the part about how Hale's wife Eden, who was no more than five-foot-five and a hundred and twenty pounds—"and that's counting her surgically enhanced D-cup ta-tas,"—came around the car holding up Hale's wedding band and started screaming that she had caught him and that he was a lying, cheating sack of shit.

"She pointed at me and called me his most recent trashy whore, too. Can you believe that?"

Luke made a show of eyeing me as if deciding whether or not I might actually be a trashy whore, then scooted away from me when I exclaimed, "Treadwell! What gives?" and acted like I was going break out some jujitsu moves.

"So then," I continued, really getting into it, "Eden throws his wedding band at him and Hale goes to catch it like it was a football." I mimicked Hale's widened stance and cupped hands at his chest. "And before I could even move, Eden whips out a set of brass knuckles from her waistband and *wham*! Hits him right in the nuts. The guy dropped to the ground faster than I would have thought a guy his size could, actually."

I'd thrown in my dramatic-gesture rendition of Eden's bowling-ball hurl with her knuckled-up fist into Hale's groin, but then I had to turn around in the dairy aisle and walk a good ten steps back to where Luke had stopped the cart in complete and utter astonishment, his eyes stunned.

"Somehow I feel like I've said this before, but you're kidding me, right?"

I said, "Nope. Not at all."

"And what did you say when you saw this woman smash her husband's nuts in with a set of brass knuckles?"

"Holy shit," I replied calmly, shrugging as if it were the only thing one could say in such a situation.

"Holy shit," he repeated like I was certifiable. "All you said was, 'Holy shit'?"

"Well," I said, "I actually *yelled*, 'Holy shit!' but, yeah, that was it for the time being." And when he seemed to be at a loss for words, I said, "May I finish the story now, Mr. Treadwell?"

"You mean there's more to the Knuckles McCafferty story?"

I rocked back on my heels. "Whoa. Knuckles McCafferty?" I asked, raising a skeptical eyebrow even though I was positively tickled. "Is that what your offering up for his new nickname?"

Luke grinned, making a slow-motion movement that mimicked Eden's blow to her straying husband, "Well, if the brass balls-buster fits…"

"Ouch." I replied. "Nice one. I don't think I could have thought of a better one myself."

"What can I say? I'm a quick learner."

I clapped a little for him and he affected a small bow in return before saying, "So, let's hear the rest of the story, Waterlane, or I want my five bucks back."

So I told him how Eden had turned her rage my way but I'd been ready for her with my outstretched arm holding my pepper spray. "Just seeing it aimed right at her eyes seemed to bring her back to her senses, thank goodness."

I explained that I'd then told Eden I hadn't known Hale was married and that she needed to leave, calm down, and do her fighting with Hale in court instead. Because, as much as he really was a lying sack of shit, I wasn't going to let her hurt him again right there in front of me.

"She glared at me like a maddened bull for another two seconds and then whipped around and left. Hale was still on the ground, groaning, but needless to say, I told him never to come near me again and then I got the hell out of there."

And by the time Luke and I came to cool our heels in the checkout line, after first going through my favorite area with all the cheeses and chocolates, where I loaded up on both and he got a small block of cheddar to shred for his Sunday baked potato, his flabbergasted mentality of the dairy aisle had mellowed into amused acceptance of the fact that I had had yet another shamefully interesting blind date. He, too, had also picked up on the fact that Shelby Waterlane and parking lots were not exactly copasetic at present.

"You know, I think we should devise some way of transporting you out of the restaurant so that you never set foot into the actual parking lot, because it seems that it's there where things go from not-so-bad to flat-out ridiculous." He thoughtfully rubbed the scruff on his face. "Maybe airlifting would be an option…"

"Shut up," I laughed as I took out my wallet from my purse.

"I'm serious. There is something weird about you and parking lots, Shelb."

Luckily, Luke didn't see it, but I had to turn away as my breath caught a little bit. You wouldn't think that someone calling me Shelb would make my heart race—I mean, it really seems like a stupid thing, right?—but it did. I guess it just meant that he was that comfortable with me to shorten my name in the same way that all the other people who truly loved me did, and it sounded like music to my ears.

And so, for a brief little moment as I gave the checkout clerk my cart so that he could start ringing up my purchases, I allowed myself to curse the fates that gave Luke Treadwell's heart to Claudia Danneberg instead of yours truly.

Then I made myself get over it, as I always did. I just kept enjoying Luke's friendship, laughing and calling him a bastard when we walked out into the parking lot and he pretended to look around for Caveman Kev and Lars the Loathsome. We talked beside my car in the warm summer air for another fifteen minutes before he eventually bade me goodbye with a, "See you Monday, Ms. Soprano," leaving me to drive home alone with my crowded brain full of thoughts of yet another odd and eventful evening that somehow ended with Luke's presence making things a million times better.

Sixteen

Lauren was, of course, completely horrified—not to mention thoroughly apologetic— when she heard the story of Knuckles McCafferty the next day. Had it not been for Luke making me laugh so much the night before, essentially taking the piss out of yet another godforsaken bad date I'd experienced, I might have gleefully skewered Lauren for a while and then extracted a promise from her in blood that she would not pull such a stunt on me again. Instead, she got off easy with a hug and a completely un-mean–sounding, "And don't you do it again, missy."

Nevertheless, I was happy to shove the Knuckles McCafferty incident to the That Which Is Best Forgotten portion of my brain so that I could return to immersing myself in planning Maggie Treadwell's September wedding and the seven other just as important weddings that were taking place in June, July, and August, respectively.

Of those weddings, it was the nuptials that would be celebrated on the last Thursday in July that I was most looking forward to because the bride was one of my longtime clients who had become both a great friend and mentor to me over the years.

Her name was Jackie Rosenstein and she was a fabulously brassy marketing executive in her late forties who had thick mahogany hair, expressive, perfectly manicured hands, sparking light-brown eyes, and a penchant for Diane von Furstenberg wrap dresses. When I first met her six years ago at the Chatsworth, when she had come in to book an event for her company, she was unhappily married to a man named Hugh but was staying with him for the sake of their two high-school–aged children. Jackie and I had bonded instantly and, whenever she used my hotel for one of her events, she and I invariably hung out in my office discussing earth-shattering topics such as sex, entertainment gossip, our love of carbohydrates, the latest incredible chocolate dessert we'd found in *Southern Living* magazine, and shoes.

Jackie was one of those people who spoke her mind always and, if you didn't like it, then tough. But I loved it and usually even looked forward to her undiluted honesty. For instance, Jackie would be the first one to look me up and down, and then use her long, graceful fingers to make air-circles toward whatever part of me she was referring to, and say, "Honey, that outfit is not doing you justice," or, "I love that you went chin-length, but those short, spiky bangs aren't working with your facial structure. Go back to the side-swept bangs and you'll be fabulous."

But beyond that, Jackie was also one of the few people in my life who openly and unflinchingly encouraged me to stay single until I had met the man who I was absolutely positive would make me happy—and yet she still insisted that I should never stop seeking out love all the same. And when she and Hugh had finally separated (after their children had finally told them to stop being ridiculous and just get divorced already) it had been I, two years later, who had introduced Jackie to the man she was about to marry.

Only I wasn't playing matchmaker like my lovely employees were currently. Instead, I had simply just finished showing the Chatsworth's grand ballroom to my latest client, Abel Schoenfeld, who was looking for a venue for his parents' fiftieth wedding anniversary. Jackie had walked in the hotel's doors as my next appointment and the very handsome, also divorced with two kids, forty-eight-year-old lawyer stopped dead in his tracks when he saw her. I introduced the two, sparks flew like mad, and Abel stayed to have a drink with Jackie and me—though I excused myself after about ten minutes when I saw my assistance was no longer needed. Being a smart man, Abel wasted no time asking Jackie for the first of many dates; three months later she was on his arm for his parents' anniversary party, and the rest was history, culminating in the fact that, after four years together, they were finally going to take the second-time-around plunge and get married.

Now while Maggie Treadwell was planning a big event, Abel and Jackie were wanting a small and elegant wedding for their second trips down the aisle. They had even specifically chosen a Thursday so that they could have an late-afternoon wedding without having to wait to get married until after sundown as required for the Friday and Saturday evenings of the Sabbath.

Once the date had been picked, the bride had then given me free rein in deciding how everything should go. "As long as it's elegant, the wedding cake has a buttercream frosting—none of that fondant crap; it looks pretty for sure, but Abel and I both think it tastes like cardboard—and the *chuppah* is covered in so many white trumpet lilies that the florist has to order more from another state, I'm going to be happy. But otherwise, Abel and I are too busy to plan the wedding and so we're happily going to pass it off on you. With refusal rights for every inch of it, of course."

I wasn't scared about planning her wedding with such little direction, though. I had been working with Jackie on various events throughout the years and I knew exactly what would make her happy and what would make those lively brown eyes narrow at me with big-time irritation. And the fact that their second wedding would only include about fifty people total, well, that just made it even easier to ramp up the elegance part of the deal.

The two things I had immediately pinned down when they'd hired me had been the venue and the invitations. After discussing a few options, Jackie and Abel agreed that they would like to use the place they met, the Chatsworth, and have their ceremony and reception in one of its smaller ballrooms. A couple of weeks later I then dragged her away from her office long enough to choose invitations from the dozen or so samples I'd obtained from both Houston-based and online stationery stores. She had taken her time with each sample, feeling the paper between her fingers, testing the look of the invitation against all its accompanying cards and the way it looked when it was removed from the envelope.

Decisive as always, though, she took little time thereafter in deciding on a cream-colored one-hundred-percent-cotton panel card framed in a sandalwood brown. Wrapping around the invitation in a gate fold was a translucent vellum overlay printed with a floral toile in the same sandalwood color. A satin bow in cream was tied around the invitation's middle, adding a touch of shine to the elegance. She chose a clean script for the invitation's wording, which was engraved onto the card stock with a chocolate brown ink. Ten days later she signed off on the proof I had ordered for her and, with space booked at the hotel and the invitations ordered, I had moved forward on my own from there, mapping out a proposal that I was confident would please my clients, even if a few details were tweaked here and there.

Since Jackie wanted the ceremony to be "short and sweet, or Rabbi Silverman won't be invited to any party we ever throw again," then it would be the dinner and reception that would make up the bulk of the evening. I would be suggesting they have a five-course meal (the wedding cake being the fifth) using round tables that seated ten people apiece. Working with Rebecca, the Chatsworth's catering director, and Chef Pevo, the talented Cambodian banquet chef who had been my friend since my own days at the hotel, I had devised two possible menus, centering each around a wine theme to play off my clients' aficionado lifestyle.

In deciding which wines to suggest, I had gone back through all my notes from every Jackie Rosenstein party I'd ever organized and had made a list of her most-requested varietals and brands. Then I had called a wine merchant friend of mine to get help with choosing the best wines for each of the five courses on both of my possible menus. Next I'd found multiple examples of the fanciful flower arrangements I had in mind for the tables, in front of the *chuppah*, and around the room, as well as samples of linen fabrics for the chair covers and tablecloths. I'd then mapped out a color scheme for all of it, using mostly the tasteful shades of creams, apricots, and soft browns Jackie preferred mixed with hints of strong sapphire blue to complement Abel's handsome olive coloring and blue-as-the-sky eyes. As for the silverware, glassware, and china, they were all to be provided by the hotel and were all top notch, naturally.

The next day at eleven o'clock, I had my appointment with Jackie and Abel for them to go over the proposal I had devised for them. When they came through the office's front door, I thought for probably the millionth time that they were a stunningly elegant couple. He looked dashing in a single-breasted lightweight wool suit and blue Hermès tie, with his thick, brushed-back, salt-and-pepper hair and sexy eyes that seemed to drink you in whenever you were having a conversation with him. And she looked like a walking advertisement for Nearly Fifty Is the New Thirty and Fabulous with her lustrous mahogany hair flying behind her, simple gold jewelry, and one of her signature von Furstenberg wrap dresses in a chocolate-brown and white print accentuating her incredible figure and beautiful legs. I went to greet her enthusiastically, my arms out in anticipation of giving her a big hug.

But instead, Jackie grabbed my left hand and used it to unceremoniously spin me around, toward where the renovations were currently under way. Abel, being the unflappably suave man that he always was, just stood behind Jackie and did nothing more than look amused and mouth a hello at me when my surprised eyes briefly caught his before being turned in the direction of where Luke and his men were working steadily away in the soon-to-be middle office, which would become Emily's personal space.

"Honey," she said, "what is that?"

I shrugged. "Construction. Renovations to make three offices for Emily, Bryan, and Lauren." I swiveled my eyes to look up another four inches at my friend. "I'm sure I told you about it—didn't I?"

She replied, "No, honey. I don't give a rat's ass about the construction, as nice as it is, of course. I'm talking about the *shaygitz* at twelve o'clock who just happens to fall in the tall and lanky categories. Why didn't you tell me about *him?*"

I wanted to sigh in (sexual) frustration. Maybe it was just me, but Luke happened to have walked in looking particularly good that day. His hair still damp from showering, he smelled extra soapy and wore a new blue KT Construction shirt that set off his eyes to such perfection that the combination caused me to have to practically hold up my Inner Wall with my bare hands as he had shown me around the previous day's progress. Luckily, Bryan and Lauren had both come in right on time and so I'd only had to keep myself from drooling for about five full minutes before I had someone to distract me.

So I told Jackie with determined blitheness even as Luke bent over to pick up a nail, giving us a clear view of his backside, "Oh, that's Luke. He's our contractor—and completely in love with a great girl named Claudia, so he's off the market."

Let me tell you, I was getting quite tired of repeating that line, too...

But unlike Hilary and my other employees, Jackie did not accept my statement as fact and let it go. Instead, she said, "Uh-huh," and turning me back toward her, she searched my eyes and said just quietly enough so that only Abel and I could hear her, "You've got it bad for him, don't you?"

And when I just made sputtering noises that sounded something like, "Nuh...uh...uh...nuh...," Jackie nodded knowingly again said, "Uh-huh. Honey, you and I are going to have a nice long talk after we go over your proposal and my handsome fiancé here goes back to the office." She then linked her arm through mine and started to walk me back to my office.

As I was being led away, I looked at Abel and my face must have looked utterly defeated and pleading at the same time to be saved from Jackie's clutches, wherein this time I wasn't so sure I wanted her total honesty, because he laughed and said, "I wish I could help you, Shelby, but you're toast."

And here I thought Jackie was at least one person on the side of Shelby Should Stay Single and Happy Until She Damn Well Feels Like Doing Otherwise. Well, she soon showed me, because it seemed that since Jackie had given in to the thought of marriage again, she had lost a little bit of her conviction that I was better off single until that right guy happened to come traipsing into my life.

In effect, Jackie Rosenstein had done a full-tilt about face and was now just as determined that I should date someone as the rest of my loved ones were.

"You need a good couple of weeks of rolling in the hay, Shelby," she informed me only seconds after Abel had kissed me on the cheek goodbye and left for the office, the both of them having been exceptionally pleased with my proposal, even though Jackie made several tweaks to my suggestions for, among other things, the color of the table linens, the first and third courses of the menu, and the types of vases for the flower arrangements. She used her wine-painted fingernail to air-draw circles a few inches from my (apparently undersexed) visage, "It's written all over your face."

"Thanks for the bulletin," I replied. "Nice to know that my single status is changing my appearance into that of a hardened, sex-deprived hag."

Jackie sat back on my sofa, not insulted in the least by my sarcasm. "It's the truth." And when I looked a little hurt, she replied quickly, leaning forward to put a calming hand on my knee, "Oh, honey, you know you have always been too adorable for words and you still are, but since you've become so set in your ways because of your recent anti-dating policy, you've just lost some of your softness, that's all. And I think I see it more so than Bryan and everybody else because I see you less, you know?"

With a dismayed sigh, I moved from my club chair to plop myself down next to her on the spot on the sofa that Abel had recently vacated, grabbing up as I did so one of the cookies that Bryan had left for us when I encouraged him to take a long lunch. Jackie was right, and I somewhat grudgingly knew it. "Yeah, I think that's what everybody has been trying to tell me in their own little ways." I laughed wryly, "Only you were the only one to say it openly and clearly. Do you ever not say exactly what's on your mind?"

"Not often, baby. Not often," Jackie replied, smiling kindly at me. "So, tell me. What is the deal with you and Mr. Lanky Contractor with the nice ass out there?"

"I told you, he's taken."

"And I heard that part. But there is definitely some sort of connection between you two, Shelby."

I was pretty floored at hearing that one. "You didn't even meet him. How could you even tell we knew each other beyond, you know, the fact that he's doing a job for me?"

"Because I saw the way he watched you when you came out to greet Abel and me," Jackie said simply.

I frowned, thinking back. "Really? I didn't see anything."

Jackie laughed, "Oh, but honey, *I* did. And so did Abel. It was when you were walking toward us. I glanced over and saw him watching you with a big smile on his face. He turned around right before you got to me."

"You mean right before you dislocated my shoulder so that you could taunt me with the sight of him bending over."

Jackie's voice was filled with amusement, "If that's how you'd like to phrase it."

I sighed yet again and said, "I hate to break it to you, Jackie, but there's nothing exciting going on whatsoever between Luke and me. I mean, you're right that we know each other from outside the office, but he's been very careful to keep things on the up and up when we're in each other's presence. He's given me absolutely no indication that he feels anything beyond friendship for me."

Jackie shifted so that she was facing me and squared her shoulders as if readying herself for taking in some important knowledge. "All right, then, tell me the whole story, honey. All of it. From how you met him to now."

So, I did. And I gotta admit that it felt good to unburden myself about Luke to someone who loved me but was just a tad bit more objective than my gang of matchmakers about the trials and tribulations of finding love—not to mention someone who was also a really fabulous secret-keeper. She listened patiently and thus heard every detail, from the Caveman Kev incident and the earning of the Lochinvar name all the way to the bit about my heart doing a little flutter when he had called me Shelb at the Central Market checkout. And, of course, since Luke ended up being involved in some way whether he wanted to or not, she also heard about Franzilla's and the Dating Brigade's determination to fix me up or die trying. She even learned about my ridiculous lust for his legs and, shockingly (or maybe not so much), she gave me a look that clearly said that she'd always known her blonde *shiksa* friend was crazy and said with the utmost pity in her voice, "Oh, *honey*, skinny legs? Really?"

Apparently I still had no takers to help me start a Bird Legs Are Hot Fan Club...

But then, just as fast, Jackie switched and went into rapid-fire question mode. "And who is this girlfriend?"

"Her name is Claudia. She's...she's just awesome. As much as I'd like to, I can't say a bad word about her—"

"And how long have they been going out?" she interrupted.

I shifted uncomfortably. "I don't know exactly. I guess I didn't want to know, so I've never asked. I know they met in college, though, so I'm guessing quite some time."

"And they're not engaged yet?" Jackie asked with a hint of disdain.

"No, not engaged as of yet."

Jackie replied, "So, you're telling me that this guy is in love with one of the greatest women on God's green Earth and they've known each other for over ten years and have been going out for at least part of that, and he hasn't asked her to marry him?"

My answer? "Um…"

"Oh, honey, this guy is either the dumbest guy in the universe or he's not as in love with her as you think he is," she declared, crossing her arms over her chest.

"That's not necessarily true," I replied quickly. "I've done lots of weddings where the couple had dated for sometimes well over a decade before they decided to get married. It's not as unusual as it sounds, Jacks."

Jackie eyed me again and said in a nicer tone, "Okay, tell me if I'm wrong. I only got one look at Luke and everything about him just screamed 'marrying type.' Am I right?"

Due to my Inner Wall doing a better job than I had realized, I hadn't really thought about Luke in that particular way. After furrowing my brow for a moment as I thought about it, I said, "Yeah. I'm pretty sure he's the marrying type."

"And this Claudia creature? What about her?"

I said dully, "Definitely the marrying type."

Jackie waited a full, pregnant second before saying, "Then don't you think that you might be overestimating what Luke and Claudia's relationship might be?"

At her words, an unexpected bright burst of hope shot through the deflective barrier that was my Inner Wall and my mind was beginning to fill with thoughts of actually getting to touch Luke, and kiss him, and shag the living daylights out of him (again, and again, and again, because I really did need a good two-week sex fest to get me and my so-called softness back up to speed).

But then I remembered how Luke looked when he was on the phone with Claudia after the night he drove me home from Lawson's. And the things I overheard Claudia saying about him to Maggie that spoke of the kind of deep love that truly overcomes all bumps in the road and lasts forever. And how Luke and Claudia had smiled at each other and how good and right their two tall, lean figures had looked next to one another as well that very first night in Bernatello's parking lot.

And the little bright spark of hope fizzled out and I was left even colder than I had been before, because I hadn't realized what I was missing when I hadn't been allowing myself to feel any real hope about Luke. And I also began to feel the figurative hands on my back again that were trying their best to shove me toward a man who was not free to return my feelings.

Thus, I became pretty darn cranky.

"All right," I said to her, making a frustrated gesture with the cookie I had yet to eat, "but so what if I'm 'overestimating' what Luke and Claudia might have together? I don't exactly see him rushing off to break up with her so that he can ask me out or anything."

"Well, have you given him any indication that you might like to go out with him?" Jackie asked.

"No, of course not. You know I don't do that kind of thing when a guy is in a relationship," I snapped. Then apologized for doing so and was forgiven.

Jackie said judiciously, "There are ways to let a guy know you're interested without being a relationship-wrecker, you know. You throw out certain hints—a long look here, a light touch on the arm there—but you temper it with very clear signals, and even statements if you have to, that you play by the rules. And if he wants you in the same way, then he'll play by the rules, too, and end it with Claudia."

I replied, "Yes, but think about it this way: Do I really want to be with a guy who will engage in any type of flirting with another woman when he is supposed to be in love with someone else? I mean, if Luke would be willing to openly flirt with me when he's supposed to be committed to Claudia, what is to say that he wouldn't turn around and do the same thing to me if it were he and I in the relationship and then he went off to another contracting job and met someone else?"

"Honey, I think you're thinking too hard about all this," Jackie said.

"No, I'm not," I huffed. "I don't want a guy who will run around on me behind my back. I've dated that type before and it sucks. I definitely do not want to be with somebody like that again. And, anyway, serious flirting with another person when you're already in a relationship is basically just cheating without the sex. It's Cheating Lite."

Jackie did her air-circles again with her finger. "So, what you're saying is that you actually respect Luke for not giving you any signals that he's interested?"

I nodded my head vigorously yes, I did respect his gentlemanly behavior. Then shook my head no, because it certainly would have been nice to know if he was interested or not, if it could happen without him being deceitful to Claudia. Obviously, the question was too hard for my frustrated, overtaxed, and undersexed brain.

"Oh, hell, I don't know," I finally cried out. "But what I do know is that it would be hard for me to respect Luke if I knew that he was just keeping Claudia—who is obviously madly in love with him—hanging around as a backup on the off chance that I might *not* be interested in dating him. Do you know what I mean? I just don't like people who keep dating someone that they're no longer in love with just because they don't want to be single and alone. I would respect Luke much more if he broke up with Claudia and then asked me out, regardless of whether or not he knew if I was interested."

Jackie eyed me again with amused consternation. "You are bound and determined to have a negative answer to anything I could come up with, aren't you?" And before I could answer, she said something that depressed me a little: She agreed with me. "But this time, I have to say that when you put it like that, you're right," she said, putting her hand over mine and giving it a squeeze. "You're a good person who doesn't want Luke to jerk around Claudia just so that he can be with you. You'd rather it be absolutely, one-hundred-percent aboveboard if you can help it at all. And that, honey, is what sets you apart from all the other women I know. Fair play means something to you, Shelby, and that makes me very proud of you." Her serious tone gave way to a self-deprecating laugh, "Because, God knows that I wouldn't have batted an eye if Abel had broken some other woman's heart just to be with me. I got lucky in that he'd stopped seeing his last girlfriend only a few weeks before we met, but I would have willingly gone mano a mano with her to have Abel in my life."

I squeezed her hand in return. "I'm glad you got lucky, Jacks, because the two of you could not be more perfect together."

Jackie reached out and gave me a big hug. "And I know you'll find that guy, too, honey. Maybe it's Luke and maybe it's not. But just keep being open and willing to take chances until you find out, okay? And have fun just being Luke's friend in the meantime, because there is never anything wrong with friendship. Especially," she said, a coy note coming back into her voice, "if that friendship keeps making you smile like you do when you talk about him."

I gave Jackie one last stubborn look and said, "Friendship is the key word, here, Jackie. Just friendship." Then I laughed and put my hand to my head like I was feeling for signs of delirium. "Especially because now I'm starting to feel really stupid about everything we've just talked about because the idea of Luke having any feelings toward me that aren't platonic is serious conjecture. As I've said before, he's given me no hints of anything that could remotely be considered romantic feelings, so I'm just going to stick with being his friend and that's that."

Seventeen

Luke's Wedgwood-blue eyes were locked onto mine. "What do I have to do to get you to say yes?" he asked.

I felt myself blushing furiously. But it was out of guilt, not something infinitely better. It was the Saturday after my meeting with Jackie and now Luke was trying to get me to leave the office to go look at office doors. And he knew I was doing my best to deflect him, too.

When preparing for my office renovations, I had made sure to make ninety-nine percent of all decorating decisions before the construction even started so that everything that needed to be ordered could be taken care of and there would be little to no hitches in how quickly the work could be started and finished. However, I had not yet chosen the types of doors I wanted for each office because I had been oddly wishy-washy about what overall look I wanted to see when all the doors were closed. Mine included, as I would be receiving a new office door as well for that cohesive look.

The only thing I knew was that I liked doors that were wood framed with glass centers because they would lend an appealing openness and approachability to the office and my employees within that a solid door did not give. But, though I had decided on the basic type when I had first discussed it with

Bob Kappler, I had soon found that there were many more options to choose from than I had anticipated. Did I want one solid pane of glass? Multiple panes? Craftsman style? And, when talking about the glass, did I want clear glass? Beveled glass? Hammered? Etched? Fluted? Frosted? Glass that looked like a sheet of rain was coming down over it? Glass that looked like it had been crinkled? I had been presented with way too many choices and, feeling oddly overwhelmed at the time, I had put off the final decision like the seasoned procrastinator I normally wasn't. And Luke wasn't having any more of it.

But that wasn't the worst of my behavior in this situation. The worst part was that I had become a big coward in the past few days. Luke had been making it clear for a couple of weeks that my deadline for deciding on a door style was fast approaching, but after Dr. Jackie Rosenstein-Freud got a hold of me and my feelings for my contractor, I had been steadfastly avoiding him as much as possible since then. This wasn't all that hard as we both had been genuinely busy throughout the week, but I felt guilty because I knew that I was working the I'm-*so*-swamped-with-work attitude for a reason: because being around Luke was suddenly too much for me to take and I needed a breather to let Inner Wall, which was panting with exhaustion, restore itself to its former glory.

It sucked rocks, but for my sanity, my morals, and my carefully guarded professionalism, it needed to be done.

However, as usual, luck was not on my side. Luke was determined to corner me and this time I had no excuse.

Except, maybe...

Trying not to sound too happy that I could skew the facts so decidedly in my favor, I looked at him from across my desk and said all cagily, "Welll...I have to work an event at six-thirty and I need to run a couple of errands before that and still be at home in time to take a shower." (That part was kinda true. My errands needed to be done, but they could technically wait.) "I also have to go by my parents' house to water my Mom's plants since they're out of town." (Glory be, that one was completely true.) I tugged at the purple Nike short-sleeved top

I was wearing. "And I was planning on going for a quick run in the neighborhood before getting on the horn to make some vendor calls. That means...," I screwed up my face so that Luke could actually see me pondering how little time I had to go door shopping with him, "I have about an hour to go to this door place with you." I tried not to cross my fingers with hope as I said, "Does that work for you? If not, I totally understand. We can do it some other time..."

Yeah, he didn't buy it.

"Shelby," he sighed, sounding like he'd had enough of my excuses, "these doors take six weeks at best to come in once they're ordered. And once they're in, they need to be fitted into the doorway. They'll most likely need to be sanded down in certain places, too, before they're stained and sealed due to the fact that the floors in this house are old and not exactly level. And all this needs to be done before the painters get here to do their job."

Feeling suddenly very stubborn, I replied haughtily, "Fine. But I'm not changing before we go. I'll be smelly and sweaty and you'll just have to deal with it if you don't like it."

"Oh, I will, will I?" Luke returned, looking thoroughly amused at my attempt at giving him the what-for. "Fine. I'll deal with it. I'm going to go to the hardware store to pick up some supplies and I'll be back here at one-thirty to pick you up. And if we run late, I'll take you to run any errand you need, so no whining."

"What? I haven't been whine—" But outraged reply was lost since Luke was already walking out the front door.

Just as he had promised, he was driving into my office's driveway at one-thirty. I was sitting on the porch steps wearing dark sunglasses against the bright midday sun, still doing the peevish thing, feeling gross since I had gotten really sweaty on my run, and hoping like bloody hell that suddenly I would find him much less attractive when I saw him.

I didn't. In fact, it was worse. That morning he'd been in his usual jeans, but he'd changed since then. He got out of his truck and walked around to the passenger side wearing the same cute-legs–baring cargo shorts he'd had on the first time we'd officially met in my office, this time paired with running shoes without socks, a baseball cap turned around backwards, and a green t-shirt with white lettering that read *Feeling Thorny? Eat at The Cactus in Burton, Texas.*

Have you ever seen how fast butter melts in a hot skillet? Yeah, that was me and my willpower. It was so not fair.

Thank goodness for sarcasm, though. I was going to make it my new best friend.

I stood up and put my hands on my hips as Luke took the sunglasses that he'd hooked onto the neckline of his t-shirt and put them on.

"You're late," I told him. He really wasn't; I was just being contentious for the hell of it. It's the way I roll.

"Your watch must be fast," he replied with infuriating easiness, the dimple in his cheek flashing at me even from thirty feet away. He yanked open the passenger side of his door and said, "Get in, Waterlane. We've only got an hour, as you were so kind to let me know. We'll need every second of it if I'm going to get you to make a decision on these doors."

"My, aren't we being a gentleman today," I replied as I sauntered slowly to his truck.

"You betcha, boss," he said, stepping back just enough so that I could pass by him and get into his truck, but not so far away that I couldn't catch the scent of him, once again reminding me of a combo of soap and wood shavings, which intensified pleasantly when I got myself settled in his passenger-side seat.

I figured I needed a mantra here. I decided on the following: I hate him. I hate him. I hate him.

Was that believable? Yes? No?

We had barely begun to back out when he said, "So, are you going to tell me what's got you all cranky today?"

I opened my mouth to reply and he said, "Don't even try to deny it, Waterlane. 'Fess up on the cranky bit or I'll make you regret it."

"Oh, yeah?" I challenged. "How?"

Putting his truck back into drive, he grinned evilly and said, "You may not remember, but you also haven't decided on a level of gloss finish for your wood, have you? There's gloss, semi-gloss, flat, satin... With your ability to vacillate on things such as this, we could be there for hours, and I'm ready and willing to make you stay for every second of it until I get an answer out of you."

"You are a truly infuriating person," I told him, crossing my arms over my chest. And then I pulled my sunglasses down onto my nose and cocked an eyebrow at him. "And *vacillate*, Treadwell? Are you trying to show off your fancy book learnin' or something?"

Luke laughed deeply and rubbed his Saturday Morning Scruff. (I hate him. I hate him. I hate him.) "You might not know this, but you happened to be talking to cum laude graduate of Vanderbilt University, not to mention the top student in the architecture department three out of four years. I'm more than just a pretty face and a tool belt, you know."

Although I gave him a deliberately skeptical look just for the hell of it, I was indeed impressed. But then I let my mouth go and asked a question that I immediately regretted in how I phrased it.

"If you're an architect, then why are you doing contracting work with your uncle in a small-scale renovations firm?"

The sunny, easygoing look on his face immediately dimmed and, as my hand flew to my mouth in embarrassment, I hastily said, "Oh, jeez, Luke, I apologize. I didn't mean it like it sounded."

He took his eyes off the road for just long enough to glance at me. "But you're not *sorry*, huh? You just *apologize*?"

"No, I'm not sorry," I said tartly. "What I said was phrased improperly, yes, but it wasn't said with any malicious intent, so I have no reason to be sorry. I only have reason to apologize. Like I told you on the first day we met, Luke, I only say those words when I've done something wrong enough that saying 'I'm sorry' will show you the depth of my remorse."

His paused and then his lips quirked momentarily upward. "It was the second time we met, remember? The first time was at Bernatello's."

My hands flew up. "What is this? Specifics Day?"

We came to a stop sign at the corner of a quiet residential street and Luke put his truck into park. Then he reached out and pulled my sunglasses back down onto my nose even as he lifted his up so that I could see the blueness of his eyes. "Have you eaten today?"

I glared at him and pushed my sunglasses back up. I waited a full, huffy two seconds, wherein I imagined kicking myself in the ass for not eating and, therefore, keeping my blood sugar and rationality on the level, before I finally said, "Not since breakfast at seven this morning."

Luke put his sunglasses back on and out of the corner of my eye, I could see him trying hard not to smile. "Hamburgers okay with you?"

"Fine," I grunted.

"Good," he replied and put his truck back in gear and switched on his satellite radio. He flipped through a few stations until he landed on a classic rock station playing a Bob Seger tune. We headed down another cross street toward Yale, which we took to a place called Loopy's Hamburger Hut. My stomach growled in appreciation of his choice as I got out.

Two bites into our fully loaded cheeseburgers, Luke braved speaking to me again. "So, you asked me a good question before and now I'd like to give you the answer," he said as he dipped an edge of his burger into a pool of ketchup.

I felt my cheeks redden. "You really don't have to. I shouldn't have butted in like that."

Luke looked at me, "No, it's fine. What you asked was perfectly valid, Shelby. It's just not something I always choose to remind myself of. And, before I go any further, I hope you'll forgive me for teasing you about the whole apology-sorry thing. I really do respect the fact that you don't throw around the phrase 'I'm sorry' like so many people do these days and I shouldn't have messed with you about it." He grinned, "Especially when your blood sugar is low."

I shook an admonishing french fry at him, which he reached out and snatched from my fingers, ignoring my, "Hey!" and dipped it into his ketchup.

"So, as I was saying... You were right that I'm not really using the skills for which I studied so hard." He popped the fry into his mouth, but the smile on his face was now mechanical, as if he was trying really hard to sound blasé.

"I wanted to be an architect from a fairly young age—ever since my Uncle Bob took me on one of his jobs when I was about six and for the next few weeks I got to watch half a house be knocked down, revised, and recreated from just about nothing. I found it so incredibly cool, but I never really told anybody about what I wanted to do...well, except for my brother when we were in high school, but even then I didn't make it into a big deal."

"Why not?"

"Oh, for the stupidest reason of all—pride. I began working for Bob in the summers from the time I was about fifteen and I knew I had talent with my hands, but I didn't know whether or not the designs I'd always had in my mind were any good. They always seemed so basic and boring whenever I would compare what my mind's eye saw to what I would see in *Architectural Digest* and what not. I was young and stupid and didn't want anyone to laugh at me. Or ask me to draw something for them, for that matter, since my drawing skills looked like that of a third grader. I also didn't particularly enjoy drawing and I didn't know whether or not I could improve, so I just kept it all to myself and vowed I would secretly take architectural classes in college."

"Secretly?" I repeated.

He took a sip of his iced tea and said, "Yep. My parents helped me pay for college, but I paid for those classes myself, so nobody knew but me. And I turned out to be much better than I ever thought I was. My designs appealed to traditionalists as opposed to modernists, definitely, but as my drawing skills improved and my confidence grew, so did my inspirations and ideas. I tried new things and my professors, for the most part at least, considered me as having talent. But then, at the start of the last semester of my senior year, I got a visit in person from my Uncle Bob."

He took a bite of his hamburger and chewed it before continuing with a wry grin. "I guess pride runs in the family because Uncle Bob came to me in secret and asked me to keep his confidence from the rest of the family. He told me that his business partner of the past twenty years, a man named Frank—who was the 'Morgan' in the former Kappler-Morgan Construction before it became KT Construction—had been diagnosed with early onset Alzheimer's and had to quit the business."

"That's terrible," I said.

"Yes, it was very sad because Frank was a good guy. He went down fairly rapidly and passed away about five years ago. It was pretty hard for Bob to take because they'd been friends and business partners for so long."

"And so? What happened?"

"Well, it seemed that Frank, before anyone knew what was wrong with him, had made some very bad business decisions and okayed some unsound renovation practices. Consequently, Kappler-Morgan was being sued by about seven different homeowners because of problems with their houses. Bob had to settle with all but one of them and it consequently stripped the company financially."

"Ouch," I said in sympathy.

"You said it. Well, he knew I was helping to renovate houses in Nashville to help pay for extra bills and so he came to me and asked me to move back to Houston after school and help him rebuild his company. He said he was starting to feel his age and he knew that his company needed fresh blood if it was going to stick around and continue to be a viable renovations firm in a very picky city like Houston. He offered me a half stake in the company, basically, with the promise that the entire company would be turned over to me without contest either at his retirement or in the event of his death. He wouldn't be able to pay me much to start, but he had a tiny little rental house in the West University area that I could live in for free for a while."

He took a breath and said, "But I would not be able to truly design houses. My architectural skills would be limited to small-scale renovations. And when I broached the subject of expanding his business to include full residential design from the ground up, Bob was thoroughly uninterested. He told me that, at his age, he didn't think he could compete with other architectural firms—and I don't think he even wanted to try, either—so it was keep the company as is or he would try to sell it, which for him would mean taking a pretty big loss and probably leaving him in financial dire straits for his and Aunt Nell's retirement years."

"Wow," I said. It was really all I could say.

"Yeah," Luke replied. "Anyway, he tried really hard not to put any pressure on me, but of course it was still there. I mean, how could it not be when Uncle Bob had been so good to me throughout my life? When I'd shown an interest in building things when I was a little kid, he was really great, taking me around and patiently showing me how things were done. He always treated me like I was intelligent and could learn to do anything I wanted to and he answered every question I ever had without ever making me feel like it was a dumb question." His mouth quirked up at the memory. "Even when they were."

I watched him intently as he said, "Uncle Bob also gave me my first job and always paired me like an apprentice with the most talented woodworkers, brick layers, and builders so that I always learned from the very best. He, along with my parents, of course, also taught me about honesty and integrity and always doing right by your clients, even if it means that you work a few hours longer than you need to only to still wake up at five a.m. the next morning to do it all over again. So, basically, I knew from the moment Bob told me about his troubles that I owed him everything and I needed to do whatever I could to help."

"But that wasn't really what you wanted to do with your life," I said, speaking out loud what the look on his face was plainly telling me.

He paused, staring off at a point just above my right shoulder, "No, it wasn't." He looked back at me and his eyes reflected a touch of regret, but not self-pity. "But you have to set those things aside sometimes, you know? You have to do what is right by the people who helped to make you what you are."

I was about to put my hamburger down, my appetite diminished with hearing Luke's story, but he growled, "Keep eating, Waterlane, or else. I don't want you to get all grouchy on me again while we're looking at doors just because you didn't eat enough."

"Who are you? The Blood-Sugar Nazi?" I asked him, scowling.

"Until the color comes back into your face, you bet I am," he replied, and then offered me one of his fries in return for the one he'd snatched for me earlier.

I took the fry and, to keep myself from going mushy at the thought of him noticing such a small thing as the level of color in my face, I said, "So, what happened, then? You've stayed on with Bob and you're still his full partner. Did you not try to get back into architecture?"

"I did try, yes. Twice. The first time was about three years after going to work with Uncle Bob. I got hired on at a friend's firm to do some part-time draft work to make some extra money, but I was working so hard at both jobs and consequently getting no sleep that I quit after six months. And then the second time was another two years later, when KT Construction was truly coming out of the weeds and I had a great guy working with me who I figured could take my place as project manager while I began working for another architectural company."

"Sounds promising...," I said.

"That's what I thought, too, and Uncle Bob supported the idea. However, by then I was five years older than the other people who were up for the same job. I was considered entry level and I was no longer interested in being at entry level, if that makes sense."

"Of course. I'd feel the same way. Especially since you'd been the boss at KT Construction for so long by that time."

Luke swiped a finger against the side of his nose as a signal that I was on the money. "You got the drift. However, I think I would have sucked it up and gone through with it anyway just to get to be an architect if it hadn't been for one thing. In fact, I did get the offer I wanted from one company—with a written assurance that I would be moved up quickly within their ranks after my first year and everything—but I turned it down."

"Why?"

His smile came out again, but this time it was much more confident and happy.

"Because the morning that I was to accept the offer I was woken up at six a.m. by one of my favorite clients. She and her husband had moved to a nearby apartment while we renovated their house and that morning she'd gone for an early morning walk with her dog to the house to check on the progress. Well, the dog was a really big, sweet Lab but he was walking around the house at one point and stepped on a piece of masking tape. For some reason, having masking tape stuck to his foot seriously freaked him out and he began tearing around the house in an effort to get it off. He knocked over a sawhorse in the kitchen, which caused a couple of pieces of specially mitered trim wood to be broken. And then he ended up thrashing around in the master bathroom, in the process knocking over a ladder into an half-finished wall, putting a huge hole into it and scraping up another part of an adjacent wall as well when he banged up against the ladder one last time and it fell crashing to the ground."

Giggling despite myself I asked, "So, how did some dog doing his best to bring down the entire house help you to change your mind about the architecture job?"

"Well, it just so happened that everything the dog broke was absolutely integral to what work needed to be completed on that very day, if we were to stay on schedule. At first I really didn't find it as funny as I do now, especially when I was surveying the damage with a hangover from having celebrated my job offer a little bit too hard with Claudia the night before—"

I kept working the smile that my laughter had turned into, but inside my insides had promptly performed a little sinking maneuver at the mention of Claudia. The masochistic part of my brain also immediately began giving me ideas of exactly what other form of celebrating Luke and Claudia had taken after they had finished imbibing in whatever frosty beverages that had given Luke his hangover the next day. Trying my best to kick start my Inner Wall into action (I had been letting it languish thus far like a complete ninny), I decided that the masochistic part of my brain could be added to my Things That Suck list.

"—but for some reason I decided right then and there that, by myself, I was going to repair everything that had been broken. Claude later told me that my hangover had made me temporarily brain damaged to take on such a project before my men got there at eight-thirty, but I did it anyway. I put to work most of the skills I had learned from Uncle Bob and the men who had helped train me and I sawed and nailed up couple of new two-by-fours in the broken wall and redid the sheetrock and got it back to where it had stood, ready for insulation. I did all the necessary repairs to the adjacent wall as well and then I re-mitered all the trim wood that had been broken. And when my guys walked in and got to work, not even having any idea that their original work had been damaged until my client 'fessed up later, it was at that moment that I realized how proud I was of everything I'd learned over the years and how good it had made me feel not to just design, but also to build and use my hands to create what I had designed."

I sat up straighter and smiled at him, understanding what he was saying, "And doing what you're doing now, you get the best of both worlds, right?"

For a few seconds, Luke said nothing; he just looked at me with a huge smile and appreciation emanating from his eyes. "Exactly," he said finally.

"Plus, you're your own boss and so you don't have to take crap from anyone but yourself." I pulled a face and said thoughtfully, "And, I guess, any client who decides to be totally high-maintenance and persnickety." Then before he could make the snappy comeback about my own ability to be difficult that was plainly on his lips, I said, "Don't even say it, Treadwell, or I'll sic Emily on your ass."

Luke put his hands up in mock surrender and I launched a fry at him.

Eighteen

June. It was a month I'd always loved. Houston is hot, but not yet too hot, and is literally dripping in green grass, blooming trees, and brilliantly colored flowers. It's also the most sought-after month for weddings, too, and we at Waterlane Events were up to our ears in them. Emily and I each had three weddings apiece and Lauren had two, with Bryan running around like mad to help all of us as much as he could.

And yet they still found time to set me up with two more guys. Lucky me.

I went on two moderately enjoyable lunch dates with the first one. Then on our third lunch at my favorite sushi restaurant, he used his chopsticks to pick up a piece of crispy salmon skin that had dropped out of his handroll and said, "You know, I wonder what human flesh would taste like. I mean, is it chewy? If you fried it, would it taste like a pork rind? Or would it be more like this salmon skin? I've always wanted to know."

Thank goodness I was sitting across the table at the time from Emily and Percy, who had been the ones to set me up with the guy. They had witnessed the weirdness firsthand; it could not be refuted. Percy had nearly spit out his sake and Emily, her blue eyes wide, had even mouthed, "Run!" when my date wasn't looking. I wasn't hassled one bit either when I chose to refuse subsequent outings with the guy we came to refer to as The Flesh Eater.

The second one? Oh, the second one was Captain Slobbersonhernose, who became an instant classic in my repertoire of not-so-great dating experiences.

His actual name was Shane and he played on the same intermural soccer team as Lauren's boyfriend Chris. If you counted the two after-work happy hours, a brunch with Lauren and Chris, and a post-soccer–match party, I went on a total of six dates with Shane, who I quickly found out had a thing for really wet kisses and my nose.

"A slobberer? Oh, this one will be *fun*." Luke smirked after I was cornered by my employees—whereby Luke had been literally dragged in as a witness—and I was forced to tell the truth about what had happened after Shane and I had finally got down to the serious snogging.

I glowered at him and replied, "Bite me, Treadwell." And, as usual, it had no effect other than to increase the cackling of all four of my interrogators.

Anyhow, Shane earned the second half of his nickname because his kisses were of the ridiculously slobbery type that literally led me to have to use my sleeve to sop up the saliva before it migrated into my nostrils by the sheer mudslide-like force of its thick viscosity.

Yes, it was that gross. So much so that I felt like hurling when he managed to do this to me a third time within the course of our otherwise enjoyable evening that had led to said foray into snogging. Oh, I tried to dodge him after the first time he slobbered on my nose and I found that I didn't like it—and definitely after the second time when I was more or less repulsed by the action—but Shane proved to be too quick for me. He would move his lips from mine and his head would move downward as if he might turn to kissing my neck (something I found quite yummy, to be honest) and then, like a bullet, he would swoop upward, ensconce my nose, and my airways would be temporarily cut off by his effusively wet lips and tongue.

But, I'd actually had some experience with guys who took wet kisses to extremes and so I had a couple of tricks up my sleeve to help remedy those more-than-damp moments.

For instance, I used every ounce of kittenish sexiness I had in me as I looked into Shane's eyes, touched the end of my still-sticky nose to indicate what he'd just done, and then said, "You know, I would just love it if you'd do that here instead," before leaning my head back and running my index finger down the most sensitive portion of my neck. Shane had gotten the drift pronto and had succeeded in performing a few tricks that were much more to my satisfaction. In fact, he wasn't half as slobbery in any of his other kisses as he was when he went for my nose. It was weird, but true.

As for the latter half of Shane's nickname, it came from each of the four people in my office incredulously using pretty much the same words once they found out about the whole nose-and-slobber thing. They all talked amongst themselves, as if asking me directly was no longer useful in their ability to believe me. Anyway, it went like this:

Bryan, looking like he might be nauseated: "He slobbered on her *nose?*"

Emily, looking incredulous: "Slobbered. On her nose. Get the hell outta here!"

Lauren, looking like a combo of Bryan and Emily: "I can't believe he slobbered on her nose! Ewww!"

Luke, looking like Christmas had come early: "That's classic. He slobbered *on her nose.*"

Yours truly, looking peevish: Hey! I'm still right here, people! Sans slobber, believe it or not. Can we get back to work now or must you all say the words 'slobbers on her nose' another hundred times so that I never, ever forget it?"

Bryan, grinning like a cat who ate the canary: "Actually darlin', we said *slobbered*, past tense, not *slobbers*, present tense. But I have to say I kind like the way you said it. So I'm calling it right now. He shall henceforth be known as Slobbersonhernose!"

Yours truly, putting my head in my hands as the others voiced their approval for Shane's new nickname: "Oh, for Pete's sake…"

But, of course, somehow just using that one nickname didn't quite work out. They tried calling him "Shane Slobbersonhernose," but, although the classic alliteration style had worked with many other of my unfortunate dating situations, it just didn't seem to have, as Bryan put it, "quite the right feel" when they said it.

But four more dates later was when things went to the birds, Shane's nickname got the extra oomph that it needed, and thus ended our brief association. Hilary got the pleasure of hearing about it first, as she and I went on one of our Saturday lunches the next day.

"You know," she told me with a look of wonder on her face, "hearing your stories always makes me realize that all the weird things Dimitri does aren't half that bad. Especially in the boudoir. I used to think that it was weirder than hell that he always wants to—"

She was sitting directly to my right, so I reached out put my hand up over her mouth before she could finish. I shook my head slowly and dramatically. "Nooo. I am not hearing any more examples of people's fetishes, especially about people I love and respect. I don't want to know about it. No, ma'am. No way. Uh-UH."

I heard a muffled, "Okay! Okay!" from my friend and, though I continued to glare at her, I removed my hand from her mouth. Once free, she patted me on the back "Still, thanks, pal. You don't know how much my marriage and I appreciate your efforts on our behalf."

I pushed my recently emptied wine glass toward her on the little wooden table we were sharing at Bistro Poitiers, having finally felt brave enough after the Lars the Loathsome incident to venture back to my favorite café. "I'm thrilled to be of service. You can thank me by buying the next round."

"We're getting drunk today, are we?" she asked, arching one of her eyebrows at me and not moving to signal the waiter.

"We are if I have anything to say about it."

"All right, look, we're doing brunch with Bryan and Gabe tomorrow. Let's get plastered then," she told me. "I'll be all for it since Dimitri is going rock climbing with his buddies. He won't be back until Monday morning so I can get good and liquored up and have time to heal from it before we have to go have dinner with my in-laws on Monday night." She pushed her fluffy golden-red curls behind her shoulder and grinned at me, "Besides, Bryan always says it's more fun to get you a little tipsy before you start telling your latest bad-date story. You're so much more entertaining when the alcohol lowers your guard and your animated side comes out. I can't wait to see you acting out the part when you and Shane were rounding second base and he started panting about how sexy you were and begged you to call him Captain..."

I watched balefully as my friend did an over-the-top impression of what Shane looked like in her own mind when he was overcome with lust and his psychological fetish came out, turning me off instantly, whereby I stopped him cold in his quest to get to third base. Initially, he was pissed that I'd had a problem with his need, which had apparently begun at age fifteen when a college girl called him her "sexy captain" while popping his cherry on her father's yacht in Rockport. But in the end I'd managed to get him to comprehend that, while I understood that everyone had certain things that worked for them, his particular need to be called Captain when we were getting busy was not one that worked for me. I'd left his apartment on decent terms, though I was fairly certain he would be avoiding me at all costs in the future.

So, when Hilary threw her head back and exulted, "Oh, Shelby, call me *Captain!*" (which was an almost dead-on impression, let me tell you), I found I couldn't stand being cool about being set up anymore.

"Hil, I'm just so tired of this!" I cried out, looking imploringly across the table at my best friend, who was still giggling from her impromptu pantomime. "I'm tired of being set up! I'm tired of going out on dates with guys who don't interest me in the first place, only to have them turn out worse than I expected! And I'm tired of being good and giving all of this dating stuff a chance!" I tried to inflect some steel into my voice, but what came out was a whine-steel alloy that just sounded fractious, "And I *have* been being good, each and every time. I haven't wanted to go on these dates, but I have done my damndest to always show up with a positive outlook and a smile on my face. I've made more than my share of an effort and you know it."

Hilary stopped smiling and focused on me. "I know you have," she replied soothingly. "You've handled all this setting-up stuff much better than I thought you would, in fact."

I gave her a dry look but spared both of us the sarcastic retort.

"You know what I meant."

"Yeah, yeah." I moodily wiped beads of condensation off my little-used glass of ice water with my thumb and thought piteous thoughts about myself in lieu of more whining.

I felt Hilary's eyes surveying me, but it took a few moments before she hesitantly said, "Let me ask you this, Shelb... Is there anyone—I mean anyone *at all*, no matter who they are or where they are in their lives—who you actually *want* to go out with?"

Although my brain immediately taunted me and Luke's smiling face, dimple and all, flashed in my mind, there was a note in her voice that still set off alarms within the still-sane part of my head. She was fishing because she knew something. I slowly raised my narrowed eyes to hers. "Hilary...what have you done?"

My friend's hands shot up in defense. "Nothing! I promise. I haven't done anything." She looked suddenly dismayed and said sort of cryptically, "Believe me, I haven't done a damn thing." And when I looked curiously at her because her expression was telling me that she really *had* wanted to do something, she nevertheless repeated, making heart-crossing motions, "I promise, Shelby. Cross my heart. After the first couple of times when I was privy to the fact that you were being coerced into a setup and I encouraged them, I deliberately haven't gone the way of your employees or Franzilla. I've stayed completely out of it."

Did the Dating Brigade know they had a member gone AWOL? Probably not, or my three generals would be on the warpath by now.

"I'm shocked," I drawled, then I rearranged my face into pleasantness and politely told the waiter no thank you when he asked if I wanted a refill on my wine. The fact that I no longer needed to get schnockered seemed to cheer Hilary somewhat and she said, "Well, at least your mother hasn't been trying to set you up lately."

And just like that, the need for lots of alcoholic beverages came roaring back.

"For Pete's sake, Hil," I cried out, "knock on some wood when you say that! Just by saying those words you could wake up the sleeping tiger and then I'd be doomed."

Grinning, my best friend dutifully knocked on our table to chase away the bad juju, but somehow forgot to turn off her mouth. "I'm just saying it could be worse. Frances could be pulling out the stops to fix you up with McGregor Elliston again. I heard he's back on the market, you know."

I blanched. I had completely forgotten about my mother's former obsession with making an official date happen with my old high-school crush. "Oh, please. No!" I wailed, flinging myself down onto our table and hiding my head under my arms, making Hilary giggle again even as she reached out and patted my shoulder sympathetically.

To explain, McGregor Elliston was the only guy from my high school for whom I ever had a long-term attraction. It started on the first day of our freshman year and continued unabated through other mini-crushes on other guys, a couple of high-school boyfriends, and graduation, until my first college man swept me off my feet. I couldn't say I really knew McGregor well, though, since I only had a couple of classes with him throughout the entire four years, and even then we barely talked.

Or, I should say, in the one class where my seat was directly next to his, he occasionally made a funny comment about something the teacher said, making me blush the full spectrum of red tones and giggle in return like, well, a schoolgirl.

But I still liked to look at him whenever I could, that was the truth. He was tall (naturally—as if that wasn't obvious by now), sliding into about six foot one or so by our senior year, with a wide smile and even teeth, a smallish nose that was just slightly upturned and worked surprisingly well on his square-jawed face, and had a combination of thick white-blond hair and brown eyes. I'd always been one for blue-eyed guys, but McGregor's were this warm, clear color of brown, like homemade caramel before it's allowed to cool. His eyes had made me weak since the first day of our freshman year when I found myself standing next to him in the lunch line and he smiled at me. I simply gaped up at him in return...and things between McGregor and me stayed just about like that for the next four years. Except for the turning red and giggling incidents, of course. This was partly because McGregor never displayed anything more than polite friendliness toward me and partly because of his girlfriend, Frederique Olivera.

Called Freddie by her friends—a tight-knit group that did not include me—she was five foot three with porcelain skin, a smattering of freckles across the bridge of her nose, loads of soft-looking black hair, and the most startlingly blue eyes you've ever seen in your life. The two of them started dating halfway into our freshman year; they broke up for reasons I never knew right after senior prom.

Fast forward seven years after high school. I was twenty-five, it was nearly one in the morning, the wedding I had just handled at the Chatsworth was long over, and I was sipping wine at a bar down the street called Pete's Lounge while catching up with one of my friends from college who had been a guest at the wedding. I had excused myself to go to the ladies' room and, on my way there, came upon a group of guys about my age who all seemed to have been partaking in the sauce for many hours. With their beer goggles firmly in place, they all stared unabashedly at me, the blonde chick in the little black dress, walking their way.

Then one guy in the pack shifted sideways and McGregor Elliston's handsome face to come into view. He saw me and frowned as if searching his blurry mind; I smiled back, easily recognizing him. And, whether it was because I had grown up exponentially or whether I was just tired from a long evening and had no nerves left in my body, I felt no symptoms of Imminent Tongue Tying when I saw him. Far from being a romantic situation, though, my years-later meeting with the guy whose warm brown eyes and wide smile still crossed my mind from time to time was a split-second encounter that went like this:

McGregor, pointing at me with his glass of beer: "You're Shhelby Wudderlane, aren't you?"

Yours truly, nodding with an amused smile: "Yes, I am. And you're three sheets to the wind, aren't you, McGregor?"

McGregor, with a squinty-eyed grin: "Yup."

Some guy in a separate pack of drunk guys: "Yo, Elliston! Get your hairy ass over here! You gotta hear what Spanky just said! It was fucking hilarious, man!"

And that was it. McGregor Elliston turned and stumbled off without so much as a second look my way and I finished making my way to the ladies' room. But luckily, by that time in life I was fully aware that a drunk man was completely uninteresting to have a conversation with (even if he was incredibly cute) and so I had only been a touch bummed that my confident, snazzy-looking self couldn't have instantaneously sobered McGregor Elliston up and, at the same time, knocked his socks off so much that he would have jumped at the chance to ask me out on a real-life date.

I will admit that I kept my eyes peeled for him the next several times I went to Pete's Lounge, though. I hoped that I would find him sober and having had weeks of impure thoughts about the vision of Shelby Waterlane walking toward him in her sexy little black dress.

Yeah, that didn't happen. In fact, McGregor Elliston wasn't even living in Texas at the time, but instead in New York, working for a consulting firm. He had only been in Houston for the University of Texas versus Rice University football game. I found all of this out not by asking surreptitiously around amongst the few people I still knew from high school, but instead from Frances Waterlane.

That's right, my mother knew more about McGregor Elliston's whereabouts than any of my friends did. She made a point to find out for me after I made a major mistake in judgment: I confided during lunch with her one day about the fact that McGregor was the only boy in my grade who I'd ever crushed on and that I'd seen him and still thought he was cute. And she took that news and ran full-tilt straight to the place I least wanted her to go. She took it straight to Mary Beth Elliston.

McGregor's mother.

See, my own dear mother had been hiding a secret from me for years and years. Or, it could be possible that I knew this fact in a vague way but had overlooked it, thinking it didn't have anything whatsoever to do with me. My mother and Mary Beth Elliston were longtime friends. Not best friends or anything, but the kind of friend that you go to lunch with once a year and could always call in a pinch if you needed something. They had known each other for ages, ever since my elementary school days when they both volunteered together through the Junior League.

Well, not being aware of the Frances/Mary Beth connection when I mentioned running into McGregor, I didn't know that I was summarily letting the bull loose amongst the china without so much as a gasp of horror on my part. I had gone home on my merry way after our lunch, not even thinking twice about the whole discussion about my high-school crush. So, when I got a call the next day from my very thrilled-sounding mother that began with, "Shelby, sweetheart, I spoke with Mary Beth

Elliston this morning about you and her son," I was more than a little shocked. I was still working at the Chatsworth at the time and, when she called, I had been twirling a pen through my fingers as I worked on the contracts for one bat mitzvah, two corporate parties, and another two weddings.

Needless to say, my pen unceremoniously clattered onto my desk after my hand froze in mid-twirl and the rest of the conversation went like this:

Yours truly, with a newfound stutter: "Ell...Elliston? As in...McGregor Elliston? You know his mother?"

Mom, radiating innocence: "Yes, dear, of course. Mary Beth Elliston, my longtime Junior League friend. We've known each other since you were about six years old or so, didn't I ever tell you?"

Yours truly: "No, you didn't. But Mom, please tell me that you didn't really discuss McGregor and me with his mother."

Mom, not only unrepentant, but also with scary bubbly note in her voice as well: "Well, I had to call Mary Beth anyway about a charity art show we Pi Phi alums are going to put on to benefit Texas Children's Hospital—did I tell you that Mary Beth and I were both Pi Phis? She went to Baylor and not U.T., of course, but still..."

Yours truly, dully: "No, that's another one you didn't tell me."

Mom, the bubbly note growing stronger: "Anyway, so after I got that business out of the way, I asked her about her son and how he was doing and all that jazz. And, wouldn't you know it, he is still single, too, and moving back to Houston from New York in less than six weeks! He's in risk management with one of those big prestigious consulting firms, you know."

Yours truly, feeling a headache coming on: "Nope, didn't know that one either."

Mom, a bit breathlessly: "Well, I told her that precious story about how you had always thought he was so nice and how he was the only boy on whom you'd ever had a big crush and Mary Beth just thought that was the sweetest thing. So, we decided that you two should be set up when McGregor comes back into town. Isn't that wonderful?"

Yours truly, crying out, with visions of McGregor thinking that I had been obsessed with him for years and years and was officially beginning my career as a stalker: "Mom, no! No! Please tell me you didn't do that!"

Mom, all indignantly: "Shelby, what are you getting all hysterical about? You're not in high school anymore and neither is McGregor. You are simply two single adults who just needed a push in the right direction to be able to meet on an adult level—and we were able to provide that for you. I must say, I'm shocked that you're acting this way. I thought you'd be pleased. Isn't this what you wanted by telling me that story in the first place?"

Yours truly, flinging my arms up in the air, trying to form words that weren't high-pitched squeaking: "How, could I have even thought that you would do this when I didn't even freaking realize that you knew Mary Beth Elliston in the first place? How?"

Mom, coolly: "There is no need to swear, Shelby."

Yours truly, through gritted teeth: "I didn't swear."

Mom, sniffing, "You may not have used the actual word, but I knew what you meant."

Yours truly, groaning: "Mom..."

Mom, using her most formal voice voice: "Shelby, just give me a moment so I can tell you what happened and then I will let you get back to work—and we can discuss this further later, if you wish."

Silence from yours truly.

Mom, satisfied that I was now listening: "Mary Beth is going to talk to her son this week and give him your phone number. Beyond that, we both decided that the rest should be up to the two of you, since you're both *adults*. She is going to let him know and if he decides to call you, then he will. Mary Beth seemed to think he'd be open to the idea, though, since he broke up with his last girlfriend a few months ago."

Yours truly, listlessly, rubbing my temples, but making myself admit that she had done this with good intentions: "Okay. Um, thanks."

But, luckily, at that second Kendra Everitt, who was still my assistant at that point, had come into the office and I was able to get off the phone with Mom lickety-split without having to really respond to anything else she could say about the potential of there being a Shelby Waterlane/McGregor Elliston Match-Up of the Century.

And another reason I was glad to not have to discuss it further was because it ended up being a moot point. The six weeks between my mom's call and the time McGregor was supposed to move back to Houston almost literally flew by and he never called me.

That sucks, right? But it didn't end there.

Fast forward another two years, when Frances Waterlane decided to bring her sister Priscilla to lunch with Mary Beth Elliston—and that's when Franzilla first truly reared her head, with McGregor serving as her first victim.

It was the Sunday before Thanksgiving and I was over at my parents' house to help Mom and Aunt Priscilla make the can-do-ahead items of pie shells and the cornbread for the stuffing. I didn't know it, but just two days prior Mom and Aunt Prilly had broken bread with Mrs. Elliston. The conversation with Franzilla went like this:

Aunt Prilly, watching me get ready to stir the cornbread ingredients: "Now, don't forget, Shelby, Alton Brown from the Food Network says to only stir the ingredients ten times, even if it looks lumpy and slightly unmixed afterward. He says any quick bread will turn out harder and less fluffy if you overstir it."

Yours truly, grinning as I began the first of my stirs: "Stir. Ten times. Ignore lumpiness. Got it."

Mom, checking the oven: "Mary Beth said she tried Alton's way after years of overmixing it and the results were amazing."

Aunt Prilly: "I know, she just raved about her cornbread, saying it was her best ever. We all had lunch at the café at

Neiman's, Shelby. Their popovers and strawberry butter were just too delicious to pass up."

Yours truly, who would have stopped stirring the cornbread out of sheer shock, even if Alton Brown hadn't suggested I do so first: "You and Aunt Prilly had lunch with Mary Beth Elliston. I'm officially frightened now. Please tell me that you didn't discuss my love life this time."

Aunt Prilly, playing Bad Cop with relish as she took the cornbread batter from me: "It was I who actually brought it up, Shelby, so you can't go getting upset with your mother. I was telling Mary Beth how Jake had met Livvie at Texas A&M but had never asked her out until years later and Mary Beth just jumped into the conversation and told Frannie how her son McGregor—I just think that is such a manly sounding name; it was her mother's maiden name, right, Frannie?—anyway, that McGregor is single again."

Yours truly, with a hint of sarcasm, and using air quotes: "Mary Beth just 'jumped in' the conversation with that information about her son, huh?"

Aunt Prilly, managing to pour a heavy bowl of cornbread batter into the glass dish and look indignant at the same time: "Yes, she did just 'jump in.'"

Mom, taking up her position as Good Cop: "She really did, Shelby. I was just floored. I thought that she would have forgotten about setting you up with her son after all this time, especially since he didn't call you the last time—"

Aunt Prilly, interrupting: "But that was because he started to see some other girl almost immediately after he moved back to Houston, right?"

Yours truly, as I went to put the utensils I'd used in the sink: "Yeah, I'm sure that was the reason."

Aunt Prilly, ignoring my sarcasm: "Anyway, then it was Mary Beth who brought up the fact that you and McGregor should go out to dinner one night."

Yours truly: "You're kidding me. You people actually want to have a repeat of that setup disaster?"

Mom, really working the Good Cop bit: "But this time it was Mary Beth's suggestion, honey. I would have never brought it up if she hadn't said if first. I promise you."

Yours truly, as nicely as I could: "Yes, but what y'all don't realize is that I don't think McGregor has now or has ever had any interest in calling me. And, what's more, I think it irks him that his mother is trying to push me on him."

Aunt Prilly, with one hand on her hip: "Shelby, have some confidence in yourself. You can't even know if that is true or not."

Mom, trying to hide the excitement in her voice and failing: "But I think he might be more interested in the idea this time, Shelby."

Aunt Prilly, excitedly as well: "Tell her why, Frannie."

Mom, opening a cabinet and pulling out two glass pie dishes: "Well, you know, historically speaking, Mary Beth and I usually go to lunch after we've run into each other somewhere and decide that lunch together would fit into our schedules. But this time she actually called me up out of the blue!"

Aunt Prilly, interrupting again: "Well, it was partly for a Pi Phi alumni thing, too, right?"

Mom, waving away her sister: "Yes, that's true, but still. I had a feeling something was up. And I was right because when Prilly mentioned Jake and Livvie and how their situation sort of mirrored yours and McGregor's in how you've known each other for years but never have gone out together, Mary Beth just pounced on the opportunity to bring up her son and you trying the dating thing on for size again."

Yours truly, eyebrows raised again with humor: "Oh, so now she's *pouncing*, huh?"

Mom and Prilly wearily, and in unison: "Shelby…"

Mom, to her sister: "She's terrible, you know. She gets it from her father."

Aunt Prilly, to Mom: "I know, honey. It's the rapscallion gene. Jake has it something fierce, and you can bet he didn't get it from me."

Mom, before I could be a rapscallion again: "Anyway, Shelby, I gave Mary Beth your number again and she's going to give it to McGregor at Thanksgiving. I think she's going to give him a talking-to because she very specifically told me to tell you to expect a call from him within a week thereafter."

Yours truly, this time with a surprised look: "Seriously?"

Mom, beaming, because she could see that I was getting hopeful despite my sarcastic manner: "That's what she said, dear! And I don't think Mary Beth would have said that unless she was very confident."

Yours truly, turning away to dip into the canister of flour with a measuring cup and trying not to tap dance with glee: "Okay, then."

Mom and Aunt Prilly in my peripheral vision, surreptitiously giving each other a high-five and stage-whispering the words that, in my opinion, officially bonded them as one big, scary, blind-date arranging monster known as Franzilla: "Hot damn!"

And yet, they were wrong again. I let the entire rest of the holiday season, including New Year's, plus an extra two weeks go by until I officially gave up on receiving a call. It was clear that McGregor Elliston simply did not want to have anything to do with me.

And being twice let down about the possibility of going out with my high school crush? Yep, it was thereafter firmly put on my Things That Suck list.

Nineteen

Unbeknownst to Hilary ("I swear!" she promised), Franzilla was indeed already plotting her next McGregor Elliston-related move. In fact, she struck in the last full week of June, the very Monday after Dierdre Zuckerman and her new husband Hunter joyfully danced the *horah* at their wedding. And this time Franzilla had a formidable ally.

I'd walked into my office after a long morning of double checking all the food preparations for Dierdre's *sheva brachot* on Tuesday. Translating to "seven blessings," the event was more or less a second reception where the wedding blessings for the bride and groom are repeated over a cup of wine. Dierdre's was to be an elegant sit-down dinner in the all-glass Skyview Room atop the forty-story Runyon Industries Tower.

Naturally, once Dierdre had decided that she would dance the *horah*, it was almost as if she did a one-eighty and went all-out Jewish, putting in just about every traditional custom she could into her wedding. In fact, she'd decided the day of her Sunday wedding that she wanted all the food at her *sheva brachot* two days later to be strictly kosher, even though her wedding had not been kosher and her family was Conservative Jewish and did not routinely practice kosher traditions.

"Oy vey," Bryan and I had said in unison as Dierdre skipped off to get dressed.

Thus, I'd spent all of my Monday morning placating Billie the caterer from Excellent Eats by Billie, who was close to tearing her spiky red hair out since she'd already received all the food for Dierdre's *sheva brachot* and had begun prepping a large portion of it, all of which would have to be scrapped since it had not been inspected by a *mashgiach*, who certifies the food, equipment, and surroundings are up to kosher status. In Dierdre's case, the *mashgiach* would be Rabbi Greenburg, who was notoriously fastidious and grumpy.

"And now I have to have this Rabbi Greenburg looking over my shoulder the whole time? Cleaning every surface with a blowtorch before I can use it?" she'd yelled, her face turning as red as her hair. "I won't even be able to light the freaking pilot lights myself because the rabbi has to do it! And my staff and I can't work after sundown? This is beyond ludicrous! How will we ever get it done in time? The girl invited two hundred and fifty people and we've got less than twenty-four hours! What is she, nuts?"

"Are nuts kosher?" I'd asked.

In the end, only a lot of soothing words and the blisteringly large check from Dierdre's parents that I pressed into Billie's hand made the caterer buck back up and get down to work.

Franzilla, too, was hardly being kosher, though it was hard to tell at first from the post-it note from Bryan that was on my desk when I walked into my office, reading, as always, *Frances requests that you call her.*

I sat down and dialed, feeling the ends of my hair and thinking I needed a trim.

"Hello?"

The voice that answered was definitely not my mother's. "Dad?" I said, surprise coloring my voice as it always did when my father answered the phone. Let's put it this way: Whenever my mother is out of town, the only way to get my pops to answer a call was to hang up and call back at least three times. He's that bad.

"You were expecting someone else?" he said in his usual dry-as-the-desert humor.

"Why are you answering the phone?" I asked.

"Your mother made me."

In the background I heard my mother admonish, "Ro*bert!*"

Giggling, I asked him why he was at the house in the middle of the day. Even though he was close to retiring from the oil company he had created, he still went to work, in a suit, every day. And he rarely came home before four in the afternoon.

"Your mother wants me to start coming home for lunch so that she can try out some of her latest Food Network recipes."

My mother shouted out, "They're healthier options than what he eats at the office, Shelby! Your father has been complaining about putting on weight!"

"Dad," I teased, as I heard Mom pick up the other phone, presumably in the Death Star. "Have you *really* been complaining?"

"Don't know the meaning of the word," Dad replied with a Cheshire Cat grin in his voice.

"Ha! You should hear the man, Shelby," Mom said. Then she told my dad to go eat his lunch and to stay away from the oatmeal chocolate-chip cookies she'd made as they were for one of her volunteer groups, though we both knew Dad would sneak one—or three—as he left to go back to the office.

"Bye, dear!" my father sang out in his best imitation of my mom, to which she replied, "You and your father! So bad, the both of you!" But in another heartbeat, she'd got down to business. "Am I correct that you remember it's your father's and my thirty-fourth anniversary next Friday?"

"Sure," I replied. I'd already called my florist to send an arrangement to their house on their wedding date.

"Well, your father and I have decided to go to Austin for our anniversary, just for a fun change."

"You going to drag Dad to the Bullock Texas State History Museum again?"

"Of course I am. It's his penance for making me go to the boat show with him last month."

"Good for you," I laughed.

"Anyway," Mom continued, "We thought that we might do a family dinner this Thursday at Café Annie since we won't be in town on our actual anniversary. Bryan already told me that your schedule was free for dinner that night, but I thought I would check again with you, just to be sure."

"Oooh, Café Annie. Swanky. Nice choice, Mom." I replied quickly, even as I scribbled a note to myself to cancel the flowers for next week and then wrote *Café Annie—Thurs.* and underlined it twice. "What time?"

"Seven." Mom said. "And, Shelby, would you mind wearing that cute green dress that you wore at your grandmother's eightieth birthday earlier this year?"

Making a that's-an-odd-request face, I said, "The strapless cotton one with the sweetheart bodice and straight skirt?"

"Yes, I thought it was so cute on you."

"Um, thanks, Mom—but why do you want me to wear it? It's not as if anyone is going to see me besides you, Dad, and Colin."

At the flustered sound in my mother's voice, I should have been more suspicious. Frances Waterlane was just as bad of a liar as her daughter. "Oh, I just wanted to get a good look at it again. You've heard me talk about my friend Peggy who volunteered with me for years at Texas Children's Hospital and has since moved to San Antonio?"

"Yeah..."

"Well, her daughter is about your size and has been looking for a cute party dress that is attractive enough to wear to a nice dinner, too. I've been trying to describe it to Peggy so that she could get one as a gift for her daughter, but I thought I could just take a picture of you in it instead and e-mail that."

I tried to be helpful. "I certainly don't mind wearing it, Mom, but I bought mine on sale last January and being as it's now a year and a half later, she probably won't be able to find the dress anymore."

Mom quickly countered. "Oh, I'm sure she'll still find it online or something."

"Um, I'm kind of doubtful…"

Mom's voice got a tad impatient, "It won't be a problem."

"I don't know…"

"Peggy's a whiz on the Internet, she'll locate it in no time."

"I really think you might want to encourage her to look for something else—"

"Shelby!" Mom said loudly. "Would you please just accommodate me for once and wear the dress on Thursday night?"

I blinked a couple of times. "Sure, Mom. No problemo."

"Thank you," she said curtly before giving me a prim, "I'll see you on Thursday, dear," and hanging up on me.

"Wow…," I mouthed, just as Bryan breezed in.

"Sugar, there's a bridesmaid revolt on line two. Candace Mapleton's girls are furious at the dress she's chosen for them. They're saying they look like stalks of asparagus and they want you to talk some sense into the bride."

"Stalks of asparagus?" I repeated, my eyebrows shooting up.

Bryan picked up the receiver of my office phone, handed it to me, said, "Asparagus is what she said. Now, *go*," and hit the flashing button for line two, where I immediately heard the squawking of the maid of honor and head mutineer.

Twenty minutes later, at Esme's Bridal Boutique in the Uptown Park Shopping Center, I was staring, horrified, hand over my mouth, at the six bridesmaids of Candace Mapleton. The group of them indeed looked exactly like the bunch of asparagus I'd bought at the grocery store two nights before. Candace herself had fled Esme's in a flood of tears; they'd seen her run into the sushi restaurant that was located about five shops down.

"Good Lord," I whispered, looking them up and down.

"Exactly," one of them replied with thick sarcasm.

Another one ineffectively tried to push down the neckline detail of overlapping scallops, which started at the clavicle area, ran upward to encircle her neck, and kept going all the way up to just below her chin. "Candy told us we'd be wearing an 'exquisite sleeveless green-silk sheath with a high neck.' She failed to mention just how high the neck would be."

"Or that we look like we need to be covered in hollandaise sauce," a third one snapped.

The other three were simply sniffling and tugging at various parts of the neck, the horridness of the dress having brought them to tears.

"Okay. Here's the deal," I told them. "Although I'll give suggestions, I very rarely interfere with a bride's final selection for her attendants..." And when they all started talking over me, begging me to appeal to Candace, I made quieting motions with my hands and finished, "but I think this time needs to be an exception." They all started cheering, and I continued sternly, "But if she relents, y'all need to not rub it in her face. You gush over her and make her feel special, like she deserves. No teasing about this whatsoever. We clear?"

All six simultaneously vigorously nodded their heads. They probably would have agreed to selling their firstborn child to get out of wearing that dress, and I wouldn't have blamed them.

"Fine," I said, digging in my handbag. "Now everybody put on some lipstick and powder your nose. We're taking a picture."

A couple of minutes later, I was pulling open the heavy door to the ultra-modern sushi restaurant, where I found my client downing a martini and motioning for the bartender to give her another.

Unlike Maggie Treadwell, this particular bride was obviously not handling the stresses of an impending huge wedding very well.

I ordered a vodka and cranberry and sipped it patiently as Candy went into a sobbing spiel over how her friends were being rude, ungrateful bitches who didn't like the beautiful dress she'd picked out and how they weren't helping her do anything and how many tough decisions she was trying to make and how she was trying hard to please everybody, etc., etc., etc.

It was your basic Stressed-Out Bride Diatribe. I'd heard it a million times.

Hiccupping loudly and pushing away her long, honey-blonde locks away from her face, Candy fixed her green eyes on me and gave me my opening. "What do you think, Shelby?"

I told her that I knew just how much she was stressed out, how I knew that all these decisions she had to make could easily overwhelm, and how she had every right to want to be the prettiest girl in the room on her wedding day, that it was every bride's right. "But I don't want to see you making a misstep about a big part of your wedding—one that you'll regret every time you look at your pictures. Here, let me show you what I mean."

I took out a small photo album from my Kate Spade tote that I kept on hand for times just like this. Bryan, ever the one to name things, called it my Little Book of Horrors. It contained pictures of every bride I'd ever worked with who had made a bad decision on her bridal gown or bridesmaid's gowns and had lived to regret it.

I slowly flipped through the bridesmaid pictures, each one showing intrepid girls trying their best to look happy as they sported their monstrosities: Iridescent orange ball gowns on a grouping of twelve—yep, twelve—bridesmaids, ten of whom did not have the coloring to wear orange, much less iridescent orange. Ill-fitting, shiny, bright-purple strapless bubble dresses on five curvy girls, none less than a C-cup and all spilling out of their dresses. Vermillion-red satin dresses, ruched from halter neck to knee, clashing gloriously on a set of three sisters who all had naturally bright red hair, milk-white skin, and gobs of freckles. Lilac mermaid dresses with tons of poofy netting at the bottom on two who were tall and thin and could handle the dress and four who were petite and stocky and definitely could not. I kept flipping until I saw Candace's face show the appropriate level of horrified.

"Now, I want to show you what the picture of you and your bridesmaids—those six girls who are your best friends—might look like in your wedding album if you decide that you want to keep the bridesmaids' dresses as is." And I held up my iPhone so that she could see the picture. At my direction, the six girls had lined up by height around a mannequin wearing a beautiful A-line gown that was similar to the one Candace had picked out. Three of them on each side of the bride, with their shoulders back, standing up straight, smiling widely, holding silk bridal bouquets provided by Esme's.

Candace shrieked, "Holy hell! They really do look like a goddamn bunch of asparagus!"

"Crisis averted," Bryan said triumphantly when I called him later with the news that the dresses were back in the hands of the seamstress to be retooled into a simple boatneck. "So what did your mama want when she called earlier? She was uncharacteristically unforthcoming, which was rather odd for her."

"Eh. She just wanted to tell me that we're doing their anniversary dinner early—on Thursday, at Café Annie."

"Yummy. Bring me a doggie bag?"

"Only if I don't finish it first."

"You're a heartless woman," he said. After informing me about two more non-emergency calls that had come in for me, he got off to "help Princess carry out some boxes of reception favors to her car so that she doesn't break a nail." Just before he hung up, I heard Emily retort, "Like you don't bitch when you forget to schedule your weekly manicure! Now get your ass over here and start hauling!"

On the rest of my drive back to work, I cranked up the radio and belted out Journey's "Lovin', Touchin', Squeezin'," blissfully unaware of both Franzilla's true intentions and if any other drivers were looking at me and snickering, which they probably were.

Thursday night came and, like the dutiful daughter, I put on my green strapless dress that Mom had demanded (fine, requested) with my three-inch metallic silver Cole Haan slingback sandals. I'd even gone so far as to redo my makeup so that I looked fresh and glowing after a long day of work. With a small bouquet of Gerbera daisies in mixed colors in the crook of my arm and a Happy Anniversary card tucked into my turquoise Elaine Turner bamboo clutch, I walked into Café Annie looking forward to a delicious dinner with my family.

"Ms. Waterlane?" the hostess asked politely when she saw me looking for my parents over the low wall that separated the restaurant's entryway from the main dining room. "Your table is waiting. Would you follow me, please?" She turned and began walking away before I could say another word.

I followed her through the middle of the main dining room, ascending a short flight of stairs to the tiny, galley-like second dining area that mimicked a balcony. My brow was furrowed by the time I made it up the last step. There were only six tables—all seating just two people—and five of them were taken already by couples. I glanced briefly at the sixth, situated just to the left of the steps; it was occupied by a blond guy in a sport coat who was reading his menu, only it wasn't my brother. Colin's hair was a dark wheat color and cut very short at present; this guy's hair was lighter and just hitting his collar.

"Miss?" I said as I rushed to catch up to the hostess. "I think you may have made a mistake. I'm with a party of four…"

She didn't reply; instead she just stopped at the elbow of the blond guy and turned to face me with a smile. "There's been no mistake, Ms. Waterlane," she said pleasantly. "I'm told you know your dinner partner?" She inclined her head toward the guy already at the table.

I turned and looked into the light brown eyes of McGregor Elliston. And I'd be hard pressed to tell you which one of us was more shocked.

He found his voice first as he quickly stood up, grabbing the napkin from his lap before it fell to the ground. "Yes, I'm sorry, but there must have been a mistake. I'm here to meet my grandfather for dinner."

"No," the hostess said, still smiling at both of us like we were silly children. "You're both here to have dinner with each other. It's a surprise from both of your mothers." She looked at me and babbled out the startling truth, "And I think your aunt as well. The three of them came in here a few days ago and planned this dinner for you two and we here have all been thinking that it's just the sweetest thing."

My jaw dropped. So did McGregor's. I didn't know what he was thinking, but I sure as hell knew what I was: Franzilla! She had struck!

And she now had a cohort in Mary-Beth Elliston, making the three morph into one really scary being: Mary-Franzilla.

Heaven help us all.

The hostess continued as she held out the menu she was carrying to me and continued on brightly, "They told us that y'all might be a little shocked to find yourselves at dinner together. I understand you two knew each other in high school?"

McGregor and I glanced uneasily at each other; he held his napkin in one clenched hand and shifted uncomfortably.

"Yes," I finally answered with a weak smile as I took the menu.

"Well, sit down, you two," the hostess beamed, seemingly not bothered by the fact that McGregor and I weren't exactly hugging each other with joy. "The check has already been paid for so all you have to do is enjoy yourselves and get to know each other again. Your waiter will be right with you. Would you like a wine list?"

"Yes," we both said, a little too loudly. Out of the corner of my eye, I could see the other diners starting to gawk at us.

The other diners could suck it.

Before my palms could start to sweat with the nerves that were beginning to flutter in my belly, I held out my hand, smiled like I meant it, and said, "Nice to see you again, McGregor. It's been a long time."

Twenty

My business line rang the next day late in the afternoon as I was transcribing notes from a meeting with a new bridal client. I heard Bryan say, "May I ask who's calling?" and then calmly, "Yes, Shelby is available. If you would please hold? Thank you so much."

Since Bryan said those words many times a day, I didn't even bother to look up from my computer screen. That was, until he jumped up from his chair and proved he really was a gay man by doing two theatric leaps over to my desk, which Luke witnessed full on since he was currently walking into my office with some wood-stain samples to show me.

"What? No jazz hands?" Luke deadpanned, as if it were the most natural thing in the world for him to be in the same room with a gaily (and gayly) leaping man.

Bryan and I locked eyes and then we both threw our heads back and whipped out the most dramatic jazz hands the likes of which would have made Bob Fosse weep with joy, amusing Luke to no end as he began arranging five different small samples of wood with as many different colors of wood stain on my desk. He opened his mouth to speak, but was interrupted by Emily and Lauren rushing in to see where the fire was. They had seen Bryan's homage to Mr. Fosse, so enough said.

"What?" Lauren said breathlessly. "What's going on?"

"Please tell me it has something to do with Shelby's potential for getting laid," Emily drawled, moving around Luke and plopping down her expense report on my desk and looking at me as if I were the two-headed lab experiment again.

"Hey!" I protested, but Emily just made a clucking noise and said, "Just speaking the truth, honey." The others weren't brave enough to meet my eye; Luke in particular kept arranging the wood-stain samples on my desk as if it were the most important thing in the world to him.

Bryan, however, could not be deterred for a nanosecond longer.

"Sweetie!" he sang out, actually wiggling a bit as he planted his hands on my desk. "Guess who is on the phone? No, wait—guess which *gorgeous hunk* is on the phone for you?" I didn't even have time to make a guess before he shouted in delight, "McGregor Elliston!"

I gave him a that's-strange look and said, "Seriously? He wasn't supposed to call until Sunday." I looked at Luke; he just shrugged.

For his part, Bryan rolled his eyes and put one hand all pissy-like on his hip. "Shelby Amelia, you are the most bizarre woman sometimes." He began faking sign language and stated, clipping his words in staccato form, "He—called—you—the—day—after—your—date. That—is—a—very—good—thing,—Shelby,—not—a—bad—thing."

Amused snickers came from the other two having-no-problems-getting-laid chicks currently occupying my office space as I made a face at my beloved assistant, said, "It wasn't a *date*, remember?" and went to pick up the phone. But when I heard Luke say to Bryan, mimicking Bryan's former sign-language movements, "Actually, I think you just called her Patricia and told her that she should go cow hunting on a smooth sunrise. Or it could have been sun*set*, I couldn't tell," I ended up busting out laughing, snorting a couple of times even, and had to yell at my ill-behaved interlopers to get out of my office pronto or I would find some way to make them regret it.

Like they really believed my threats, but still…

Anyway, it took me two deep breaths before I could get my laughter under control, but once I answered the phone, it officially kicked off my budding relationship—yes, relationship—with McGregor Elliston.

I know. Who would have thought it, right?

Basically, once I accepted I was stuck having dinner with McGregor, I realized I was starting at rock bottom with him and there really was no place for me to go but up. And thus I proposed something radical.

"McGregor," I said, after we'd both taken altogether overly healthy slugs of our respective glasses of wine, "This sucks just as much for me as it does for you, but it's ridiculous of both of us to pout about it. Why don't we just do our best to just enjoy ourselves and be friends?"

He paused, then stated doubtfully, "Friends…"

"Yes, friends," I repeated. "I figure that if we could tell our mothers that we had a nice time, even enjoyed each other's company, but, you know, it didn't work out chemistry-wise, then they would finally give up. I just think that if we could both go back to our moms and say that, if we saw each other at an event somewhere, that we had a nice enough time with each other that we'd *want* to go say hello to one another, then they would be happy." I grinned, "Maybe not as happy as they would like, but at least happy enough to give us a break."

McGregor had stared at me with those lovely brown eyes. Warily at first, then, slowly, with increasing humor. "Okay, you've got a point in that we need to do something to get our mothers to ease up," he finally said, holding out his glass. I clinked mine with his, we smiled at each other, and got down to the business of creating a friendship.

I did my part by making him laugh with stories of wacky things that had happened at some of my weddings and he got a kick out of hearing how some of my brides were so nervous on their wedding day that they had to take a dose of tranquilizers or tequila (and sometimes even both) before they could make it down the aisle. He reciprocated with funny stories about the apartment building he'd lived in while in New York with all its eccentric tenants and how he sometimes missed the crazy old lady in 3B who thought he was the reincarnation of her husband Melvin and the lazy Sundays he and Frederique— "You remember Freddie, don't you? Frederique Olivera? She and I are still good friends."—would go to breakfast at Pastis when she was there for a visit. I learned that he and Freddie still went to lunch at least once a week and often acted as each other's plus-one when one or the other had a function to go to.

Spearing a fried Brussels sprout from our plate of appetizers, I asked, "It just seems that you two really understand and care for each other, so why are you just friends?"

He'd searched my face and when he couldn't find any trace of stalkerish ill-will, he'd explained that Freddie had major trust issues that stemmed from the fact that she had come from a set of immensely wealthy but screwed up parents who always put their needs and dramas before her. "When we dated as teenagers," he explained, "she was always testing me and could never quite believe that I really was faithful to her. But it was weird—she wasn't wildly jealous per se, more just completely unable to comprehend that she could truly trust me. Anyway, it finally wore me out around prom time and we broke up."

I nodded, finally understanding what had ended their relationship. "But you remained close."

"Yeah, that aspect of it just kind of happened. We never stopped caring for each other and we kept in touch." He shrugged, looking at a point just over my shoulder, "And since then, we've just been friends and nothing more."

He'd smoothly changed the subject after that and we'd kept talking about everything under the sun, laughing and joking, surprising ourselves with how easily we got along. It was about the time I had truly gotten into my role of friend to McGregor that I had begun to notice that, each time he looked at me, it was a little bit more of a lingering gaze. Still, I didn't let the thought go to my head. Nor did I freak out with joy when he asked if we could hang out again sometime as we stood outside the restaurant at the end of our three-hour, thoroughly fun dinner. I didn't even lose my cool when he hugged me, his scent much different than Luke's, much sweeter, somehow reminding me of maple syrup.

I did, however, let loose as I drove home, bouncing with excitement in my seat and calling Hilary first and then Bryan to tell them the whole story of my first good setup in many, many moons. Although as soon as he heard my happy voice, Bryan wouldn't let me say another word until he put me on speaker so that Gabriel could hear everything, too. Franzilla would have been so proud of him, no?

So, McGregor Elliston and I began spending time together and I let him set the pace. For starters, we went to dinner again on Sunday. We did Italian, sharing fried calamari and sampling each other's entrees like two people who were already comfortable around each other. And though his schedule and mine were both very busy, we carved out time to have lunch with each other and also found two more nights where we had dinner. Still, it took him until our fourth true date—our first semi-date having not counted as agreed upon by the entire Dating Brigade—to kiss me. But when he did, he made it worthwhile.

"You're so sweet, Shelby," he said, pulling me to him and wrapping his arms around my waist as we stood on the very spot within Pete's Lounge where we'd seen each other at twenty-five. "You didn't think I remembered seeing you here all those years ago, did you?"

"No," I said, shaking my head, amazed.

He laughed and held me closer, his brown eyes twinkling. The manly-yet-mapley scent of him filled my senses as he told me, "I wasn't all that drunk that night. I just pretended to be sloshed so that I wouldn't embarrass myself by slobbering all over you when you walked up to me in that dress you were wearing." He released me just enough so that he could look down and take in my current, updated, little black dress I had worn for our romantic dinner at the upscale Mark's American

Cuisine, "Not that it could compare with how you look tonight."

I felt giddy all over. "You're not kidding, are you? You *really* remember that night?"

"I can't exactly say that I remember much after that because of the three tequila shots in a row I was, er, encouraged to down by the yahoos I call my friends, but yeah, I remember exactly how you looked and how you smiled at me. I couldn't believe how hot you were and how I'd never seen that in high school. You had me literally tongue-tied." He put a hand up and gently pushed a stray lock of hair away from my completely stunned face. "Anyway," he said, clearing his throat, "I certainly realize that I haven't kissed you yet..."

"No," I said, "you haven't."

"It's not that I haven't wanted to," he said, an adorable little flush coming on to his cheeks. "I just...I've just rushed into things a few times before and it didn't work. Once I got to know you, I realized I didn't want to rush it." And by the slightly confused look I gave him, he laughed and said, "That may be a put-down when some guys say it, but I assure you, for me it's a compliment. Things that are special to me, I take my time with."

And before I could even catch my breath, he took my face in his hands, lowered his head, and kissed me. And kissed me good, too.

"So why the hell didn't you call in this morning to tell us you were going to be late because you were up all weekend doing the squelchy with your tow-headed hunk?" Emily asked me on Monday morning, narrowing her eyes and looking me over like I might be deliberately hiding the fact that I relinquished my Kinda-Sorta-Self-Imposed Chastity Belt, or at least made a dent in its armor.

"Yeah," Lauren seconded.

"Ditto, sugar," Bryan said, taking a sip of his cappuccino.

I replied, "Because it was already nearly midnight when he kissed me and he had a fishing trip to Matagorda planned for literally the crack of dawn on Sunday. He left at five in the morning with his father and he didn't get home until nearly midnight. And naturally he was exhausted, so I didn't even get to see him when he got back."

What I didn't tell them was that I thought I had detected a note of relief in his voice when I'd replied that I understood and that he should stay home and rest instead of coming over to put his hands all over me.

Luke walked past my office at that point and Emily yelled out over the construction noise coming from across the hall, "Hey, Luke, if you had a beautiful and willing new girlfriend, you wouldn't take four dates to ravish her, would you?"

Luke had stopped beyond my door frame and had to take a step back. At first his face was cautious, but when he looked at me to see my hounded expression, his dimple flickered. "What do you think?" he said and walked off again.

My employees whooped and hollered after him in appreciation as I slunk down into my chair and whimpered. Not only was I unravished by the hands of McGregor Elliston, now I had visions of Luke taking way less than four dates to ravish me, too! Curses! This was so not fair.

Bryan turned back to me and said, "So do you think he'll sex you up soon?"

When I initially said, "Huh?" it was because my naughty mind would not let go of the thought of Luke sexing me up, but then I turned my Inner Wall back up to full blast, my mind back to McGregor, and replied, "I'm damn sure going to let him know I want him to, that's for sure."

Seven days and three dates with McGregor later, I was still unravished, thoroughly sexually frustrated, and once again being pelted with questions from the Dating Brigade.

"Is there something wrong with this guy? Is his penis malfunctioning or something?" Emily asked.

Lauren rephrased. "She means, do you think he's nervous about his performance, Shelby?"

"Definitely not," I said.

"Then what's the problem?" Bryan said.

I had no idea, and I told them so. "He seems to really care about me. He's always telling me how wonderful I am and I can't get within ten feet of him without him kissing me, which is awesome, but in the three times we've had the chance to rip each other's clothes off and go at it, something has always gotten in the way."

Lauren held up her hand, "The first time was my fault, I admit it."

I reached across my desk and put my hand over hers. "Lor, sweetie, your migraine was making you sick as a dog and no one else was available but me to take over at the Scherfenberg Foundation gala. You had no choice but to call me and I don't blame you at all." I remembered how quickly McGregor had buttoned his shirt back up and had booked it out of my bungalow, however, and I couldn't help but look dismayed.

"And the second time was when he had to drive to San Antonio at some ungodly hour of the morning to be with his sister, whose baby came early with complications." Bryan told the other girls, since he already knew the story. "Everything turned out fine, but McGregor stayed at the hospital with his parents and brother-in-law all day and drove home. Shelby went over to his house for their date to find him sound asleep on the couch. Snoring like a pig with a sinus infection, too, from what I understand," he finished with a what-a-shame look on his face.

"So, what did you do?" Emily asked.

"What could I do?" I replied. "He was so worn out, I just covered him with a blanket and left." I could still see the three pictures that were right above his head on the side table, the biggest of which was of McGregor and Freddie, looking beautiful together, their respective eyes glowing as they grinned ear to ear and cheek to cheek. He'd had lunch with Freddie the day before and they'd gone to an Astros game the previous Saturday when I'd been working a wedding. Though he'd said nothing more than a casual, "Sure, it was fun," when

I'd asked him over the phone if they'd had a good time, there had been a definitive ring of happiness his voice.

"And so the third time was last night, then?" Lauren asked. "What could have possibly happened?"

"Well, he seemed determined to make it up to me after falling asleep. He'd brought over a bottle of wine to my house and everything was going great. We were doing some serious making out, with a condom package ripped open and at the ready, I might add...and then his boss called. One of their biggest clients had come in town unexpectedly and wanted to take McGregor and a couple of others to dinner as a thank-you—and it was more of a command than a request. I could hear the tone in his boss' voice myself. McGregor was gone again not twenty minutes after he came over."

The Dating Brigade let out a collective groan. I had groaned inwardly at the time, too, because McGregor had not even hesitated at his boss' request. Not even for a millisecond. His sense of relief that we had been interrupted yet again had been even more evident, too.

What's worse, when he left my house he made no mention of making it up to me, again. He would be out of town for work during the last week in July and then he'd be on vacation at his family's cabin in Montana through the first week in August. He gave me one last quick kiss, telling me a little too cheerfully that he would see me the weekend he returned, when I would be going as his date to a Houston Livestock Show and Rodeo charity gala. Frederique would be there, too, he said, his cheeks flexing into a smile when mentioning her name, since she was a volunteer on one of the three Rodeo committees that were hosting the event.

"Great," I replied, feeling bummed that I wouldn't have any more dates with McGregor until then.

Though oddly enough, during the time McGregor and I were apart, I did get the chance to go on a date with Luke Treadwell.

Twenty-One

Okay, sort of. Luke ended up getting conned by his little sister into being my platonic plus-one for Jackie and Abel's wedding. In fact, Maggie turned out to be quite the little Franzilla wannabe, even though it was totally unwitting on her part.

I was just glad the Dating Brigade hadn't witnessed Maggie nimbly traversing the verbal minefield that Luke and I both laid out for her to keep her from shoving the two of us together. They would have been frothing at the mouth to get her to defect over to their side, yessiree.

It was Tuesday afternoon in late July, just two days before Jackie's wedding. Maggie was in my office so that we could go through her checklist and make a plan for how we wanted to tackle all that we had to do in the next six weeks before she walked down the aisle. The office was completely quiet other than sweeping noises coming from the other side of the house, where Luke was cleaning up debris while he waited for Maggie and I to be finished. The Treadwell siblings were then going together to a family dinner in a couple of hours. Luke was driving Maggie to the restaurant, with a quick detour to his house to change beforehand.

For the bulk of our meeting, I was sitting with my feet up on my desk while Maggie was in one of my barrel chairs concentrating on typing in various updates to the file she'd titled "My Big Fat Episcopalian Wedding" on her iPad. But the title of her document file was about as humorous as she was getting at the moment; otherwise, she was in full Intense Bride mode.

She had been dropped off by Barton a little after four o'clock and she walked in looking like a put-together beauty. Her normally long, straight hair curled into soft waves and I told her that rhubarb hue of her knee-length sleeveless linen shirtdress and the claret of her lipstick were doing wonders for her skin tone.

But by four-thirty, when my three employees had left for the day—Emily for a hair appointment, Lauren to go pick up printed t-shirts for an upcoming event, and Bryan to go sofa shopping with Gabriel—Maggie's fresh-linen state had deteriorated. She'd run her fingers through her hair so many times, at one point hastily pulling her hair back into a ponytail to get it out of her face, that her waves had drooped to nothing more than a vague bend at the tips. Her linen dress had also become covered in wrinkles from getting up and down with the need to pace as she talked to me out loud about timetables and seating charts. And with the fact that she would tuck her lower lip under her upper teeth as she contemplated her next nuptial-related move, every trace of claret lipstick was gone from her kisser. So, when she finally looked down at her dress that was doing its impression of a shar-pei, she naturally had a meltdown.

"Oh, no!" she wailed. "I'm all wrinkled!"

"No biggie," I said. I had just come back from the kitchen with a glass of sauvignon blanc for each of us.

But Maggie was trying in frenzied vain to smooth out the wrinkles that were all over her dress. "Oh, I should have known not to wear linen! I'm a total mess! And my grandmother's coming, too—I wanted to look nice for her since it's her birthday! I bet my hair looks horrible now, too!" She kept making fretful noises until I called out, "Hey, Maggie. Over here."

I had moved to the closet, opened the door, and was standing to one side; with one hand I was holding my wine and with the other I was making dramatic game-show–hostess motions as to the contraption that was located just inside the closet.

"You have a steamer!"

"You got it." I smiled. "And I've got a curling iron and tons of makeup and perfume samples and a fluffy robe and just about anything any girl might need to get spruced back up again. So get as wrinkled and as mussed you like. No one will know by the time you get to your grandmother's dinner."

Maggie plopped back down with a relieved laugh in her seat, the wrinkles in her dress now left to their own devices. "Does anything ever faze you, Shelby?" she asked.

Ahh, someone who I've managed to fool… (And obviously the girl did not remember the first time we met… Thank goodness for small favors, no?)

"God, yes," I laughed. I handed her a glass of wine and winked. "I just know how to fake it really well."

Then Jackie called and my bold statement crumbled right in front of Maggie, who managed to go back to intently typing into her wedding document and still witness the Fazing of Shelby at the same time.

"Shelby," Jackie's throaty voice was all business when I answered my office line. "You haven't replied to me with the correct spelling of McGregor's last name for the place cards."

I replied, "What? No, I'm not bringing a date…"

Jackie *tsk*ed me and retorted, "Honey, I sent you an invitation that very specifically said *Ms. Shelby Waterlane and Guest.* I even mailed it directly to your house, instead of to your office."

"Yes, but I figured that was just an accident in what address you gave the calligrapher."

I started to hear my friend's I-love-you-but-you're-exasperating-me tone that signaled she was under stress and losing patience. "It wasn't an accident."

"Jackie," I said, hoping to nip the conversation in the bud before it went where I thought it might go, "you know I don't bring guests to my clients' weddings, even if my client is also my good friend. I'm there for *you*, not to pay attention to a date." I saw Maggie lift her head and look at me with mild curiosity before getting back to her typing. Since Jackie's voice was so damn loud, I figured Maggie was hearing her every word.

Jackie said, "I'm the bride, right?"

I'm not stupid. "You bet."

"And it's my day and I'm supposed to get everything I want, right?"

Need I repeat that I'm not stupid? "Absolutely." I saw Maggie glance up at me again, a smile playing at her lips.

"Then I'm not *asking* you, my sweet friend, I am *telling* you that what I want is for you to bring a date and to have as good a time at my wedding as Abel and I and all my other guests are going to have."

"But Jackie…"

"No buts, Shelby. I know you're worried that everything won't go smoothly, but I'm telling you that it will. I've already had the florist phone me to gripe that you've called to triple-check everything and, if I know you, you've done the same thing with everybody else from the limo driver to the cake designer to the catering manager at the hotel. I bet you even went to the Chatsworth yourself just so that you could check personally with Chef Pevo that every last haricot vert and grain of Arborio rice for the mushroom risotto were accounted for, didn't you?"

"Er…," I blushed furiously because she had pegged me. In fact, just before my meeting with Maggie, I had just come back from one last walk-through of the menu with Chef Pevo and Rebecca, the hotel's catering manager. Still, this was Jackie's way of telling me how impressed with me she was that I was going to extremes to make sure her day was perfect. So I had been most definitely blushing with pleasure. I briefly met Maggie's eyes and felt my cheeks burn more since she was now watching me intently. I guessed that she was wondering if I would be doing the same thing for her. She didn't know that I already had been double-checking the few things I could, which turned out to be a good thing because the tuxedo rental shop had somehow gotten the wrong date for this weekend's groomsmen's fittings, even though I'd had a computerized printout stating the correct day had indeed been scheduled.

"Yeah, I knew you had," Jackie laughed, her voice finally softening. "I told Abel about it and he's been calling you my Super Shiksa all week. Speaking of, he can't wait to dance with you at the reception. He remembers how well you jitterbug and, I don't know if you noticed when I gave you my play list for the band, but he specifically included some peppy Rat Pack tunes so you two can cut a rug when I'm, as he put it, 'talking my way through my throng of adorers.'"

I grinned. "Tell Abel that I can't wait."

Jackie heard the note of acquiescence in my voice and pounced on it. "So you'll act like my guest then and bring that cute new boy of yours?"

I shook my head ruefully. I had walked right into that one. But I still had one trick up my sleeve in my quest to make sure I could still do my job at her wedding the way *I* wanted to.

Trying to keep from looking smug, I said, "I'd love to, Jacks, but McGregor is out of town for the next two weeks. And since Bryan will be helping Lauren with a big corporate event on Thursday, that leaves my well of men bone dry as usual, so I'm going to *have* to come stag." I gave Maggie a quick, conspiratorial wink, but she just thoughtfully smiled me in return before dropping her eyes to her iPad once more.

I heard Jackie sigh dramatically on the other end of the line. "Shelby, honey, why didn't you tell me this ages ago? You knew that I had places for forty-eight guests exactly and I've told you at least ten times that everyone invited was either part of a couple or bringing a date. Even Abel's and my kids are bringing dates. So who exactly did you think my forty-eighth guest was going to be?"

Cue the official Fazing of Shelby... The fact that my desire to be the Deliberately Dateless Wedding Coordinator might have been messing with Jackie's carefully planned numbers was the one detail I hadn't even thought about.

Crap....

"Um..." My mind sped up as I tried in vain to think of even one single, available guy I could ask last-minute to go with me to Jackie's wedding...and failed.

The irritation had come back full-force in my friend's voice. "Honey, is there not *anyone* you can bring to even up the tables? Colin, maybe?"

I said weakly, "He's working the late shift this week. Low resident doctor on the totem pole and all that..."

"So there's no one?"

I pulled out the proper words: "I'm so sorry, Jacks, but—"

"You can take Luke."

I didn't realize that I was hanging my head. I snapped up to see Maggie looking at me patiently. (I was right. She obviously had been able to hear everything Jackie had been saying.)

"Huh?" I replied in disbelief just as Jackie said suspiciously in my ear, "Who's that you're talking to?"

"It's Maggie Treadwell...Luke's little sister."

"And what did she say?" Jackie demanded.

Maggie piped up again, leaned forward, and raised her voice loud enough so that Jackie would undoubtedly hear. "I told her that she should take my brother to your wedding."

Even as I began to shake my head, Jackie practically shouted into my ear, "Luke! He's a cutie! You're bringing Luke, Shelby! Done deal."

Finally, I stammered at both of them, showing Maggie just how fazed I could get, naturally, "Wha...? Nooo... I can't..."

Maggie raised her eyebrows as if I were being completely irrational, "Why not? I know you're seeing someone right now, but you and Luke are still friends, right?"

I pushed my hair self-consciously behind my ear and said, "Of course, but..."

"But, what?" Jackie chimed in.

I would have liked to believe that both women knew just how much they were torturing me, but I could only say that of one of them. Maggie's entire body radiated innocence as to what she was doing. And somehow, that just made it that much more frustrating, don't you know.

Thus, I tried for the easiest way out. "I'm sure he has other plans with—"

Maggie cut me off with an eye roll and a dry reply. "I assure you, he doesn't have other plans, but let's ask him anyway." Then before I could stop her, she turned toward the doorway and screamed out, "LUKE!"

"I'm loving this girl," Jackie chuckled softly in my ear. Since Maggie's eyes were trained on the doorway, I closed my own for a moment and gave a small, mortified shake of my head.

Within seconds, Luke sauntered in, giving Maggie an irritated-brother look that clearly said *What gives that you're yelling for me like a banshee at my jobsite?*

Maggie herself showed just how unfazed she could be and got right to the point. "You doing anything Thursday night?"

I tried to leap up from my chair, but I only managed to stumble forward, the receiver still glued to my ear, and bang my hipbone on the edge my desk. I said, "Oh, crap, ow—" right as Luke warily replied, "Not much. Why?"

"What'dja do, smack yourself?" Jackie laughed in my ear, bawdily, of course, and completely without regard for my pain. For her part, Maggie looked amused. Only Luke seemed aware that I might have fractured my hip on my very hard wooden desk.

Obviously, my dramatic side was coming out to help cover for my being fazed in front of a client...

"You okay?" he asked.

Maggie cut in again before I could even pathetically wince in return. "You're going to be Shelby's date for her friend Jackie's wedding, okay?"

"Huh?" Luke replied. He stared at his sister as if she might be a little nuts.

I tried to jump in. "Luke, you don't have to—"

"Oh, but you know he will," Jackie said softly, lasciviously into my ear. I groaned inwardly, turned away, and hissed, "Jacks, cut it out."

Luke spoke sternly to his sister. "Maggie, Shelby is seeing someone now. You can't just go—"

"I'm not," she retorted. "You two are friends and Shelby— *your friend*—needs a plus-one to Jackie's wedding." She leaned back, and crossed her legs primly. "Jackie needs forty-eight guests to make sure that each of her tables are evenly filled. Shelby's boyfriend is out of town and, since he can't come, that makes the number forty-*seven*. It's uneven, Luke, and Jackie doesn't want the number to be uneven. And it's her wedding and she deserves her wedding to be just like she wants it to be." She batted her eyes as if double-dog daring her much bigger, older brother to contradict her. "So would you please go with Shelby? You've told me a million times how much fun you have with her, so just be her good friend in return and *go*."

Although I blushed at the third-party compliment, I must admit I felt a ripple of fear run through me. If you put a Neiman's credit card in Maggie's hand and turned on the Food Network on a nearby television, she could be a forty-years-younger Frances Waterlane. It was truly scary.

As Luke and I just stared at Mini-Franzilla sitting comfortably in my leather barrel chair, I heard Jackie's voice once more. She ordered me to hand the phone over to Maggie. I did so like a slack-jawed zombie and Maggie popped up with a grin and put the receiver to her ear. For once, Jackie's voice could not be heard by the entire world as she spoke with my other current bridal client. I dared not look at Luke; I just watched Maggie's face flush like she'd just been complimented as she grinned and laughed. "Oh, absolutely. Us brides have to stick together, right?" More laughter. "I'm happy to help." She looked at Luke and then at me. "And by the fact that neither has been silly enough to say otherwise, I'm thinking you just got your forty-eighth guest." Even more laughter. "No problem. Have a wonderful wedding day. Thanks—it was nice talking with you, too. Okay, here's Shelby again."

And she handed me back the phone, I finally looked at Luke and we simultaneously shrugged helplessly. Then he rushed his hand through his hair and said, "Jesus, Shelby. Now I know how you felt these past months." Jerking a thumb in the direction of his conniving baby sister, he looked (a bit wide-eyed) at me, "There wasn't anything I could have said that would have made any difference whatsoever in that one-sided conversation, was there?"

I grimaced weakly, "Not really, no."

"Holy mother of God."

And with those words, I had myself a date with Luke Treadwell.

Twenty-Two

"Have you seen Rabbi Silverman?"

The bartender shook his head as he finished cutting up a lime into perfect wedges. I quickly moved to another grouping of hotel staff.

"Has anyone seen the rabbi? He's about five-nine...? Short gray beard...? Glasses...? Yarmulke...?" I hastily motioned to the area of the head where the small skullcap was traditionally worn. In their turn, each staff member I questioned shook their head no as well.

And by the time Jorge, the longtime headwaiter, replied, "I'm sorry, Shelby, I haven't seen him since he arrived," I was starting to sweat. The good rabbi had indeed turned up in the Chatsworth's second-floor Mayfield Ballroom on time at five fifteen and I had greeted him warmly. We'd met on many occasions at Jackie's other events, not to mention the eight weddings he and I had worked together on in the past. But not long thereafter he had shown up at my side and murmured to me that he would be right back.

He hadn't come right back, though. He was officially missing in action.

I looked at the time on my phone. It was twenty minutes of six. Jackie's and Abel's ceremony was due to start at precisely six p.m. and Jackie had absolutely insisted that everything should happen on time. ("Two things I've never been fond of about other people's weddings, Shelby, are when the ceremony doesn't start when the invitation says it's going to and when the bride and groom wait until the damn cows come home before they cut the cake. My wedding will have neither of those problems, yes?")

Yeah, maybe I shouldn't have replied with a cocky, "*Absolutamente*, Jacks. And if I fail ya, you don't owe me a cent."

My eyes roamed the stunningly decorated room until they lit on the rabbi's wife of forty-eight years. Greta Silverman looked classy in her black St. John knit suit with white-tipped collar and cuffs, though her lipstick, which was just a shade too dark, and her hair, which boasted a lot of teasing and a lot of hairspray, belied her humble Brooklyn upbringing. She seemed calm and unconcerned about her husband as she chatted away with Abel's mother near the—as requested—white-trumpet-lily–smothered *chuppah*.

As for the bride, she was up in the bridal suite having her stylist put the finishing touches on her loose chignon. Her mother Miriam was with her, no doubt fussing over every last detail. Sanity for Jackie would come in the form of her daughter Norah and two other female friends, all three of whom were serving as bridesmaids. The five of them would not come down until the very last minute. Abel and his three groomsmen, which were his two boys Matthew and David and Jackie's son Philip, were in a second hotel room relaxing and, I was sure, watching the Astros game on television until the alarm I set on David's watch buzzed at five fifty-two.

That meant I had exactly twelve minutes to find Rabbi Silverman before anyone would notice his absence.

Heading down the hotel's marble staircase as fast as I could in my floaty black-chiffon cocktail dress and my four-inch Stuart Weitzman heels, I thought about Rabbi Silverman. It was no wonder that Jackie invited him to all her parties. Spry and still very active at seventy-six, he was an intelligent conversationalist who could discuss both the secular and the religious with an open mind. His blue eyes also seemed to permanently dance with good humor and he had a plethora of little time-worn jokes he would tell that were always short, clean, and flecked with Jewish (that he would add at will, even if the original joke had none to speak of). I hadn't forgotten the one he told me the first time we met over five years ago. He had taken my hand in both of his and said, "Shelby, my dear, you must listen to me. I have a little joke for you. You'll love it, I promise."

"I'm all ears, Rabbi," I'd grinned.

Looking pleased that he'd found a new buddy and making emphatic motions with his wide, capable hands, he'd begun: "So a grasshopper walks into a bar and says, 'Barkeep, whatcha got that's good?' And the bartender replies, 'Well, we've got a drink named after you, would you like to try that?' And the grasshopper looks surprised and says, 'I can't believe it! You got a drink named Herschel?'" As he'd burst into a shaking belly laugh, I had been thoroughly charmed and thereafter always looked forward to seeing him.

Needless to say, it also went without saying that it was not like the rabbi to go missing when he had a ceremony to perform. In fact, of all manner of marriage officiates I'd dealt with over the years, Rabbi Silverman was the only one with whom I'd yet to have a single problem; hence, my ever-increasing worry over where he could have gone with so few minutes before the ceremony.

Striding quickly through both the hotel's highly rated restaurant and then its dark, pub-style bar, which was already filling up with those looking to start celebrating the weekend early, I scanned every nook and cranny for the silver-haired rabbi. No luck. I checked with the hostess at the entrance to the hotel's restaurant. She hadn't seen him, either. I went back inside and started heading toward the lobby. I was about to breeze past the Castlemaine Ballroom, but I stopped short. Murmuring, "Just in case," I slipped inside, passing as I did so a large sign outside of the closed doors that read:

O'Connor-Hageman Wedding Reception
7 p.m. to 1 a.m.

The spacious room was opulently decorated for what obviously would be a huge reception. The theme colors were red and silver at their most dramatic: The tablecloths were distressed red silk, the color of hunt coats. Three deliberately mismatched silver vases per table held rounded, tightly packed bouquets mixed with classic red roses, oxblood calla lilies, crimson peonies, cardinal-red gerbera daisies, and tulips the color of cherries. A handful of votive candles in red-glass holders were positioned around the vases, waiting to be lit. The chairs—ten per table for this wedding—were covered with silver distressed silk and tied at the back with a matching hunt-red sash. Red starched dinner napkins were laying in a simple pocket fold atop a silver charger plate; a menu card in red with silver writing was nestled in the napkin's pocket. And as if all that wasn't enough, the wine and water goblets were both made of dark red glass.

I felt a smile—no, I had to admit it, I felt a little smirk coming to my face and I momentarily forgot about Rabbi Silverman. I had seen this particular setup before. I also knew instantly who was the wedding coordinator for the O'Connor–Hageman wedding.

"Recognize 'Red and Silver Combo Number One'?"

Looking over my shoulder, I saw Rebecca, the hotel's catering manager, coming in the doors. As she stopped at my side, I replied, "You know, for all of Kendra Everitt's talent, you'd think she wouldn't try to pass off the exact same theme time and time again to any bride who happens to like red."

"Tell me about it. But wasn't it you who designed this particular look for the Castlemaine Ballroom, more or less?"

"More or less, yes," I said, surprised that she'd even known. "But that was years ago, when this look was still fresh and new."

"Yep," Rebecca nodded, "I knew it. Kendra's still ripping you off, all these years later." And when I looked at her with astonishment, she replied, "I may be newer to the game, honey, but don't think I haven't figured out what's what and who's who."

My flattered face said what my lips didn't. "I'd love to stay," I told her, "but it seems I've lost my officiate. Seen Rabbi Silverman wandering around by any chance?"

Rebecca's face went to thoughtful concern. "No, I haven't. But that's not like him to go MIA. Do you want me to put out an all-hotel-points bulletin?"

I was about to say yes when we heard voices out in the hall. Not a moment later, a skinny, long-legged platinum blonde breezed in carrying a clipboard and wearing a sleek black pantsuit and black-and-white Manolo Blahnik spectator pumps. A necklace with a pear-shaped diamond pendant outlined in smaller diamonds was around her neck, matching pear-shaped studs at her ears. Her long blonde hair was in lots of chicly tousled layers. In her wake hurried a petite red-haired assistant in her early twenties, lugging a heavy cardboard box, wearing an unattractive brown shift dress and looking positively frumpy next to her glossy, manicured-to-the-hilt, feline-like boss.

Both of them stopped short when they saw me. The redhead looked surprised, but Kendra Everitt's baby-blue eyes—after flicking quickly out into the decorated ballroom—glittered with palpable animosity when she locked them onto me.

"What the hell are you doing in here?" she demanded, her free hand, French-manicured talons and all, on her hip.

Out of the corner of my eye, I saw Rebecca shift nervously. I knew she couldn't afford to lose Kendra's business and was worried about what I might say.

I smiled politely, clasping my hands calmly in front of me, hiding any reciprocal cattiness. "Hello, Kendra. I was just looking for the rabbi for my wedding upstairs. He left the ballroom and now I can't seem to find him. I ducked into here to see if he didn't accidentally go into the wrong ballroom.

Rebecca here saw me and came to say hello. We were just saying how beautiful the room looks."

"Doesn't it though?" the redhead gushed. "I just love the red and silver combination. It's so dramatic and feminine at the same time." She shifted the box she was carrying to one side and threw out her hand eagerly. "You're Shelby Waterlane, aren't you? I'm Darcy Rutger, Kendra's new assistant," she shook my hand enthusiastically, "it is *such* a pleasure to—"

"Darcy!" Kendra snapped. She turned to her assistant and bared her teeth into her version of a smile. "Would you please take the box of favors and begin placing them just above each charger plate...*please*?" Cheeks flaming, Darcy slunk off with her box. Rebecca murmured that she would go help and left me standing alone with the woman who was my former assistant.

I had fired Kendra Everitt just a week before I met Bryan. The weeks preceding her firing had been some of the worst of my professional career, with vendors left and right doubting me, refusing to return my phone calls, and generally acting as if they were unwilling to work with my clients, all because Kendra had been dishing out lie after lie, saying that I had been bad-mouthing all those who I'd worked with over the years. But, to be honest, I would have been willing to relive those moments all over again for the very fact that such a difficult and stressful situation had led me to such a wonderful and deserving person as Bryan, who would never sell me down the river just to advance his own career.

After I'd fired her, Kendra had gone on to be the catering director at a much smaller, much less luxurious hotel. She stayed there for two years before, seemingly out of nowhere, she'd left her job to marry one of Houston's most wealthy playboy bachelors named Chad van Ingelsdorp—who, we'd heard, was both a taco short of a combination plate and not exactly known for keeping his enchilada in his pants. We were hardly surprised when, not long after they wed, I saw Chad at one of my events chatting up a woman who plainly wasn't Kendra. Though when Bryan saw him a few months later at a club dancing with "someone who plainly wasn't a woman," we'd howled with laughter and dubbed him Bi-Curious Chad.

Now, looking at her otherwise attractive face made ugly with hatred, I felt no desire to laugh. I only felt pity.

"The room looks beautiful?" Kendra repeated, looking me up and down with obvious distaste. "Let's cut the crap, Shelby. I thought you never told lies—or at least that's what you'd like people to think, isn't it? I know you pride yourself in taking credit for this particular reception design, so don't tell me that you and Rebecca weren't slamming me for it."

With a distasteful look of my own, I did respond with a lie, but one for the good of another: "Rebecca did nothing of the sort. *She* was the one who said the room looks beautiful, and I simply agreed with the statement. Though you are right, I don't respect your lack of creativity in the design." I straightened my shoulders and added a real compliment, "Still, your bride will be very pleased. The room does look wonderful."

Kendra knew me well enough that at least my last statement was a truthful one. Thus, she changed tactics and the subject. "I heard you landed Maggie Treadwell's wedding,"

"I did," I replied.

"I wasn't really surprised," she sniffed. "Especially once Maggie said that you'd hired her brother to do some work on your office. Smart move, Shelby. Tug on the family heartstrings and it gives you a natural edge."

My eyebrows shot up as I fought back an incredulous laugh. "That's not quite the reason why Maggie signed with me, Kendra, but if you'd like to believe what you've concocted in your own mind, then go right ahead."

She practically spat, "So you're denying that you and Luke Treadwell are sleeping together?"

Okay, how in the hell did Kendra Everitt even know who Luke was? And why did she sound *jealous*?

"Excuse me?" I returned.

"I saw him, Shelby. He was looking for you when I walked in." She gave me another disdainful look. "I told him that, thankfully, I hadn't seen you."

And she had talked to Luke, too? What gives?

"That doesn't mean that I'm sleeping with him," I snapped, crossing my arms over my chest. I didn't bother to explain further. (Nor did I remember to state that I was, in fact, dating a very handsome guy named McGregor. Well, crap…)

Kendra watched me, reading between the lines. She had always been very good at that. "Oh, but you sure as hell want to, don't you?" she hissed. "Is that why you're wearing such a sexy little number tonight, Shelby? You were the one who taught me to always look professional," she mimicked my voice perfectly (she'd always been very good at that, too), "'for any event to which you put your good name.' You certainly don't look professional tonight, honey. You look like you deliberately picked a dress with easy access. Like you're ready to drag that tall drink of water into the service elevator, hike those layers of chiffon up, and beg him to bang your lights out while you go up to the twentieth floor." She cocked her hip and sized me up. "You may be too short to do it with him standing up, but I've felt his arms before. He could hold you up against the wall while he's screwing you."

About ten nasty comebacks came to mind and I was choosing the nastiest of them when my cell phone vibrated twice, signaling a text message. It was from He Whose Ears Must Have Been Burning, otherwise known as my accidental plus-one for the evening. He had written:

Found rabbi. Come to lobby. Luke

Working my face into a calm smile, I said, "It seems my rabbi has turned up. I'm *so* sorry, but I have to go now." I quickly texted back a one-word reply: WHEW!

"You're just a pillar of professionalism tonight, aren't you, Shelby?" Kendra snarled, her eyes narrowed in hatred, "Wearing a slutty little dress? Losing your officiate? My, aren't the mighty slipping."

I replied, "Oh, but the mighty know not to bad-mouth their competitors, Kendra. You should know that Maggie Treadwell was yours to lose. I told her the truth—that you are a very talented wedding coordinator and that she should sign with you if you and she clicked together. It was your response when she asked you for your opinion of me that sold her firmly back my way." And with an unimpressed look at her pissed-off yet thoroughly stunned face, I gave her a cheeky little wave and started to walked out. Then I stopped and whipped around. "I nearly forgot. How's that handsome husband of yours doing?"

Kendra Everitt looked positively furious; her cheeks flushed and her jaw clenched. But she didn't answer.

She didn't need to. The three-carat pear-shaped rock and diamond-encrusted wedding band that she had sported and flaunted for the past three years were gone from her left hand. They had been made into a beautiful necklace.

I strode out of the ballroom, grinning wickedly to myself and wondering whether Chad had left her for a she or a he (probably both). Looking at my watch, I now had eight minutes until Abel and his boys made their way down to the Mayfield Ballroom. I picked up the pace big time and headed for the front of the hotel.

Luke's voice called out to me as soon as my high heels hit the lobby's marble floor. "Shelby, over here."

He was standing in the doorway of the concierge's office, directly across the lobby from the reception desk. I was out of breath by the time I reached him, but it was not just because I'd practically sprinted to the lobby. It was just as much because of Luke himself, making Kendra, her drama, and all my questions for him about how they knew each other fly out of my mind.

He looked more handsome than I'd ever seen him. He wore a tailored dark suit with a silk twill tie in a cornflower blue liberally dotted with tiny red-and-white convertible sports cars, adding a lighthearted tone that was perfect for a wedding like Jackie's. Peeking out from the French cuffs of his white dress shirt were some simple gold cufflinks monogrammed with his initials. But it was the comfortable way he wore all of it that really did it for me. I was pleased to see that Luke wore his suit easily; it made him look every bit the gorgeous businessman and less the equally gorgeous khakis-and-work-boots–sporting contractor I had grown to know and love.

Whoa, there. Scratch that. Grown to know and have around as nothing more than a cherished *friend*. Yeah, that's what I meant, friend. I was dating the equally-hot-in-a-suit McGregor Elliston, who was aware that I was bringing Luke to the wedding and had seemed thoroughly unperturbed, saying only, "Well, I see it this way. If you're okay with the fact that I go have lunch with Freddie, I don't really have room to ask you not to have one of your guy friends escort you to a wedding since I can't, do I?" Therefore, I was in no way expecting or wanting Luke and I to have a quickie in the service elevator, with my floaty chiffon dress proving that it did indeed offer easy access, with Luke's strong arms holding me up so that I could wrap my legs around him, gripping him as he...

I'd no more felt a surge of panic because my Inner Wall wasn't going up like it should than Luke tilted his head toward the concierge's office. "He's in here."

The serious look on his face had me back to my senses in a heartbeat. I whipped into the office to see Rabbi Silverman sitting in a chair, looking worn out and sipping on a Sprite. The concierge, Jonas, was standing off to the side. "Hey, Shelby," he said, his dark face breaking into a smile.

I reached out and squeezed Jonas' fingers even as I knelt down next to the rabbi.

"Shelby, my dear," Rabbi Silverman said, reaching out for my hand, "have I ever told you that I am mildly diabetic?"

"No, sir, you haven't," I said.

"Well, there you go," he said. "But not only am I diabetic, I'm also a fool."

"Oh, no—" I protested, but he squeezed my hand to stop me.

"Yes, I am a fool, because I didn't listen to my wife and eat properly today. I did too many errands without stopping to eat, which doesn't do much for keeping my blood sugar level. I started feeling weak when I went out to my car to get my reading glasses. Thank God your young man was there to help me back in."

Feeling my cheeks heat up, I looked over at Luke, but I didn't contradict the statement since it wasn't the time. He just smiled modestly.

"And," Rabbi Silverman said brightly, suddenly sounding like his usual happy self, "he gave me a peppermint! Saved my life, he did."

He was so cute about it, I broke into a huge, relieved grin.

When he went to get up, though, I put my hand on his arm and said, "Rabbi, I know you're tough as nails, but are you sure you're okay? Do you want me to delay the ceremony another few minutes or anything?"

Rabbi Silverman looked at me with his big blue eyes that were once more clear and sparkling with humor and said, "Shelby, would *you* want to ask such a thing of Jackie Rosenstein?"

I laughed. "I wouldn't dare, Rabbi."

"And neither would I, my dear." He nodded toward Jonas. "This fine man over here was kind enough to bring me a soda and a grilled chicken sandwich while I was recovering." He angled to the side and I could indeed see a mostly eaten sandwich. "I feel healthy as a horse now." And when I gave him a *really?* look, he said, "I promise. Now, let's go and conduct a beautiful ceremony for two beautiful people."

Twenty-Three

After Jackie and Abel had been showered with rose petals and drove off in Abel's vintage convertible Mercedes and after the last guest had chosen their own personal favor from the table filled with bottles of fine wine, all was finally quiet. For some, it might have meant feeling wistful that it was all over, but for me, the peaceful moments after the reception venue had cleared out and I knew that my clients had left happy were moments I used to close my eyes, breathe deeply, and take in the good aura that seemed to permeate the venue's air for another precious few minutes, quietly dissipating with each moment until all that was left was the memory of an event well planned and enjoyed.

I lived for that feeling. It was just another thing that reminded me that I had made the right career choice.

When I opened my eyes, I realized Luke had been watching me. "You're savoring the peace and quiet, aren't you?"

"I like it. There's good vibes after a happy party like this. I'm drinking them in." I demonstrated the fanning of said good vibes into my face.

"I know what you mean. The day that we put the finishing touches on a project and everything suddenly goes from a work space to a transformed room and the client walks in and says, 'I love it!' gives me the same feeling. But next time I'll have to remember to breathe them in and do this..." he trailed off, mimicking my theatric hand movements.

"That would be *wafting*, Treadwell. The proper way to take in good vibes is to waft them upward, then breathe them in gently."

"Ohhh, okay," Luke nodded. "You'll have to remind me to waft and breathe gently when you tell me how much you love your new offices."

"And what if I don't love them?" I said, my hand on my hip, my eyebrows raised as if he was being supremely presumptuous.

Yeah, he wasn't intimidated.

"Oh, you will," he said, flashing me a toothy grin. "You'll love them so much that you'll want to remodel the rest of your place because it will pale in comparison to how incredible those three offices look."

I slipped on the little bolero jacket that matched my dress. "Is that right? My, awfully cocky, aren't we?"

"You betcha," he grinned. Then, before I knew it, he had stepped forward, closing the already short gap between us. "Here," he said, reaching out and gently sliding his thumbs under each side of my jacket, near my clavicle, "You're all turned inward." He pulled the upper corners out that had inadvertently gotten tucked under.

I felt the slight roughness of the sides of his thumbs sliding against my skin. I could smell him. I was looking up, watching his mouth, wanting suddenly so bad to kiss him. And goose pimples popped up all over me.

Turned inward, my ass. It was more like I was turned inside out.

"Thanks," I managed to say, looking hastily away, my throat dry. I picked up Jackie's guest book and the box containing the silver pen from the table. She would pick it up from my office when she and Abel got back from their honeymoon in Italy.

All evening, Luke had been the perfect date, doing no more than wave me off with a grin, saying, "Go, do your job, I'll be just fine here talking with Mrs. Blumenfeld. Right, Muriel?" when I'd apologized that I'd have to leave him alone, sitting with Jackie's octogenarian aunt, so that I could actually earn my keep with Jackie. I'd barely got to converse with him during the five-course dinner, too, since our other table companions, including Rabbi Silverman, kept up most of the conversation. In fact, our longest discourse had lasted about ten seconds after I'd watched him take yet another big bite of the wild-mushroom risotto cooked with shallots, garlic, chicken stock, some Pinot Noir, and topped of with a splash of green-tinged basil oil.

"What are you doing?" I'd asked.

Luke, scooped up another forkful. "Eating every last bit of this risotto. It's awesome."

"You do know that's *rice*, don't you?"

He gave me his sideways look. "Of course I know it's rice. I love rice. Eat it all the time."

"No you don't," I said with supreme confidence.

Luke looked at me like I was batty. "Whatever gave you that idea?"

I was about to say, "Claudia told me," (which was sort of true) when Rabbi Silverman called my name from across the table and asked me to recount the story of our mutual friend Father Desmond, a Catholic priest who no longer allowed wedding rings to be tied onto silk pillows. This was because of an incident where, when the knots holding the rings wouldn't come loose and he had asked the groomsmen in an undertone if any of them had a penknife on them to cut the knotted ribbons, one of the groomsmen had whipped out a six-inch switchblade and the entire congregation had freaked out, thinking that said groomsmen was trying to attack Father Des. Possibly due to my exuberant gesticulations, our entire table was in stitches by the end of it, and Luke's and my discussion about his rice-eating habits was quickly forgotten.

He and I never got to dance, either. During the few songs that I wasn't doing something for Jackie, or helping the photographer set up a group shot, or doing something silly like getting bottles of water for the band, Abel had claimed my jitterbugging talents. Luke danced several times, too, either as Norah Rosenstein's partner—after I'd whispered in his ear, inadvertently breathing in his soapy-woody scent and going a bit weak-kneed, "Her date refuses to dance and she's dying to. Would you mind?"—or with various female guests who brought him out to the dance floor when they saw that the long-legged *shaygitz* could actually cut a rug.

But we smiled at each other a lot from across the room, I will admit that. And, though my Inner Wall seemed to be up and in place, I found myself holding his gaze for as long as I could without actually staring.

Truth be told, I'd almost completely forgotten about McGregor. Was that bad?

As I put Jackie's guest book and pen into my Kate Spade tote, Luke asked me, "So have you ever had a wedding go really wrong?"

"Oh, most definitely." I replied. "No planner would ever be able to claim that they haven't, in fact. No matter how hard you try, whether it's a simple thing like a groomsman losing his boutonniere before the pictures are taken or something big like the bride or groom having second thoughts just as the wedding march cranks up, there's always things that just get out of your control. Just look at tonight and how Rabbi Silverman had gone missing when I thought I had everything in hand and quadruple-checked. Speaking of which, I really would have been in deep crapola had you not rescued him." I nudged him with my elbow, "And given him a peppermint, of course. The rabbi and I were both very grateful."

"Yeah, I know. Me and my peppermints. I got 'em all over the place. I could help out a diabetic every minute of the day practically. I just have a thing for mint, I suppose. Even before Uncle Bob stopped smoking."

"Let me guess," I said. "You ate toothpaste as a child and your favorite ice cream is mint chocolate chip."

"Toothpaste was practically my after-dinner snack," he grinned.

"Well, that explains a lot about what's wrong with you, Treadwell. Obviously all that toothpaste you ingested as a kid made you a little, you know, off." I tapped at my temple.

"Oh, yeah?" he called out when I scooted away from him, laughing. "And what's your excuse?"

As we walked out, Luke carrying the Bryan-dubbed Suitcase o' Tricks that had only doled out a handful of bobby pins and an extra pair of men's black socks, he said, "So are you going to tell me what your best wedding-gone-wrong story or am I going to have to tell Jackie that you never jitterbugged with me like you promised you would? You know she'd have my back if I did."

I couldn't help it. I went weak, thinking how much I'd love to do the horizontal jitterbug with this man. For a second it was as if my Inner Wall had developed human traits and was tapping me indecisively on the shoulder, asking, "Do you need me? Yes? No? Because I'm thinking I could just take a break here…"

NO! Inner Wall, don't fail me now! Get cranking!

"Oh, so now you're blackmailing me, are you?"

"If I must," he replied.

We opted for the stairs, taking them slowly, and I obliged, telling Luke of the second wedding Bryan and I had ever done after I'd started Waterlane Events, where everything went wrong, from the bride being a real bitch—"starting the moment we met, when she sat down, crossed her legs like Sharon Stone in *Basic Instinct*, only without the crotch view, thank God— and proceeded to tell me that if she was going to hire me, I was to do exactly what she wanted, when she wanted, and without talking back, *capisce?* And yes, she actually said *capisce.* "

"Nice."

"Yeah. She was a real piece of work and the negative attitude she brought from day one almost seemed to pervade every aspect of planning her wedding. This girl would have a hissy fit about anything. She yelled at me when I told her that the reception venue she wanted would not hold the number of people she wanted to invite. Ditto for when I told her that, even though it would cost extra money, not having cocktails and hors d'oeuvres to start off the reception was sure to unduly frustrate her three hundred hungry friends and family while they all stood around and waited for the newlyweds to arrive after they took their first pictures as a married couple. And when her salmon-colored bridesmaids' dresses she'd ordered came in and had all been altered to fit her attendants, I thought she was going to break a blood vessel when she got in my face and screamed that the color turned out 'fresh salmon' instead of 'smoked salmon.'"

"There's a difference?"

"Well, the fresh-salmon color has a touch of pink in it, when she wanted more orange undertones, not that she'd bothered to tell me that little detail when we spent six hours looking at dresses and color swatches. I even made her take some of the swatches outside in the daylight so that she could see the colors in all lights. I told her that the pink undertone would flatter her four bridesmaids more than the orange undertone, but she wouldn't listen. Despite the fact the bridesmaids looked gorgeous in them, she still said they were ugly and that she should make me absorb the cost of them since it was I who had recommended the salon where she bought the dresses."

Luke looked incredulous and I grinned slyly, "My reply was to wordlessly highlight the paragraph in her contract where it stated in plain English that the bride is always encouraged to shop around and neither Waterlane Events nor I are responsible for any final choices the bride makes. She was livid. But those weren't the best parts of my time with the bride from hell."

"You're joking. It got worse than that?"

"Sure," I replied as we reached the lobby. "For instance, her recently divorced parents had a knock-down, drag-out fight in my office as to whether or not the mother's new, lecherous husband should be allowed at the ceremony. It was like an episode of the *Jerry Springer Show* in my office. It took Bryan and I literally pulling them off each other to get them to stop. Then on the day of the wedding the florist got into an accident on the way to the church so that the flowers and unity candle weren't delivered to the church until seconds before the guests started filing in. And right before the bride was due to walk down the aisle, her wedding gown split at the side-seam."

"It actually split?"

"Yep. We had to delay the ceremony while I stitched her back up," I told him. "She berated me the entire time even though I had warned her that her lightweight, tight silk dress would be susceptible to strain and so she needed to maintain her weight. Let's just say it wasn't an accident when my needle slipped and poked her in her left boob..."

Luke laughed and I said, "The reception had a few mishaps, too. The band's lead singer got in a tiff with his bassist and walked off the stage. I had to play mediator like a kindergarten teacher until they made up while Bryan got the groomsmen to karaoke 'When a Man Loves a Woman' up on the stage. And then an hour later we ran out of booze and Bryan had to make a mad dash to the nearest liquor store to buy some extra before the guests started to riot. But on the upside of it all, I still picked up three new clients off of that wedding and soon had enough business that I got to hire Emily. So it was a major trial by fire that Bryan and I didn't know whether we'd get though alive, but it came out good in the end. That wedding taught both of us a lot about how to handle things without having the help and resources of a hotel behind us, and it also made us realize that, if we could get though a disaster like that and still want to come to work the next day, then we were definitely doing the right thing by going out on our own."

Nodding, he said, "Sometimes it takes something like that to make you realize just how much you love what you do, right?"

I smiled at him. He knew exactly how I felt. "Right."

A group of drunk wedding guests suddenly stumbled out of the Castlemaine ballroom. "Speaking of receptions," he said. "It looks like another one is still going strong."

Suddenly remembering Kendra's comment about Luke and his strong arms, I replied, "Actually, that particular reception just so happens to have been organized by the one person I consider to be my rival—Kendra Everitt. I happened to run into her when I was looking for Rabbi Silverman. I understand that you two know each other…?"

Luke shrugged. "Yeah, a little. I did a small closet-remodeling job for her seven or eight years ago."

I could see in his face that there was more to the story. "And?" I said.

But he grinned back without guilt. "And nothing, nosey. On my last day of the job, she cornered me and kissed me. I politely told her I wasn't interested and got out of there. I haven't seen her again until tonight."

"So, was it you who introduced Maggie to Kendra, then?"

He stood up straighter, looking proud of himself, "Actually, no, I didn't. Kendra was doing the wedding of one of Maggie's friends and that's how they met." Inclining his head, he said, "Although I will admit to telling Mags that she was welcome to tell Kendra that she was my sister if she thought it would help her in some way, but that was before I'd even met you."

I laughed at him just to tease him. But I felt ludicrously happy at knowing that Kendra Everitt had tried to sink her claws into Luke Treadwell and had failed spectacularly.

"Excuse me, Ms. Waterlane?"

We turned to find the hand-wringing form of Kendra's red-haired assistant.

"Hi, Darcy," I smiled.

She stepped forward, glancing nervously first toward the ballroom, where her boss was no doubt inside. "I was just coming back from the lobby when I saw you. Um, well, I know this may be a horribly tacky thing to do, but I thought I would take the chance. I've known I've wanted to work for you for a couple of years now, ever since I happened to be invited to three weddings in a row that you organized."

She named the weddings, explaining them in glowing detail to Luke when he looked curious.

One had been an ultra-romantic outdoor affair at a beautiful ranch in Helotes, Texas, northwest of San Antonio, the sunny open fields bursting with springtime bluebonnets and canopies of huge oak trees filtering soothing dappled light over the guests. A second had been a smaller, more intimate affair held in the Museum of Natural Science's Cockrell Butterfly Center, with seemingly hundreds of colorful, magical live butterflies fluttering around every guest, making them smile in wonderment.

And the third, a December wedding, had been a Winter Wonderland theme in the Skyview Room of the Runyon Industries Tower overlooking downtown Houston. In addition to the luxuriant table decorations in silver, gold, and white, I'd designed varying sizes of floral-foam spheres covered in white roses that hung at different heights from the ceiling, mimicking huge, fragrant snowflakes drifting downward. I'd also had dormant, leafless crepe myrtle trees brought in and lit up in golden-hued tiny lights from base to each limb's tip, making the guests feel as if they were in a place where faeries might pop out to greet them at any moment. They had been three incredible weddings indeed.

"I'm really flattered," I replied. "Thank you."

Darcy smiled widely, then stole another nervous glance toward the ballroom. "Only you've never had any openings for jobs that I've ever heard of. Um, so, I thought I would ask since I finally met you in person if there might be any chance of you having an opening at Waterlane Events for an assistant. Is there any possibility?"

Luke put my suitcase down and said, "Things not working out with Kendra, huh?"

Darcy turned beet red, "Oh, um, yes and no. Kendra's weddings are incredible and I've learned a lot in the six weeks I've been with her, but business has been slower lately and, besides that, I'm just not…"

"Clicking with her?" I finished for her gently.

"Yes," she said, sighing loudly, looking distressed at having to admit it. She looked down at her dowdy outfit. "For instance, this is the first wedding I've officially done with her and she waited until yesterday at three o'clock to tell me that I was not allowed to wear black. She said that black is her signature color and she didn't want me wearing it, too. But at the same time, she told me I had to wear a dark, neutral color to blend in and not take any emphasis away from the bride and her wedding party. All this would be fine, but I just graduated and right now all *I* have are black suits, too! So, I had to rush out and find something in the two hours I had free before the rehearsal dinner."

She pulled at her ill-fitting brown dress as if she couldn't wait to take it off. "Obviously I didn't find anything that flattered and there was no time to get it altered. And then I had to wear it again tonight because I didn't have a second outfit. Anyway, I guess I just feel like she deliberately waited to spring this detail on me just to be mean, and…well, I just don't know how long I can work for a person who does those kinds of things."

I couldn't blame her. (And she'd nailed her assessment of Kendra.) But unfortunately I also couldn't afford to hire anyone else at present and I had to tell her so. "And probably by the time I'm able to hire another assistant, you'll have too much experience to be one."

Darcy's shoulders sagged dejectedly and she looked like she was desperately trying not to tear up at the thought of having to continue working for Kendra Everitt.

"However," I said, "I might be able to give you a few leads on other jobs. My e-mail is on the Waterlane Events website. If you e-mail me on Monday and can wait a week or so for me to gather some information, I'll be happy to pass along your name to a few people. After that, it's up to you to do the impressing and then the hard work that comes with the job." She gushingly thanked me, promising that she wouldn't let me down, and I said, "The only thing I ask is that you not mention me or our talk to Kendra at all. And I mean *ever*. You just tell her that you found the leads on your own and I'll consider that your thank-you gesture, okay?"

She crossed her heart and shook both of our hands happily before bidding us good night and heading back into the Castlemaine ballroom.

"That was nice of you," Luke said.

"She's a nice girl," I replied. "And she deserves to have a boss who will show her a shred of respect. Besides, Rebecca's assistant here is pregnant and leaving permanently in two months. Rebecca will need a replacement and she seemed to get along with Darcy really well earlier. I'll have to talk to Rebecca first, but it might be good timing."

"Could be," Luke agreed.

"I wonder what she meant by business being slow," I mused. "I haven't heard any gossip through the grapevine and the other coordinators I know are all doing great..." I shrugged my shoulders in apathy even as I said it. The music coming out of the ballroom was peppy and I didn't want to think about Kendra a second more. "Hey, are you tired yet?" I asked.

He grinned slowly, putting his hands in his trouser pockets. "Nope."

"You want to go have a drink at the bar? Maybe get one jitterbug in before I turn into a pumpkin and have to call it a night?" I chose my words deliberately, so as not to insinuate that I wanted anything more than a little extra friendly time with him. It had been a great night and I was happy; happy and with Luke.

Happy *with* Luke. And I didn't really want the night to end. I smiled at him, holding my gaze steady to his without thinking. Luke was smiling widely back at me. He tilted his head toward the direction of the bar and angled his right elbow out for me to take his arm.

But as if to remind me that my emotions were seeping uncontrolled though my Inner Wall and that was not a good thing, I was just about to slip my hand in the crook of his arm when I felt my phone buzz from inside my purse. Still smiling, I took it out and found a text message.

From my boyfriend.

"Oh," I said. "It's a text...from McGregor."

I kept looking at my phone. I finally heard Luke say, "Anything exciting?"

"He just wants me to call and tell him how it all went." I laughed hollowly. "He says he drank too much coffee this afternoon so he's wired on caffeine and wide awake."

I looked up into Luke's eyes and neither of us spoke for a long moment. Finally, he stuck his hands back in his pockets and stated, "Well, then, I guess we'd better get out of here so that you can call him, right?"

"Okay... Right."

Rats.

Twenty-Four

To her credit, Hilary tried really hard not to smile when she said, "I can't believe McGregor's mother and her cobbler interrupted your attempt to have phone sex with him." Her jaw worked back and forth. "That is just… Just… Oh, hell, Shelb, that's freaking hilarious!"

Through my best friend's peals of laughter, so hard they shook my sofa, I poured myself a second frozen margarita from the blender pitcher on my coffee table and ruefully remembered the moment when, over cellular air waves and lots of heavy breathing, I clearly heard Mary Beth Elliston knock on McGregor's bedroom door at the Elliston's Montana cabin and call out, "McGregor, honey? I made a peach cobbler. Would you like some?"

"Freaking mortifying is more like it," I grumbled, sinking back into the cushions of my sofa to sip my drink. Though I was nearly fifteen hundred miles away, I'd scrambled along with McGregor to sit up and adjust my clothing. We were both so embarrassed afterward that our long-distance attempt at *l'amour* quickly ended, even though he tried to salvage some of the moment by reminding me how he was looking forward to taking me to the Houston Livestock Show and Rodeo gala.

Hilary grabbed her margarita glass and leaned back with me. "So when is he coming home?" she asked.

"Tomorrow." It was Thursday night, a week since Jackie's wedding, and I'd spent the last seven days in emotionally tortuous ride of highs and lows. While I talked to McGregor every night (putting me on an instant high), I kept feeling like something was holding him back from me (giving me a resulting low). And during the day? During the day I was tortured by Luke, who smiled at me, laughed with me and at me, and would have ravished me by now if he were free. Which he was not, of course. So every day I said silent thanks for my job, for it had kept me busy, and therefore giving those around me the impression that I still had a firm hold on my wits.

"You don't sound all that thrilled," Hilary said. "What gives?"

I licked some salt off the rim of my margarita glass. "I just feel like we keep going one step forward and two steps back, you know? I adore McGregor and I want to be with him, but all of this is wearing me out a little."

Hilary's voice was confident. "It's just because your relationship is new, Shelby, that's all. You're both still getting used to each other and a little bit of awkwardness is completely normal. Give it more time."

"I suppose you're right," I sighed and took a sip of my drink.

"Of course I am," Hilary grinned. "So, yesterday you told me you were thinking about getting a room for the two of you since the Rodeo gala is at the swanky new Hillmorton Hotel. What did you end up deciding?"

"I decided to do it," I replied with more moxie than I felt. "I've had enough of this waiting around crap. I'm going to end my moratorium with McGregor Elliston on Saturday night whether he likes it or not!" I raised my glass in salute to my determination.

"*Olé*, baby," Hilary replied, then slurped her margarita.

McGregor showed up on my doorstep on Saturday night looking dashing in a dark suit and carrying a bouquet of hot pink and bright yellow roses. His celadon tie matched perfectly with my form-hugging sleeveless dress and I told him so.

"Freddie helped me pick it out a few months ago," he told me. "You had shown me your dress and I realized it was the same color, so I decided to wear it for you." He looked so proud of himself and kissed me so passionately that I decided to ignore the feeling in my gut that always seemed to happen when he mentioned Frederique. Instead, I pinned one of the yellow roses behind my ear, grabbed my vintage Mark Cross evening bag that I'd stuffed with a ream of condoms for luck and we were off to the museum district and the Hillmorton Hotel.

When we arrived, the junior ballroom and its adjoining three-thousand-square-foot outdoor terrace were rocking. People were everywhere; McGregor and I kept running into so many friends and acquaintances that it took us a full half hour to make our way to the buffet line.

We were both all smiles. He held my hand the entire time we waited in line, squeezing my fingers at one point to get my attention and pointing outside to the artfully lit terrace where people were dancing, telling me that he wanted to boogie with me just as soon as we finished eating. I felt like I was walking on clouds until the couple who were in line ahead of us moved away and the girl standing in front of them happened to turn around.

With the exception of staring at her picture in McGregor's house, I hadn't seen her since high school, yet Frederique Olivera had scarcely changed. Still as beautiful and petite as ever, with her dark hair in a layered, shoulder-length cut, she was wearing a strapless dress the color of lapis lazuli that did wonders for her intensely blue eyes.

And boy, were those eyes stunned. Not because she didn't expect to see us there, of course, but rather I got the feeling that it shocked her to finally see McGregor and me together, looking like we were an actual couple.

Which, I gotta give myself props, we did. I'd caught our reflection in one of the hotel's huge mirrors and McGregor and I looked downright fantastic at each other's side.

But when she looked at us, our smiles, our hands linked in easiness, and how we were even color-coordinated with McGregor wearing the tie she had helped him pick out, her face looked like it would crumple at any moment. I also felt McGregor's hand go limp in mine, even though he didn't let go until I released it to return Freddie's hug. I felt very strange standing there as the new girlfriend of a former couple who were still the best of friends. But eventually we made it to the head of the buffet line and Frederique and one of her committee friends, introduced as Ashley, went on one side of the buffet while McGregor and I went on the other. Our side of the line moved faster and we were soon too far ahead to see Freddie clearly through the plexiglass sneeze guard. Not that I noticed McGregor looking. It was more that I could feel his eyes glancing back every few seconds.

By the time we got to the bar and ordered our drinks, that sinking feeling was firmly back in my gut. And it only got stronger when I saw my boyfriend, who I'd barely seen drink since we started dating, drain half of his vodka tonic before he even handed me my white wine.

It was a big clue, yes. But I still let it roll off my shoulders as we sat down at our table. I had figured that the first time we were in Frederique's presence things would be a little weird, so I couldn't say I was all that surprised at her reaction. But then I saw something that made me smile once more.

Leaving McGregor to start eating, I walked over to where Luke Treadwell was standing with a beer in his hand. "I didn't know you'd be here," I told him, thinking again how handsome he looked in his suit, this time with an apricot-colored tie sporting little green frogs, the occasional one springing up in a hop.

He gestured with his beer to a stocky guy in a cowboy hat standing a few feet from us at the bar. "My friend Trent and I are both on the Bar-B-Que Committee. His wife had to go out of town for work at the last minute and he'd already bought the tickets, so I'm his plus one for the evening."

"You're everybody's plus one it seems," I grinned. "You should start charging."

"Nah," he returned. "It's my way of giving to the needy."

I called him a bastard and he laughed. "But I didn't know you'd be here, either," he said, then he gave me his sideways look. "Did you mention it to me and I'm just not remembering?"

I hadn't. Ever since I'd decided that I was going to pounce on McGregor and end my moratorium, I'd found that I didn't want to talk about my love life with Luke, as if discussing my happiness with my boyfriend would tarnish the moments I had every day with my contractor who had become my friend. I realized, too, that as the office renovations were progressing, my days of having Luke near me every day were decreasing, and somehow that made me want to mention McGregor even less.

So, I changed the subject.

"You're looking very nice tonight, Treadwell. Just so you know."

"I was just thinking the same thing about you," he returned, giving me an appreciative once over.

Suddenly feeling hot down to my pink toenails, I glanced around the room as I said, "So how's Claudia? I haven't seen her since we shopped for Maggie's dress."

If Luke responded, I never knew for I had stopped listening. Instead I was focused on watching Frederique stare at McGregor from across the room.

I excused myself, distractedly telling Luke I would talk to him later, and went back to my boyfriend. Once I was back at his side, everything seemed normal for a while. McGregor was attentive to me as we ate dinner. We laughed and joked and he even gave me a kiss when I'd offered to go refresh his drink. But the joy that had been in him when he'd shown up at my door with an armful of roses was noticeably fading. I'd caught him several times looking around the room and I could sense that he was searching throngs of partygoers for any signs of a lapis-blue dress. I pretended not to notice, and pretended that I wasn't back to being hit over the head with more clues, too. I was determined to take it all in stride. I was going to do whatever I needed to make this a successful and complete night with McGregor, yessiree.

But I have to admit that I had to try especially hard to stay unfazed when, the one time I did look around the room, I saw Frederique and her friend Ashley being introduced to Luke, who was shaking Freddie's hand as if he was looking at the goddess of love herself in the flesh and couldn't believe his eyes. "Maybe he needs his own Inner Wall," I grumbled under my breath.

"Did you say something, Shelby?" McGregor asked me, his lips smiling but his eyes obviously not feeling the same emotion.

"No, nothing," I said hastily, tearing my own eyes away from Luke and Frederique, who were still talking as if they were the best of buds. McGregor seemed all too fine with not having to make further conversation as he drained his second vodka tonic.

I still wasn't not ready to give up quite yet, though. The band started up on a slow song and I pulled my handsome man to his feet. "Come on," I said. "You promised that we'd trip the light fantastic all night long and I'm holding you to it."

McGregor smiled and took my hand with a confidence I could see he didn't feel. But still we danced. And I felt myself melting against him like I'd wanted to do for years. We fit together nicely, it was true. So I ignored the two other clues that were being effectively lobbed at my head: One, the way McGregor would only briefly meet my eyes when I looked up at him and, two, the fact that I could sense the unhappiness in him. It was reverberating through his body, and my hands and my heart, both of which were holding McGregor close, could feel it.

My forced obliviousness did a good job for a while, though, as the eclectic band went into a series of fun country songs.

McGregor and I both grinned as we jitterbugged our way through the band's rendition of The Charlie Daniels' Band's "Drinkin' My Baby Goodbye," and he put his lips to my ear to tell me that I was a great dancer when Shenandoah's "Two Dozen Roses" moved us into an energetic two-step. But it was when the band slowed again, going into the distinctive waltz beat of George Strait's romantic "You Look So Good in Love," that I felt McGregor momentarily stop cold.

I turned my head to see where he was looking. It was as if the world was standing still, but not for me. McGregor was staring at Frederique, who was looking back at him with huge, stricken eyes at the edge of the dance floor. There was no jealousy in those eyes, no acting, just pure, deep hurt and longing. And I was pretty sure McGregor's were mirroring hers. Then she turned and rushed back though the crowd.

I felt McGregor take two deep, halting breaths and then he started to move me to the music again.

And I think it was his determination not to ruin another night for me that made me finally let all the clues rain down into a big river of truth.

The force that had been holding McGregor back from me was now confirmed. It had porcelain skin, a smattering of freckles, and those fantastically shocking blue eyes.

Not only was McGregor still in love with Frederique, which I pretty much knew from the start, but had hoped against hope like a fool that it truly had fizzled into nothing more than a lasting friendship, but seeing me with him had made Frederique finally realize that she was undoubtedly, full-on, crazy in love with McGregor.

I waited until the song ended and then I walked with my date back to our table. "I'm going to go to the ladies' room, okay?" I told him.

McGregor Elliston lifted his handsome face up to mine and smiled. "Sure. I'll be waiting right here." He gave my fingers a light squeeze for emphasis.

I nodded. He was a good man. He would have stayed. I turned on my heel and weaved my way through the crowd, giving a grim wave to Luke when I saw him looking at with a puzzled look on his face. I walked out and made a quick trip to the hotel's front desk before heading to the ladies' lounge, where, as I suspected I would, I found Frederique sobbing, her friend Ashley next to her on one of the two small sofas that occupied the carpeted lounge area just prior to entering the tiled bathroom portion.

Frederique's blonde friend looked up at me with conflicted eyes, not knowing whether to ask me for help or to bare her teeth at me.

I said, "Would you mind if I spoke to Frederique alone?"

Ashley got up and left us, saying to Freddie, "I'll come check on you in a bit, okay?"

I sat down and pulled out another tissue from the box for her. I went to speak. Instead, it was Freddie's teary voice that started first.

"I'm sorry," she said with a sniffle. "I didn't mean to do that. Interfere, I mean. I ho—hope that it didn't ruin your evening."

I held out the tissue for her and she took it, looking down at her lap and not at me. I felt like I was stepping off of a cliff, but I did it anyway. "You figured out just now how much you love him tonight, didn't you?"

Even her reddened nose and gaped mouth didn't diminish how beautiful she was as she raised her stunned eyes to me. The look in those blue, blue eyes said it all.

Yes.

With a hiccup, she then stunned me by saying, "McGregor told me that you tuned into things before other people did. I never knew that about you. I never knew it, but I was jealous that he'd said it all the same. He really likes you, Shelby."

"Yes, he does," I said simply, for it was the truth.

Well, yeah, that started the tears up again but good. She was a blubbering mess in seconds.

It was just what I wanted.

I got up from the couch and held out my hand to her. "Come with me," I said.

"Why?" she asked thickly as she wiped her nose with one hand. The other reached up and took my outstretched hand.

"You might have heard that I used to work at a hotel," I told her and she nodded, a fat tear sliding down her pretty face. "Well, some hotels keep an emergency room for situations just like this, when someone has a," I smiled at her so that she knew I wasn't being cruel, "bit of a meltdown and need a place to recover and touch up without being stared at like a sideshow. It's a little-known secret, but I thought you might need it right now, so I used my connections and got the room for you."

It was well-meant truth-stretching, but I couldn't exactly tell her I had reserved the room myself in hopes of pouncing on McGregor like a deranged sex fiend, could I?

"You did?" The way she looked at me made me realized that Frederique Olivera, for all her beauty, was just a little girl on the inside who had experienced, as McGregor had told me, all too little unconditional love.

"Yep," I said. "And you can stay there as long as you want. I'll send Ashley up to be with you as soon as I can find her." And then I led Freddie out the ladies' to the elevators and then to room 518. Swiping the plastic card key in and out of the slot, the lights turned green, and I opened up the door, revealing a small sitting room in plush shades of cranberry that also sported a wet bar and a television and, next to it, the bedroom and bathroom. The room was fresh, beautiful, quiet as a tomb, and also calming. Just what Frederique needed. I grabbed out one of the bottles of water from a small basket of complimentary goodies on the bar, unscrewed the cap, and handed it to her. "Here, have some water and sit down. I'll be back with your friend in just a couple of minutes."

I went to the door, but turned back around as I heard her say, "Shelby."

"Yes?"

"You didn't have to do this for me. Thank you. I promise you I won't get in your and McGregor's way."

I smiled. "I appreciate you saying that." I then paused and said without heat, "I honestly don't know why you never allowed yourself to trust him, Freddie," calling her by her nickname even though she hadn't formally asked me to. "I don't think I've ever met someone who's as faithful and loyal and deserving of your trust—of any woman's trust—than McGregor. He is truly a very good man and I've never met anyone else like him."

Except Luke, was the unbidden thought that popped into my head. Shaking my head sadly and slipping out the room before she could reply, I still couldn't miss the strangled sob emanating from Frederique before the door finished closing.

Back downstairs, I aimed in the path of where I could see McGregor still sitting at our table, looking thoroughly miserable, starting on his third vodka tonic. Before I could get there, though, Luke caught up to me and took my elbow.

Even though we were a good thirty feet away from where my date sat, unaware I was even approaching, Luke still spoke in an undertone. "Is everything okay, Shelby?"

I looked innocently up at him, "Yes, of course it is. What would make you say that?"

Luke rushed a hand though his hair, making pieces of it stick out at odd angles. His tone was frustrated now. "I was just over there talking to your boyfriend...," he said. Then he paused, and he flung his hand up for emphasis. "Do you not see it, Shelby? Are you that blind?"

I crossed my arms over my chest and eyed him coldly. "See what, Luke? To what exactly are you referring?"

His expression was pained and pleading at the same time, as if he was silently begging me not to make him say it. I squared my shoulders in defense and said, "Just say whatever's on your mind, Luke. You obviously have something important to tell me."

"Oh, for God's sake, Shelby," he exhorted, but said nothing else. Seizing the moment, I changed the subject, gesturing with my head to a point behind him. "There's a man passing behind you with a tray of champagne. Would you please grab me two glasses while I go get McGregor and my purse?"

Luke turned his head to see the waiter and then looked back suspiciously at me. "Why?"

I batted my eyes and said airily, "Because I have a room waiting upstairs and I don't want to waste another second."

Luke looked like I'd just rinsed his mouth out with acid-laced soap. He said with deadly calm, "I really don't want to be the one to help you take that guy to bed, Shelby."

My hackles rose a bit with his tone, but I stopped them dead. Reaching out to him, I put my hands on either side of his arms (and couldn't miss the hardness of his muscles, by golly), "Do you trust me?" I asked him, looking up into his face.

"Yes," he said quickly, his face fierce with intensity. "Absolutely and explicitly."

I smiled again, this time easily as my heart soared with his words. "Then trust me now." I said. "You won't be sorry." And, when his face registered some acceptance along with the confusion and frustration, I turned him and said, "Now, please, go get me those glasses of champagne."

He looked unhappy, but he went and got me the glasses all the same as I went over to McGregor and pulled him to his feet with a playful smile. "Come on," I said to my longtime crush, "I want to take you upstairs."

I nearly laughed as McGregor's face took on that of a cornered puppy who knew he was going to the vet. I pretended not to notice as gave him a quick but sultry kiss and whispered, "Come on," again into his ear, using my teeth to ever so gently bite his earlobe. "I've waited long enough, McGregor Elliston."

I could see that he wanted to talk me out of it, but I happily pulled him to his feet and grabbed my evening bag, slinging its short strap over my shoulder. Luke appeared, glowering and looking surly even as he held two dainty glasses of champagne. I thanked him with a sassy grin and took the glasses, handing one to a stunned-into-submission McGregor. Luke turned on his heel and stalked away disgustedly without saying a word, making me want to laugh even more.

And men say that us women are dramatic? Ha!

I pulled on McGregor and led him through the throng of people toward the bank of elevators. As if it knew we were coming, one of the elevators was already waiting and, giggling like it was I who'd been chugging vodka tonics, I pulled him into the car and punched the number five button. I turned and handed him my other glass of champagne so that he was holding one glass with each hand while I began digging in my handbag.

"Shelby…," he finally said, a note of pleading in his voice, holding the glasses of bubbly up and out to each side of him to keep them safe from spilling. He looked like a well-dressed, champagne-swilling refugee from the sex police who had been caught and was now surrendering unhappily to his fate, and it tickled me to no end.

"Shush," I commanded him as I pulled on his tie to bring his mouth down onto mine. I wrapped my arms slowly and sensually around his waist, feeling him suck his stomach in a fraction in one of the most basic of sexual responses. (At least I still had *some* feminine wiles, no?) "Mmmmm…," I said softly when I pulled away, my eyes closed as if in a blissful moment, "That's so nice." I turned around to face the elevator doors so that I wouldn't have to see how uncomfortable he looked, but I allowed myself to lean up against him just one more time before the elevator pinged, signaling that we'd reached our floor.

Taking a discreet deep breath, I opened my eyes and set them with purpose toward the hallway that would take us to room 518.

And then I led McGregor to his destiny.

Stopping at the door, I finally turned around to look my former crush in the face. He was valiantly trying to hide the fact that he didn't want to be there with me and I found it endearing. I smiled. "McGregor, I have a present for you. *Just* for you."

Watching his handsome face, I saw his brow knit and his pretty caramel eyes show confusion. He was still holding the glasses of champagne. "I—what do you mean?"

I had tucked the key card for room 518 into my dress, right above my left breast. I pulled it out with a grin and handed it to him. "Open the door and you'll see."

It took McGregor a whole two seconds of obvious contemplation before he finally bent down to put the glasses of champagne on the floor and then reached out to take the card from me. His desire to balk was absolutely palpable, but his commitment to me was keeping him still. He searched my face continually the whole time, as if watching for that moment when I would say, "Is something wrong, McGregor? Do you not want to do this?"

But I didn't do anything more than smile sweetly at him, and so he eventually swiped the card in the electronic lock and turned the handle when the lights glowed green.

And when he pushed open the doorway, revealing a quivering, wide-eyed, and hopeful Frederique standing before him, I turned and walked away. And a smile came easily to my lips as I heard Freddie's choked-up scream of delight, McGregor's happy, "Freddie!" and a noise that suggested that Freddie had leapt directly into the arms of the man she loved more than anything in the world.

At the hallway before the bank of elevators, I heard McGregor call out, "Shelby!"

I turned around to see two happy people entwined in each other's arms, the happiness glowing from both of their faces. I just winked at them and said, "Check your pockets. There's another little gift from me in there."

With a grin, he felt his pockets and, from the right one, came up with a ream of three condoms. Freddie giggled, her hand over her mouth, and looked at me with thrilled surprise. She then buried her face blissfully in McGregor's strong chest. I didn't know why I thought it, but I could tell from her face that she loved the way he smelled, too. I looked once more into his warm brown eyes and handsome face as he wrapped his arms around the woman he'd loved for so long. "Thank you," he mouthed silently, gratefully to me.

I quickly blew him a kiss and turned the corner into the bank of elevators. Once again, one was waiting open for me and I stepped into it. The last thing I heard before the doors closed was the sound of two happy people giggling in a way that said that they were going to have some really great sex.

A few seconds later (and thoroughly exhausted from voluntarily giving up a good man to another woman, I might add), I was back down in the hotel lobby, stopping Ashley just as she was dialing Freddie on her cell, and told her the news.

"I've never heard of anyone actually doing something like that," Ashley told me, her eyes half impressed and half disbelieving.

I shrugged, not really wanting to discuss it. "Just do me one favor, okay? If Freddie ever questions McGregor's love again, remind her that she got lucky once, but no other sane woman would ever let that boy go again, so she needs to hold on tight this time."

Ashley nodded thoughtfully. "I'll do that. It was nice to meet you, Shelby."

I told her likewise and, eyes beginning to droop, I dragged myself out to the cab stand outside of the hotel.

As exhausted both emotionally and physically as I was, I did feel a shred better when, as my cab was pulling out of the hotel driveway, I caught a glimpse of Luke rushing out the front doors looking for me, his tie flying and his suit jacket flapping open with how fast he was moving. At the last possible second, he saw me smiling tiredly through the cab's window at him. He held up a hand—did I detect relief in his face that I was leaving, unravished by the hands of McGregor Elliston?—and I waved goodbye back to him in return.

And twenty minutes later I had to be woken up by the cabbie when he pulled up to my house. I'd fallen dead asleep seemingly a moment after waving to Luke.

No doubt, trying your best to get a relationship off the ground when fate just won't have any of it is tiring stuff. It's definitely not for the weak-hearted, that's for sure.

And it is most definitely on my Things That Suck list.

Twenty-Five

Appointments on Monday kept me out of the office until nearly quitting time. Walking in wearing my power outfit and my shoulders squared, I summoned the Dating Brigade in after me almost immediately. And as an afterthought when I saw Luke coming out of one of the offices with a broom in hand, I called out, "You. Treadwell. Get your hindquarters in here, please." I pointed into the realm of my office for emphasis. Shockingly, Luke did as he was asked (okay, ordered) without any more comment than a curious face.

When the four of them were standing at my desk—Lauren with wide eyes, Emily with one hand defiantly on her hip, and Bryan and Luke looking at each other and shrugging—I went around to the other side and sat down in my chair, leaning back a bit, and steepling my fingers together as I surveyed them with narrowed eyes.

"Don't you need a white cat to stroke when you do that?" Luke asked me, making my three employees start sniggering. But when I gave him a withering look, he held up his hands in surrender, pretended to lock his lips with a key, and said, "Gotcha. Shutting up now."

Finally, I said. "I've asked you three to come in here—along with you, Luke, because you've been either willingly or unwillingly sucked into the gang—to make an announcement."

"This ought to be good," Emily wisecracked. Because I knew my lovely Emily would only glare back at me if I tried to take her down a notch, I opted just to ignore it.

"As all of you are now aware, courtesy of Bryan calling the two of you yesterday with the news," I used my first two fingers to point at Emily and Lauren, "and because you," I pointed at Luke, "were there to witness it—" I grimaced a bit, "more or less…McGregor and I are no longer dating. Now, this may be where one or more of you start getting that scary little gleam in your eye that says you've been eyeing some guy with whom to torture me with by the means of another blind date, but I am here to put a stop to it right now."

I stood up, placing my hands flat on my desk and leaning forward with what I hoped was a hard look on my face. "There will be no more setting me up on dates. No more. None. Nada. I'm done." I pointed at my chest, "If *I* happen to meet a guy who I would like to go out with, I will handle the situation myself. Because I *can* handle it myself, see? I'm a big girl and I can get dates when and if I want them." I waved my right arm wildly and dramatically up in the air, my voice getting louder, "Are we freaking, absolutely crystal clear on this point, people?" And, before they could even answer, I said even more loudly, pointing back to myself with my thumbs, "Well, we'd better be, because otherwise y'all are going to see this chick open up a big ol' can of whup-ass on each and every one of you. Got it?" I finished by pointing once more at each of them in turn.

Yeah, I should have known that saying something like that last positively ridiculous bit wouldn't get me very far in the Taken Seriously department. I should have stopped when I was ahead. Especially when all four of them had been forced to cover their mouths with their hands in order to not bust out laughing in my face.

Emily, of course, spoke first, her hand back on her hip. "And is 'whup-ass' the term you used with your mother when you warned her off, too, Shelb?"

I crossed my arms over my chest. "I did discuss this point with my mother already, yes. And she and my aunt both are now once and for all aware that this effort to set me up with each and every single guy who comes within arm's length of them has come to an end."

I didn't mention that this so-called telling off of Franzilla had begun with a short but intense screaming match between my mother and me when she'd heard—from a thrilled-for-her-son-and-grateful-to-me Mary Beth Elliston—that I'd handed over McGregor to Frederique Olivera (on a condom-laced silver platter, no less). In fact, "What the hell were you thinking, Shelby? Have you lost your mind?" were her exact words that began the phone call and precipitated said screaming match. Basically, it really had just showed how much she'd temporarily lost her senses when it came to the idea of marrying me off and getting to brag to all her friends about it. Not to mention family, random acquaintances, and anybody off the street who would actually listen.

But my mother finally stopped and began listening when I'd broken down in tears, crying out, "Why, Mom? Why can't you just understand that you can't force love to happen between two people and that I'm really okay with being single until I do meet that right man? I promise you that I want to meet that right guy and get married, but trying to force it to happen will never make me happy!" I think she also realized how crazy she had sounded, too, which is never a bad thing.

In the end, she apologized to me from the heart, promised me that she would back off (and then laughed when I growled, "Mommm...," and promised she'd make Aunt Prilly back off, too), and then we talked for a long time about how finding the right person was the most important thing because of all the trials and tribulations that a couple, no matter how compatible they are, will eventually go though in life. The conversation ended with the both of us laughing hysterically as she told me some of the stupid things my father did that drove her crazy and we both agreed that he was a big, sixty-one-year-old baby who'd never be able to function if it weren't for the good women in his life. In all, it turned out to be a fruitful conversation that reminded me how grateful I was for both of my parents, for they and their relationship they had together had set a very high standard for me. A love like theirs was what I wanted, and what I had yet to find.

But, damn it, *I* was going to find it. Me. Moi. Yours truly. Nobody else.

"So," I said, keeping my beady stare going to each of the bright-eyed ruffians standing before me. "Are you four going to be good and stop setting me up?"

Luke was first to answer. "No problem on my end. I was just an innocent bystander for all of it anyway." He grinned and spun the broom he was still holding around on the end of its handle.

"Traitor," Bryan said to him out of the side of his mouth. But when I glared at him, Bryan hastily said, "Okay, I give. No more setting you up, sugar. I promise."

"Swear on your chocolate-chip cookie recipe," I demanded.

Bryan looked scandalized for a moment, but he finally said it with high drama, holding his right hand up as if swearing in court. "Fine. I swear on my award-winning cookies that I will not set you up again," he paused, and then said, "unless you ask first."

I gave him a sour look, but I then turned to the female members (biologically, at least) of the Dating Brigade. Raising my eyebrows, I said, "And...?"

"Sure, Shelby," said Lauren, nodding earnestly, ever the person I could trust to be sweet and compliant when the chips were down. "In fact, I was surprised it took this long for you to blow."

"Thanks a lot," I grumbled.

"Oh, okay. Fine. I give up, too," Emily exhorted suddenly, looking like it was akin to major torture to her to even say the words. "No more fixing you up, Shelby. I won't set you up even if I meet the cutest guy in the world and he is so perfect for you that the entire world knows it and is shouting it from the rooftops. I won't do it. No way, no how." And then she added, "Not *even* if you ask."

"Fabulous. Thank you," I said. Sitting back down in my chair, more relieved than I realized I would be, I said, "Besides, Maggie's wedding is coming up in five weeks and, it being the biggest wedding I've done all year, I wouldn't have time to go on a date with a guy if I wanted to." I smiled in Luke's direction, "And I want to devote my entire concentration to making it as incredible as Maggie wants it to be. She deserves it to be the fairy tale she's always wanted, just like every bride does."

Luke's dimpled grin came out like the sunshine. Stepping forward with his broom, he said, "While you're all here, I wanted to let you know that we're in the final stretch of the remodeling. The painting should start next week and, all things staying on course, you should be in your new offices by the last Friday in August."

The cheers were deafening. Lauren and Emily grabbed Luke into a hug, kissing his cheeks enthusiastically, and Bryan called out, "A happy hour at Lawson's to celebrate! Luke, put up that broom and dust off those boots. Girls, grab your handbags and let's go!"

I could tell that Luke had something that he either wanted to ask me or say to me, by the way he shifted around on his feet and fiddled with the broom, but didn't move. I told Bryan, "We'll be there in a few. Save us some seats, okay?"

"No problemo, sugar," Bryan called back. Lauren and Emily were already walking out the door, talking excitedly about getting their boyfriends to help them move in the furniture they'd ordered for their respective offices. Within moments, I was alone with Luke and the only sounds came from his men, who were sweeping up across the hall.

I said, "Why don't you let your guys go home and then come back in here, where you're welcome to ask me or tell me whatever it is you'd like."

He looked surprised, and then not-so surprised. "When did you learn to read me so well?"

I pretended to stroke a nonexistent white cat in my arms and looked smugly evil, "It's a gift from God, Treadwell, and you should fear it."

Shaking his head in amused despair, Luke saluted me with the broom handle and walked out the door to let his men go home. He was back in under five minutes, minus the broom, and sat in the leather barrel chair opposite my desk. And, it being a long, sucky past couple of days and all, I ducked down under my desk.

"Um, Shelby…? What are you doing?"

I popped back up with my bottle of Wild Turkey and two rocks glasses. "You drink bourbon, cowboy?"

"Are you kidding me? You actually have a bottle of Wild Turkey hidden under your desk?"

"Sure," I replied, setting down the glasses and pulling out the bottle's cork with a soft *pop*. "Doesn't everybody?"

Luke watched me pour a scant finger of the amber liquid in each glass and his grin grew wider. Taking his glass when I pushed it toward him with my own, he picked it up, we clinked glasses, and he said, "Well, hell, if people don't, then they should."

"Damn straight, my friend." I said. "Bottom's up."

His eyes practically bugged out. "Seriously?"

I snorted. "What are you, a big ol' titty baby? I said drink, pal." I threw back the shot of whiskey like I did it every day.

And then coughed and gagged until tears ran down my face in little rivulets. Which, of course, made my buddy Luke, who was obviously a lot better at whiskey shooting than yours truly, laugh like a long and lanky hyena until he nearly fell out of his chair.

"God, I love you, Shelby," he gasped out, his face red from laughter.

Well, you'd think that Luke saying this would freak me out with ridiculous hope or something, but I took it in stride, figuring he meant it in the same way I'd say the same thing to any of my beloved employees. Besides, he was in love with Claudia. To my knowledge, that hadn't changed a shred.

"Yeah, yeah," I croaked, my throat still seared from the Wild Turkey, "That's what they all say."

Luke had taken in a sharp breath and had looked down at the glass in his hand, his face still red. I took that in stride, too.

"So," I rasped, "I'm guessing you'd like to know what really happened Saturday night, huh?"

Glancing up at me, where I was dabbing my eyes with a tissue and pouring myself another half finger of whiskey anyway, he held out his glass for another as well and said, "Actually, I just wanted to tell you that I figured out what you were doing about thirty seconds after I gave you that champagne."

"You did?"

"Yeah… You weren't blind about him, were you? You knew he'd been in love with that dark-haired girl the whole time. And you took him up to that room because she was already there, didn't you? You got them back together."

I cocked an eyebrow with a distasteful look. "Let's not rub it in, shall we?"

Luke sat back in his chair regarding me. Nodding, he then said, "You did good, Waterlane."

My eyebrow went up again, but this time in amusement. "And you were worried about my virtue, weren't you, Treadwell?

Luke threw back his second shot of whiskey like a pro and then scoffed, "Nah."

"Oh, no?"

Getting up he leaned his long body over my desk and said in a low, gravely voice, "Nope. Your virtue was obviously lost a long time ago, Waterlane. I was just trying to watch out for the best interests of my client." And then he had the audacity to reach out and touch my nose with the tip of his finger.

"Hey!" I said indignantly as he straightened up. "My virtue is still front and center and in perfectly good working order, thank you very much."

"Oh, absolutely," he nodded, grinning as if talking to an asylum escapee. "Of course it is." Then he proved even more infuriating by changing the subject. "The Thursday before we finish the offices is Mag's bachelorette party—you going?"

I batted my eyes all uppity-like, "We're calling it a 'hen party,' Luke. 'Bachelorette party' is so passé."

"Ah, yes. I stand corrected." He affected a British accent, "A *hen* party, of course. Will you be attending?"

"Well, I can't make it to the Lake Austin Spa with them that weekend, but I am going to the dinner and, ah, festivities on Thursday. In fact," I said, inspecting my fingernails as if bored, "I need to make sure to get myself a whole heapin' wad of singles," I looked up at him, "You know, for the boys' G-strings and all. It's important to tip them well."

Yeah, that got him back. Luke was your typical male. He couldn't take females talking about salivating over oily, cheesy, well-muscled men gyrating around in gold lamé banana hammocks. He made a face like he'd just been force-fed a handful of maggots. "Please, spare me the explanations. The idea of it makes my skin crawl."

"Good," I shot back, trying to look mean and failing. There was a moment where we were both there smiling at each other, and then I said, "C'mon. Let's go to Lawson's and finish getting plowed. I think we deserve it."

This time, when Luke offered me his arm, I took it without another thought. And I decided the Wild Turkey was the reason my Inner Wall didn't go up like it should have.

Well, come on, something had to be to blame, right?

Twenty-Six

I dressed in a slinky navy blue cashmere tank top, white straight-leg trousers, and my Jimmy Choo strappy sandals. Fluffing up my freshly highlighted hair and adding some big gold hoops in my ears, I grabbed my handbag and headed out to Leonora's Tex-Mex Cantina to meet Maggie and fourteen of her best girlfriends for the first leg of her four-day hen party.

On my way there, I called Luke's cell. I had given him my spare office key when he asked if he might stay late to finish making a few tweaks before the furniture was moved in. "Are you sure you don't need anything?" I asked him.

"I'm good, but thanks for asking," he said. "I'm hoping to be finished by eight or so." I told him to feel free to utilize the little portable television in my office to watch the Astros game while he tweaked, and he told me that I was his best client ever and to have fun "doing all that chick stuff."

A night of unbridled chick stuff was just what I'd decided I needed, actually. Even better, Claudia wasn't able to make the dinner portion, so thankfully I didn't have to listen to how she and Luke were so in love and how he was the greatest guy in the world both in and out of bed—sex and men being the topics *du jour* around our table for fifteen of randy, margarita-laced girls, naturally.

After dinner, as we were waiting in the parking lot for our party bus to come and take us to Steele, the cheesiest male strip club the maid of honor could come up with, I had just finished entertaining the girls with the story of Knuckles McCafferty when my cell phone rang. Moving a few steps away, I answered my phone as I watched one of Maggie's friends pull out a cheap bridal veil adorned with brightly colored condom packages and place it on Maggie's head. I saw my client's horrified expression just as I heard one of my other client's voices in my ear.

Candace Mapleton sounded like she was inches from screaming. It seemed that Diego, her really sweet but often absentminded fiancé, had accidentally shredded her finalized seating chart with some other papers, and she was desperate to get a copy of it.

"I've got to make sure that Diego's cousin Tessa is sitting in the equivalent of the boonies and not anywhere near my Uncle Jay and Aunt Stella, who doesn't yet know her husband was seconds away from screwing the little piece of trash when I walked in on them last night during our couples shower," Candace told me before I heard her turn to shout at Diego. "And *'She was just showing Jay how to salsa,'* my ass! They were in my aunt's walk-in closet and Tessa was naked and wearing one of Stella's favorite furs! So how do you say 'thieving, home-wrecking slut' in Spanish, Diego? Because that's what she is!"

"All right. Let's take a breath, Candace," I said in a calming tone. As it was my standard practice to have my clients give me copies of every possible document they created for their nuptials, I had a copy of the seating chart in her file at work. "I can scan your chart and send it to you first thing tomorrow," I told her as I saw Maggie becoming more and more stressed out while her tipsy girlfriends attached the condom-infested veil to her head.

But when Candace went into hysterics and started screeching at Diego again, I said, "Candace, I'll get it to you within the hour. Just sit tight and calm down, okay?" Then I practically hung up on her as I rushed to Maggie's side. All the girls had loaded the party bus, except Maggie. She had turned away, one hand up to cover her face as the other reached back, shaking, to the condoms in her veil. There were tears forming in her huge hazel eyes.

Needless to say, I wasn't very surprised. There is always a breaking point with every bride—and it's usually something stupid; something that they would probably laugh at normally—that makes them dissolve into a heap of nerves and tears. While Maggie had borne every inch of her wedding preparations thus far with good humor and aplomb, not to mention making moving arrangements to London at the same time, she finally lost it when the humiliation of having to wear a bridal veil decorated with condoms sent her over the edge. Going to a male strip club was, to her, a silly rite of passage, but a condom-laden veil was very clearly over-the-top tacky and hideously ugly in her book. It was simply too much and all the stresses that were on her shoulders of planning a huge wedding in five months were finally coming to the surface.

I was there in an instant, hugging her and saying softly, "It's okay, sweetie. Don't worry, I'll take them right out."

Using my little scissors I always kept in my purse, I began wedging out the staples that held the condoms in place. Each one that I extracted from the veil's cheap white mesh was dropped into my purse for lack of anywhere better to put it. In less than a minute, they were all out and I was handing Maggie a tissue and making her laugh, telling her about Candace and her seating-chart histrionics and other stories I had of other brides who'd fallen apart at much sillier things, such as the one who went into floods of tears after a valet parking attendant had adjusted her car's rearview mirror, and another one who sat down in the middle of a restaurant and started bawling because another diner was nice enough to stop her and tell her how beautiful she looked. By the time Maggie had applied a new coat of lipstick and powdered her nose, she was relaxing again and looking ready to get into the bus and join her friends.

"Thanks, Shelby," she said, fingering her now condom-free veil and grinning shyly with relief. "I don't know what I'd do without you."

I waved off her thanks, saying, "Honey, you are one of the few who would have been just fine without me. You're tough as nails and don't you forget it."

Her grin widened, "And stubborn as a mule, too, or so says Luke."

Feeling a touch nostalgic since I'd just then realized that all too soon I would no longer be in the company of either Luke or Maggie Treadwell and I knew I would have lost something good in my life because of it, I said, "The more I know you, the more you look like your brother, you know? Especially when you smile like that. You've got a dimple in your right cheek, too."

Maggie giggled. "John has one, too. We get it from Mom," she told me proudly. "Mom is always telling us that we look like her little clones when we're all standing next to her and smiling in a picture. Dad's the only one in the family without any dimples."

"And is your mother where you and your brothers get your stubbornness from, too?"

"Oh, no," Maggie said, her pretty eyes now dancing with humor. "That trait *definitely* came from Dad. He's absolutely terrible!"

Putting my hand on her arm, I said, "Honey, I don't know about John, but that other brother of yours is just as bad. The apple obviously didn't fall far from the tree."

Maggie turned and said something, pointing at me for emphasis, but her response was drowned out by the revving of the bus' engine and the music her friends had started playing. Still, as I waved goodbye, I could see that she was laughing and at ease once more, and so I didn't bother to ask her to repeat what she said. It didn't matter so long as she was having fun.

I walked into the Waterlane Events office to the sounds of cheering baseball crowds coming from the television in what was about to be Emily's office. Luke had been shooing us away from the renovations all week, saying that he wanted the end result to be a big surprise. Feeling sneaky, though, I peeked around the doorway and said over the din, "Did someone score?"

"Jee-sus!" Luke yelled, jumping backward from where he was touching up the paint on a part of the built-in shelving. He reached over to turn down the volume on the television, which was perched on one of two folding chairs that was in the room. He had changed from his standard chinos and oxford to an old red polo with a wide navy stripe across the chest and a pair of sexy skinny-legs–bearing khaki shorts.

I had every intention of pointing at him and laughing (hey, it's what I do), but the sight of the completed renovations got to me first. I stepped inside, put down the clear plastic to-go box containing a two pieces of *tres leches* cake I'd purchased from Leonora's before heading to the office, and put my hands up to my face much like Maggie had earlier. But my gesture was one of pure joy.

"Luke, I love it!" I exclaimed, taking in the shelving on both side walls that was painted white with just the merest of peach undertones. A huge, cedar-lined closet that could hold a big, poofy ball-gown wedding dress, was angled into the corner. The windows at the back of the room—Emily and Lauren both had one while Bryan had the windows that looked out over the front yard so that he could see clients coming up the walkway—were framed with plantation shutters. Recessed lighting made the office glow and the wood floors, which were mostly covered with drop cloths for protection, gleamed from applications of stain and sealant.

The doors Luke and I had chosen on the day we'd had burgers together were just right, too. The wooden portion of the office door, which had a large single pane of hammered glass in the middle for an accessible look, matched the floors and the overall look was both professional and stunning. I went into the room, standing where Emily would put a seating area much like my own for talks with her clients and whirled around saying, "Oh, Luke, it's absolutely gorgeous!"

Recovered from my sneak attack, his grin split his face in two before he closed his eyes and began fanning his face.

"You're wafting, aren't you?" I said.

"Am I doing it right?" he asked.

"Do you feel happy and peaceful at the same time?"

"Definitely."

"Then you're doing it right," I laughed.

"You look great, by the way," he said. "But why aren't you still at Maggie's hen party?"

I picked up the box with the *tres leches* and handed him one of the plastic forks they'd given me, grinning toothily. "Thanks. One of my other brides had some drama that I could only fix here. Here, you look like you need a break from all that wafting. Enjoy yourself while I go send Candace her seating chart."

"Do you want any of this?" he asked me as I walked out.

"What are you, nuts? Of course I want some," I replied. Then went back into exultation mode at finding that Luke had installed my new door as well. It was inviting without being too see-through, just as I'd hoped. I turned back to find Luke was standing in Emily's doorway, wafting while he savored his dessert.

Once Candace had confirmed receipt of her seating chart, I walked back into Emily's office a few minutes later to find Luke sitting on one of the folding chairs with his feet up on the other, finishing off his slice of cake. Using my knees to bump off his feet from the chair, I pulled it closer to him (and his cute legs, that I had to make myself not look at, don't you know), and we began sharing the second piece.

"So are you going to go back to the party?" he asked me.

"I might," I shrugged. Now that I was sitting with Luke, I was feeling ridiculously selfish at that moment to have a moment alone with him, even if it was only a platonic moment. Part of me felt like I was going to be losing Luke to Claudia very soon and so, since our office renovations would be done as of the next day, this would probably be one of the last times I got to speak with him without anyone else around. Even though we were talking about nothing. Even though we'd never be anything but friends. Even though...

I realized that I had been staring at him, taking in every inch of his face, and he was staring at me, too. The office, with the two of us sitting just inches from each other, was suddenly so quiet I could hear my heart beat. Electricity of the lustful variety was slowly, heatedly filling the air, too. Still, I couldn't look away. Didn't want to look away.

I watched emotions roll over his face. The pupils in his blue eyes were dilating. I drew in a shaky breath.

He sat forward and spoke, his voice was low and husky.

"Shelby."

It must have been the rarely used Emergency Alarm on my Inner Wall that woke me up. I stood up, knocking my chair over with a clatter. "I should go," I whispered.

Luke reached out with both hands and covered mine with his own. The tips of his fingers were on the backs of my wrists and he gently closed down and pulled me forward. I felt the slightest bit of stickiness from his palms and my mind lit up with the notion: He was nervous.

"Shelby," he said again and I could feel my own palms starting to perspire, "I've been trying and trying to rein this in, because I didn't—I couldn't tell for sure if you felt the same way I did. But I feel like I've got to take the chance while I have it."

"Luke, please," I said, feeling a little desperate as I didn't know which way to turn.

He pulled on my wrists again, gently but firmly, and I took a step forward. He stopped pulling and spoke.

"I've never understood it," he said in a gravelly voice, "when somebody said that they would die or go crazy or whatever if they didn't kiss somebody. I always felt like that was the most ridiculous thing I'd ever heard. But I know what they're talking about now, Shelby. I've wanted to kiss you for so long. And if I don't kiss you now…"

And my Inner Wall came crashing down.

He pulled once more and brought his knees together in one smooth action so that when I came forward I could straddle him. My arms went limp as he took my face into his hands and looked deeply into my eyes for a long moment.

And I assure you, the look that he was searching for was right there in my face.

I guess I expected a hard, rough lip lock like you see in the movies. After all, I'd been in lots of kissing situations before, but never in this particular situation. Instead, though, he brought his mouth to mine in a long, slow, intense, emotion-filled kiss.

That kiss told me that, at long last, I was finally kissing the Right One. It filled me with a deliciously hard shiver in my body. And, with my hands now on his chest, with his heart ramming against his rib cage, I could guess that he was probably feeling the same.

Oh, blessed day. I mean night. Heck, it didn't matter—oh, blessed everything!

It took a while, but eventually, in between what felt like the twenty-eighth and twenty-ninth long, sexy kiss, I managed to find the brain cells to say, "Claudia…"

He instantly leaned back just enough to look me in the eyes. He looked like he couldn't wait to get it out of his system. "Shelby, I'm not dating Claudia."

It was the words I'd longed to hear, but never thought I'd hear, and I was filled with an even more intense, not to mention astounded, happiness that made for a huge, thrilled smile. "You…you aren't?"

Ladies and gentlemen, please excuse us while we pause for another few minutes of ecstatic kissing…

Coming up for air again, I repeated, shaking my head side to side in incredulous hope, "You really aren't?"

"No," he said, grinning. And then his expression went serious. "I'm not dating anyone, Shelby. I'm completely and totally free. You can ask my friends, my family, anyone. In fact, I *haven't*—"

Suddenly feeling like I'd been fasting for years on end and then been told I could go eat a fully loaded pizza, I grabbed the collar of his shirt with both hands and yanked him toward me, ending anything else that he could have told me at that point. The next second I could, I pulled the polo he was wearing up over his head and felt like I might go a little crazy when he angled in and ran warm kisses up my entire neck.

And multiply that thought by five when he pulled my cashmere tank top off of me, popped open my bra strap with one quick movement (with a boyish grin, no less), and my skin touched his for the first time as we came back together in barely contained anticipation.

Let us just say that Emily's office got christened that night. As did the pull-out bed in my toile sofa that I'd used on occasion when I had to work into the night. And those condoms of Maggie's that I had stuffed into my purse after detaching them from her bachelorette bridal veil? Yeah, those sure came in handy, too.

And when we finally crashed for the night, me snuggling in his arms as he sleepily murmured romantic things in my ear, I finally bid a happy adieu to my dating moratorium.

Twenty-Seven

"What time will the gang be starting to come in with their furniture?" Luke asked as he nibbled on my neck.

"Eiff-furty," I replied. The watch on Luke's wrist read seven forty-two.

He took a big bite out of the other end of the chocolate-glazed doughnut that I was stuffing in my mouth, his blue eyes laughing into mine, and rolled out of the sofa bed in his red polka-dot boxers to fetch the bottles of water we'd stupidly left on my desk instead of within easy reach by the bed. The only time we had dressed was to make the fastest early morning Shipley's Donut run known to man. Then we'd ecstatically gotten undressed and squelchy with one another again, with a box full of doughnuts on the side. Now I was wearing his polo shirt and nothing else and feeling utterly blissful.

And the fact that Luke proved to be a non-slobberer in addition to being fabulous in bed? Icing on the cake, baby. Icing on the slobber-free cake.

"Has anyone ever told you that you have really sexy legs?" I asked him as I licked chocolate glaze off my fingers and eyed him unabashedly, my Inner Wall finally taking a well-deserved rest.

Holding two bottles of water, Luke looked down at his legs, then back at me as if he feared for my sanity.

Apparently even guys who have bird legs think I'm nuts. Who knew?

Outside, the morning sun was already blazing and peeking through my shutters. Birds were singing and every thought in my mind was a lovely one, except one.

"Um," I said, trying hard to concentrate when he fell back into bed and started kissing me again. I straddled him once more, loving the feel of his body against mine. "I'm meeting Maggie and her bridesmaids at You Beautiful Bride at noon," I mumbled between kisses.

"Mm-hmm," he breathed in my ear.

"The out-of-town bridesmaids are having their final fittings before we all go to lunch to discuss who is in charge of helping Maggie with what task and all that stuff. Then they all head to Austin for their spa weekend."

"Sounds really girly," he grinned, before pulling the polo neck to the side and planting kisses on my clavicle and shoulder.

"And um, your ex is going to be there," I said, my fingers running through his soft hair like they'd wanted to for four months now as his tongue went lower and lower. "I didn't get the chance to let you explain when and how you broke up," I grinned wickedly, "because your talents were making my thought processes go absolutely blank. So should I keep my trap shut for a while and not mention...us...to anyone yet?"

Luke had stopped making shivers run up and down my spine. He'd leaned back enough so that we could look into each other's faces. "What are you talking about?" he said.

I gave him his own sideways look, confused. "Claudia. She'll be there as one of Maggie's bridesmaids and, in my experience, most ex-girlfriends aren't real thrilled to know the guy they just broke up with is already seeing someone else. Especially someone they know."

"Shelby..."

My heart began to pound, but not in the good way. Had I totally jumped the gun? Did Luke just consider this some little rebound fling?

"I thought you understood," he said.

Oh, crap. I *had* jumped the gun.

"Understood what...exactly?" I returned.

"Shelby, I was never dating Claudia. She's just my best friend. Only my best friend."

Okay, that wasn't what I had expected him to say. I stared at him for a full two seconds before starting to babble. "But she was always talking about you. How much she loves—loved you. How you washed her car and put that shine stuff on it. How you don't like rice, but you just smile with your dimple and her knees went weak..."

Luke laughed. "So that's what you were talking about at Jackie and Abel's wedding. Shelby, she was talking about John. Claudia is dating my brother, who is the weirdo who doesn't like rice. She's been dating him for the past three years. John, not me. Claudia and I were never a couple."

I stared at him some more, unable to answer. All I could think was that it was so... So...

Obvious.

The way Luke always looked weirdly uncomfortable when I mentioned Claudia. The way he'd answer her calls with the casual, you're-just-my-pal, "Claude. What's up?" The fact that he hadn't put a ring on her finger after knowing her and loving her for so many years...

It was because she was just what he had said. She was his best friend. And only his best friend.

Yeah, all that was obvious *now*.

Another two seconds went by as my suddenly queasy stomach switched gears to make room for another feeling: anger. "Are you kidding me?"

Luke's blue eyes blinked and his words began to rush out. His hand gripped my knee as he'd felt me tense up. "It's what I've been wanting to tell you all this time. Claudia and I have been best friends since our freshman year in college. We went on two dates when we first met—we kissed once and realized instantly we weren't clicking that way. There were zero sparks. We've never even slept together, I promise. She met my whole family over the years except for John, until about three years ago when she moved to Houston. They met and were nuts for each other instantly. And they're great together. John's even going to ask her to marry him on her birthday in October..." He blinked again as his voice trailed off. It must have been the furious look on my face that did it.

"You've been single this whole time?" I asked with deadly calm.

He nodded, searching my face.

"And you never thought to correct me?"

"No," he said. "I mean, yes. I wanted to correct you several times, but something always got in the way. Shelby, it was just a misunderstanding from the beginning..."

I was having a hard time wrapping my head around it, but I was sure of one thing: It wasn't just a misunderstanding. In my opinion, it was an outright lie. Luke had been lying to me from the moment we met. And for the past four months, I had been suffering because I had fallen for him even though I thought I could never have him. I had worked my Inner Wall to the bone because I hadn't wanted to be unprofessional or be that girl who screwed (both literally and figuratively) with someone else's relationship. But all my professionalism had been for naught.

I picked his hand off of my knee and got off of him and the bed. He scrambled out after me, taking my hands. His voice was serious, with the lower vibrations in his voice humming loudly, signaling to me that he was in no way just telling me what I wanted to hear. "Shelby, I never even told Claudia about the misunderstanding because I felt like such an idiot that the whole thing had gotten away from me. I kept hoping that you would find out somehow from some member of my family or Claude herself, but it never happened. But what matters is that I was more than wrong not to correct you the very first time you misunderstood my relationship with my best friend and

I'm sorry for it." His mouth quirked upward for a second, "And I mean that 'I'm sorry' in the way you say it, when you care enough to use those words. I'm not just throwing it around. I'm so very sorry, Shelby."

I'd gotten my apology, but at that moment in time it didn't make me feel that much better.

It did cause my voice to choke up, though, as I looked up at him.

"Why?" I asked him in barely more than a whisper. "Why did you even allow me to misunderstand in the first place? And what did I do that made you feel the need to keep me in the dark for such a long time thereafter?"

"Do you not know?"

I shook my head, I turned my palm over beseechingly and my mouth opened, but no words came out. I had absolutely no clue.

"It was because of your moratorium."

Yeah, the anger came right back on that one. "*What?*"

I must have looked really pissed, because a little fear came into his eyes. "Shelby...you said you didn't want to date anyone, that you weren't ready to date..."

"*So?*" I shouted. Then it hit me. "Wait a minute. So you thought that if I believed you to be in a relationship then I would want what I couldn't have and suddenly *wham!*, I would *want* to give up my moratorium just so that I could date you? Is that it?"

"That's not exactly how I would put it," he returned.

"Yeah? And why not, Luke? It sounds like it's the truth to me."

He shot back, "It also sounds sordid and cruel, Shelby! Like I thought myself the Puppet Master and was deliberately manipulating you to achieve my own ends! I only wanted to give us a chance to get to know each other without you feeling like I would be pressuring you to go out with me!"

"Is that so?" I shot back, my voice becoming louder and infinitely more sarcastic. "And tell me, O Pious and Unmanipulative One, what is more sordid and cruel on basing a relationship on lies in the first place? Because that's what your so-called misunderstanding really was—a lie!"

He looked away and rushed his hand through his hair again, knowing I was right.

And it made me cold. I turned abruptly away. I needed to get out of the office and away from all of this so that I could think. I pulled off his polo in one fell swoop and threw it at him before pulling back on my white trousers and navy cashmere top that were in a heap on my desk along with Luke's clothes I'd torn off of him in Emily's new office. My bra and white lace G-string—which I had defiantly put on the previous night before Maggie's hen party, announcing loudly and stubbornly to my reflection as I did so, "I don't care if I'm going to end up sad and alone with no one but my six cats ever seeing my sexy unmentionables ever again, I'm wearing 'em!"—were grabbed and stuffed unceremoniously into my purse.

"Shelby..." His voice was pleading. It gave me momentary pause.

Finally, I said, "I need some air," and began to walk out of my office. Then, without turning around, I said in a calm, cold voice, "I don't want you here when I get back, Luke. And I don't want you to come back, either."

"What?" he was astounded. "Shelby, come on, don't..."

I interrupted him as I put my hand on the door knob, "The project is finished...and apparently so are we. E-mail me your final bill and I'll send you the check by mail." I turned just enough that I could see he'd lost some color to his face and his eyes were worried.

Good! Serves him right, damn it.

"If Bob or your men want to know why you're not here to supervise your last day, make up a reason. You're obviously good at it," I said, though I could feel my eyes start to burn despite the unrelenting tone in my voice. "But I don't want to see you here again."

And I walked out my office door to find Bryan holding a painting for his new office and smiling, but he stopped dead in his tracks when he saw me.

"Sweetness? You okay?"

I didn't meet his eyes. I just shook my head no before running down the steps to my car.

Twenty-Eight

I beelined it to Hilary's so that I could cry on her shoulder. My best friend, however, had another shock to my system to give me instead after I tearfully told her the whole story.

"I knew he wasn't dating Claudia," she told me, handing me a glass of orange juice she'd laced liberally with champagne after seeing my tear-stained face and mussed hair. "I've known for ages."

We were sitting on a bench in her back patio and two seconds went past of my staring, wide-eyed and incredulous, at Hilary's face before I could speak. (And even then, it wasn't really intelligent speaking.)

"Excuse me?" I said, barely able to understand what I just heard.

"I figured it out on day one," Hilary said.

"You did? What...? How...? What are you talking about?" I sputtered.

"Shelby," my friend said, looking at me with a mixture of happiness, love, and pity, "You forget that I was there on that day the living room wall got torn down. Luke had lunch with us and I watched him react to you. And you to him, for that matter."

I could scarcely get the words out as I raised my palm in desperate supplication even while my voice was defensive. "I wasn't flirting! I was only being *friendly*! And *nice*! That's it!"

"I know," she said soothingly. "You did nothing wrong."

"And neither did he!"

Hilary nodded in confirmation. "No, neither did he."

"Then what the hell are you talking about, Hilary?" My voice had become high, screechy. The dolphins out in the Gulf of Mexico could probably hear me loud and clear by that time.

"I'll tell you," she said patiently. "Do you remember when you told me that it was Luke and Claudia who had helped you out with that guy Kevin?"

I nodded quickly, silently urging her on.

"You were looking at me when you called Claudia his girlfriend. What you didn't see was his reaction to you giving Claudia that label."

My eyebrows knitted for a moment and I went to open my mouth to say that I'd seen something out of the corner of my eye, but I had just assumed that…well, I didn't know exactly what I assumed. Hilary apparently already knew this and went on before I could say anything.

"He about choked on his food when you said that and, if he hadn't had the good manners to not talk with his mouth full, he would have set you straight immediately. He was trying to when his curiosity over my calling him Lochinvar got the better of him."

My eyes were staring over her right shoulder at nothing in particular as she spoke, my ears taking in everything she said. "But then why didn't he say anything after that?" I asked.

"Because, just as soon as you had explained all the nickname stuff, your moratorium came up and had to be explained. One conversation simply flowed into another. Then, if you remember, he asked you if you were still on your moratorium, and I watched every inch of his face as he said it. He was hoping you would say something that would give him a clue that you would be interested in being asked out."

"No," I said, not wanting to believe that what Luke said about my moratorium being responsible for my current heartbreak was the truth.

"Yes. You were listening to him, Shelby, but I was truly *hearing* everything he said," she said. "But when you answered him, you stated clearly, for all the world to hear, that you were not yet ready to date. 'I happen to like being single and I'm not ready to start dating again' is pretty much exactly what you said." she quoted, mimicking my voice.

I looked at her finally, frustration narrowing my eyes. "I know what I said, but so what? He *knew* I was going on dates regardless, so why the hell didn't he just jump in there and ask me out sometime within, I don't know," sarcasm filling the air, "the past four months!"

"I think he would have," Hilary said, not unkindly, "if it hadn't been for what you said after that."

What was this woman, a freaking Dictaphone?

"Yes?" I inquired archly.

"It was what you said much later...on the porch after lunch, actually. About how you were not going to all of the sudden fall in love just because everybody wants you to. You said it would have to happen naturally or not at all."

Even though I of course remembered saying that (because it was and still is how I felt), I looked at her like she was nuts. We had been alone on my office's porch and, as far as I knew, there were no listening devices planted in my porch swing. Hilary read my look correctly and added in the part I didn't know.

"You were looking down when you said that and you didn't see that Luke had already opened the front door. I just saw his hand open the door, so he didn't even know I'd seen him. But didn't you notice how he came out and stuffed his hands in his pockets all self-consciously? I'd only known the boy for an hour and I already knew that it wasn't like him to be all nervous like that. He heard what you said and, I believe, took it very much to heart."

I laced my response with acid. "So—what? He thought that by lying to me this whole time about being in a relationship, I would just get to know him and then think that he and I had fallen in love naturally?"

"Look," Hilary returned sternly. "You know that I don't abide by lying. If you remember, I even broke up with Dimitri for two weeks that one time before we got engaged because he lied and told me he wasn't feeling good one night just to get out of going to dinner with my parents, and then I caught him out having beers later with his friends. He had to beg on bended knee to get me back and he's known ever since then not to even try lying to me. I certainly don't agree with Luke's decision on how to handle things, but I can see his point."

"Which was?"

"That *you* had to be the one to figure out you were in love— he couldn't force you or beg you or even try to convince you in any way, shape, or form. Within a day or so of meeting you in the parking lot of Bernatello's, Shelby, he learned that many people, myself included, were trying to steer you in the direction of dating and loving someone when you didn't want to be steered. He knew that if he tried to do the same, then you would probably just run for the sake of running because it had become ingrained in you."

"I'm not Pavlov's dog," I snapped. "I'm intelligent enough to not run away from something good if it had been presented to me properly."

Hilary looked at me sadly. "Are you sure about that, Shelb?"

My fangs at the ready, I opened my mouth to snap at her again, but was foiled by Dimitri coming outside with her cell phone. "Hil?" he said tentatively (obviously so as not to set off the she-wolf sitting next to his wife), "Your teacher's assistant is on the phone. She says it's urgent and can't wait."

Taking a risk as I'm sure I still looked a bit rabid, Hilary reached out and gave my hand a quick squeeze. "I'm always, always here if you need me."

I didn't respond, but waited until she had gone inside, pushing Dimitri ahead of her to stop him gawking at me, before I got up, grabbed my purse, and let myself out using the back gate.

I drove for a good fifteen minutes without being able to do much else than stare stonily forward as I relived the conversation I'd just had with Hilary. After another ten minutes (and at a stop light, thank you), I grabbed my phone and dialed Hilary's number. She answered immediately.

In a tone of voice that said I was not yet ready to play nice, I said, "Would I be right in thinking that the reason you did not ever take the chance to correct my assumptions about Luke and Claudia was because you figured out what Luke was trying to do and wanted to see how it played out without interference?"

"Yes," she confirmed. "Like I said, I didn't approve of his lie of omission, but it only took a couple of times of hearing you talk about him to realize that his patiently waiting for your mind to catch up with your heart was working. If I was wrong in doing so, then I'm so sorry, Shelby."

I was still steamed to think that my best friend did not have my back, as she should have. Through gritted teeth, I said, "I'll talk to you later," and hung up on her. When I had to blink my eyes several times to be able to read the street sign at the next light, I realized I had started crying again.

Twenty-Nine

Recently Added Items to My Things That Suck List:

1. Finally getting to be with the man you are totally crazy about, only to find out he had been keeping a huge truth from you for the past four months.
2. Being so blind/stupid/trusting/obtuse that you did not clue in ages ago to a fact that now seems absolutely and painfully undisguised.
3. Figuring out that, when all was said and done, both the guy you were crazy about and your semi-meddling best friend were right: I had to figure out on my own that I was in love.

Yes, I probably really would have emotionally hightailed it away from Luke if he had pursued me from the get-go. I would have been scared off because I wasn't ready to fall for anyone—much less the man I now knew was my Right One—when he met me. I was running away from dating for the sake of running because I had gotten all too used to being on my own and not having to deal with anyone else's crap, be it good crap or bad crap. And also because I, Shelby Waterlane, did not like to be pushed into absolutely anything, and evidently I didn't like to be pushed more than even I already knew.

What's worse, I didn't even like to be led into anything when I wasn't ready to be led, either. Even if I could logically tell you that where I was being led to was a good place, I still didn't like it. I liked to walk into it on my own free will and in my own sweet time. And Luke, after hearing all the little things I had said to him (when I believed him to be taken) and overhearing what I had said to Hilary on his first day of being my contractor, had had the patience to understand that it was I who had to decide to fall in love. Even presenting love to me on a silver platter would not have worked until I was ready. But I had to see that for myself.

I get that now. I am truly a stubborn, impossible, hard-headed woman. I own it like a rock star, that's for sure, but it's still the truth.

Now, as I slowly pushed my cart through the aisles of Central Market on the Thursday afternoon before Maggie's wedding, I imagined that I saw Luke's face or heard his laugh at nearly every turn, and each time it was as if my stomach dropped into my toes afresh. I sucked it up, though, and kept going.

In truth, I would have liked to say that I had been a drama queen in the past two weeks—because I really wanted to be one, don't you know—but I didn't really get the chance. I was too busy putting out fires instead.

It started just seconds after I had walked into You Beautiful Bride, barely a couple of hours after I'd walked out on Luke. A hard run in the heat and then a long shower where I'd stood until the water ran cold had done a great deal for my ability to not break down at the sight of Maggie and Claudia, who were waiting for me just inside the salon. A text message beeped from my phone as the two rushed to my side.

"Luke called us," Maggie said.

"And he told us what he did, the big dumbass of a doofus," Claudia added. "No offense, Mags."

"None taken," Maggie replied. "It's the truth. My brother is an idiot. But Shelby, we're so sorry!"

My voice would have gotten choked up if I hadn't heard a second text-message beep from my phone. Still, I responded, "What do either of you have to be sorry about? You didn't do a thing."

"Still. I'm so mad at him right now I could spit," Claudia fumed, "I mean, what was he thinking pulling a stupid stunt like that? But I still hope you give him another chance. Shelby, that boy has been bananas for you since the night we met you in Bernatello's parking lot."

"Really?" I found myself saying as a third beep came from my phone.

Maggie nodded along as Claudia replied, "Like you wouldn't believe. He was in love with you from the moment you called that guy—what was it? Oh, yeah. 'Fred Flinstone's less-socialized cousin.' He's probably repeated that scene to me a dozen times since then."

"You're so good for him, Shelby," Maggie chimed in as a fourth beep made me finally look down at my phone even as my stomach was swooping with misery and longing. "Just please promise me you won't leave me before my wedding."

My head snapped back up. "What? Oh, Maggie, of course not! Wild horses couldn't drag me away, I promise." I reached out to hug her and she started crying instead of me. Claudia's eyes were misty, too, as a fifth beep came from my phone, then a sixth soon after. I finally checked the texts; they were all from Bryan. And they read, in order:

Called Amali's Cakes to confirm time they want florist to deliver accent flowers for Maggie's cake. Something wrong with order. Am having them double-check.

BTW, Luke told us what happened before he left. We were furious for you! But I think Luke beating himself up more. Are you OK? We're sending you hugs!

Amali's Cakes called back. Problem with the cake order.

Urgent! Her cake order has been cancelled! Am checking on groom's cake order.

Groom's cake still OK. Won't re-sched Maggie's cake. Said YOU cancelled order! Please call them!

Feeling my stomach swoop for an entirely different reason, I texted Bryan back at lightening speed (Didn't cancel cake! Calling them now!) and then excused myself with Maggie and Claudia, sidestepping the reason why and wishing them lots of fun on their trip to Austin. Then I sped over to the tony River Oaks area of town, talking on the phone the entire time with Nadine Takahashi, the manager of Amali's Cakes.

"You called two weeks ago and canceled," she told me.

"Nadine, I promise you I didn't," I said, trying to keep my voice calm.

"Well, then someone who sounded exactly like you did," she said, sounding like she felt no need to cut me any slack. "She said that she had found another baker but was too embarrassed to cancel the order herself, so she had relegated the task to you, her wedding coordinator."

At a stop light, I closed my eyes wearily and said, "And as my name was down on Maggie's order as having the authority to make changes, you didn't question it…"

"No, we didn't," Nadine replied. "We normally won't cancel an order unless the bride or someone she authorizes actually comes into the store, but everyone here knows your voice and so we believed it was you on the phone and canceled the cake."

I inwardly groaned as I turned into River Oaks Shopping Center. Maggie's cake was sure to be fabulous. The entire five-tiered cake was to be Red Velvet, each rectangular layer having its edges rounded off before being swathed in perfectly smooth cream-cheese icing and spray-painted with food coloring in the distinctive tartan of the Hamilton clan, though using Maggie's colors of raspberry and peach with apple-green accents for the plaid instead of the traditional red and blue with white accents. Each tier of cake would then also separated by the same groupings of flowers in Maggie's bridal bouquet, giving the bright and just a little bit cheeky cake a polished touch. Maggie had come up with the design herself and I had loved it that, while being traditional in almost every other way, she had gone against the grain with her wedding cake.

At the bakery I looked at the order, which had been stamped *CANCELLED* with the date and time written in. Checking my phone's calendar, I had been at a lunch meeting with a new client at that time. Nadine also showed me the fax they had supposedly sent me confirming the cancellation. Even though I almost exclusively used a scanner and e-mail now, I still used my fax every so often. But the number on the invoice was not mine, nor was it Maggie's or Virginia's. When I dialed it, all I got was a fax tone.

With no way to explain what happened, I resorted to pleading, which got me a lot further with Nadine. But my saving grace was that Amali herself had walked in and, the two of us having had a long and fruitful association, she had agreed to put Maggie's cake back on their order list.

I breathed a sigh of relief. Maggie would never know how close she was to not having the cake she wanted at her wedding. However, since my mind was still reeling from learning that Luke hadn't been truthful with me, I hadn't thought too much thereafter about the cake mishap, figuring it was somehow just a weird accident. I went back to feeling miserable over Luke, though it got a little better when Emily, Lauren, Bryan, and Gabriel came over later bearing an extra-large pizza, three bottles of wine, and a half gallon of my favorite Blue Bell Fudge Brownie Nut ice cream. Sitting out on my porch in the evening warmth, we'd all got promptly schnockered and devoured all of it with relish.

Yet, I was able to add another item to my Things That Suck list—specifically *Friends who don't tell you that the guy you're crazy about may, in fact, be single so that you don't have to bother your Inner Wall at all*—when, after the first bottle of Pino Noir had loosened up my friends' tongues, Bryan had said thoughtfully, "You know, I have to tell you that the three of us had our doubts about Luke and Claudia. He never acted for one moment like he was truly in a relationship with her—right, girls? We've discussed this amongst ourselves several times." Lauren and Emily had nodded earnestly, and Gabriel had to pull me into another hug when my shoulders drooped dejectedly.

The rest of the weekend I'd helped Lauren and Emily out with their events so that I would have as little time to sit around and mope as I could. Even Colin did his part to entertain me after finding out from Bryan what had transpired. Of course, "entertaining me" came under the disguise of driving me up the wall when he dragged me to the Galleria with him on Sunday afternoon "because Izzie says my wardrobe needs updating" and proceeded to be the most annoying grown-up little brother on the face of the planet by questioning every suggestion I made, telling me my taste sucked when I said he should try on the Ferragamo loafers instead of his usual Cole Haans (and then smirkingly buying the Ferragamos anyway), and threatening to call Mom and tell her that she was "this much closer to grandchildren, but then Shelby blew it...again," when I got pissed off and said I was going to take a cab home if he didn't shape up and stop being obnoxious.

But that was all the respite I got, because I was too busy to think after that. Emily's great uncle in Fort Worth passed away on Thursday and she immediately flew off to be with her family. With Lauren already prepping for a huge weekend-long corporate event at the Houston Polo Club, I took over the final details and the handling of a small outdoor wedding on a ranch in Chappell Hill, about an hour northwest of Houston.

Most everything went according to Emily's well-executed plans; however, at the reception, Bryan slipped on a set of stone stairs and wrenched his left knee. By the time we left for the trip back to Houston, it was swollen up like a balloon and so it was I who ended up helping Lauren with the Sunday portion of the Polo Club event.

Though my free moments were rare, I spent them missing Luke and staring at his phone number on my cell-phone's screen, with my thumb hovering the button that would actually dial his number. Invariably something that needed my attention came up, though, and so neither my thumb nor I got to reconnect with him.

And then the week of Maggie's wedding came, and the chaos truly began.

On Monday, I showed up early at the Post Oak Country Club to meet a new client for a site visit. There I'd found Sarah, the club's special events director, and was chit-chatting with her about how their wedding business was booming since they'd begun allowing non-members to book their nuptials. She'd then said, "Speaking of, I meant to call and ask you why the Treadwell-Hamilton reception was reduced from four hundred and eighty guests to three hundred and eighty. Did the bride go that far over budget that she had to cut back a hundred people?"

I didn't panic. Instead, I merely cocked my head and gave her a quizzical look. Neither Maggie nor I had made any such change. In fact, I'd called a few days prior to set in stone the total at four hundred and eighty, and I told her so. After consulting my notes, I told her, "I spoke with your assistant, Brianna."

Sarah rolled her eyes when she heard the name. "I sincerely apologize, Shelby. Brianna obviously mixed up the number." She looked at me dolefully, "Unfortunately, this is not the first time she's made a mistake like this." She wrote herself a note on her clipboard about Maggie's reception numbers, underlining it twice for emphasis. "I'm glad I asked and we caught this in time. I'll be sure and change the number back and I'll e-mail you a confirmation. There will be no more problems on our end, I assure you. I'll make sure of it personally."

"I'd appreciate that," I replied easily, and we were soon immersed in the details of my current client's ideas for her dream wedding. I received Sarah's confirmation e-mail about an hour later, and, once I knew the situation had been cleared up, my thoughts had moved on. We'd caught the error in more than enough time; it was nothing more than a minor hiccup.

I'd barely gotten back in the office and weepily marveled over how much more incredible the new offices looked in the daylight and all decorated to the hilt by their new owners, thinking how I should be holding Luke's hand and telling him again what a wonderful job he and his men had done, when Bryan had found me and told me that they'd just heard the weather report. A tropical depression that had formed in the Gulf a few days back was heading our way.

"Tropical Depression Hyacinth," he said. "It's only predicted to become a tropical storm, thank goodness, and could possibly even fizzle out if we get the cold front they mentioned. But if it doesn't, they're saying it'll hit the Houston-Galveston area either next Friday or Saturday."

"Oh, for heaven's sake!" I exhorted, feeling pissy and exasperated. Then I took a steadying breath and got back to business. "I had Maggie put down a deposit for two covered walkways but do you think we could use a third?"

"It wouldn't hurt," Bryan replied with his reassuring smile. "I'll go call Farnon Tents—from my new *gorgeous* office— and see if we can get another."

A few minutes later, I was shaking the copy of the cancellation order that had been faxed to me, with my name clearly in the "Person Requesting Change of Order" box and a fax number that looked the same as the one I'd seen at Amali's Cakes written in at the top of the document, insisting to the snappish customer service associate on the other line who had identified herself as Kristina that there'd been an error. "I'm telling you, I did *not* cancel the order. And neither did the bride. There's a tropical storm coming and we need those walkways. We absolutely must have them. Is there anything you can remember from that day that might help me so that I can figure out how this might have happened?"

Kristina replied curtly, "The only thing I remember is that the woman I spoke with said that fax for the number we have on file for Waterlane Events wasn't working and asked me to fax the cancellation order to another number. The first time I tried to send it, some guy picked up the phone on the other end and asked if I would wait five minutes because they were switching out ink cartridges in that machine. I asked where I was calling, and they said it was a Copy in a Flash store. And that's all I can tell you."

By the time I hung up, Bryan was already at my computer, typing in the keywords "Copy in a Flash" into the search engine, plus the fax number we already had, to get the store location. "It's the one on Bissonnet," he'd said softly. "Bissonnet and Harvest Street..."

We exchanged glances. He then typed in another website address, clicking on the "Contact Us" link when the site came up. The address for Elegant Events by Kendra Everitt said 508B Harvest Street with a notation in parentheses: *(Just off Bissonnet)*.

And all became clear. Kendra Everitt was taking a shot at me. Again. But this time it was a shot at me through Maggie...

"This isn't happening," I whispered, my hand on my forehead in disbelief. Bryan gave my shoulder a reassuring squeeze as he murmured, "I'll go start calling other tent companies."

Another company ended up having the walkways, but we would soon not need them as the predicted cold front came through, cooling the waters under Hyacinth's swirling winds and shifting her eastward at the same time.

Hurricane Kendra, however, was still trying to come straight at us.

At seven thirty on the dot on Tuesday morning, Galliana, the owner and head florist of Bella Arrangements, her Italian accent still fairly thick even after nearly two decades in America, called me.

"Oh, Esshelbee, I am glad I catch you. I want to make esshure of change to Treadwell customer order before I make arrangements, yes?"

I should have expected it, but I didn't. Still, this time, there was no confusion on my part, no pathetic, "What? I didn't know about any changes..." I immediately asked, "Galliana, do you remember exactly when this supposed change was called in?"

"Last Friday," she answered promptly.

The previous Friday was when I had done my week-out vendor checks. Kendra, my former assistant, would have known that.

"My new asseestant, Rosa, took message," Galliana said. "I see that client want carnations—pink carnations—as main flower in every arrangement and I think, 'Thees is not correct. Carnations no good for pretty wedding, yes?' But, Rosa, she say customer herself call and make change. Customer say Esshelbee push her into using ranunculus when she really want carnations. But I remember customer tell me she love ranunculus—ees her favorite flower, no? So when I see change this morning, when I go to start arrangements, I immediately call you."

"I'm so glad you did," I replied as I trotted up the porch steps and breezed into my office to locate Maggie's file so that Galliana and I could check off every last flower we'd ordered for the bouquets, boutonnieres, and reception arrangements. Basically, the floral theme was an ode to the ranunculus with a hearty nod in the direction of the English rose and the hydrangea, all in Maggie's raspberry, peach, and apple green colors, with ribbon accents in a coffee-with-cream brown. And if any or all of Maggie's floral pieces had shown up with common pink carnations instead? Yes, I was pretty sure that no matter how easygoing she was, Maggie would find that a reason to hit the roof. And I wouldn't have blamed her for a second.

But Kendra would. Kendra *wanted* Maggie to lose it—and then she wanted Maggie to blame me for what went wrong.

My jaw set, I dialed another number.

"Post Oak Country Club, this is Brianna. How may I help you?"

I spoke with Sarah's assistant, the one who had supposedly accidentally shaved an entire one hundred people off of Maggie's reception guest list, for less than five minutes. She confirmed my hunches that a woman posing as Shelby Waterlane had called, giving Brianna a song and dance about how the bride had gone wildly over her budget and would have to drop a hundred guests from her reception. The caller had then pulled the broken-fax-machine stunt again, giving Brianna the exact same fax number as she'd given Farnon Tent Rental and Amali's Cakes.

"She sounded just like you," Brianna said.

"Yes," I replied darkly. "She was always very good at that."

I asked Brianna to transfer me to Sarah's voicemail, where I left a message exonerating Brianna of any wrongdoing and warning them both to be on the lookout for any more unauthorized changes or odd mishaps courtesy of one Kendra Everitt.

Then I'd called a Waterlane Events pow-wow.

"No shit? You really think Kendra is out to sabotage Maggie's wedding?" Emily said. Lauren had been too stunned to do anything but gape at me. Bryan, however, had just rubbed his temples as I gave them the lowdown on Kendra's subversive activities, and Bryan only rubbed his temples when he was really stressed.

"It's pretty clear Kendra wants to find a way to ruin Maggie's wedding to punish Maggie for signing with us instead of her. And by doing that, she hopes to punish me by making Maggie hate me."

Bryan said, "She's also hoping that by ruining Maggie's wedding, Maggie will spread bad press about Waterlane Events and others won't sign with us. She is evil!"

I agreed. "You know it. That just pisses me off and I won't have it for another second. Not with any of our clients, but especially not with Maggie."

"Kendra is obviously unstable," Lauren stated, her usually soft brown eyes now hard and fiery.

"You just tell us what you want us to do, Shelby," Emily said, fierceness in her voice. "We'll do whatever you need. That platinum-from-a-bottle bitch won't get away with hurting you, Maggie, or any of our clients."

I told them just to check with their own clients for signs that Kendra had been messing with their events and then to keep their eyes and ears open beyond that. Afterward I headed to see every one of Maggie's vendors in person—Amali's Cakes, Bella Arrangements, and the Post Oak Country Club included—and I explained the situation to whomever was in charge, asking each of them to include a password that had to be given before any changes of any kind could be accepted. Meanwhile, Bryan made calls to the vendors of any of my brides who I knew had interviewed Kendra before signing with me. We covered our bases but good.

It was lucky that we did, because only hours later Kendra had tried to pose as me in order to cancel Maggie's videographer, telling the guy she'd hired that, at the last minute, Maggie had decided to let her cousin film the nuptials. Naturally, she mimicked my voice perfectly. But when the videographer had asked Kendra for the password, though, she had, as he put it, "choked on her lying-ass words and hung up."

Now, the more I thought about Kendra trying to sabotage Maggie's wedding, the more pissed off I became. "Damn it!" I said, temporarily forgetting I was currently in a grocery store. Irritation prickling at my entire body, I grabbed my shopping cart and jerked it around fast to the left so that I could hightail it to the chocolate and cheese aisle.

And then I had to stop short when two different arms reached out to keep my cart from colliding into them, the shoppers who had seemingly come out of nowhere.

Thirty

I looked up to find two guys, standing in almost the exact stance that could only happen from sharing the same genetic code. Both were in chino shorts and running shoes. One wore a red t-shirt that said *Accountants Like to Get Fiscal*; the other's was white with *Vanderbilt Commodores* across the chest.

On two of us, (yours truly being one) our expressions could have been the benchmark for shocked surprise. The third showed merely interested curiosity, sort of like I was the two-headed lab experiment again.

"He's not following you, Shelby, I promise," John Treadwell smiled. Though he was about an inch shorter than his brother and had straight brown hair instead of Luke's curly-at-the-ends variety, his eyes were the same Wedgwood blue and his voice was warm and deep, almost a copy of Luke's, making a squeezing feeling come onto my already thumping heart. "Tonight is Maggie's *polterabend* and Mom sent us out on a food run."

My stomach did an extra dip. Maggie was in love with wedding traditions and she and I had spent hours researching customs she could incorporate into her wedding that would honor both her English and German roots as well as Barton's Scottish heritage.

Barton's family had already thrown her a Scottish show of presents. Similar to a sip 'n' see, tea and cakes were served as the guests mingled and viewed Maggie's wedding gifts. Following Scottish tradition, Maggie would also be receiving a strip of Hamilton tartan from Barton once they were pronounced husband and wife. It would be clipped onto her dress as a symbol that she was welcomed into the Clan Hamilton. Then for her English roots, she had already had a small silver horseshoe charm sewn into the hem of her bridal gown and a sixpence for luck would be placed in her left shoe by her father just minutes before she walked down the aisle.

Tonight, though, was all about her German ancestry. Maggie's aunts from the Kappler side of her family would be hosting a German *polterabend* for the couple at Maggie's parents' house. Guests would toss old dishes at the threshold to the bride's parents' house as a symbol of good luck for the bride and groom; Maggie and Barton would then clean the mess up to indicate that they would work together as a couple through all the messes in life.

As a fun gift, I'd bought Maggie and Barton each a pair of Wellington boots to wear for the cleanup—black for Barton and white for Maggie. Bryan had even decorated the tops of Maggie's boots with colorful fake crystals in her wedding colors for, as he put it, "that extra sassy look." After the dish-tossing was a huge party filled with food and dancing, the invitation indicating that the party would go as long as the guests wanted it to. It had sounded like such fun and I had been looking forward to being there. In fact, I was still trying to convince myself that I was okay with not going, and still wasn't succeeding.

Nevertheless, showing I was still somewhat of an adult, I moved around my cart and offered Luke's older brother my outstretched hand. "It's a pleasure to finally meet you, John," I said politely.

"And you as well," he replied, shaking my hand and smiling with ill-concealed and Treadwell-dimple-producing enjoyment at how self-conscious his brother and I were at that moment.

"I've heard a lot about you, from everyone it seems. You have a big following amongst my family and my girlfr—." He caught himself and made a hilarious damn-I-totally-said-the-wrong-thing face. Out of the corner of my eye, I saw Luke close his eyes in mortification. There was a massively pregnant pause.

And it amused me.

Wrestling my twitching lips into submission, I said in all honesty, "Claudia is really incredible and I've come to think of her as a friend, too. You have yourself a great girl."

John Treadwell positively beamed and thanked me, telling me what I already knew, that he was a lucky guy. Then he caught his brother's expression. Luke was giving him a look that said *Really? Are you really gushing about Claudia RIGHT NOW?*

"Right," John said with a wry grin. Jerking his thumb over his shoulder, he said, "Well, I'm going to go get the flour and the nuts. Um, Luke, you just…," he made a gesture that said he knew he had a small window of correct words to say, "do whatever and I'll find you later." He turned back to me, said, "I sincerely hope I see you again, Shelby. It was very nice meeting you," and then turned, grabbing a jar of ground ginger before booking it away from the hot zone.

A few seconds passed as Luke and I watched each other, but said nothing. Shoppers passed us by, giving us curious glances.

"Shelby…," Luke finally began. His voice sounded hoarse, like he hadn't properly used it all day. Just then, my phone beeped. I could hardly bear it, but after all that had gone down with Kendra, I tore my eyes away from his long enough to see that it was a text from Bryan.

Bernatello's calling. Kendra there in person – saying she's you! – and trying to cancel M's rehearsal dinner. Mgr keeping her talking until you get there. Am on my way too.

"Shit!" I exclaimed.

"What?" Luke said, looking alarmed.

"I've got to go." I said. "Kendra's trying to sabotage Maggie's wedding." I left my cart where it stood and was already heading out of the spice aisle to one of the exits, texting Bryan back and saying over my shoulder to Luke, "Don't tell Maggie—please! I don't want her worried! I've got it under control!"

But he had already caught up to me.

"I'm coming with you," he said when I stopped in my tracks and stared at him. "You can stay mad at me if you want, Shelby, but if Kendra's trying to make my sister and you unhappy then you're not going to stop me from helping you." Then he held out his hand.

Without hesitation, I took it and we raced out of the store to my car.

He drove while I gave him the rundown of Kendra's misdeeds. "She can mimic my voice perfectly. She was so good at it when she was my assistant that I occasionally had her call vendors for me, as me. No one ever knew the difference. She also knows how I do things and so she waited to do most of it after I had made my week-out confirmation calls. If two of Maggie's vendors hadn't thought to mention the discrepancies to me, we wouldn't have found out about most of them before it was too late. Oh, it would have been a mess!"

Luke's expression was determined as he gunned it through a yellow light. "Well, we're going to fix it now, even if you and I have to track Kendra down and put armed guards on her until Maggie and Bart are safely off on their honeymoon. I'm not going to stand for her to mess with either of you another second."

I looked at him and I couldn't help myself. I told the truth. "I love you," I blurted out.

We sped through another yellow light as Luke's rogue grin, dimple and all, came out in full force. "Yeah? Well, it's about time you caught up with me. I love you, too, Shelby Waterlane."

There wasn't time for me to do anything but laugh out loud because we were finally in Bernatello's parking lot. "The scene of the crime," Luke winked as he grabbed my hand again right at the spot where Caveman Kev and I had taken pot shots at each other. We raced inside the doors to find Bernatello's as calm, peaceful, and darkly lit as ever—except for the fact that the four tables of well-dressed senior citizens were not enjoying their early suppers, but instead had their eyes trained on the kitchen. Two waiters stood just outside, peeking in the little round windows. As if on cue, we heard a crash and yelling. I looked up at Luke. He looked back at me and we streaked toward the swinging double doors.

I feared the sight of a crazed Kendra Everitt wielding a chef's knife, so I almost busted out laughing when I saw portly Chef Umberto, a huge stainless steel bowl on his head like a helmet, brandishing a long-handled steel chinois strainer at Kendra as he played chicken with her, trying to keep her from getting past him. His dark eyes were narrowed at her and his double chins shook with each surprisingly quick move he made with his doughy body.

Kendra was holding a head of romaine lettuce, raised like she was about to launch it at him like a football. Another box of lettuce heads sat to the left of her on the stainless-steel prep table, right next to a glass vase filled with pink roses that Umberto would use to garnish his homemade rose-infused gelato. I saw no evidence that she'd yet hit him with a head of lettuce, though a couple were already on the floor. From the red stains on Umberto's chef's uniform, though, it was clear she'd already made contact with a couple of tomatoes. They were both making enraged-bull guttural noises at each other as they danced from side to side. Rafael, Bernatello's manager, was standing to our left, holding a much scarier-looking meat-tenderizing mallet and looking ferocious. It was no wonder Kendra had decided to get past Umberto instead.

She was dressed in a little black dress and Christian Louboutin satin platform peep-toed pumps, their signature red soles the color of fresh blood visible every time she picked up one of her feet. Her platinum hair was spilling down her back and sparkles seemed to radiate from her with every move. But the closer I looked, I could see that Kendra was a mess. Three inches of roots showed in her hair, which looked dry and brittle. Always skinny, she looked like she'd dropped another ten pounds; her cheeks were hollowed, her shoulders bony. The makeup she'd applied, heavy on the foundation and smoky eye shadow, did nothing to help. And the sparkles were because she was apparently wearing every bit of expensive jewelry she owned. A ring, sometimes two, was on every finger. Her engagement ring-cum-diamond necklace was around her neck, just peeking out from under two different-length pearl necklaces. Four diamond tennis bracelets, one mixed with pink sapphires and another with rubies, were around her right wrist; her left had a diamond-studded Rolex and two more tennis bracelets. Her pear-shaped diamond earrings were the only thing that seemed to be worn by themselves, I could see them as she whipped around to face me. She was only surprised for a split second.

"You bitch!" She screamed and hurled the head of romaine at me. In a move Luke would later describe as "one of the most awesome things I've ever seen," I caught it and fired the lettuce right back at her, pelting her hard on her left shoulder. It barely stopped her. More agile than I expected in such high stiletto heels, she then made a grab for the flower arrangement and managed to lift it over her head to throw at me. But I'd closed the gap between us and reached up, grabbing the round glass vase so that we both had a hold of it. Another frustrated scream had her shoving the vase at me, which Luke deftly snatched away before it could do me any damage. I merely was rocked back a few steps, grabbing a pink rose out of the arrangement by accident as I did so.

In the melee, Kendra had booked it. She'd darted around Umberto and was heading toward the back exit, throwing assorted produce at any shocked kitchen staff who tried to block her. Luke and I took off after her, but I feared she would get away.

Not for the first time, though, had I underestimated the Dating Brigade.

Kendra tried to lunge for freedom, only to be stopped just outside the back door by a sultry brunette standing beside a sassy blonde with Texas Big Hair. Emily and Lauren blocked Kendra's way, their faces set, their hands on their hips. Behind them I saw the faces of their boyfriends, Percy and Chris. Kendra could see them, too; it showed by the cornered-panther look on her face.

The next moments happened so fast I wondered later if I had somehow willed time to speed up so that the drama could be over sooner. Bryan had arrived, coming up behind us. And before Kendra could bolt again, Luke and Bryan each grabbed her wrists with one hand, lifting her up by her armpits with the other. Emily and Lauren backed up as the two men swept the skinny blonde out of the restaurant before she could even really struggle.

"How did you know?" I asked Lauren and Emily.

"We were still at the office when Rafael called about scarecrow over here," Emily replied, giving the cussing and fuming Kendra a disdainful look.

Lauren said, "Percy and Chris were with us, helping us rearrange some of our new furniture, and so they were both available to be extra muscle." She grinned widely over at Luke, who was easily holding Kendra still all by himself while Bryan made a phone call. "But it seems you brought some good lookin' manly muscle all on your own. Care to explain, Shelb?"

Off to the side, Kendra called Luke a bastard and he replied, "Hey, only Shelby gets to call me that."

Laughing, I said, "Happy to, once we figure out what to do with the wicked witch of Space City over here."

But the witch decided to get some things off her chest first.

"You."

I stood two feet in front of her, casually smelling the rose I still held. "Yes? Is there something you'd like to tell me, Kendra?"

Her eyes were narrowed slits; her lips thinned with meanness and curled back. "I'm losing my business, losing everything!" she yelled. "And it's all because of you!"

Emily drawled, "Yeah, Kendra? And how exactly did you come to that asinine conclusion?

Kendra ignored her, jerking against Luke and snarling at me. "I never had a chance against you. You were always the one clients loved, always the one who they asked for, always the one who the vendors still ask about when I call to place an order. Perfect little Shelby, with her capable attitude and her disgusting desire to be honest. Every time something went wrong and I thought you would lie about it to save your ass, you never did. And you always came out smelling like a fucking rose. And every time I tried to do the same, I got my face slammed in the door because of it."

I arched an eyebrow. "Oh, we're rewriting history now, are we? Because I don't remember you ever taking the high road when a lie was much easier for you. Although I do like it that you're conveniently forgetting all the times I lost a potential client or, hell, even a client I'd already signed because I'd screwed up somehow and they didn't give a crap that I was taking responsibility for it. I didn't come out smelling like a rose those times, did I, Kendra? But instead of whining about it, I had to suck up the bad times, keep going, and try to do better. *That's* what has made me successful, Kendra. I've worked at being better each time I've made a mistake. So maybe you should try working on yourself instead of just trying to trip me up to bring me down to your pathetic level."

My former assistant's head snapped back in surprise at hearing the harsh truth, but her eyes went back to furious slits only a moment later as she started listing the names of the brides who she'd lost to me since starting her own business, spitting out the names of each bride as if they'd tasted bitter on her tongue for too long and she couldn't wait to rid her mouth of them.

Chris was calmly videotaping the whole incident on his iPhone as Lauren interrupted Kendra with thick contempt,

"And why is it that you think these brides came to Shelby after interviewing with you, Kendra?" she said. "Possibly because you're a repellent bitch who bullies her clients into aspects of their weddings that they don't want or can't afford? I've heard that the clients you do have don't want to recommend you to their friends because of how miserable and stressed out you made them before their weddings. I, for one, am never surprised when they come running back to Shelby after spending even twenty minutes in your cold, pain-in-the-ass presence."

My jaw dropped. And even better, so did Emily's and Bryan's. Kendra, after figuring out that she was being recorded and that her entire ridiculous diatribe was caught digitally, went wild. Jerking furiously against Luke, she bared her teeth at Lauren and a low scream began discharging from her mouth, from deep down in her angry gut. It got louder. And louder. I sent a look at Chris and he stopped filming.

And then I put a hand behind Kendra's neck and stuffed the big pink rose right into her mouth, shutting her up instantly to more of a muffled gagging sound.

I smiled. "Now *that* just makes everything rosy, doesn't it?"

Thirty-One

Despite everything I did, Maggie's wedding still did not go off without a hitch.

Nope, the photographer had a family emergency and was an hour late, sending Virginia into enough of a nervous tizzy that I had to sit her down for a few moments with a glass of wine. One of the bridesmaids also forgot her underwear and Bryan had to make a Target run to get her some knickers, only to have to repeat the trip when he accidentally grabbed the wrong size. Then one of Barton's uncles from Scotland couldn't find his heart medication and Bart's father nearly missed the start of the ceremony because he had to help his brother tear apart his hotel room in search of his pill bottle, which ended up being in the uncle's jacket pocket, where he had put it in the first place.

After the ceremony, the four-year-old ring bearer Callum wouldn't stop crying long enough to be in the pictures and it was only Luke and John, being so adorable and hilarious that Claudia and I both got utterly weak-kneed again, who got the little boy to smile again just in time for one last group shot. At the reception, the valet parkers got backed up and some of the guests got a little testy at having to wait in line for so long. But those, thank goodness, were the only major issues. The rest of it could not have been better.

Everybody enjoyed the food and went crazy over Maggie's gorgeous tartan Red Velvet cake and Barton's all-chocolate groom's cake, which was in the shape of Texas and covered in colorful and amazingly lifelike marzipan renderings of all Bart's favorite things about the Lone Star State: a bottle of Shiner Bock beer; a barbeque plate with sliced beef brisket, sausage, baked beans, and potato salad; a representation of Texas A&M's Kyle Field with little Aggie and U.T. Longhorn football players battling it out; a small swath of bluebonnets; a hamburger with jalapeños on it; a glass of iced tea; a bull bucking off its cowboy at the Houston Rodeo; and a miniature replica of the San Antonio River Walk abutted by the famed Alamo.

Maggie's wedding favors—two stacked two-ounce tins, one filled with Maggie's favorite Earl Grey tea and the other filled with Bart's favorite dark-roast coffee, were wrapped in a Great Britain-themed tea towel and decorated with a tea infuser basket and coffee scoop—were complimented left and right. And friends, family members, and couples happily waited their turn to have their picture taken in the photo booth, each taking home a 5x7 print showing four different poses. A copy of each photo card was then inserted into a scrapbook by the guests, who wrote their good wishes to the newlyweds underneath their pictures.

And best of all, the guests literally danced the night away until the band stopped playing at one in the morning.

Luke and I finally got to dance, too. When Maggie's train had been bustled, every last important picture had been set up, and the cake had been cut, she finally told me, "You, missy, have done your job!" She hugged me tightly, saying in my ear, a smile in her voice, "And a little bird who shall remain nameless but who happens to make award-winning chocolate-chip cookies has told me just how much you've done, too." She pulled back and looked at me with shining eyes. "And I love you for every last inch of it. Now you go and dance! And make sure you keep my brother wrapped around your finger so that I can call you my sister-in-law before too long." So, I didn't feel guilty that Luke and I were the last ones to leave the dance floor, having jitterbugged and slow-danced to our hearts' content, Kendra Everitt and her drama never once crossing our minds. We did find out what had made Kendra go off the deep end, though. Or rather, my intrepid assistant found out for us and came out onto the dance floor to tell us, with Lauren and Emily in tow, both of whom who had showed up to celebrate Maggie and Barton's reception after their other events had ended.

"All of you remember the two gentlemen who showed up to cart Kendra away at Bernatello's, yes?" Bryan said, looking around at our expectant faces.

We nodded. While Luke had been single-handedly keeping Kendra from escaping, Bryan had been off making a phone call. He had not elaborated on who he had called, though, merely telling us that he needed to pry out more information from his source before spilling any beans. And within seconds of my stuffing a rose in Kendra's mouth, two well-dressed men in their thirties had shown up and taken Kendra off our hands. A curt thank-you was all they said as each grabbed one of her bony elbows and marched her to the Mercedes sedan idling a few feet away, not even bothering to remove the rose from her mouth until they put her inside the car. Lauren had wondered aloud if they were undercover police, but I thought otherwise. One reeked of being a lawyer and the other reeked of Eternity for Men.

"Well," Bryan continued to our rapt faces, "The shorter of the two wearing the slim, custom-fit Ralph Lauren polo in that detestable mauve color was Gabriel's ex-boyfriend, Cory. The other one in the gorgeous tattersall Brooks Brothers dress shirt was Grant, Kendra's lawyer. Her *bankruptcy* lawyer."

"Seriously?" I exclaimed.

"No kidding?" Lauren said.

"You don't say," Emily smirked.

"Please," Bryan returned. "I couldn't make anything up this good." He paused for dramatic effect. "So, I'm in Starbucks a few days ago and I ran into Cory. I never really liked the guy because he's a bit of a priss, but he starts talking to me like we're friends and I felt it would be rude to brush him off. He tells me that he remembered that I'm in the event-planning business and he asks me if I know Kendra. In case he's baiting me, I keep a poker face when I really want to gag on my café Americano, and I tell him that I'm acquainted with Ms. Everitt."

Emily said, "Did you tell him that your version of 'acquainted' means that you say, 'Hello, cheap slag,' when you cross paths and she replies, 'Good to see you, butt licker,'?"

Luke let out a bark of laughter and Bryan said loftily, "I felt that was better left until some later conversation."

I couldn't stand the wait. "C'mon! I need more!"

Bryan's eyes sparkled. "Well, so Cory tells me that the reason he asked is because Kendra became Grant's client a few weeks ago. Then he realizes that he probably gave away more pillow talk than he should and shuts up. I tell him that I won't tell a soul, but later I ask Gabriel for Cory's phone number, just in case Kendra keeps up her shenanigans."

"Bryan, you are so freaking awesome," I told him.

"Of course I am, shug," he replied. "So then Kendra tries to cancel Maggie's rehearsal dinner at Bernatello's. I called Cory so that he could get in touch with Grant, but they were already together, heading to the Galleria to go shopping. I heard Grant yell, 'Kendra! For Christ's sake! I told her to keep her nose clean!' as I'm on the phone, so I figure there's more to the story than meets the eye." He winked at us, "But I figured that Grant wouldn't spill, so I had to get it all sneaky-like from Cory..." He paused dramatically again and his grin was wicked, "who just so happens to owe Gabriel a favor. Gabriel brought him to the reception tonight and I've spent the last half hour in the hotel bar getting the most delicious scoop."

"Ooo, do tell," Lauren grinned.

"I shall. Let me tell you, it only takes one apple martini and Cory the Priss starts going on and on about how Kendra's business expenses and spending habits have far exceeded her income and she's losing her shirt."

"Get *out*." I said.

"Oh, it gets better," Bryan continued with morbid excitement. "Kendra hasn't been receiving any money from her divorce from Chad van Ingelsdorp like we all thought she would. It seems that Kendra had signed a prenuptial agreement exonerating Chad of owing her any kind of financial support in the event of a divorce if, wait for it...*she* had been unfaithful. So it wasn't Bi-Curious who had done the cheating after all, it was Kendra!"

"Holy crap," I said.

"What she said," Lauren seconded, pointing at me.

"And that's not even the best bit," Bryan said excitedly, his eyes locked in unblinking incredulity onto mine. "Kendra didn't just cheat on her with any random guy, she had an affair with one of her client's fiancés! The bride in question is even suing her for two million dollars, citing emotional distress because not only did she have to cancel her huge wedding, but she found out about the affair when she came home early from her Vegas bachelorette party and caught the groom banging Kendra from behind in the kitchen of the bride's condo, where the guy had been living."

"*No*."

"*Yes*. Apparently there was truffle-infused olive oil involved, too."

"Oh, sweet Jesus."

"I know. It paints quite the raunchy hetero-sex picture, if you ask me," Bryan said, making a face at the thought. "Kendra is apparently is in deep, deep shit, and none too happy about it, too."

I realized then that Kendra's apparent business success had merely been the result of a good public relations campaign rather than the actual truth. In reality, she had lost client after client—mostly to Waterlane Events, Bryan said—and her emotional health had, as Cory had apparently put it, "gone down the toilet along with her business."

I let the news digest in my brain for a few minutes, and then I made a decision.

After Maggie and Barton had been sent off on their honeymoon, Luke and I sped over to Bernatello's, making it just minutes before the staff went home for the night, and with some effort, I convinced Chef Umberto and Rafael to drop the charges they'd levied against Kendra for the damage she inflicted, promising them that I would steer more clients their way if they would.

"Train wrecks may be some people's thing," I told Luke later as I snuggled into his arms, "but they're not mine, you know? I just felt it was the right thing to do."

"Wow," Luke replied. "I think that was just the perfect opening to ravish you again. Come here."

Speaking of, in the past two weeks I had learned a lot about Luke Treadwell that I hadn't known during the time he worked for me. I found out that he ate the same breakfast every morning—oatmeal with banana slices and a spoonful of brown sugar on top—and the only time he could be enticed away from this boring fare (in the opinion of yours truly, at least) was if we physically went out for breakfast. None of my offering to make him my famous chocolate-chip pancakes or peanut-butter-stuffed French toast would sway him, though he would devour my breakfast treats with finger-licking gusto at any other time of the day. I told him he was weird; he just shrugged and shoveled another bite of oatmeal in his mouth.

The man was also ninety-nine percent laid back...unless he couldn't find his keys. Then I called him Grouchy McCrabbypants as he cussed and stormed through the house in a furious search, and then he continued to be one serious grump for a good while after he actually recovered them. From this I learned that, though it was rare for his ire to get up, once it did, it took a while to simmer back down and he was best left alone until his naturally easygoing disposition showed back up for duty.

Actually, after being single for so long and not having to deal with anyone's crap but my own, I had no desire to give him the time of day when he was being that pissy. And I told him so.

His reply? "I can't say that I blame you."

In addition to this, he was your typical man, whining like a big baby whenever he didn't feel well, leaving the toilet seat up, forgetting to change out the toilet paper roll when it was done, and having no concept of the romantic brilliance of Jane Austen books or movies based upon them. He also refused to be in the room if I turned on any entertainment-news program, telling me that my brain cells were deteriorating with each minute of that "load of crap" I got a kick out of watching; did not agree with me that crème brûlée was a delicious dessert, instead insisting that it had the texture of congealed phlegm; and would very nearly flip out during tampon commercials, whereby he would scrabble for the remote control, changing the channel as fast as he could while yelling out, "Ugh! Why the hell do they have to talk about stuff like that! It should be illegal!"

And this coming from the man with both a girl as his best friend and a sister.

Basically, the man was much more infuriating than I thought he was. If he had been anyone else, I wouldn't have been able to handle it. His quirks would have driven me up several walls at the same time and I would have been gone. Vamoosed. So long. Buh-bye.

But here's the thing—he wasn't anyone else. He was that person who made me *want* to handle it. Just being who he was every day, with all his weird things he did and all the incredibly wonderful things he did, too, made me want to stay. Not have to. Not need to. *Want* to.

There's a big difference, you know. And I told him so the night after Maggie's wedding, both of us relaxed in shorts and sweatshirts as we sat on the front porch of my house and looked at the stars. He said that he felt the exact same way.

"The exact same way. You want to know how I can say that?"

I leaned back and snuggled up against him, enjoying the feel as he wrapped his arms around me. "Sure," I replied. "Hit me with your best shot."

"Well, there's one thing you've never asked me since you found out that Claudia and I were just friends…"

I did a split-second mental search for things I hadn't asked him and came up with nothing. We'd had some good, long conversations in between our many rolls in the hay and though I found out more about him every day, I was sure I knew the things that mattered most. "What's that?" I asked.

"Well…you've never asked me how long I've been single before I met you."

I sat up straight so fast that I bumped my head on his chin, making us both wince and say, "Ow."

The top of my head recovered first and I turned around to look at him. He was working his jaw and made a show of checking a couple of teeth to see if they were loose. "You've got a hard head," he grumbled.

"That's not news to anyone," I retorted. "Now spill it, Treadwell. How long were you single?"

He rubbed his jaw another second before a slow smile began to spread on his face, his dimple creating a crevice in his right cheek. "Longer than you."

"My ass," I retorted, though with a less-than-certain face.

"Your ass is cute, but I still was single longer than you and I can prove it. I was on a moratorium myself."

I stared. He grinned roguishly and stared back, mocking my widened, unblinking eyes.

"You were not." I stated confidently. Then: "How? When? Where? What happened? What started it?"

He gave me his sideways look. "Oh? Believing me now, are you?"

My jaw jutted in stubbornness. Then I grabbed his sweatshirt and pulled him into a hard and hot kiss, breaking it off when I could feel his heart racing and his hands went for my boobs. "Uh-uh," I told him, shaking my head. "Those paws don't touch me until your gums have sufficiently flapped and I am satisfied."

He was breathing hard. "Damn those feminine wiles!"

I did my best Evil Saucy Wench laugh and then looked expectantly at him.

Putting a hand on each of my knees, he began. "It started when John and Claudia started dating." I felt his fingers tighten on my knees; he must have felt my surge of fear as my old worries tried to resurrect themselves, for he quickly said, "Babe, no, I wasn't jealous, I promise. I'm going to say it again—Claude and I figured out very quickly we weren't meant for each other in that way and that has never, ever changed. What I meant is that, for truly the first time, I saw up close what a good relationship should be like. One where two people weren't just dating to date or sleeping together, but were really meant to be together. I'd had other friends in good relationships, but I'd never taken true notice of it." He shrugged, "Maybe it just wasn't the time for me to take notice of it until Claudia and John—two of the people I'm closest to in my life—got together. But no matter what, it put a harsh light on the relationships I'd been having up until then, which were basically decent, but were on the whole meaningless relationships that would never go anywhere."

"So you didn't have any doozies like mine?" I asked.

He grinned and drawled, "Darlin', I dated a few seriously irritating women, but the closest thing I ever got to one of your oddball relationships was when I dated a vegan who kept trying to convert me throughout our entire six-week relationship. I broke it off with her for good when she came over uninvited during one of my Sunday steak cookouts with my friends and threw a pail full of sand on my new barbeque grill, where all our food was cooking, and then started screaming and crying that we were all cow murderers."

"*Nice.* I like that story. Did you give her a nickname?"

"Other than Psycho Vegan?"

"Simple and descriptive, I approve. Now, please, continue with your explanation."

Chuckling, he said, "There's not much more to say, really. I stopped dating and I've been single for three whole years." He tapped the end of my nose with his finger. "So a whole year longer than you."

My eyes were wide again. "No dates?"

"Nope."

"Not even one setup or anything?"

"Well, I will admit that the first year and a half I had an ex-girlfriend who wasn't interested in a relationship but was willing to do the friends-with-benefits thing on occasion," He smiled at my I-knew-it look and continued, "But we're talking maybe nine or ten times in eighteen months—not exactly a big deal. Plus, she ended up meeting her husband and moving to the West Coast with him and so I'd been completely without sex for a year and a half when I met you, and completely dateless otherwise for three years. In fact, the day I met you in the parking lot of Bernatello's was because Claudia was kind enough to remind me that it was my three-year anniversary of not having a pointless relationship. That's why she and I were out to dinner—she took me out in mock celebration."

I let what he said roll around in my head for a minute and asked, "So were you even interested in dating when I met you?"

"Sort of, meaning I wasn't against the idea. I think the only difference between your situation and mine is that I never really consciously declared myself to not be dating like you did—I just *didn't* date for a while and kind of kept it up by sheer fact that no one made my head turn until I met you." He put his hand up and cupped my face, his thumb stroking my cheek, smiling at me because he could see in my face that he'd said the right thing.

"Well, hot damn," I whispered as I looked deep into his eyes, my heart finally feeling what it was like to be about to burst with love.

Thirty-Two

But I would soon be in damn hot water. For the one person I had yet to tell that I had found my Right One was my mother. And since my Aunt Priscilla was very protective of my mother? Oh yes, Franzilla was not very happy with me.

So why did I take so long to share my news with the parents I loved and respected? Well, let's put it this way: I'd been waiting for a really (*really*) long time to be able to bring the man that I truly loved—not just the man I was dating, but the man I truly was in love with—to meet my parents. In fact, my parents had only met maybe two or three of the guys I'd dated over the years because I always knew in my gut that the relationships weren't right and I didn't like the look of thrilled anticipation my mom always got on her face whenever I'd introduce her to whatever guy who turned out to be, metaphorically speaking, really nothing more in my life than another little turn in the road on my way to meet Luke. Thus, having my parents see me finally with a man who made me really, blissfully happy, a man whose hand I wanted to hold for the rest of my life, was something I'd longed for and not really been totally sure that it would ever happen.

Anyway, I'd wanted Luke to meet both my parents together and then later be introduced to my aunt and uncle and other various relatives, but it was Franzilla herself who got a hold of us first. And the both of them were spitting mad at me.

See, I had done Franzilla's version of high treason and waited another two weeks after Maggie's wedding before I started thinking about taking Luke to do the Big Parental Introduction. Though Luke warned me that my parents—"or, specifically, your mom, I should think,"—would not be happy with our concealing our relationship from them (especially when his parents had already had us over for dinner), I just wanted Luke and me to have some time alone to date, quietly, just the two of us. In reality, I wanted so badly to tell my parents, but Luke and I were feeling a little overwhelmed with love from all those who already knew about our relationship and were thoroughly over the moon for us and I just wanted a little more time before we added my mom and dad to that mix.

Only this did not sit very well at all with Frances Waterlane and Priscilla O'Keefe when they found out that I was actually dating someone, not to mention actually in love.

This was because they found out not from me, but accidentally from Bryan.

Believe it or not, I'd actually had a big notation on my calendar that read: *Call Mom in a.m. to schedule dinner with Luke & me for when Dad back from hunting trip.* Only I had been busier than expected all morning and hadn't yet made the call. Bryan, though, did not know that when he traipsed out of the office at nine to run errands. I had told him confidently I was going to call my mom, "Sometime between my nine fifteen meeting with Molly, the bride who wants the beach wedding in South Padre, and my eleven a.m. with Gretchen, the bride who wants her wedding and reception at the Junior League building."

So, when Bryan ran smack-dab into Franzilla (at the Neiman Marcus café, naturally) and he ecstatically blurted out, "Isn't it fabulous about Shelby and her new gorgeous hunk o' man, Frances?" my mother was naturally taken aback. And then felt incredibly hurt.

Which then went to being really pissed off because she was the last person to know her daughter had found the Right One.

And Aunt Prilly was madder than a wet hen at me for making my mother upset.

I was in the doghouse with both of them, big time.

So, when Bryan came literally skidding into my office after he'd run into Franzilla at Neiman's, I could only give him a baleful look and say beseechingly into my cell phone for what felt like the tenth time, "Mom, please don't be mad. I'm really sorry! You know I love you more than anything. Luke and I just wanted to take things slowly for a couple of weeks! I'm really, really sorry!"

Bryan apologized to me over and over in a whisper, looking distraught. "It was past noon—she looked so happy when I ran into her—I thought you'd already told her! And then she and Priscilla dragged me into the Neiman's café and made me tell her *everything!*" His big, mossy green eyes got even bigger with the apparently scary memory. "They wouldn't let me leave! I tried to call you to warn you, but I forgot my cell phone on my desk. Sweetness, I am *so* sorry!" His eyes were filled with such remorse that, my phone glued to my ear, I still gave him a hug to reassure him that all was okay and I still loved him.

Nevertheless, I got an earful for another ten minutes from my mother (with Aunt Prilly making sarcastic comments in the background every so often) and she only let up when I said, "How about this: Dad won't be back from his trip yet, but I don't think he'll mind. I'm free for lunch on Saturday and so is Luke. How about we meet you and Aunt Prilly for lunch then? I'd really love for you to meet him. Would that work for you two?"

Mom's voice was still hurt, but she replied, "Why don't you just bring him to the house? Prilly can bring her spinach salad and I'll make roast beef. I'll serve your grandmother's Spanish chocolate cake for dessert."

I smiled into the phone. "That sounds incredible, Mom, thank you. Luke will go crazy over your cooking, without a doubt."

Proving to me for the umpteenth time that Luke was really the right man for me, I found I wasn't remotely nervous about having him meet Franzilla. In fact, I was kind of excited to introduce him to my beloved mother and aunt. Squeezing his hand as he drove my car down Memorial Drive, I told him, "Hey, I've seen you handle Bryan, Lauren, and the scariness that is Emily with absolute finesse. If then you can handle them, you can definitely handle my mother and Aunt Prilly. We call them Franzilla as a whole, but they're both pretty marshmallowy on the inside. Plus, you'll love my parents' house. Parts of it are over a hundred years old. Bob has remodeled it a couple of times, but my parents never touched the old parts."

Mom and Aunt Prilly were waiting for us on the brick front porch as we drove up. "I am so happy to finally meet you, Luke, though I must admit I had *no* idea that you and Shelby were dating until yesterday," my mother said with a sweet twitter in her voice, really working the I-was-the-last-to-know bit, though she warmly shook his hand.

"Oh, yes," Aunt Prilly smiled, managing to shoot me an accusing look even as she smiled and giggled right along with her sister, "Bryan telling us about the two of you just about shocked the hell out of Frannie and me. You could have knocked us over with a feather right in the middle of Neiman's, I'm telling you."

Luke smiled widely and turned so that he was standing between my mother and my aunt, hands casually on his hips, shaking his head like I was an impetuous schoolgirl. "Well, I told Shelby that she shouldn't wait too long. I knew that my own mother would have had my head on a silver platter if I had gone this long before introducing her to the girl I was crazy about. But your daughter, Mrs. Waterlane, well, I hate to break it to you, but she is just a touch stubborn."

"Wha...?" I sputtered. I fear my eyes bugged out a little in shock.

But you would have thought Luke was the Pope himself with the way Mom and Aunt Prilly started fawning over him. And agreeing with him.

"She's been that way her whole life," Mom told him, patting his arm.

"For heaven's sake, Luke, you should have heard the way this girl used to talk back to me when she didn't get her way as a teenager!" Aunt Prilly told him, throwing her head back and practically cawing with laughter.

"She takes after her father, Luke, you should know this," Mom told him. "The two of them are the most stubborn people I've ever known in my life. And if they're hungry? Well, it's just not worth speaking to them until you get some food in their stomachs."

Luke winked at me, "I've already figured that one out, Mrs. Waterlane."

"Good for you, dear," Aunt Prilly congratulated him as they turned and walked inside.

"Traitor," I hissed at Luke when he stood back to let me go ahead of him, then swallowed a squeal as he pinched my butt and whispered, "You love me, admit it," even as we heard Mom call back to us, "Feel free to have Shelby show you around the house, Luke. Lunch will be ready in a few minutes."

Following Mom's suggestion, I showed him around their spacious one-story house, chattering away the whole time and pointing out the places that Bob had remodeled. I'd noticed he'd become quiet as his eyes took it in, his hand running along a wall or a bit of molding every so often, but I didn't think anything of it. Until we passed the kitchen and Luke froze just steps away from my mother's office.

"Wait a minute...," he said under his breath. My mother, my aunt, and I watched curiously as he covered the ground between the family room and the office in three of his long-legged strides. Once again, he stopped in the doorway, this time spanning his arms out to either side of the extra-wide doorway. He then stepped inside the office and spun back around, looking at me with excited eyes.

"I thought there was something really familiar about this house. I can't believe it. This...this is the Death Star!" He pointed at the floor of the office.

Aunt Prilly gave me a searing look as my mother admonished, "Shelby, I can't believe you would tell him about that silly name."

"No, Mrs. Waterlane," he grinned. "I know about the Death Star—I mean your office—because I worked on it!"

"What? You're kidding!" my mother and I said in unison. The three of us followed him into the office, looking around almost as if we were seeing it for the first time: butter-colored walls glowing warmly in the daylight from the large bay window, Mom's computer monitors a matte charcoal black on top of a oak desk, chintz chair-and-ottoman combos with huge candy-pink cabbage roses predominant, and a half-moon's worth of bookshelves filled to the gills with books of all ages, sizes, bindings, and genres.

"Seriously, I did. I helped build this office," Luke said, nodding as he looked around my mother's beloved sanctuary with a grin that wouldn't quit. "Mrs. Waterlane, you might not remember meeting me back then because I was only sixteen, but this was my very first job working for my Uncle Bob as an actual employee."

My mother stared at Luke for a moment and then a look of wonder stole over her face. "I do remember you," she said. "Or I remember a gangly young man who always said 'yes ma'am' and 'no ma'am' to anything I said." She gave him a fond, motherly look. Luke blushed; I felt happy and proud. Then a realization hit me.

"Wait a minute," I said. "If you were here working on my parents' house, then did we ever meet?" I gestured with my finger from my chest toward his, "Because I don't remember seeing you..."

I mean, seriously, I'd been hot for tall, lanky guys since I was about five years old. If a cute boy like Luke Treadwell had been anywhere near me—especially at my house, no less—I would have been all over him like flies on a rump roast.

Okay, strike that. I was only fifteen at the time of the house remodel and I was a good girl until college—and no cute boy would have got me to give in before I was ready—but I would have been all over him in all the relatively chaste ways possible, without a freaking doubt.

Mom answered for him as she reached out and pushed a stray lock of hair out of my face. "No, dear, you were at summer camp at the time, remember?"

I did remember. I was also hit me square between the eyes with the wild realization that Luke and I could have met when we were kids. But knowing what I now knew about myself and what I needed to do with my life before falling in love, I realized just as quickly that the seventeen-plus year wait hadn't been in vain. He and I, as we were now, were worth the wait.

"Your uncle was so proud of you, too," Mom said to Luke. "But how incredible is it that the boy who worked on my favorite room in the house should be the handsome man standing here right now! I can hardly believe it!"

Luke said, "My uncle was definitely great. He'd taught me all sorts of woodworking skills over the years and he'd pay me to be on the cleanup crews whenever I had extra time, but this office was my first time creating built-in shelving with a real construction crew on a real house." He was entranced as he looked around the office, like he'd just seen an old friend after far too many years apart. Then he said, "In fact…," and he swung around, hands out, as if some unseen energy would pull him in the right direction, "all of us who worked on the office signed our names on the framework."

With his back to my mother's desk at the bay window, he went back and forth between the centermost set of shelves and the set that was directly to the left. He finally chose the set slightly to the left and chose a shelf that was about as tall as I was, tapping Colin's hardback set of the entire *Hardy Boys* mysteries that my mother kept for safekeeping in the Death Star.

"I'm pretty sure it was right behind here. And I remember you being so great about letting us sign your wall, Mrs. Waterlane. You made it into an event, bringing us each a cold Coke to drink, letting us use your black marker, and watching as we all put our John Hancocks on the two-by-fours at the end of our work day."

He looked at me, his face beaming. "Your mom was so cool about it. She clapped when we were done and we even took a picture with her. I probably still have it somewhere." He turned back to my mother. "It was a pretty big moment in my life, actually. It was the first time I really felt like a true craftsman."

Mom's and Aunt Prilly's eyes were shining and had their hands over their hearts. They were completely speechless.

Well, if this wasn't freaking dandy. I'd been trying to shut Franzilla's yap for years now and Luke had gone and done it in the span of fifteen minutes. So not fair.

Later, somewhere in between the time we'd devoured my mother's roast beef and were working on pieces of my grandmother's cinnamon-infused chocolate cake, I had an epiphany.

See, though it was obvious my mother was totally taken with Luke and seemed to approve wholeheartedly of him, I just kept getting the impression that something with her was still a little off between us. Deep down, she was still upset. I could tell by the way she wouldn't quite hold my gaze, instead shifting her eyes away more quickly than usual as if, I don't know, a little sad.

Then it hit me: Mom loved being a matchmaker for me and, in her heart, even though she was probably telling herself that she was being silly, she had wanted to be the one to introduce me to the man of my dreams. I knew my mom well; she would get over these feelings within a day or so and would soon feel guilty that she'd thought that way to begin with, but for right now, she was the slightest bit melancholy that she couldn't congratulate herself on a match well made.

But that was something I could definitely fix.

"Hey, Mom," I said. "You know what?"

"What, dear?" she said politely, using her fork to cut off another dainty bite of her cake, yet not looking at me.

"I just realized that, in a way, you're responsible for Luke and me meeting one another."

My mother's blue eyes raised to mine; they were questioning, curious, and hopeful all at the same time. "I am?"

"Sure," I replied, nodding toward Luke, who sat to my right at my mother's dining room table. "You were the first of many friends, family, and neighbors to hire Bob Kappler and his crew, which included Luke, to remodel your house. Had you not, Bob might never have gained such a reputation amongst various people I know and his name might never have stuck in my head as the contractor I wanted to hire to redo my offices. And had you not allowed a sixteen-year-old to help build your office, Luke might never had such a great and memorable start to his career."

Mom looked back and forth at Luke and me with wonder. Luke's face said he knew exactly what I was doing and approved of it.

I continued, "Now, Bob had a hand in things, too, by being clumsy on the golf course and breaking his leg, but if you had never hired Bob back then, then I would never have hired Bob all these years later and then met his nephew, who," I looked shyly at the man I could now call my boyfriend, "is who I've been waiting my whole life to meet and who I love very much." Luke reached out for my hand and I said, "So, Mom, I have you to thank for all of it."

I knew I'd made my mother happy when, eyes welling up, she had to dab her eyes with her napkin before she hugged me. But the icing on the cake was the fact that my Aunt Priscilla, always the tougher judge of the two, winked at me from across the table in the best, you-did-well kind of way.

Could it be? Yes! I had tamed Franzilla!

Yeah, well, kind of. Once Luke and I got married, Franzilla just turned into the champion of the phrase, "Do you and Luke have a little announcement for us yet, Shelby?"

And the Dating Brigade morphed easily into the Bump Watch Brigade, don't you know.

I would never be free!

But I'm all right with that. And so is Luke. We kind of like it, actually. But don't tell my loved ones I said that, okay?

2445438R00176

Made in the USA
San Bernardino, CA
22 April 2013